Born in Carlisle, Margaret Forster is the author of many successful and acclaimed novels, including *Have the Men Had Enough?*, *Lady's Maid*, *Diary of an Ordinary Woman*, *Is There Anything You Want?* and most recently *Over*, as well as bestselling memoirs (*Hidden Lives* and *Precious Lives*) and biographies. She is married to writer and journalist Hunter Davies, and lives in London and the Lake District.

ALSO BY MARGARET FORSTER

Dame's Delight
Georgy Girl
The Bogeyman
The Travels of Maudie Tipstaff
The Park
Miss Owen-Owen is At Home
Fenella Phizackerley
Mr Bone's Retreat
The Seduction of Mrs Pendlebury
Mother Can You Hear Me?
The Bride of Lowther Fell
Marital Rites
Private Papers
Have the Men Had Enough?
Lady's Maid
The Battle for Christabel
Mothers' Boys
Shadow Baby
The Memory Box
Diary of an Ordinary Woman
Is There Anything You Want?
Keeping the World Away
Over

Non-Fiction
The Rash Adventurer
William Makepeace Thackeray
Significant Sisters
Elizabeth Barrett Browning
Daphne du Maurier
Hidden Lives
Rich Desserts & Captain's Thin
Precious Lives
Good Wives?

Poetry
Selected Poems of Elizabeth Barrett Browning
(Editor)

MARGARET FORSTER

Isa & May

VINTAGE BOOKS

London

Published by Vintage 2011

2 4 6 8 10 9 7 5 3

First published in Great Britain in 2010 by Chatto & Windus

Vintage
Random House, 20 Vauxhall Bridge Road,
London SW1V 2SA

www.vintage-books.co.uk

Addresses for companies within The Random House Group Limited
can be found at: www.randomhouse.co.uk/offices.htm

The Random House Group Limited Reg. No. 954009

A CIP catalogue record for this book
is available from the British Library

ISBN 9780099542094

The Random House Group Limited supports The Forest
Stewardship Council (FSC), the leading international forest
certification organisation. All our titles that are printed on
Greenpeace approved FSC certified paper carry the FSC logo.
Our paper procurement policy can be found at:
www.rbooks.co.uk/environment

Mixed Sources
Product group from well-managed
forests and other controlled sources
www.fsc.org Cert no. TT-COC-002139
© 1996 Forest Stewardship Council
FSC

Printed and bound in Great Britain by
CPI Bookmarque, Croydon, CR0 4TD

I

THE HARDEST thing to tell Isa and May was where, and how,
I met Ian. I thought seriously about lying. I could claim I'd
met him at a party, which would have satisfied May but maybe
not Isa. Isa is the sort of morally upright person who can
sense a lie at once. She would have wanted to know who had
given this party, where it had been held, and a load of other
questions hinting at her suspicions. So I told the truth, but
not the whole truth. I said I'd met him at an airport. I didn't
say I'd tried to pick him up. The meeting place was scandalous enough for them.

My grandmothers hated me going abroad as soon as I
graduated. To May, 'abroad' represented desertion; to Isa
it meant evasion of some sort. They ought to have been reassured by the fact that I was going to teach, but teaching
English to foreign students, in several countries, was not
what they regarded as respectable. My parents didn't
approve either but were resigned to my evident need to
spread my wings. I e-mailed my parents often, and sent
regular pretty postcards, as well as letters, to Isa and May,
and I phoned on special occasions. But they missed me.
And I found I missed them too.

The airport was exceptionally busy, with long and
confusing queues at every stage. I was standing at the end
of one queue, praying it would be the last before reaching

the departure area, when a man standing in a parallel queue caught my attention. There was nothing remarkable about his looks (medium height, dark hair, slim build) or his clothes (jeans, black jacket, white T-shirt) but his composure struck me as unusual. He had a serene air, a calmness, that contrasted with my own agitation and that of everyone else I could see. There was I, fussing because my queue wasn't moving, and there he was, not bothered, relaxed.

Then he did something unexpected. The woman immediately in front of him was elderly. She had white hair, caught up with clips in an untidy bun, and she was wearing a weird assortment of clothes. She had a long, bedraggled flowered skirt topped with a bulky red anorak, and round her neck she wore a brown woollen scarf that half obscured her face. She looked hot and uncomfortable and was forever turning round, as though searching for someone. She was quite stooped, but had a bag on each shoulder. The bags were clearly heavy, because she kept shifting their weight, constantly readjusting the straps. She shuffled her trainer-clad feet all the time. I was watching her, feeling sorry for her, when the young man tapped her on the arm. She swung round, alarmed, and though I couldn't hear what he said, I saw him point to her bags. He was offering to carry them for her. At first she shook her head, and looked afraid, and then, when he smiled and made a gesture indicating that he understood, it was fine, she changed her mind. He was given her bags. She stopped moving from foot to foot, but repeatedly checked that her bags were still there. This old woman was nothing like elegant Isa or plump little May, but I immediately thought of my grandmothers and how they would have reacted to the stranger's kindness. It made me feel sentimental and a little tearful.

When we got to the front of our respective queues, we were still level with each other and I heard the woman, who was American, thank the young man effusively. He said it

2

had been a pleasure, no trouble at all. He was Scottish. And then I couldn't resist speaking to him. I said, can I just say what a kind thing that was to do. He looked a little embarrassed, and shrugged, and said it was nothing. I asked him where he was flying to, and he said London. So was I. Maybe we were on the same flight, I said, flourishing my boarding card. But he was on a later one, and had arrived much too early. He didn't say why. We walked together to the departure lounge. I went on trying to engage him in conversation. It was hard going. I could tell he was amused by my persistence, but wary, too. I carried on chattering, the way I do when I'm nervous, telling him what I'd been doing the last few years. He listened politely but didn't reveal anything about himself. I did all the talking, acting entirely out of character, but he wasn't to know that. At that point, my flight was called. I said it had been nice meeting him and here was my mobile number – 'Here is my mobile number!' Oh God.

Now, how could I tell Isa and May this? May would say that Ian might be an axe murderer, you never knew, and Isa would say – well, she would *look* rather than say. She doesn't like the unexpected. Mysteries intrigue her, but my inexplicable behaviour and the lack of information about Ian would make her very uneasy. A strange young man standing in a queue at an airport – a foreign airport – would strike her as an untouchable. So, what I said was that I'd met Ian in an airport and, extraordinarily, he turned out to be a friend of my school friend Beattie. They both know Beattie, so that seemed all right. Just.

It was a tough time, those first few weeks when I came back. There was the question of money, for a start. I had none. Everything I'd earned had gone on keeping myself, and doing a bit of travelling. I had to go back to living at home, where I was made very welcome, but it felt like putting the clock back. I wanted my own flat, but that meant finding money for rent. Meanwhile, I was applying for a grant to do an MA – that was a laugh. I discovered I could get accepted on a course OK but I didn't qualify for a grant (hardly anyone does any more).

My parents offered to 'lend' me the money that would be needed, but I refused their offer. They've been generous enough to me in all kinds of ways. Instead, I had to take really boring temping jobs. It was such a shock, that sort of work – May laughed at my dismay. She reminded me that half the population get up at six and don't get home until seven or eight in the evening, and that the work they do is boring. May said I carried on as though I were down the mines instead of sitting on my backside in offices. Being a temp was to her the life of Riley. Isa, on the other hand, was 'pained' that I had had to resort to such 'undistinguished' employment. She was quite alarmed when I explained my job as that of a sort of stand-in secretary. 'To whom are you a secretary?' she asked. I said to different people; that I just filled in for various people in big organisations when someone was ill or taking leave. I was sent by the agency I'd enrolled with and was never anywhere more than a month. Isa thought this 'low' employment, and was surprised my father allowed it.

It took me almost three years to save up enough to finance my MA course. I would never have got through those years without Ian. He called a week after I got back. He told me later that I'd stuck in his head, refusing to fade from his mind, but that he had been ready to find either that the mobile number was a joke, just made up, or that I would have no idea who was calling and no recollection of giving my number to a strange man I'd encountered in an airport. We met at a Café Rouge. After that, things happened fast. Skip another month, and we'd met ten times. Skip six more weeks and we were renting a flat together (with Ian paying the major share). I'd kept him a secret up to that point – I was twenty-six, and felt entitled to. I'd told my parents, of course, that I'd met a

4

really interesting man, but Ian hadn't met them yet. He said he'd rather not, which upset me a bit. His reason was that he preferred not to get involved with family. I didn't mention him to Isa nor May for another six months, fearing the inevitable inquisition, and then I told them the Beattie lie.

It will be obvious by now that I am obsessed with Isa and May, my grandmothers, or, more precisely, I am obsessed by their significance, without being sure what that is. There is nothing special about these two old women. They are not famous or anything, but that's not the point (we'll come to what the point is later, I hope). I am named for both of them. It's an awkward name: Isamay, pronounced Is-a-may. Isa is my paternal grandmother's name (shortened from Isabel) and May my maternal grandmother's (it comes, somehow, from Margaret). The amalgamation is, as you see, strictly alphabetical. Life, I feel, would have been much easier if they had chosen Maybel. But Isamay it is, reduced to Issy by my friends but never by my grandmothers. They are pleased with, and proud of, the name, and want me to be. I wish I could oblige.

I owe rather more than my odd name to my grandmothers. I owe them my life, and not merely in the genetic sense. The tale of how they delivered me, of how I was born, has grown in the telling, as such stories do, but the facts seem to be real enough. I was a Christmas baby, though not due to arrive until three weeks later. It was Christmas Eve, no snow, but driving winds and rain, and my parents had just moved into their first flat the week before. My grandmother May had come to help her daughter Jean 'get organised'. My mother didn't want to be organised by May but there was no denying her. What she hadn't told May was that she had been having pains that she thought might, or might not, be contractions. She knew May would make a fuss and insist that she go to the hospital and she didn't want to do that only to be told it was a false alarm and find herself sent home. So she was waiting for more definite signs. I'll cut short what happened next – no need for the gory details, though these are gone into every Christmas. My mother went into labour and May called an ambulance. Before it arrived, my other grandmother, Isa, came to deliver a present (a china tea set, never used). She came by taxi and kept it waiting, intending merely to drop the present off. May, expecting the ambulance, flung open the door, and then there followed some confusion about whether the taxi should be used to take my mother to hospital. The grandmothers argue about exactly what they each said, but anyway it doesn't matter: I took things into my own hands. There and then, on the bathroom floor, I was born, with May and Isa managing things between them.

God knows how. It is unimaginable, knowing them as I do now. The paramedics who turned up in the ambulance minutes later apparently congratulated them – 'good team work, ladies' (or something like that; again, there are arguments about what was said). Isa and May, a team? I don't think so. Isa and May are as different as it is possible to be (no, that's not quite true, they could have been of different races and nationalities, which they're not). In the few meetings there had been up to my birth they had not got on. They were mutually suspicious. A lot of this was due to class, but the hostility that always hung in the air between them had, I think, a much more basic explanation. There was, and is, a sort of animal-like antipathy there, a cat/dog reaction, which neither of them, not even Isa with her emphasis on good manners at all times, can quite conceal. I make it worse. They are jealous, because of me. They each have always wanted more of my time than the other is getting, each wants me to prefer her company. Isa has no other grandchildren so her need is greater. May has others but they are boys and she's never seen them because they live on the other side of the world. Isa and May don't actually fight over me, but I've always felt they could. I take care not to provoke them.

My grandmothers loom large in my life, even now, when I am almost thirty years of age. I would not have chosen to do this work if it were not for their importance. I love them both, though I love each of them in a different way. But I am trying, and will go on trying, even if I fail, to keep my love out of it, to keep the personal in the background.

In the foreground, at the moment, is another grandmother: Elizabeth Fry.

I selected Elizabeth Fry because of May. She looked like May in George Richmond's portrait of her, which I came across in the National Portrait Gallery. The clothes are different, of course, especially the cap, but that face is my maternal grand-mother's – same plump cheeks, same rather long, straight nose, same pointed chin, and, most striking of all, the same shrewd expression in the eyes.

This is not a good reason to have chosen Mrs Fry. I won't tell Claudia. I'll think up some suitably convincing explan-ation as to why I picked her. She did, after all, draw attention to the state of prisons in the early nineteenth century, espe-cially for women, and did much to help reform them. And she had eleven children, *eleven*, the last born on the same day as her first grandchild in 1822. That fact alone self-selects her, surely. For my purposes, Mrs Fry should be perfect, mater-nity personified. But the first surprise has been to discover she was no great shakes as a mother, never mind what she might have been like as a grandmother. She always put her work before the comfort and welfare of her children, reck-oning it was all right to leave them in the sometimes doubtful care of servants while she went off to do it. When that last child was just six weeks old, the exhausted forty-two-year-old mother travelled seven miles from her home in Essex to visit the damp and filthy Newgate prison. 'My dearest babe,' she wrote, 'suffered much by the rides to and from town, so that its little cries almost overcame me.' 'Almost' may even

7

have been an exaggeration – nothing was going to stop her doing what she felt she had to do. And the six-week-old boy was still an 'it'.

So, the question, the question for me, is did Elizabeth Fry see her role as a grandmother in the same way as she saw her role as a mother? Or did she regret never putting her children first and decide that being a grandmother gave her a chance to make amends? That seems unlikely, from what I've learned so far. She was no more inclined to stay at home and teach her granddaughters to bake cakes than she had been to teach her own daughters. Domestically, she remained as uninterested and as inadequate as she had always been. It wasn't in her nature to organise and preside over a well-run household – she wanted to be out and about, managing things on a larger scale, striving for the public good and not for harmony at home. This makes her an exciting figure, in my opinion. She was a grandmother who rejected the traditional roles for women and set her granddaughters an example of public service.

But did she have any real influence with them? That's what Claudia will want to know. Her granddaughters and grandsons (how many of each did she have, how close was she to them?) may have admired her without wanting to follow in her footsteps. Or they may have privately thought her quite wrong to have lived her life as she had, and turned back with relief to an easier pattern. They may well have respected her achievements, but how much does respect matter? How much does it mean to respect a grandmother? The one it matters to is surely the older person. May brings up the *lack* of respect in the young, i.e. me, but I don't think it is respect she really wants. It is not what she's after, and I suspect it was not that important to Mrs Fry either, but we'll see.

What May wants is love. She wouldn't call it that – talk of love is 'soft', and she doesn't hold with it. She craves company and affection and attention, lashings of it. She feels starved of it these days, and it makes her grumpy, not that she would admit that this is the reason for her increasingly cross moods. I used to love May extravagantly when I was young – she was so cuddly, unlike Isa, who was never comfortable being cuddled and whose lean frame didn't lend itself to a child's embrace. May was better than any soft toy and I loved the very feel of her plump tummy. I'd put my arms round it and hug her, and she'd pick me up and put me on her knee, and then I'd switch my eager arms to her fat neck and lie on her chest. May liked the contact too. She only had this physical closeness with small children. With older children, even me, she became distant, the hugs perfunctory and only given if offered first by the child, and with adults there was no close contact. I've never seen her touch my mother. But May wants love still. She hasn't grown out of that. She wants exactly what I now find hard to give her, because I'm no longer a child. She wants me to be at her side, in her house, as often as possible, preferably once a day for at least an hour. She wants me just to *be* with her. I would have been a better granddaughter to Elizabeth Fry. She would have sympathised with my love of studying even if she would have deplored my lack of involvement in any kind of reform work. She approved of girls being well educated, writing in her journal when she was seventeen that she hoped to gain more knowledge and to have her mind in greater order. Her poor grasp of grammar bothered her, and her spelling wasn't up to much (she spelled 'went' as 'whent' and 'wrong' as 'rong'), so she set herself to read Lindley Murray's *English Grammar* to correct her deficiencies. A granddaughter such as myself, of a scholarly disposition, would not have dismayed her.

It dismays May.

Today, I spent four hours in the British Library studying Katharine Fry's two-volume transcript of her mother's forty-six volumes of journals – pleasurably, but probably pointlessly

– and then I took a bus to go and visit May. She lives off the Holloway Road in the small terraced house she's lived in since she was married in 1947. It had been damaged in the war, but not seriously, which was why the rent wasn't out of her husband Albert's reach. He soon put right whatever was wrong – something to do with a chimneypot going through the roof – and eventually he was able to buy the house when his plumbing business did well. I don't know how much this modest little place cost, though I'm sure May remembers to the last penny, but it's worth half a million now. This thrills May, though she doesn't really believe it, and every now and again she fantasises about what she could do with the money if she sold the house. 'Not that I'm moving,' she always ends. 'They'll carry me out feet first.'

But she really should move to somewhere more suitable now that the narrow, steep stairs are a trial to her. She only goes up and down them twice a day, and claims the exercise is good for her, but it gives her arthritic knees hell (or 'gyp' as she calls it). Watching her go up them isn't as scary as watching her come down. Going up, she sort of crawls, and though pathetic to witness it looks safe enough, whereas coming down she sways on each step and a catastrophic fall seems imminent. There's a stair rail on one side, but not on the other, and she clings to it with both hands, putting her off balance.

It's impossible, travelling along Holloway Road in a bus, to imagine the quiet streets that run off it, just a few minutes' walk away. The traffic is so heavy and thunderous on that major artery, and then suddenly it fades and there are these enclaves of small houses with hardly a car driving past. In May's street, a couple of houses have recently been painted, one cream, one a heathery lilac, and a few window boxes have appeared on upstairs sills, the geraniums startlingly colourful against all the drab rendered concrete walls. May doesn't know if she approves of them or not. 'This ain't Chelsea,' she mutters. That's her comment on a front door that has been stripped down to its pine wood. 'Folk trying to pretend they're living somewhere else.' She likes front doors to be a seemly black, with a brass knocker always kept polished, as hers is.

May's house does not have a bell. There is no need for newfangled things like bells, which she maintains scare the life out of you and are always going wrong. A knocker that alerts the whole street to any visitor trying to gain entry is good enough for her. My parents have been trying for years to have not just a bell but an intercom put in for her, or at the very least a spy hole – but May won't hear of it. She says she can look out of her parlour window to see who's at her front door. 'In the dark?' my mother asks. May says that she doesn't open the door after dark anyway, and if she wants to know who's knocking she can shout through the letter box and ask. That's what I had to do today, because I'd forgotten my key, shout through her letter box after I'd hammered away with the knocker without result. No face had appeared behind the net curtains of the parlour window, no sound of shuffling footsteps along the passage inside. 'Granny May!' I yelled. 'It's me. Isamay.' A door banged inside, and I heard her shout, 'Hold your horses!' and at last she made her way to the front door and opened it.

There was no great welcome. Instead, she scowled and said, 'Where you bin, eh?' I said I'd been busy working, which met with the usual snort of derision – 'Working! Working, she says! As if she knew what working was!' I followed her down the passage – it is always called 'the passage', never the hall – with her still muttering that real work was something I was unacquainted with in spite of my recent years temping, and that my grandfather could have told me a thing or two about work. May loves to talk about Albert and his 'emergencies', as though he'd been a doctor, a surgeon, forever rushing to save lives. She was describing one of his emergencies as she led me into her back kitchen – 'Middle of the night it used to be sometimes, the banging on our door 'cos someone had a flood, something had burst, and send for Albert, it was, and off he'd go . . .' Any minute and we'd be on to the toilets he'd had to sort out – 'now that was work' – and the unmentionables he found in pipes he unblocked, dirty work, hard on his knees, wore his overalls into holes, all that kneeling . . .

I always try to listen humbly, even though I've heard all this, or versions of it, so many times. May is right. I don't know what 'real' work is. My maternal grandfather's work was real and hard, and, at the time, not well paid (though it would be now – last week I paid a plumber a £60 call-out fee just to come and look at our leaking shower). When May finished her tirade the way she always finishes it, with the repetition of the words 'you don't know what work is', I agreed. The moment I agree, she changes her tune. 'Mind you,' she always says, 'brain work is good. If you can get it. You're smart, you are, and your dad and your mum, my Jean, going for the brain work. No flies on you lot. I'd have gone for it myself if I had the brains. I'd have done the brain work and laughed all the way to the bank instead of down on me hands and knees scrubbing other women's floors.' It was never any good protesting that my particular brain work was making me in *debt* to the bank at the moment, with no prospect of things changing financially for the foreseeable future.

May does have brains. She hasn't had much education, but she's clever, she could have done 'brain work' if things had been different. Hers is the usual, or rather common, story of a woman of her era and class. Class: that was what made the real difference. Left school at fourteen, got a job in a factory making parachutes – it was wartime – and then in a shop selling hardware, an ironmonger's, and that's where she met Albert and married him when she was two weeks away from her eighteenth birthday. After that, it was four children and going out charring for ten years till Albert prospered and she could

12

stay at home. She could have educated herself, true, but as she puts it, she didn't have 'the habit', and anyway she was always exhausted and had no time or energy for book learning. May is not philosophical about the opportunities denied her. On the contrary, she's resentful. She envies her own daughter, my mother Jean, and she envies me. But at the same time she can never make her mind up, it seems to me, whether she admires women who've succeeded in doing brain work for a living, or whether she despises them. It isn't easy to tell.

'What you bin up to, then?' she asked when she'd made us some tea and we were settled at her kitchen table, which was covered with brass ornaments she was cleaning. They were so familiar – the jug (usually full of artificial flowers, lurid things made of plastic), the plate, the bell, the three monkeys, all polished to a high shine every six weeks. Even the Brasso tin made me nostalgic for all the times, so long ago it seemed, when I'd been excited to be allowed the privilege of smearing the smelly khaki stuff on to the ornaments. I touched the tin with the tip of a finger and was at once told not to do so, I'd get my hands dirty. She used to make me wear gloves to do the polishing, which was all part of the charm – oh, how vigorously I would rub away with the soft cloth she gave me, rubbing and rubbing until the brass shone. 'Can you see your face in it?' May would ask, and if I could, the job was done to her satisfaction.

She asked again what I'd been up to, complaining that I was away with the fairies from the look of me. I told her about Elizabeth Fry. She frowned and asked why was I going on about this Mrs whoever-she-was. Mrs Fry, I said, you know, the famous prison reformer. That was a mistake. May said, excuse me, I ain't never heard of her, being ignorant, and what's the point you reading about her? Without thinking, I asked did there have to be a point, couldn't learning be for its own sake, and May was furious – 'Don't get clever with me, madam!' she shouted.

Somewhere, I have May in me. I am said to be stubborn, like her. Like a mule, when I don't want to do something. Can't be moved, just like my grandmother. And I have a temper, just like her, sudden flashes of rage that used to come over me (hardly ever now). May used to watch me, when I was a small child, in the middle of one of these tantrums, with a strange expression on her face, half horrified and half sympathetic, a slight smile playing round her lips though verbally she'd be expressing disapproval. She would say that she used to 'carry on' like that but that her dad thrashed it out of her. I wasn't thrashed, rather to her disappointment, I think, though she would never have wanted to see me hurt. 'The sight of a belt would do her good,' she'd tell my mother, who ignored her (which took some doing). May never gave me the sight of a belt, but she often shouted at me, when I was in one of these states, that any minute I'd feel the back of her hand, and she'd raise her arm over me to warn me that it was going to come down and slap me if I didn't stop. It never did end in a smack. Once the raised arm, and threatening words, had intimidated me, she'd slowly lower it. She only liked to see me suitably cowed.

But this is only one side of May, the grumpy side. Unfortunately, it's the one we all see most often these days, though I try to cling to the memories of the other May, the grandmother who doted on me and was so cosy to be with and laughed with pleasure at everything I said and did . . .

'Are you wandering again?' she asked me. I said sorry, I was day dreaming. She said she knew what I was doing and if that was all I was going to do, 'gather wool', I might as well go. I said I had to be off anyway and she said she didn't know why I'd come at all if I was hardly going to warm a seat and had no chat. I got up and gave her a peck on the cheek and said I'd see myself out and that next time I'd come for a proper visit. 'Don't bother if it's going to be a trouble,' she said.

'Bark's worse than her bite' is what my grandfather apparently used to say (he died, both grandfathers did, before I was born). I'm not sure he was right.

No British Library today. No safety. No leaving Euston Road behind, the noise, the traffic, the dust and dirt, and entering all that silence and clarity. Clarity? Whatever do I mean? But yes, clarity, of purpose. Whereas today it was a supervision day and all was confusion. Not that Claudia's room is in any way confusing or muddled. It is orderly, as she is herself, dressed as she always is in her calf-length skirt and her boat-necked long-sleeved top, the skirt always black, the top always some vivid colour and its neckline followed by a silver necklace of impeccable taste. The colours of her tops change but never the design. I admire how she sticks to her quaint yet elegant style of dressing. It gives her an old-fashioned but somehow glamorous look. I make an effort on supervision days. I get out of my jeans and sweaters and try to look reasonably well turned out, though probably Claudia wouldn't think so.

I dread going to see her. I dread the uncertainty, the slight panic. I know that I am going to feel, every single time, that I have to prove myself, to show that I know what I am doing, which of course I don't. To get the subject for my dissertation accepted, and to start on this course, I was obliged to make the subject matter sound more authentic, worthy of research, than it actually may turn out to be. It was a struggle, touch-and-go, whether it was suitable for an MA in Women's Studies (Hums.). I know there *is* something worthwhile here, but trying to summarise it had me desperate, scrabbling around at the edge of my mind looking for a firm hold. Claudia undoubtedly knew this, so it was good of her to accept me. But naturally, she expects results. She's not going to allow me to drift along exploring half-baked theories only to discard them. She wants to see a clear line of enquiry leading to an original and interesting conclusion.

15

She doesn't like me. It's childish to say that, even more childish to care about whether it is true, but that is the trouble – Claudia Harmsworth makes me feel a child. She's an unusual woman, not like most people's idea of an academic at all. I think people might guess she was an actress, what with her beautifully groomed hennaed hair, pageboy style, and her bright red lipstick and nail varnish, and the habit she has of continually raising her carefully plucked and shaped eyebrows, which gives her an air of permanent astonishment. She's a very still, alert person. 'Still' and 'alert' may sound like contradictions, but in Claudia they combine. She sits the whole time I am with her without moving, legs neatly together, hands clasped in her lap, and she watches me intently. I see her eyes following my own gesticulating hands, noting how many times I fiddle with my hair, taking in my restlessness. I annoy her, I am sure. I feel she wants to shout at me to stop jerking about like a marionette on a string, to be calm, as she is calm. And my speech, in her presence, is equally all over the place. I start sentences, then interrupt myself and start again, only to remember what I really want to say, and so I have to begin once more. The more rope she gives me, by allowing me to rant on, the more securely I verbally hang myself.

I confessed about Elizabeth Fry. At length I tried to explain why I'd thought she would fit into my dissertation (without mentioning the likeness to my grandmother May as the real starting point for my choice, of course). Claudia listened, she raised her eyebrows, and then she asked several questions I couldn't answer. Had I looked, she enquired, at the early tracts about Mrs Fry – 'Illustrious Woman', 'Angel of the Prisons', for example? No, I hadn't. Did I think she was a precursor of the feminist movement? Or was she rather a figurehead of philanthropic endeavour? She quoted the Reverend Sydney Smith, who apparently said of Mrs Fry, 'We long to burn her alive. Examples of living virtue disturb our repose and give birth to distressing comparisons.' What

16

weight did I give to that? She was checking out that I was doing my research properly, and that upset me, though I know she's entitled to, it's her job.

But she ended that supervision by being quite encouraging. Elizabeth Fry, she said, might yet prove promising for my purposes. She agreed that a grandmother ready to put her work before her family was surely sending out a very strong message to granddaughters. I might find that, far from being an exception that proved a rule, she altered the rule itself. It was worth investigating.

I felt quite heartened for once when I left. No clearer about what I am really trying to prove, but at least reassured that the trail I'm on might lead somewhere.

There are other matters to attend to. Next week it is Grandmother Isa's eightieth birthday. Isa – who likes to be called Grandmama, not Grandma, and certainly not Gran or Granny or Nana – cannot bear the idea of being old. All her life, I am told, she has concealed her age (and, I've begun to suspect, other things) from those who would like to know it. When I was around four or five, I asked her how old she was, and she told me that a lady never reveals her age and that it is rude to ask (when I asked May how old she was, she said she was twenty-one). So facing up to being eighty is hard for Isa, though my father predicts that there will now be a volte-face and his mother will start boasting about her age.

In any case, Isa is prepared to come out and celebrate being eighty with a party. She has spent months on preparations, writing all the invitations herself. My father was dumbfounded when he saw the list of guests, claiming he had never heard of half of them. It includes two cousins, both women, from Canada. Isa has never met them, but claims to have been in correspondence over the years with one of them, Mary-Lou, youngest child of her father's brother. There are also to be members of her dead husband's family at this party, in-laws

17

from Somerset with whom Isa says she has kept in touch, though none of us can imagine how, when there has never been any previous mention of these relatives-through-marriage. And she has invited May. My mother wishes she hadn't. Very kind of Isa to include May (who loves a party), but it fills all of us with foreboding. May accepted, though she was sarcastic about the invitation from 'Lady Muck', and commented she'd thought Isa had turned eighty years ago. This was not just unkind but the implication was unfair. Isa does not look older than eighty. She doesn't even look eighty. Her appearance is impressive, whatever May says. She has good skin, with few deep wrinkles, due, she says, to never sitting in the sun. A tan is an abomination to her. Her hair, though white, is still thick and healthy-looking, and she has it cut and shaped every three weeks by a hairdresser who comes to the house. It's true that her neck is scrawny, but she hides it with silk scarves, ever so artistically tied, and she dresses in such a way that the emphasis is on her still very neat waist. She is slim but not too thin. The only age-related thing she can do nothing about is the backs of her hands, which are quite heavily covered with dark brown patches. Isa is vain, and so these blemishes distress her, but she knows that compared to her contemporaries she looks wonderful – she has not let herself go. Nothing, she says, is more lamentable than letting oneself go, and that includes the putting on of excess weight or becoming slovenly about dressing.

My contribution to this party is to write a poem in cele-bration and recite it. A parody is the obvious route to take. I have got as far as the first verse:

> You're not old, Grandmama,
> This birthday comes as a shock.
> Your family agree, credulity's strained,
> *Can't* be eighty that's up on the clock.

The next verse will have to contain compliments, in some detail, about her appearance, and then move on to her achievements, I suppose. That's going to be tricky. What exactly has Isa achieved in her eighty years? She's been a wife and a mother and a grandmother. That's it. None of those roles have been very onerous. She was quite a spoiled wife, so far as I can make out. Grandfather Patrick looked after her very well and had the means to do so. She only had one child, who was sent to prep school at the age of seven, and then to Rugby. And I am her only grandchild. An empty sort of life, I would say, but mustn't.

I'm never sure whether I like Isa or not – not love, but *like*, quite different. There's something so detached about her, a sense that she is keeping herself apart, that she fears intimacy – even with her own son – as much as May seeks it. I've watched Isa and Dad together hundreds of times and they are painfully polite to each other. They never argue as Mum and May do, but instead, if some disagreement threatens to surface, they carefully register their different views and then move on to other topics. Yet Dad is quite proud of Isa, proud that she looks after herself and that she is well dressed and groomed, and that she at least attempts to read her *Times* (though complaining constantly that it has 'gone tabloid' in style as well as size) and keep abreast of world events. She is, in many ways, a model eighty-year-old mother.

I tried again to bring up the subject of his so-formal relationship with his mother when he took me out for lunch last week. He treats me as often as work permits and I look forward to these dates. The places he takes me to vary but are all similar – cafés rather than restaurants, family-run and cheerful. He is always there before me, though I am never late, sitting studying the specials board with an anxious air. He only relaxes when the order has been taken and his glass of wine has arrived. Then he asks me how 'it' is going. I tend just to say fine, and get on to something else, but last week

I was back to feeling lost, so I said 'it' was going badly and I wished I'd never started, I wished I'd chosen something straightforward, the growth of women's literature in the twentieth century maybe. He said why didn't I change my mind then. I said it was too late, and anyway I never change my mind. Your grandmother's granddaughter, he said, stubborn as her. There's no virtue in not changing your mind, he said, it isn't really anything to be proud of. Minds should change as circumstances do, it's a sign of strength, not weakness, to realise a decision or an opinion has been wrong.

Perhaps he's right, but I'm not just being stubborn. I tried to explain to him that I do feel what I'm trying to do has a purpose but I can't see it clearly. Dad hasn't had much need to find a sense of purpose in his work. It's been all too obvious: someone's hip or knee has worn out, he replaces it – bingo, job done. He knows exactly what he is doing, and why. He tried to cheer me up by pointing out that there could be a satisfaction in my kind of work, a creative element, which there wasn't in his, but that didn't help. Then our moussaka arrived, and after we'd eaten it, we went on to discuss Isa's coming party.

One of the many things Dad couldn't understand was why on earth his mother had invited some members of his father's family whom she could only have met a few times, long ago, at weddings and funerals and so forth. Even more puzzling to him was why these people had accepted her invitation. Her brother-in-law's widow, a woman of eighty-five, was coming all the way from Somerset, and a man referred to as Uncle George, though he was not an uncle. Dad swore he had never met them, or several others, but Isa insisted he had. Then there were the Canadian cousins. What was the connection with them? He'd found that this, at least, was relatively easily explained. It seemed they had been planning a tour of Scotland, to visit the places their ancestors came from, and they were fitting in Isa's party on the way. Mary-Lou, the one Isa had been in correspondence with, is tracing the history of the Macdonell family, of which she and Isa are both members. Dad said he knew he ought to offer to have them to stay, but he couldn't face it, and had invited them for lunch instead the day after the party.

We tried to make up some more verses to my poem, over the pudding, but without much success. Dad agreed there should be some compliments about Isa's appearance, her clothes, and how marvellous she always looks. She's fussing at the moment about having nothing to wear, and has been to Harrods (by taxi, as ever) but found nothing satisfactory and may have to fall back on a Worth frock she's had for years. We both smiled, agreeing that her obsession with clothes was extraordinary, at her age, but we couldn't decide whether it was by now a bit pathetic and somehow unseemly – but then Dad and I set no store by appearance, so we decided we were being snobbish, mocking poor Isa just because we ourselves don't appreciate fine clothes. Dad said he used to be so pleased with her when she came to his school – she always looked stunning and made everyone else's mother look dowdy. I couldn't resist saying, so that's what you most admire about your ma, is it? Her dress sense? I was mocking him now, and he knew it, but he said, quite calmly, that what he admired more was his mother's ability to hold herself together whatever happened. But, I said, nothing much has happened to test her, has it? He was silent, then seemed about to say something but didn't. I pressed him, but he changed the subject. He said he had a message from Mum: would Ian be coming to the party? I said no. He patted my hand and smiled. 'Don't be cross,' he said. 'She was just hoping you'd bring him.' I said I knew what she was hoping, and that there was no hope.

I must be missing the obvious ones. The grandmothers I'm after should spring unbidden into my mind . . . but they don't. I have to go looking, and then I get ambushed, one of them leaps out at me from the thicket of history and demands attention, and I waste time assessing her and usually find she's an impostor and was hardly a grandmother at all.

At least in that respect George Sand was genuine enough when she stopped me in my tracks. She was definitely an influential grandmother. She was far better as a grandmother, in fact, than as a mother. Her first grandchild was born when she was forty-four, but lived only a week, and it was her second, Nini, born the following year, who proved so significant in her life, and she in Nini's. Nini's mother, Solange, went into a convent and Nini went to live with her maternal grandmother, who was by then the famous author of several novels proclaiming and defending sensual love as a right for women. Nini, then almost five, completely fascinated her grandmother. The two of them spent hours gardening, each with a wheelbarrow (Nini's a tiny copy of her grandmother's). Nini, said George Sand, 'worked like a little horse'. All she wanted for her granddaughter was happiness – 'I try to stuff her with happiness,' she wrote. She couldn't bear the thought of Nini's individuality being suppressed to fit her into society. But this 'stuffing' didn't last long. Nini's father claimed her, filing for divorce from Solange and applying for custody of the child. Nini was taken from her grandmother and sent to a boarding school. Soon after, she contracted a fever and died.

The death of her granddaughter was an experience so profound for George Sand that it came close to breaking her. She had found grandmotherly love something she was more able to sustain than any other sort, and she had felt herself changed, very much for the better, by it. She had so much to pass on, now that she had white hair and had survived the emotional turbulence of her youth.

She had two more granddaughters, her son's children, and though she adored them, she didn't feel about them the way she had felt about Nini, the only one given into her care. Nini had made her take pride in her grandmotherly role, which contrasted sharply with her sense of failure as a mother. She decided that society needed grandmothers—

No, that's me. George Sand never said that. She may well have come to that conclusion, but I haven't found that she said so, much though I would like her to have done. It would make my job so much easier. But she at least gives me a lot more hope than Mrs Fry did.

Going to visit Isa is not like going to visit May. I can't just drop in. We have to make an appointment, and since Isa likes to keep up the pretence that she still has a crowded diary, this takes some doing. She's always been like this. When I was at school, I used to complain about this formality, and Beattie would say that maybe Isa needed to have time to hide a secret lover in the wardrobe, ha ha. She likes me to visit between five and six in the evening (after her 'girl' Elspeth has left), which is when she has her daily glass of sherry, the Bristol Cream variety. I think sherry tastes horrible, but I do love the glasses it comes in, so I always accept the offer. These delicate, lace-patterned glasses belonged to her grandmama. My father calls them 'thimbles' because they hold so little sherry, but that suits me. I like holding my glass by its fragile stem and twisting it gently round so that the light catches the amber fluid and lightens the colour. We sit opposite each other by the fire (real) if it's the least bit cold, Isa in a Queen Anne armchair (real again, and again bequeathed by her grand-mama) and I in a similar style of armchair though of Parker Knoll vintage. We converse. We do not chat, we do not gossip, we do not merely pass the time of day. Isa is proud of keeping abreast of world affairs, which lately has meant a lot of discussion about global warming. I find this boring but try not to show it.

Isa's attitude to my MA is different from May's. She herself did not go to university ('One didn't in my day,' she is fond of saying, though since she was born in 1928, this is not quite

23

true), but she is approving of my education, though not for the same reasons as May. Isa has decided that having a degree, and being in the process of achieving another academic qualification, will find me a good class of husband, not that she would ever use the word 'class'. She sees me marrying a professor, preferably an Oxbridge one, and that thought pleases her. She used, I think, to be frightened of highly educated women, but since my mother married into the family, this fear has faded. Nobody could be intimidated by my mother. Isa's relationship with her daughter-in-law is rather strange, changing, I think, quite substantially over the thirty-odd years they have known each other. When my father first took my mother home with him, all he'd told his parents was how pretty and clever Jean was and how he loved her and wanted to marry her as soon as possible. What else was there to tell them? Why, a very great deal, in Isa's opinion, such as what her father did, a question probably carefully phrased by Isa, and what sort of family this girl came from. My grandfather Albert's job as a plumber and his Isle of Dogs background did not go down well.

But Isa, I imagine with a struggle, managed to overlook my mother's lowly social status because, after all, the girl had been to Oxford, which in her eyes counted for something. She was also relieved that her son's girlfriend did not have the same accent as she later found May and Albert to have. Jean's vowels had been smoothed out during her time at Oxford, and while still not what Isa regarded as perfect (Isa had her own standards of perfection in all things), they gave little away. After first meeting Jean, Isa told my father she had been 'pleasantly surprised' by how 'refined' the girl seemed, and even how elegant, 'considering'. My father managed not to be appalled by his mother's patronising attitude and just said he was glad she approved (though Isa hadn't said anything about approving).

My mother had, of course, been overawed both by the

Symondsons' house – a veritable manor house at the time, near Bath – and by Isa. She was upset that my father hadn't given her an inkling of what she was going to experience. All he'd said to her was that his parents lived in the country, in 'an old, rambling place', and that his mother could be a bit 'iffy' sometimes but was all right once you got to know her. His father, he'd reassured her, was 'a sweetie'. At least that bit was accurate, according to my mother. Lieutenant-Colonel Patrick Symondson was a distinguished man but, as they say, he wore his distinction lightly. I wish I'd known him personally, and not just his history. He was born in India, where his father, an officer in a Gurkha regiment, was stationed. Patrick was sent to Rugby, then went to Sandhurst and was himself commissioned into the 1st Gurkha Rifles. I'm not sure of the details, but I know he was taken prisoner during the war, by the Japanese in Malaysia. He died in 1976, when my dad was twenty-three. Isa loves going over his army record, recounting instances of his bravery, though he himself is said to have been a reticent, modest man.

My mother told me that on the first awful occasion, when Isa was at her most distant and superior, Patrick himself was casual and relaxed. When Isa invited Jean to 'tell us about your family', Patrick interrupted to say that he'd far rather hear about Jean's studies and what she wanted to do. Mum didn't really know what she was going to do. The finals results weren't yet out and she didn't know if she would qualify for a research grant. Patrick asked her what it was she wanted to research, and she tried to explain about her interest in the communication networks of proteins and their involvement in human diseases. Biochemistry definitely wasn't Patrick's field, but he said he was fascinated and asked her to explain. Mum did her best. And remembered being pleased because Patrick seemed to grasp the essentials and asked intelligent questions.

Afterwards, Isa apparently got her husband to explain what

25

my mother had explained to him, and slowly, with the help of my dad as well, she managed, roughly speaking, to understand what biochemistry was and became quite proud of being able to toss about bits of terminology – not enough, of course, to engage in a real discussion with a biochemist but enough to impress those (like May) who knew nothing. Isa likes accumulating that sort of superficial knowledge. She has picked up a lot of medical lingo from her son, too, and can astound her friends (the few she has) with information about their hip and knee operations. I was never good at any of the sciences at school, which mystified my parents. Dad even thought I'd deliberately acted stupid as a sort of rebellion, but I don't think that's true. Well, maybe a bit. I sort of understand my mother's job, but not the detail. She's presented papers at the European Molecular Biology Laboratory in Heidelberg and got drug companies all excited about the possibilities opened up by her research. And I'm proud of her, but her work remains a bit of a mystery all the same.

Ian's is a mystery to me, too, though not such a dense one. He works at the National Physical Laboratory at Teddington, a hellish place to get to from our flat. What he works on has to do with time, trying to make an even more accurate optical clock than exists already. Asked to explain, he launches into descriptions of lasers trapping a single charged atom in a force field and then giving it a poke, and then – and then I'm lost. I tell people just that he works on the ordering of time. That baffles them. I told May he works with clocks, which immediately conjured up in her mind the image of a man my late grandfather Albert used to take his watch to, to be mended. She liked that, though she thought it an odd career for a clever young man. She asked me if Ian would have a look at her wedding present, a 1947 clock, and gave it to me to show him. It amused him to oblige. (Actually, he is good at things like that and did succeed in mending it.)

26

He isn't in the least bothered that May misunderstands what he does, and he doesn't care that my knowledge of his work isn't much more profound. It's fine by him. He has his colleagues to talk to about what he does, and doesn't need me. When I worry about this and say that one whole side of his life is in effect barred to me, he says that's how he likes it, a complete separation of the professional and the personal. He is willing to share in my work, though. In fact, he is quite keen to hear about it. So is Isa. 'A sad story,' she said, when I'd finished telling her what had happened to Nini. She asked if George Sand had had any other grandchildren and I told her the little I knew about them. I threw in that her dying instruction to her two surviving granddaughters had been to 'be good', which I thought disappointing somehow. But Isa approved. 'Goodness is so important, don't you think?' she said.

Well no, I don't think it is really. I was tempted to ask Isa how she would define 'goodness', but I didn't. She would think it obvious. We'd finished the sherry at this point, and I had an urgent need to go and clean my teeth to take the taste away. Leaving Isa is not difficult the way leaving May can be – an hour is enough for a visit to Isa, she has 'things' to attend to, or so she believes. As I gave her the regulation peck on the cheek to bid her goodbye, she murmured, 'Will you be bringing your young man to my party, Isamay?' I said no, I would not. I didn't give a reason, I didn't make up any excuse for Ian.

Isa, in this at least, is in agreement with May: she wants to see me 'settled', i.e. married. She wants to see me have a child. She wants 'the line' (her line, of course) to be continued. She's going to be disappointed.

II

'GRANDMOTHERS ARE figures of authority in society.' The moment I'd written that, I knew it was rubbish. I don't need Claudia to enjoy pointing it out. If I am to get anywhere, I'm going to have to stop thinking that the place of *my* grandmothers in *my* life is the norm. I know full well that it is not. My friends (except for Beattie) don't have grandmothers who have the kind of influence on them that Isa and May have had, and to a certain extent still have, on me. The majority don't have grandmothers at all – they are long dead, even memories of them have faded. Beattie is the only one who still has a grandmother alive. For other friends, all that remains are recollections of driving in the school holidays to visit the grandmothers and finding them at first delighted to see them and then, by the third or fourth day, critical of their behaviour, or clothes, or both. Leaving was a relief. None of my friends remember any Nini-type adoration by grandmothers. It simply never had the chance to grow and flourish. The ones who had grandmothers who came to stay tend only to recall the tension of these visits, with their mothers endlessly fretting over how to make Gran comfortable and happy.

Yet it seems to me relevant to what I'm trying to work out that Isa and May were a real presence in my young life. I once lived with May for a few months, when my mother was in hospital, flat on her back; trying to hang on to her second baby (she failed). I was not quite three, but the memories are distinct, though I expect heavily influenced by what I've been told. 'You were as good as gold,' May says, and then she boasts, 'You didn't miss your mum one little bit.' But this is possibly true. I was certainly very fond of my granny till I was about ten, extravagantly so. She was no George Sand, but in her own way she too tried to stuff me with happiness. And sweets, especially the lethal barley sugars, the cure for all unhappiness. God knows how my teeth survived.

Happiness, to May, lay in being well fed and having plenty of sleep. I only had to let out the merest whimper of discontent to be told I was tired and a good sleep would see me right. Either that or I was surely hungry and needed a biscuit or some cake to get me through to the next meal. My mother frequently remonstrated with May about stuffing me with food, but was told that what the child doesn't want she won't eat and it was doing her no harm. May overrode my mother at every turn and did what she liked with me until I myself began to rebel and say I wasn't tired or – less often – hungry. That didn't go down well. That was giving her 'lip'.

As I grew older, I gave May a lot of lip. Sometimes I was unthinkingly cruel. I'd tell her she had a funny smell. She'd never laugh that off – funny smells to her meant dirt of some sort, and she had an obsession about cleanliness. She'd tell me she'd had an 'all-over wash' that very morning, and her clothes were fresh on from the skin outwards, so no more talk of smells. I was too young to be able to stipulate what exactly I could smell or to say that it had nothing to do with being dirty. It was May herself who had a distinctive smell, a mixture of soap and soap powder but also of her particular scent, a kind of yeasty aroma, a bit like the kitchen after some baking had been done – far too complicated for a young child to explain. I hadn't meant anyway that 'funny' equalled 'bad'. But she took it that way.

I commented on her accent and grammar as well, which was naturally very offensive to her. But I wasn't sneering; I was just eager to show off that I knew how to say things properly once I'd learned to. After I'd moved into the juniors section of my primary school, I didn't like May coming to pick me up, which she was always eager to do. There was one girl who mimicked May's grammatical slips, trying to get the others to laugh at the dropped aitches, and the ain'ts. I hated the girl but was at the same time embarrassed by May. As for May herself, she could handle this kind of thing in public. She'd just turn and stare at the girl, if she heard the sneers, and ask, 'Anything else to say, madam, while your mouth is warm?' Everyone would laugh and May would pass round the forbidden barley sugars and the incident was over. But my embarrassment remained and I was ashamed of it and didn't understand it. May was my grandmother. I shouldn't have this uncomfortable feeling about her, surely.

I was glad when I moved on to secondary school that I no longer needed May to pick me up. She thought I still did, but my mother agreed that I was perfectly capable of getting myself to and from school even though it involved crossing a major road. Anyway, May's arthritis was beginning to bother her, and it was now too far for her to walk. So everything changed. Instead of seeing her every weekday I saw her only at the weekends, and not always then. I began saying 'Do I have to?' when my mother suggested I go to visit her on Saturdays, and I absolutely refused to stay the night if I did condescend to visit. The days of being tucked up with May in her big, sagging double bed were long over. I expect she was hurt by my sudden lack of interest in being with her, but if so, she was too proud to show it. When I trotted out excuses, around the age of thirteen or so, she asked why I thought she cared, she'd plenty to do, didn't have time to entertain me as once she had done.

It was around then that I switched my allegiance for a

while to Isa. Isa took me for tea at posh hotels after we'd been to some art exhibition or other. For a couple of pre-teenage rebellious years – I was a late starter – I was impressed. Isa took taxis everywhere, and that alone was impressive. I was even quite agreeable to 'looking nice' for her, and wore clothes she'd chosen for me quite willingly, down to the Mary Jane shoes. I listened respectfully to Isa's lectures on artists, and dutifully studied the expensive catalogues she bought. Then, inevitably, the thrill wore off. I still relished the teas, though I was reprimanded frequently for never, ever leaving anything for Miss Manners. My greed was beginning to annoy her – it was not ladylike. Worse still was my growing habit of contradicting her. Rather than standing humbly beside her, a little overawed, while she interpreted a painting for me, I offered my own opinions and told her I thought she'd got it wrong. Instead of being pleased with my independence of thought, she was offended. There was no tea at Claridges on those days.

Remembering that period in my life makes me see that this was when I first became fascinated by what my two grandmothers represented, not that I thought of them as 'representing' anything at the time. They were so contradictory, pointing me in entirely different directions. I knew virtually nothing about them, of course, though I was constantly asking for information. Isa would produce photographs of herself as a child, but May only had one blurred snapshot of herself at around the age of seven. In spite of not knowing much about them, I regarded them both as figures of authority when I was young. It was this conviction that, between them, my grandmothers *knew* all the things that mattered that led me, eventually, and in a very convoluted way, to what I am doing now. They are the source of my idea: grandmothers matter.

But how? Why? Where's the evidence?

* * *

Isa mentioned, before I left her, that there was to be a Millais exhibition soon and that perhaps we might go to it together. What she means is, will I take her, because she can now no longer quite manage on her own, in spite of having a taxi there and back. I said that of course I would go with her, and I will, though I loathe all the Pre-Raphaelites, especially Millais. Isa actually looks a bit like one of Millais' portraits, a portrait of Effie Millais, though all I recall of it is that the woman is wearing a dark red velvet gown with a lace collar and that she has another bit of lace sitting on top of her hair.

Effie Millais had eight children. I looked her up. I looked up the wives of all the Pre-Raphaelite artists – Rossetti's, Madox Brown's, Holman Hunt's; it's possible to spend ages doing that sort of thing, and I am an expert at it. Because Isa wanted to go to a Millais exhibition, I justified pleasantly passing an hour or so gathering useless information. Except in this case, it wasn't quite useless. I hit on Edith Holman Hunt, a rather terrifying, and therefore promising (for my purposes) grandmother. She was a tall, bony woman who lived in a bizarre house full of paintings, gongs, church candlesticks and all kinds of other curious things. Her grand-daughter Diana wrote that her throat used to be 'sore with worry' when she was deposited on her grandmother's doorstep. The welcome she got was warm, but also uncomfortable – Edith would embrace her, and all the brooches and buckles adorning her person would press into her.

Like Isa, Edith saw it as her job to educate her grand-daughter. She'd take her to the Tate Gallery and go from painting to painting lecturing her. These lectures in the Tate were not as agonising as one that took place in the crypt of St Paul's Cathedral, where, at one time, Holman Hunt's painting *The Light of the World* hung. Edith would gather a small crowd round herself and her granddaughter and before beginning to tell them all about the picture would announce that she had the honour of being the artist's widow.

Afterwards, she would take Diana for tea, but it wasn't the sort of tea Isa treated me to. No plush hotels for Edith. She'd choose a modest café, and once settled at a table ask for two cups and saucers and a jug of boiling water. When these items arrived, she'd produce a muslin bag of tea leaves from her reticule, and an envelope of powdered milk, and proceed to make tea. The tea drunk, she'd dip her finger into the salt on the table and massage the gums of her lower jaw. By this stage her granddaughter would be beetroot red with embarrassment, but her ordeal was not over. On the way home, Edith would make a commendably regular habit of stopping to give pavement artists money. This was fine, but where she got her purse from was not: she wore it under her skirt, and so, to retrieve it, she had to crouch down and lift her skirt. She also kept printed cards in her purse, and one of these would be given with the money to the artist. They read: 'Prudent thrift permits the luxury of giving.'

Diana Holman Hunt spent her childhood being shuttled between her grandmothers when she wasn't at boarding school. Now, what effect would that have on a child? How did she turn out? There couldn't, surely, have been more influential grandmothers, but how did this strong influence make itself felt? Did Diana become rigidly conventional? Or did she follow the pattern of eccentricity laid out for her? And what kind of grandmother did *she* become, if she became one? I felt quite excited just thinking about her – her experience links into what I'm looking for, the thin (as yet) thread slowly unwinding.

I try to imagine myself at seven, the age Diana Holman Hunt was when she went to live with her grandmothers, first with one, then the other, and it scares me. This is odd, because I was closer to both Isa, and to May, then, than at any other time. I loved going to their respective homes and being the centre of attention. But I wouldn't have wanted to live with either of them, I know that. I was always glad when my parents collected me, though sometimes I'd pretended to make a fuss about leaving, doing it to please the grandmothers. It used to irritate my mother a little, particularly when I acted reluctant to leave her own mother, May. 'Why do you do it?' she would ask. 'You don't really want to stay with Granny, do you?' I'd just smile and say I didn't know why, but of course I did. I sensed the need in May for me to make her better loved than her daughter, and sometimes I played the game she wanted me to play and let her think she was my favourite. This sounds sophisticated for a child, but it was merely instinctive. I couldn't have explained exactly how I felt.

I would have turned out quite unlike the person I am now if either of my grandmothers had had sole care of me. How lucky I am that this never happened. My grandmothers have stayed just that, grandmothers, mothers once removed, as it were. Grandmotherhood brings a sense of distance, however close the involvement, as George Sand found out. It's what makes their influence valuable, I think.

Party day yesterday, and thank God it dawned warm and sunny, one of those late September days more summer-like than any we've had since May. I rang Isa straight away, as soon as I looked out of the window and saw the thin mist, low on the ground, already lifting, swirling away, and the blue of the sky unmistakably heralding a perfect day. Isa was ecstatic. She boasts every year that her birthday is always blessed with beautiful weather.

May couldn't care less about birthday celebrations, no need for them. The fuss some folk make is ridiculous . . . Told that Isa was going to have a big party for her eightieth, May was as usual dismissive. She wondered aloud why Lady Muck would want to. Parties were for the young. It was just showing off at the Duchess's (another of her alternative names for Isa) age to have a party. Who would want to go? Well, May for one. She might detest Isa, she might scorn her party, but if she had *not* been invited she'd have been livid.

Isa herself had been in some doubt about inviting May. She had tentatively discussed it with me. She did not wish, she said, Mrs Wright to feel excluded, but on the other hand, if an invitation was dispatched, she did not want it to place Mrs Wright under any obligation to accept. I told her not to worry about it, just to do what she felt comfortable with. The invitation came through May's letter box while I was visiting one morning. Thick, cream-coloured envelope, first-class stamp, hand-written address, the postcode neatly underlined in red. I handed it to May. She fingered it suspiciously, yet with respect. She doesn't get much post and none of it comes in stylish envelopes. It took her a long time to open it, after many turnings-over and minute examination of the hand-writing, which yielded no clues. 'Get me a knife,' she ordered. 'Don't want to spoil an envelope like this,' which made me snigger. 'What you cackling about?' she said. 'You don't know how it might come in useful. We made use of all kinds of things in the war, no waste then.' I just went and got a knife and handed it to her silently, not prepared to get involved in a daft argument.

May stared at the embossed, gilt-edged card and finally said, 'I can't read this fancy writing, it's that posh sort. You read it out.' The script was ornate but perfectly legible. I read out Isa's invitation to a luncheon party on 27 September. It said RSVP by 5 September. I read that out too. 'RSVP means—' I began, but May cut in crossly, saying she wasn't born in a bog and knew what it meant, everyone knew what it meant. I apologised, and meant it. May was just as likely to have gone the other way, pretending she did *not* know, and I was trying to forestall her game. Anyway, the details read out for a second time, May pondered. She said she would have to think about it. She thought she was going to have her toenails cut at the clinic that day. 'What,' I said, 'on a Saturday

35

lunchtime? I don't believe the clinic is open then.' I pushed her. I said why bother to invent excuses if she didn't want to go to Isa's party, why not just say no, Isa wouldn't care. 'I know that,' May snapped, then she said, 'I suppose there will have to be a present.' The worry about an appropriate present sat heavily, and Isa's request that there should be none was treated as a come-on by May. 'Course I have to take something,' she said. 'Can't go to someone's house empty-handed.' Her face was creased with anxiety. I suggested maybe just something like a bunch of flowers from her own garden. Isa would appreciate that. She didn't like stiff arrangements from florists. A bunch of home-grown flowers would be just the thing. 'Home-grown, eh?' May said. 'From my garden? You blind, or what? You taking the mick? Come and show me what to pick,' and she held out her hand. I took it and she led me to look out of the kitchen window. I looked. A tiny square of tired-looking grass, surrounded by borders that had nothing in them but a few straggly-looking Michaelmas daisies together with some unidentifiable shrubs. No flowers to pick, yet in my head was such a strong image of myself standing on that grass and May handing me red and pink and yellow flowers to hold, straight after she'd cut them from among masses. She was watching my face. 'Sorry,' I said, 'I thought . . .' 'That was in them days,' she said, 'not now, can't do it no more.' Of course she couldn't. But I could, and should. 'Sorry,' I said again. She gave another of her little grunts, open to many interpretations. She likes being apologised to, though she is never gracious about accepting apologies. She never responds with 'you're forgiven' or 'never mind, we all make mistakes'. A grunt, a nod, that's it. We returned to the vexing question of what she could give 'her'. Finally, we settled on chocolates.

Next fuss was over what kind of birthday card to get, should it have 80 on the front or not? I said I thought not. Cards that had figures on the front tended to look cheap.

May said there was nothing wrong with cheap. I sighed, and she asked me what I had that face on for, and did my card have an 80 on it? I said no. I hadn't bought a card, I'd made one. I told her about my card to distract her from any more grumbling, describing the collage of photographs I'd assembled of Isa at different ages, starting with one of her as a baby on her mother Clara's knee. Clara was a strikingly beautiful woman, much more beautiful than Isa turned out to be. There's one photograph I've used in which Isa, aged about five, is standing between her parents, holding their hands. Clara stares straight to camera, but Isa is looking up adoringly at her father. He is not a handsome man, big and heavy, with one of those fearsome moustaches and not much hair. In the later snaps, the resemblance between Isa and me is pronounced, as everyone always points out. Even I can see it. It's not just the colour of our eyes (which can't be seen, naturally, in these sepia-tinted photographs) but their shape, slightly tilted upwards at the corner. And then there is our bone structure, such strong cheekbones (from my grandfather, by the look of him).

I said I'd take May to buy the chocolates and a card, and she grumpily fixed a day and time.

It was my job to collect May and take her to Isa's party. I'd rather have been given the task of picking up the Canadian cousins from their hotel, but that fell to Dad. Mum couldn't be spared to do either because she was in charge of organising the caterers and carrying out Isa's orders, something neither Dad nor I would have managed to do without making a mess of it and upsetting Isa. Mum doesn't always find dealing with her mother-in-law exactly easy – Isa can be so bossy, so peremptory – but she prefers allocating her services to her rather than to her own mother. I think it's because there is little emotion in her relationship with Isa, whereas there is a lot of suppressed feeling of one sort or another in her relationship with May. Mum and May don't fit. Their personalities as well as their looks and temperament are totally different. I am more like May than my mum is. I am more like Isa than my father is. Sometimes I wonder if anything about me is my own or whether I am made up entirely of my grandmothers.

I knew May would be in a faff, and I was right. When she opened the door she was wearing a heavily patterned short-sleeved dress that for at least a decade had been her 'going-out' outfit, worn with a beige jacket that could no longer be buttoned owing to her increased girth. She looked at me defiantly. 'I know it's a bit on the neat side but there's nothing else.' There were so many things wrong with this dress that there was no point in mentioning any of them. May's body is now a travesty of what I'd seen from photographs it had once been, but she made no allowances for all the extra weight and its distribution. In my mind, I defended her. She liked the dress. The fact that her upper arms were now so fat that the edge of the sleeves cut into them and produced a painful weal was neither here nor there, neither was the display of wrinkled chest revealed in the generous neckline, nor the visible straining of the rather thin fabric over her large tummy – none of these things mattered if May was happy in her dress. But she wasn't. That was the point. She was waiting for me to make even a mild comment about it no longer fitting as well as it had once done, and then to flounce off, declaring she wasn't going to the party. All I said was 'Very nice.' I wasn't perjuring myself. The dress, once upon a time, had been 'nice', if also ordinary. 'I'm not wearing it,' May said. 'It don't fit no more and if you can't see that you need glasses.'

Half an hour later (still with plenty of time because I'd known there would be this fuss) we left with May clad in black. It was her funeral outfit. A black skirt and a black top with white piping round the square neck and round the cuffs of the long sleeves. She'd said she couldn't wear black to a party, what would folk think, and I'd said they'd think her very smart and stylish. She insisted on wearing a cardigan with it 'to cheer it up'. The cardigan was red but it didn't look too bad. And she added her fake pearls, given to her by Albert on her fortieth birthday. 'What a carry-on,' she muttered as we finally left her bedroom, after a dab of lipstick had been dashed on to her thin lips and a brush pulled through her still thick hair. 'I can't be bothered,' she said, 'all this tarting up.' But I could tell she felt quite pleased now with her appearance. I thought, as we drove off, how the elegant Isa would inwardly shudder at the sight of May dressed in her best. Dress, to Isa, is such a serious business. She is appalled by women of her age who go on dressing as though their arms are still firm, their cleavages wrinkle-free, their legs unscarred by varicose veins. 'Clothes, Isamay,' she once said as though it was a brilliant insight, 'are to enhance one's best features when young and disguise one's worst when old.' Quite so. I wondered if, logically, the disguise for most women would have to end up being a burka.

Because the day was warm and sunny, the French windows of Isa's sitting room could be opened wide on to the terrace so that guests could, if they wished, sit outside on the cushioned benches or wander round the garden, admiring the late-season roses. The food was inside, arranged on a long table stretching from one end of the room to the other. Guests had to help themselves, but staff had been engaged to stand by and assist them if necessary. 'Staff' consisted of Elspeth and two girls she had found. The guests were mostly elderly but they were all in terrific good humour. Delighted to be there, pleased to see people they hadn't seen for years. Isa looked fantastic in her old Worth frock, with her immaculate white hair in a chignon. She moved about the party with a grace and ease that belied her age, laughing (but not immoderately), smiling (but not falsely), kissing cheeks far more withered than her own, and shaking hands lightly, quickly. Her colour was a little high perhaps, and once or twice I saw her reach for a chair to hold on to for a moment, but her poise was remarkable. I couldn't help but be impressed, and proud of her.

She greeted me warmly and May politely. 'How good to see you, Mrs Wright,' she said. May thrust her box of chocolates at her. 'Here,' she said. 'Happy birthday, don't eat them all at once.' Isa smiled, glacially, took the chocolates, and invited May to help herself to some food and a drink. May turned at once to the table, dragging me with her. She worked her way from one end to the other, piling up the plate I was obediently holding. She took something of everything, regardless of the indigestion she claims to suffer from and regardless of whether or not she recognised what it was. 'Do you really like aubergines, Granny?' I whispered. 'And anchovies?' She said it was a party; she'd give them a go. When she was satisfied she'd missed no delicacy, she led me to a little wrought-iron table on the terrace and told me to get a couple of chairs. I said I thought this table was just to put drinks on, and pointed to the four garden tables arranged further along the terrace, each with pretty cloths on and places set for six. 'I want this table,' she said. 'Fetch two chairs, quick, before they get snatched.'

So I found myself crouching at this ridiculous toy-like table, feeling embarrassed at so pointedly separating myself from the rest of the company, who were gradually taking their place at the proper tables. May was not in the least bothered. She applied herself to the food in a determined fashion, pausing only to sniff certain items before putting them into her mouth. She spread duck pâté over the slices of smoked salmon, dipped bits of chicken into cream cheese, never putting her knife and fork down until her plate was quite clean. 'Very tasty,' she said. 'Mind you, it should be, it'll have cost her enough.' At that

40

point, the Canadian cousins appeared. They stood beside us, only drinks in their hands, and asked if they could say hello. They were Mary-Lou and Beth, from Ontario, related to 'the birthday girl' through their fathers. May eyed them suspiciously, a little alarmed by their aggressively tartan outfits. They both wore not only tartan skirts but tartan jackets over red blouses, and on their heads they had tartan berets. They were, though, aware of looking a joke, and got in first with their own amusement at their rig-out. 'We couldn't resist it,' Mary-Lou said, gaily. 'Let's go the whole hog, we thought, let's be out-and-out Scottish for the party.' She then told us, without being asked, that the tartan was the Macdonell tartan, and that they'd given Isa a jacket the same as theirs.

I left Mary-Lou and Beth regaling May with every detail of their lives, from how many children they had to what kind of cars they drove – they never seemed to be going to draw breath. I went straight to Isa's side and tried hard to be the granddaughter she wanted. She was talking to a man in a wheelchair, whom she introduced to me as Uncle George. A handsome man, strong-looking, with broad shoulders, he sat very upright in his chair. I should have guessed he'd been a soldier.

'So you're related to Grandmama?' I asked. Both he and Isa laughed.

'No, no,' she said, 'the "uncle" is an honorary title, isn't it, George?'

'Big honour,' he said.

I was lost – this wasn't Isa's style, it was May's. She was always referring to 'Uncle this' and 'Auntie that' in her tales of her childhood, and they always turned out to be neighbours and not relatives at all – everyone in her street was Auntie or Uncle to children.

'What was the honour?' I asked George.

'Oh, it's a long story,' Isa said quickly. 'I will tell you some other time.'

George's helper – a grandchild of his, a bit older than me, I thought – appeared with his food, and as she pushed him to a table outside, another woman came up to Isa and said, 'Lovely food, Isa, such a treat.' Isa introduced me. Her name was Gertrude Symondson, widow of my grandfather Patrick's brother Harry. Dad joined us. 'Ah!' said Gertrude. 'The son!' Dad smiled, did a mock bow, said he was the son indeed. 'The longed-for son,' Gertrude said. 'You don't know the joy the news of your birth brought, my dear.' Dad said he was glad to hear it. 'Longed-for, longed-for, my boy,' she whispered. It was embarrassing, but Dad dealt with her well. He realised she'd had quite a bit to drink and very little to eat, and he steered her away towards the food table. 'That woman is a menace,' a voice said, quietly, in my ear. 'How do you do? I am a second cousin of yours, I believe, Frederick Macdonell.' I shook his hand, looking sharply at him, and we moved out on to the now very busy terrace. He told me he had known Isa when they were both young, but lost regular contact after she married and moved to London. 'A big surprise, that,' he said. 'Both families were rather upset. They didn't see the point of London, you see, and it was all rather sudden, I seem to remember.' This was not what I wanted to hear so I tried to get him to describe what Isa had been like when young. 'She looked like you, my dear,' he said, 'just as lovely,' and he put his arm round me and squeezed. Well, he was an old man, so I tried not to cringe. Luckily, I could hear May shouting my name and saw her waving her napkin in my direction, so I had a good excuse to leave him.

The Canadians had moved on to wanting to know about May, a trade-off for all they'd shared with her. They were saying how proud May must be of me, and of her daughter. May responded with her usual grunts, which could have meant anything. Clearly, the cousins were having trouble equating what seemed a grumpy, greedy old woman with her gentle, pleasant, concerned daughter. I saw them look from May to my mother Jean in confusion – some mistake, they were thinking. I saw exactly what they meant. Mum was going from guest to guest, hovering over each one, bending down to listen to them, smiling at them, getting more food or drink for them. What had this woman they were looking at to do with May?

Then Isa came over to ask the cousins if they had sampled the desserts yet, and recommended the zabaglione, which had just been brought out from the kitchen.

'The what?' asked May.

'Zabaglione, Mrs Wright,' Isa said. 'It's a special Italian sweet with—'

'Oh, Italian, is it?' May said. 'Not for me, too fancy.'

'Would you prefer some chocolate mousse, Mrs Wright?' said Isa, her tone still ever so light, 'I know you're fond of chocolate.'

'Not specially,' said May, ready to interpret a love of chocolate as Isa's way of saying she was fat.

'Or I believe there is apple tart,' Isa said, blandly. 'More your kind of pudding, Mrs Wright? I'll leave you to decide,' and she wafted off.

'Damned cheek,' May muttered, almost inaudibly, but the cousins caught it. There was a little throng round the table of desserts by then. May and I were left sitting together just outside one of the open doors, still at the small table, our backs to the house. I said nothing, I just waited. After a few minutes, May sniffed and said: 'Nice garden. She has it kept nice. Albert would've liked it.' This was a peace offering, her peculiar kind of way of apologising. She said it without a sneer, even if a sneer was implicit in 'She has it *kept* nice' rather than 'She has it nice.' I knew how the 'kept' could have been made to sound. I still said nothing. I could play May's games very well. Sometimes I felt she was the child and I was the grandmother. It was tempting to scold her, but

43

neither the place nor the time was right. I got up, to go and get May some sort of acceptable dessert, but she said, 'You leaving me on my tod?' I said, 'Just to get you some apple tart.' 'I don't want any,' she said. 'I'm full. I want to go home.'

It was so plaintive – 'I want to go home' – the cry of a four-year-old who was tired. We would be the first to leave, it would look bad, very pointed. I leaned towards her and whispered that we would go soon, but I had to go and be with Isa for a while. I'd tell Mum to come over so she wouldn't be on her own. 'Suppose so,' May said, grudgingly. She looked both fierce, frowning away, and vulnerable, clutching her napkin and twisting it around as though strangling it. She had no social graces at all, was only at ease with her family. But it was Isa's day, and I had to put her first, so I went and circulated, giving Mum a quick nudge and a look towards May, still at the table. Isa was by then sitting down at one of the other tables, and I joined her and chatted away to her guests, smiling until my cheeks ached. They all said how like my grandmother I was, and we were requested to stand together to be photographed and our likeness preserved and marvelled at. I never got straight who was who, but I took them all in, so that I could ask Isa later. There were more women than men, and not one of them had aged as well as Isa. She looked the youngest and healthiest woman there (not counting the Canadians). What I couldn't work out was how these guests regarded Isa – I sensed a strange mixture of respect and something like caution, but what made them cautious? Did they think she was frail? Were they afraid of offending her? Or maybe it was just that I was mistaking caution for admiration. Whatever – there was suddenly an air of hesitation, as though these relatives and friends didn't feel quite comfortable, in spite of all the laughter and good humour.

Isa herself was unaware of this, I'm sure. Her party was going with a swing and she was content. At three o'clock, twenty minutes after May had wanted to go (so she'd be furious with me), Elspeth brought out a cake and we all sang 'Happy Birthday', which Isa endured graciously, though she doesn't like that kind of display. Then Dad stood up and made a little speech. Well, he had to. Mum and he had laboured over it, and he delivered it with just the right mixture of seriousness and light-heartedness. He stressed his mother's independence of spirit, her dignity, her generosity, and he reminisced, just a little, about his father and how proud he had been of his wife. Then I spouted my doggerel, which went down very well. That was supposed to be it, with coffee and cake to follow, but to her own family's surprise Isa stood up and said she would like to say a few words while she had the opportunity. She began with thanking people for coming, and Jean for doing the organising, but then she moved on to talking about her late husband in, for her, surprisingly emotional terms. She said he had made her the happiest of women and his death had been the cruellest of blows. Everyone knew of his bravery but few appreciated his other virtues: his kindness, his sensitivity, his constant concern for others. Being his wife had made her so proud and as his widow she had tried to lead her life, bereft as it was, according to his standards.

There was quite a bit of throat-clearing at that point, a lot of it due to embarrassment, I think. I didn't dare look at May, whose opinion of Isa's eulogy would be one of scorn – she'd be muttering that she didn't believe a word of it. But Isa then moved on to talk about her son, my father. James was the perfect son, handsome, clever, devoted – Dad looked slightly bewildered – and his wife Jean was the perfect daughter-in-law. (Her perfection, though, was not gone into.) And then it was my turn. I was her only and much-loved grand-daughter. I was 'very precious'. What was precious about me was not just my particular qualities, but what I represented. 'Isamay,' said Isa, 'carries forward the family banner. When

I am gone, I will live in her, which makes me so happy.' She was so desperately serious no one quite knew how to react. There was a tentative clap from someone, picked up with relief by everyone else, and then we all relaxed. There was an urgent pull on my sleeve. 'I want to go, now!' hissed May.

'What was she on about?' May asked, crossly, as I drove her home. I didn't reply. I felt exhausted, though I'd done nothing but hand out plates of food, and chat.

'All that banner business,' May persisted. 'What banner's that? Eh?'

'It was a sort of metaphor,' I muttered.

'Oh, thank you very much. A met-what's-it, eh? Baffled by long words, am I?'

'You know what she meant,' I said.

'Would I be asking if I did?'

'Yes, you would, you often do, just to make a point.'

'And what point's that, then, madam?'

'You think Isa was showing off and being ridiculous and over the top. Pretentious, in a word.'

'You'd know it, o' course, never heard of it meself.'

'Well, you know it now.'

'You're being cheeky, talking like that to your grandmother what isn't educated like—'

'Oh, Granny, stop it!'

There was silence after that little outburst until we got to her house. Once there, I spent twenty minutes helping her look for her indigestion tablets in case she needed them. When she commented, as she was showing me to the door, that it had been a very nice party anyway, I knew that was, again, a peace offering. I agreed that it had been. 'It made Isa happy,' I added. May obviously decided that to let that go was too much. 'Happy?' she echoed. 'She ain't had nothing to be *un*happy about, that woman, never done a hand's turn, never had to wonder where the next penny was coming from, never lost a child, life of Riley she's had.'

'Are you jealous?' I said it before I had the sense to stop myself. I got the usual response – 'Did I say I was?' – and didn't pursue the accusation. I knew it was an unkind one, even if May had provoked it. Then she suddenly said, 'You're my granddaughter too. She forgets that, with her banner. Thinks you're all hers, just because you look a bit like her. Looks are nothing. You're more like my side than hers.'

I turned back from the door and gave her a hug. She looked so defenceless, her old face all screwed up with resentment against Isa's claim on me, vulnerable and yet fierce, like a small animal determined to defend itself against some predator. My hug, I could tell, relieved her – she relaxed against me, patting my back, and saying I was a good girl. It was as touching as Isa's speech had been. God, the pathos of being old, old and envious; what a combination. I thought ugly feelings like that belonged only to the young, I thought jealousy was an emotion we grew out of. How foolish. Maybe it lasts until death, until the victory of one rival over another is final.

I was lolling on the sofa, recovering, when Ian came home. He doesn't understand this family stuff. Soon after I first met him, and was starting to get interested in him, I made the mistake of trying to find out about his family. I think I asked him a harmless question, such as where did his parents live, and he asked why I wanted to know. He didn't say this aggressively, but there was a definite feeling that he resented the enquiry. I quickly said it didn't matter, I just wondered, and I suppose I expected him to laugh and go on to tell me. But he didn't. Another time, when I was regretting that I am an only child, I asked him if he had any siblings. He made the same reply: why did I want to know? That time, I defended my innocent question. I said surely it was normal, wasn't it, to wonder if someone had brothers or sisters. He said something about not wanting to be defined in terms of his family, and I told him not to be so pompous. But he was, and is, secretive. He won't give anything away about his family. This, of course, makes me more and more curious.

The fuss over Isa's eightieth birthday party had puzzled him. Why have a party if everyone dreads it? he'd argued. I'd said Isa didn't dread it, and neither did the rest of us, not really; we just worried about it turning out the way she wanted. He shrugged, and said it still seemed not worth the tension, the agonising over arrangements. So when he came in and found me prostrate on the sofa, he wasn't going to ask how the party had been, but I told him anyway.

Somewhere, Ian has a family. He must have a family, even if the members of it are all dead, or unknown to him. His parents may not be alive now – are they? I don't know – and he may have no siblings (has he?), but he was once part of a family. He will at least have distant relatives he doesn't know about, to whom he is genetically connected. But he denies them all. As far as he is concerned, he comes from nowhere, and I have to accept this. He stands on his own, uncluttered, or so he likes to think. Naturally, with this kind of outlook, he doesn't want to start a family of his own. Doesn't bother me. Bothers my grandmothers. Isa drops hints; May approaches the subject full frontal. When, they ask in their different ways, is Ian going to marry me and give me children? They've taken to pointing out that I am nearly thirty, and mustn't leave it too late. I laugh, and point out that today women are having first babies at forty, and that anyway I'm not considering maternity. I have my dissertation to nurse. Ian and I are perfectly happy as we are, together and childless. They'll just have to get used to it.

Ian eventually met them, my parents and my grandmothers: my family. He had gone on being highly resistant to meeting any of them, but I pleaded with him. What harm could it possibly do, and it would be such a relief to them – their imaginations had been working overtime, thinking his

48

reluctance to meet them meant he had evil designs on me, or else there was something spectacularly wrong with him. Ian said he just didn't want to get involved. That was it, quite simple. I more or less had to issue an ultimatum: if you take me, you take my family. That's the package. We argued a long time about this – he rejected absolutely that I was part of a package, and I argued that everyone is – but when he finally met my parents it came about accidentally. They came round unexpectedly to give me a surprise birthday present and Ian was here. He was suspicious that it was a put-up job, but it wasn't.

Naturally, when it came to the crunch he was charming. Well, maybe not charming, but polite and friendly and inter-ested, which is better. My father liked the fact that Ian is a Scot, and they chatted about Scotland, with Dad boasting of his Macdonell heritage. My mother didn't ask him anything, but he asked her about the project she was working on (I'd told him about it, obviously) and he made more sense of her answers than I had ever done. After they'd left, with invita-tions to come and have a meal issued (and deftly sidestepped by Ian), I said that wasn't so bad, was it, I told you they are nice. He said he'd never doubted that they were, it was more that he feared their niceness sucking him in, into a set-up he wanted to stay clear of. I was offended. My family is not a 'set-up'.

But it was done, the meeting, and for the time being I was satisfied. Ian is a very private person and I didn't want to push him further. I bided my time and engineered an intro-duction to May. Funnily enough, he didn't fight against that so hard. I asked him to pick me up from her house. I said he needn't come in, he could just knock on her door and I'd come straight out. But he did step in when May invited him (this time it *was* a put-up job – I knew that if my granny opened the door, he wouldn't turn his back on her). Ian, I'm sure, had known perfectly well what would happen, and so by going along with it he was complicit. May made him a cup of tea, and he said it was good to have it properly made, with loose tea in a teapot, just like his own grandmother used to make. I almost choked – did he realise what he'd let slip? He had, or had had, a granny who made tea in a teapot! What a revelation! What a sensation, this tiny sliver of family news! But I didn't tease him. I was just glad to hear it. We only stayed long enough for Ian to finish his tea, and then we were off. May's only comment, later, was that he had good hair. She likes a man with good hair.

Isa, by then, had learned that my parents had met my young man, and was aggrieved that he had not been brought to be vetted by her. She invited me to bring him along for sherry, and when I said Ian was never home in time for sherry, it was an impossible time of day for him, she said surely he didn't work on Sundays. I said no, but he played football. This scandalised her and kept further invitations from being issued for quite a while. But when she heard from Dad that May had met Ian, she became absolutely determined to see him. On and on she went, ringing me up and giving me a list of dates when it would be convenient (for her) for me to bring my young man to her house. I made desperate excuses, knowing Ian would never agree to anything so formal. And then one day he answered the phone to her, and said her voice sounded so quavery he hadn't the heart to turn down her suggestion. So he agreed to some of what she wanted, i.e. accepting her invitation to a cup of coffee on Sunday morning, but making it clear he only had half an hour to spare before another engagement. He meant going off to football, of course, but the use of the term 'engagement' was a masterstroke.

It was quite a tricky occasion. Isa is always elegant and beautifully coiffured, but I noticed that extra effort had gone into how the vital silk scarf round her neck was tied. Ian, mercifully, had conceded that it would be insulting to wear his tracksuit, and so had on proper trousers and a shirt, but the shirt was open-necked and he didn't wear a jacket. I saw Isa run her eye over him and find fault, but the way he drank his coffee (in Isa's opinion there are *vulgar* ways) passed muster. Conversationally, he kept his end up, playing her at her own game of exchanging pleasantry with pleasantry very successfully. When Isa moved on to an ever-so-delicate line of enquiry regarding career, family, etc., Ian ever-so-delicately blocked her. He timed the agreed half an hour to the second without once looking at his watch, and when he rose to leave, his manner was impeccably correct. Isa reported to my dad afterwards that Isamay's young man was a disappointment in some respects but she thought him clever and certainly not the 'undesirable' she had feared.

When I told him today about Isa's speech and the banner remark, he smiled. I asked him what he found so amusing. 'Oh,' he said, 'nothing.' And he wouldn't explain.

III

THERE IS no escaping her. Queen Victoria it will have to be. You will need to examine Queen Victoria closely, of course, Claudia had said, but I'd instantly felt rebellious. Why 'of course'? There is no element of surprise about Victoria as a grandmother – it is all as would be expected. Obviously, she set an example to her granddaughters. Obviously, she was an influence. And I won't be able to make a connection between her and grandmothers in general. She was a queen, she was different. She is not what I am seeking (and what is that, pray? I can hear Claudia asking).

However. Here we go: so far, I've found thirty-eight grand-children, of whom twenty-two were girls. Six of them were named after her. Dutifully, I've listed them all, and an impres-sive, even overwhelming, list it is. From 1859 to 1886, Victoria was being blessed with grandchildren. What surprises me – there, a surprise already – is discovering that the Queen was not thrilled to become a grandmother in the first place. She was not pleased when her daughter Vicki, married to the Kaiser's son, announced that she was pregnant. The news, she wrote, was 'horrid'. She'd wanted Vicki to have at least a year free from pregnancy, and there she was, practically having a honeymoon baby. There is little pride and joy to be found in Victoria's correspondence about becoming a grand-mother at thirty-nine, and absolutely no burbling about how she looked forward to holding the baby in her own arms. In fact, she disliked small babies. To her, they were ugly and unappealing, especially naked, so perhaps it was just as well that she didn't see her grandson, Vicki's baby, until he was eighteen months old.

But Victoria had no doubts about what her role as grandmother was: to be a fount of wisdom. In the interval between her grandson's birth and her first sight of him, she bombarded his mother with detailed advice and instructions to do with his care and upbringing. Yet in spite of the hectoring tone of some of the letters I quickly read, there seemed to be a good deal of sympathy there for what Vicki would be going through in her pregnancy and childbirth. The Queen herself had hated being pregnant – it made her feel like an animal – and thought women who enjoyed this state 'disgusting'. As for giving birth, the pain was terrible, her sufferings 'severe'. The indignity of it all, as well as the physical agony, outraged her. But to her credit, she did not pass all this on to Vicki – she told her not to dread the birth, there was no need to.

But Vicki suffered far more than the Queen had ever done. It was a breech birth, during which the poor mother almost died and the baby's left arm was damaged. 'How I wish I could have lightened the pain for you,' wrote Victoria. She felt helpless. A grandmother ought to be there, supervising the care of both baby and mother. Once Vicki was pronounced well, and her son thriving (though his arm remained withered), the Queen began to enjoy being a grandmother – it was, after all, 'fun' to 'look and feel young' even so. She intended to be fully involved.

That sounded promising for my purposes, but I had to stop at that point, just as I was beginning, and with all those relationships with the twenty-two granddaughters to come, and high hopes of useful material emerging . . .

* * *

May is ill. Mum rang to tell me, and to ask me to look in on her some time this afternoon. She, Mum, has been round already and thinks it isn't anything serious, just overindulgence at Isa's party. May's been sick half the night but wouldn't hear of the doctor being sent for. She is blaming 'them fancy dishes' and not her own greed.

I don't like to think of May lying alone in her house. The image is a pitiful one. I see her white hair, probably with a hairnet in place, peeping out from the pink satin eiderdown, which bulges round her plump little frame. She'll have her wincyette nightie on, and her red candlewick dressing gown will be hung over the end of the bed. At least she'll have the curtains open and won't be lying in gloom. She and Albert always slept with the curtains open so that the light could wake them for work – 'better than an alarm clock'. (It used to puzzle me. Dawn breaks at around four at the height of summer – why would they want to wake up then?) The curtains wouldn't have kept out much light anyway. They aren't lined, and the material is thin, but May made them herself and likes them because they 'wash easy and dry in ten minutes'. She'll be lying in that saggy old bed, watching the pigeons coming and going on the guttering . . . I'll have to stop, I'll be in tears in a minute. My poor old granny, ill and alone, nobody to look after her, having given her life to looking after others, etc., etc.

I remembered to take my door key this time. The moment I opened the front door I yelled out so May wouldn't be scared. I half hoped – very mean, this – that I'd find her blissfully snoring, and that all I would need to do would be to refill her flask with tea and tuck the bedclothes in. But she was awake, and told me there'd been no need to shout, she wasn't deaf yet. The radio was on – a repeat of *The Archers*, I realised – and I was told to be quiet till it finished. I sat down on the hellishly uncomfortable chair beside her bed and studied her.

She had her eyes closed, to concentrate. That made her look worse than she probably was. Her colour wasn't good, it had a yellowish tinge, but otherwise she looked robust enough. The programme over, she told me to put the wireless off and go and make her some toast because she felt peckish.

I couldn't work the grill on her old cooker. She hasn't got a toaster, won't have one, claiming the grill is perfectly adequate for the making of toast. It isn't. Getting the damned thing to light is a challenge to start with – it hasn't an automatic switch, and I didn't remember at first that I'd have to find matches, and so the kitchen filled with the smell of gas before I could light it. The first slice burned – I'd turned the flame too high – and I had to throw it away, but I didn't dare put it in May's waste bin. I put it in my pocket instead. Taking a successfully toasted and buttered slice up to her, I was greeted with an accusing stare and 'What you bin and gone and burned then? And don't say nothing, 'cos I've got a nose.' I confessed. She grunted and said I was too clever to make toast, brain work had made me stupid. I humbly agreed. She nibbled at the slice I'd given her, then pushed it away – 'Here, you eat it, do you good.' So I did. 'Always had a good appetite, you did,' she said, and then began a recital of all the dishes I'd loved best when she made them for me: the apple crumbles, the roast chicken, the fishcakes – 'Oh, you weren't faddy, you ate anything, not like your mum at all. You took after me.'

Mum was faddy, Mum was fussy, Mum had made May despair. I know all that. Nearly died of malnutrition at six months, etc., etc. May's never forgiven her for the shame of it. '"Madam," the man at the hospital says to me, "madam, this child is wasting away, she is dying of malnutrition."' As the tale goes (and it goes regularly, even now), May had just had all her teeth out and her milk was affected. The baby was fed, but she wasn't getting the nourishment she needed. She survived, obviously, but was for ever after a picky eater. The opposite of her brothers, the opposite of her mother.

It was the first sign that she was a cuckoo in the nest, as May loved describing her – 'I dunno where your mum come from.' But she knows where I came from. I am from her. Greedy. Stubborn. I am her, through and through. There's no point in arguing, no point in listing all the ways in which I am *not* like her.

I didn't even think of doing so this afternoon. I humoured her, nodded and smiled and agreed, and all the time wondered how soon I could get away and still be in time for my supervision with Claudia. I didn't feel bad about leaving May. She looked comfortable, and Mum would be coming again. She called me a good girl as I left, though in order for this not to go to my head, she added that my shoes could do with a polish. I stood for a moment in the narrow hall before I opened the front door. I wanted to hear if the radio had been switched back on, and when I heard it I was relieved. May was tucked up, and listening to the wireless. All was safe.

I arrived for my supervision late. Only about ten minutes, but late. This was bad. Claudia will never listen to excuses, she isn't interested in them. She holds her hand up like a traffic policeman when I begin to explain, so I've learned only to apologise and then sit down looking humble. It was tempting to tell her about visiting my sick granny – surely it would place me in a good light – but I resisted. I don't know if Claudia has grandmothers still, or whether, if they are dead, she knew them and was fond of them. Since she never indulges in idle chat, when this kind of information might emerge, it's impossible to guess. There are plenty of other academics who I've heard are quite chummy with their postgraduate students, but she isn't one of them. She treats supervisions as I've been told psychotherapists treat their clients – all detached and distant, their approach scientific rather than humane.

I tried to impress her with what I'd learned so far about Queen Victoria's attitude to becoming a grandmother, but that was a mistake. She asked if I'd consulted the letters the Queen wrote to Princess Victoria of Hesse. Oh, you mean Wilhelm's mother, I said brightly, and was about to launch into a précis of what I'd read when she said no, not Wilhelm's mother, that was Vicki, the Queen's eldest daughter. Princess Victoria was the Queen's granddaughter, her second daughter Alice's child. She told me about Alice, who died at thirty-five from diphtheria, leaving Princess Victoria, as the eldest, aged fifteen, to look after her three sisters and her brother. The Queen, said Claudia, had told the Princess to 'look on me as a mother'. She said it might be interesting for me to look at what the difference is between being a grandmother and yet acting as a mother, if indeed that was what the Queen went on to do.

We then spent the rest of the supervision discussing this. Naturally, I was eager to show off what I'd learned about Diana Holman Hunt's experience, but though Claudia listened politely, she seemed to think this had no great relevance to my dissertation and certainly none to Queen Victoria's mothering of her granddaughter. What I had to study, said Claudia, was the *essential* difference between being a mother and being a grandmother. Obviously, said I, a mother actually gives birth; she goes through the physical process of pregnancy and childbirth, whereas a grandmother does not. But, on the other hand, it is an experience she *has* gone through herself and so she can identify with it. And once the child is born, the grandmother can do everything the mother can do, apart from breastfeeding (which many mothers don't do anyway). In Queen Victoria's case, she clearly meant, I thought, that the Princess should turn to her for guidance in all matters, as she would have done to her mother. But Alice had been quite different from Queen Victoria. Alice breastfed her children and was intimate with and close to them, the kind of mother to whom children could turn without fear of criticism or scolding. According to Prince Albert, Victoria was not that kind of mother. He wished she could be more relaxed with the children, more inclined to play than impose her will upon them. As a grandmother who wanted to be looked upon as a mother, Claudia asked, did the Queen change? Did her role as grandmother enable her to reinterpret the role of mother?

Claudia ended by telling me something I didn't know (well, compared to her I know nothing) that struck me as important. When someone assumes a new role in life, she said, they tend to copy or to reject the example of whoever has filled that role for them. Claudia said that Queen Victoria had no role model as a grandmother. She never, within her own family, saw grandmothering in action. She had to invent the role for herself, as many women have to. Is grandmothering, then, all about second chances? Or about repetition?

Claudia always ends with questions.

No chance to get down to any work today. The Canadian cousins want to meet me 'properly'. Dad picked them up again from their hotel and brought them to his house for lunch, where Isa and I were already waiting. Isa was tired after her party, but still keen to see the cousins again and hear about their forthcoming tour of Scotland. They were not wearing their tartan outfits this time but grey pantsuits (Isa, of course, loathes such garments). Almost the moment they were through the door, they were telling Isa they had a big surprise for her, she was going to be so thrilled, so amazed . . . Isa, with her dislike of surprises, looked alarmed. The surprise turned out to be a genealogical chart of the Macdonells, tracing them back hundreds of years and going up to the present day. They could hardly wait for lunch to be over to get the table cleared and their chart laid out. I put Isa's apparent lack of enthusiasm down to her general exhaustion, and her irritation with how the cousins, Mary-Lou in particular, shouted.

The chart was secured at its corners to Mary-Lou's

satisfaction with a salt cellar, a pepper mill, and two small china bowls, and then she began what amounted to a lecture, impossible to interrupt. She, with Beth's help (Beth beamed her pride), had traced Isa's family, the Macdonells, back to the Jacobite rebellion period. Her great-great-great-grandfather Gavin Macdonell was killed by the musketry of Pulteney's Regiment on Culloden Moor, together with his chief, Alexander Macdonell of Keppoch, and scores of others. His son, also Gavin, inherited the land leased by the chief to his father, but in 1772 he, together with an estimated 5,400 others in that year, emigrated to Canada. Mary-Lou, who was proud of knowing the history, informed us that this early emigration movement was not the desperate affair it was to become in the next century, when starving Highlanders were cleared from the land to make way for sheep – Gavin Macdonell and his fellow emigrants had some money and left because they could see better opportunities in North America. This Gavin bought some land on the Gulf of St Lawrence and prospered. He had three sons, the eldest of whom (Gavin, of course) was Mary-Lou's great-great-grandfather and the youngest, James, Isa's. James returned to Scotland – Mary-Lou didn't know why – and became a businessman, ending up owning a steelworks and becoming wealthy. Mary-Lou's side of the family hadn't been so fortunate. We listened politely as she detailed their hardships. My father yawned, and Isa's fixed smile and head-nodding became irritating to watch. Mary-Lou kept pausing, as though for gasps of appreciation or astonishment. But you don't have to be clever to unearth this stuff. It's just a matter of having computer skills and being patient and dogged.

On and on it went, with Beth jumping in to finish Mary-Lou's sentences. Their excitement should have been infectious – they were so thrilled by all this family history – but instead was slightly embarrassing. Mary-Lou was particularly thrilled about the longevity of the name Gavin. 'There are,' she announced, 'at this moment in time *seven* Gavin Macdonells alive!' She pointed them out among the crowded lower branches of the family tree. They were all Canadians. Mary-Lou said she'd been unable to trace any Gavins on this side of the ocean and asked if Dad knew of any. That made Mum and me smile – Dad hasn't a clue about *any* of his relations. He didn't recognise any of them at Isa's party. Realising what his blank expression meant, Mary-Lou asked him, in a rather incredulous tone of voice, if he didn't keep in touch with his family on his mother's side. Dad said he was afraid not. This admission temporarily silenced Mary-Lou. I took the chance to ask a question. I'd been studying the chart, concentrating on Isa's side and not the Canadian lot, and I'd noticed a tiny question mark written next to Isa's name and date of birth. I pointed at it. 'What's that there for?' I asked. Mary-Lou said it was there to signify that Isa's parents had had a son, born in 1930, but that there was no information about him other than his date of birth. 'I wrote to you, Isa, do you remember?' Mary-Lou said. 'About your brother?'

We all looked at Isa. Mary-Lou had at last got us truly interested. Isa was smiling, but it was that fixed, glacial smile she specialises in when she wants to intimidate someone. 'I had no brother,' she said, speaking very clearly, slightly separating each word. 'As I told you, Mary-Lou, I had a sister, who died of diphtheria, aged three. You made a mistake.' As far as Isa was concerned, end of subject. But Mary-Lou was not so easily thwarted. She was mutinous. I could see it in the way she flushed and her mouth became set. 'I know about your sister, Isa; she is there, on the chart, see. But there was a brother too. I have his birth certificate. I offered you a copy, do you recall, dear? But you said not to trouble myself.' 'How fascinating,' I said, quickly. 'What do you suppose happened to him? What was his name?' 'James,' Mary-Lou said, and then added, 'I think. The writing is almost indecipherable.' 'I had no brother,' repeated Isa. 'This is all a nonsense.'

The tension was marked in both Isa and Mary-Lou, but I

couldn't let the matter of the mysterious brother rest. I wondered aloud what had happened to this baby Isa knew nothing about. 'Maybe he was stillborn, and it was kept from Isa,' I suggested. But Mary-Lou didn't think so. She said there would have been a record of his death, and that, in fact, the birth was registered six weeks later, showing the child had at least reached that age. But there was no death certificate for a James Macdonell born on 1 June 1930. She had searched and searched and found nothing. 'Because there is nothing to find,' said Isa. 'But you weren't quite two,' I said. 'You wouldn't necessarily have known about the baby, Grandmama, and—' My dad nudged me, and said, 'I'm sure Mother is right and it's all a mix-up. Anyway, it's all in the past, it doesn't matter.' 'Oh!' said Mary-Lou, 'But the past *does* matter!' Dad hurriedly muttered something about the past always being a bit unreliable anyway, and then Mum started serving the coffee and the atmosphere lightened.

After that, my parents both worked hard at steering the cousins away from their precious chart, asking them about the Scottish trip they were about to set off on. They gave us their itinerary in bewildering detail. Isa had by then quite obviously gone off them and seemed relieved when they made the first move to leave. I offered to drive them back to their hotel. It gave me the opportunity to give Mary-Lou my address and ask her to send me a copy of the intriguing birth certificate. 'You'll find there's no mistake,' she said, and offered me a copy of her whole chart if I'd like one. I said I'd love a copy, but I must pay for the copying and the postage. She wouldn't hear of it – I was *family*. Before we parted, I asked her why she thought my grandmother had been so angry about this brother, why wasn't she fascinated instead and curious to know what had happened to him. 'She is offended she didn't know about him,' Beth offered, but Mary-Lou wasn't sure that was the reason. I pressed her to give me her opinion, but for a woman who was normally so garrulous, she was curiously reluctant. I couldn't get anything out of her, if there was anything to get.

The letters Claudia had told me about, from Queen Victoria to Princess Victoria of Hesse, showed a grandmother who, though she had indeed written 'look on me as a mother', and been full of sympathy for the young princess's plight, was also highly critical of the girl's behaviour. She obviously took offence easily and insisted on the highest standards. 'Two letters I have received from you,' she wrote in 1879, 'but never the one thanking me for mine.' Not to thank her was inexcusable. She was also shocked by Princess Victoria's tomboyish ways, especially her love of hunting – 'it is not ladylike to kill animals and go out shooting . . . only fast ladies do such things'. All this struck me as typical grandmotherly stuff, but what was more interesting was the Queen's attitude to her granddaughter's girlfriends. She advised her never to make close female friendships – 'girls' friendships and intimacies are very bad and often lead to great mischief'.

Really? I sat and thought about that. Friends are important to girls, especially in adolescence. I thought about my own friends at that period and knew I'd have been lost without them even though I wasn't as dependent on friends as some girls are. Beattie, especially, was important. We told each other everything, spent hours in each other's company planning what we were going to do in the future, how far away from our boring lives we were going to move. Other friends didn't matter as much but we, Beattie and I, still needed them to give our activities more point – we needed them for parties, and to play games with, and to move around in a pack with when we wanted to seem powerful. So why did Queen Victoria think this kind of thing was bad? A grandmother who had wanted to be thought of as a mother forbidding her granddaughter the kind of friendships that could bring her so much comfort and pleasure – it was odd.

I don't think there can have been any sexual undertone. Wasn't the Queen famous for believing lesbianism couldn't exist? So she can't have been warning the princess off girl-friends for that reason. It was such a strange piece of advice to give a young girl, and I raced on through the letters looking for clues as to what the Queen meant, but there weren't any. She had other extraordinary things to tell her granddaughter, though, but I was interrupted before I could absorb them.

Mum rang. May is in hospital. How she comes to be there is a drama she will relish describing once she is better, featuring as it does hammering on her party wall with a heavy torch (her dead husband Albert's) to attract the atten-tion of her neighbours, the Patels, and then the Patels calling the police, who used a ladder to get in her bedroom window to find her lying in her blood-soaked bed . . . all true, appar-ently. No good asking why May hadn't used her telephone to call someone. She hasn't a phone in her bedroom, won't have one, won't have a portable or a mobile, and says the bedroom is no place for dratted telephones. She was lucky the Patels heard her and acted swiftly. May has not exactly been a good neighbour to them, restricting herself to good morning and nice day type pleasantries, though she does give their children barley sugars. She admits that Mrs Patel keeps her family in good order and that Mr Patel is very polite and always puts her bin back in its proper place if the bin men have left it on the pavement. But she has never invited them into her house and I doubt she'd accept an invitation into theirs, if it was offered.

Mr Patel, when he heard the noise, was afraid his neigh-bour was being burgled. He didn't have her telephone number, so he rang the police, afraid to confront intruders himself. The police banged on May's front door first, got no reply, and then went through the Patels' house into their garden and over the wall into May's. They climbed up to her bedroom, opened the window easily, and found her unconscious, half in, half out of her bed, clutching a pillow sodden with blood. They called an ambulance and rang Mum (her number was written in large print beside the downstairs telephone). It's a call she's been anticipating and dreading. She went straight to the hospital, where May was still in A & E in a cubicle, and stayed with her until she was moved to a short-stay ward. She'd had a haemorrhage, but they don't know the cause yet. Mum is going to work soon. I am to take over, and visit this afternoon.

I've been trying to remember how many people I've ever visited in hospital. Not many. I'm not the hospital visiting type. It's not that I don't care when friends or family are ill, just that, like many people, I have a weird phobia about hospitals. OK, it's cowardice. I always worry that I'm going to faint at their bedsides. I only have to walk into the building and the palpitations start. Sometimes, when I'm visiting someone, I only just manage to get into a corridor, or stumble to a toilet, before my knees give way, and I end up lying on the floor. These dizzy spells are over quickly. I get up, splash my face with cold water and rush out of the place.

So, going to visit my granny was not easy. I dreaded disgracing myself and upsetting her. For ages I stood outside the main entrance of the hospital, with the smokers, and tried to brace myself. I took deep breaths, and shivered – though not with fright but from the cold, from the sting of the wind whipping its way from the north, round the concrete pillars. Going into the place was at first a relief because of the warmth. I relaxed a little, and lectured myself, and vowed I was going to be fine this time. I almost ran up the stairs, scorning the lifts, and felt better for the exercise. I hoped it would have given my cheeks some colour so that May wouldn't tell me I looked like death warmed up. I found the short-stay ward but paused to read a printed list of instructions about wearing protective clothing because of the threat of MRSA. I had to put on a kind of apron, made of plastic, I think, and a pair of gloves, after I'd removed my jacket. This helped, funnily enough. I felt protected against my fear, too.

There were only four beds in the ward, all of them occupied, though one patient was out of her bed, standing looking out of the window. May was nearest to the door. She was propped up on pillows, awake and watching the two women opposite her with what looked like pop-eyed surprise. 'Granny,' I said, and went to sit on the chair beside her bed, pulling it close. For a moment, I thought she didn't recognise me, but then she said, 'Well, you've come; I'm glad someone's come, 'cos I don't know what they're doing to me here.' I said they were finding out what was wrong with her and then they'd make her better. 'Huh,' she said, 'if you believe that you'll believe anything.' But she said it in a mild tone, her heart not in it – usually, that phrase comes out searingly sarcastic. I thought she might relish telling me what had happened, but she hadn't the heart for that either. The spirited account I'd imagined never came. Instead, she sighed and mumbled about the blood, and the pain in her belly, and how she was all on her own and didn't know what to do. 'Right carry-on it were,' she said. I was just about to try to reassure her, as well as praise her for managing to alert the Patels, when a loud 'Fuck that!' rang through the ward. May jerked her head round to trace where the swearing had come from, and I did the same.

It had come from the woman who, I'd thought, had been standing just looking out of the window, with her back to us. I saw now that she'd been struggling with some sort of oxygen mask, which she'd wrenched off and flung on her bed. The other two patients appeared to have slept through this interruption, but the woman could see that May and I were mesmerised, staring at her, probably with our mouths hanging open. 'I'm fucked up,' she said, but in a resigned way. She came towards us, pointing at her chest. 'Lungs fucked,' she said, and then, moving her finger down, 'liver fucked. I tell you, I'm bloody well fucked, good and proper, and as for that fucking nebuliser, it does no fuckin' good.' Neither May nor I said a word. A polite 'how interesting', or a caring 'I'm so sorry' definitely would not do. May clutched my hand tightly, and I cleared my throat. 'That your gran?' the woman said, perching now on the end of May's bed. I nodded. 'Thought so, poor old sod. Brought her in in a right state, early hours this morning. Haemorrhage, was it? Stomach ulcer, was it?' I said I didn't know. 'They don't know either,' she said. 'They know fuckin' nothing.' I cleared my throat again. 'Want a Strepsil?' she asked. I nodded, and a packet was produced from her jeans pocket. 'I'm Jess,' she said. 'Don't mind me, I just get that fuckin' angry, know what I mean?' I said I did (but do I?). 'I'm sick of being told this is all my own fuckin' fault. Do they think I don't know that? Course I do. But I can't help it if it's my own fuckin' fault, can I? Do they ever think of that? Course they don't.'

At that point, a nurse came in. I waited for Jess to scurry back obediently to her bed, but she didn't. She greeted the nurse with 'Where the hell have you been?' and the nurse, perfectly amiably, said she'd been bringing a patient up from A & E. 'Have you used your nebuliser, Jess?' she asked. 'Course I fuckin' have and it's fuckin' useless,' said Jess. I waited for the reprimand, but all the nurse said was that she'd check the nebuliser to make sure it wasn't blocked. 'This thing on my arm is killing me,' Jess complained, holding out her shockingly thin arm, where there was a patch of something stuck on the upper part. The nurse said it was probably sore because Jess was reacting to the antibiotic. 'Of course I fuckin' am!' Jess shouted. 'So do something about it, get another antibiotic going. One I ain't allergic to. I'm not having this, it's itching like mad, I want it off or I'll rip it off myself! Go on, scarper, get a doctor!' The nurse, completely unfazed, gave a little laugh, as though Jess had made a joke, and went off again. Jess went back to her bed.

May and I looked at each other. 'In *hospital*!' May whispered. She was astounded more than outraged. Sick people didn't swear. Sick people revered doctors and nurses. She was stunned, and so was I, with less excuse. Why shouldn't Jess be angry and complain? Why shouldn't the nurse just overlook the swearing, knowing it was Jess's normal language and she didn't mean to be offensive? But May's attitude had passed over to me in spite of my different upbringing. She'd always been in awe of doctors and hospitals. She'd wanted her clever daughter to be a nurse, not a scientist (but at least she had married a doctor, the one thing my mum ever did that really pleased May). Now I sat there, as uncomfortable as my grandmother, eyes only for Jess, who was walking up and down the short length of the ward, talking to herself furiously. Then a phone rang, and she produced a mobile from her pocket. May and I gave each other another shocked look. 'A phone, in *hospital*!' May whispered. 'They ain't allowed!'

We were either out of date (and we were) or else Jess was defying orders. 'Tony!' she yelled. 'You wanker! Yeah, I'm in again, fuckin' prison, not even a telly. Just had the place done, it's a new ward they say, and no bloody telly, can you believe it? What are they like? What are their priorities, yeah? Taxpayers' money, and no telly, for Gawd's sake, bloody ridiculous. What? Yeah, my dad's been, wish he hadn't, he says Stacey wants to visit. I ain't having that bitch anywhere near me telling me it's my own fuckin' fault, yeah, that's what she does, bloody cheek.' There was a longish pause. Neither May nor I could drag our eyes away from Jess, who seemed entirely oblivious to the presence of anyone else. 'What?' she started again. 'What? At my age? Forget it. I'm going to be forty in July, *forty*. I'm a fuckin' miracle I am, only four pounds when I was born and that was in a toilet, no, honestly, stop laughing, I was, I come out head first into a toilet,' and then Jess screamed and laughed and wiped her eyes on her sleeve. 'What? Right, see you then, love you, babe, bye.'

She came back to May's bed in high good humour and said: 'Don't mind me, I'm hyperactive. It don't mean nothing, I can't help it. You won't be here much longer, darlin',' she assured May. 'They shove you out of here pretty quick, don't you worry. They'll be sending me up to Alexandra any minute. I fuckin' hate it there, full of old women moaning away.' I looked at May, worried she'd think she was being insulted, but she was beyond any kind of angry response. Jess hypnotised her. May's expression was almost one of awe that anyone could be so voluble and loud *in hospital*. But Jess turned her attention to me. 'Nice tan you've got, for the time of year. Been away?' I'd been with Ian in September to Crete but I felt embarrassed at admitting this – it seemed so flash – and so, stupidly, I said yes, I'd been away earlier in the year to an island. 'Ireland?' Jess said. 'I didn't know you could get a tan in Ireland, fuckin' amazing, I thought it was all bogs and rain.' She'd been perched on the bed but now she stood up. 'I'll have to leave you,' she said. 'This place is doing my head in. I'm going out for a fag. If anyone comes for me, tell them I'm in the toilet, yeah? Won't be long.'

'Thank the Lord,' one of the women in the other beds murmured, still with her eyes shut. 'A fag!' May said, still whispering, 'with her troubles.' 'Maybe she didn't mean it,' I said, but of course I knew she did. I wondered where exactly she would go. It was a long way to get outside the building – maybe there was some outside space halfway down that I didn't know about, but no, balconies and rooftops would be too dangerous. Jess would have to go all the way down, it would take her ages. Without her, the ward was deathly quiet. May didn't like the sudden silence. It made her nervous. She started sighing loudly, and groaning. 'I want out,' she said. 'Where's my clothes? I'm all right now, I want to go home.'

I patted her hand and said I'd go and find a nurse and try to find out what was happening. 'Get my clothes,' she said.

I couldn't find a nurse. The place seemed empty, though it couldn't be. I wandered round the corridors, looking into the different wards, each with four beds, but all I could see were beds with patients in them. There was a long desk at the point where two corridors joined and I stopped there and waited. A nurse finally came and I asked her what was happening about my grandmother. 'Dr Almed is with her now,' she said, 'and then in half an hour, with luck, Dr Smith will be along and we'll get a report.' I wandered back to May's ward, knowing I'd have to stay till the report was made – presumably a diagnosis and a decision about treatment – but as I neared the entrance to the ward I heard a man's voice, a rather loud, hectoring voice, say: 'May, I want to ask you some questions, OK?' I stopped. May's dignity would be outraged that a stranger, even a revered doctor, should address her by her Christian name. I thought I wouldn't interfere – I'd just lurk and listen, and then when he'd finished, go in.

The doctor repeated his request, and I wondered if May had fallen asleep, but surely he'd be able to see that. Eventually, I heard her grunt. If she'd been asleep, he'd woken her up. Bit thoughtless, surely. Jess would've told him off. It's strange building up an image of a person just from hearing their voice. Listening to the doctor, I imagined him as tall and heavy, with thick black eyebrows and old-fashioned horn-rimmed spectacles. I wondered if he was wearing a white coat, though hardly any of them seem to now. May would want him to wear a white coat and have a stethoscope round his neck.

'Now, May, when were you born? Can you remember?'

'Course I can. January the fifteenth, 1930.'

'Very good. Now, May, listen carefully – your hearing is all right, is it? Good, good. Now, what I'm going to do, May, is give you an address, OK? Then in a few minutes' time, when I've asked you some other questions, I'm going to ask you what that address was. Right? I'll speak very clearly. The address is forty-two, North Street. Quite simple. I'll repeat it: forty-two – North – Street. Got it? Forty-two, North Street.'

'Never heard of it,' May said, not objecting, but registering how puzzled she was. 'Who lives there? Do I know them?'

'No, that's not the point, May. Don't worry about it. The point is just to remember it. That's all I want you to do, just remember forty-two, North Street.'

'If you say so.'

'Now, May, can you count backwards from twenty to one?'

'Why?'

'Never mind why, May. It's just to see if you can do it. It's a sort of game.'

'I was never very good at games.'

'Come on, May – twenty, nineteen, eighteen . . .'

'You've done it yourself, so that's good. Anyone can do it, can't they?'

A sigh from the doctor. 'May, who is our monarch?'

'Elizabeth. She's married to Philip and she's got four children, Charles, Anne, Andrew and Edward, and they've all let her down, *three* divorces, imagine, and what she's had to put up with, what with—'

'Thank you, May. Now, can you remember that address I gave you?'

'Yes.'

'Good. What is it?'

But May was becoming suspicious. This wasn't how doctors were supposed to behave. I could hear her losing her respect for this man, and sounding more like her true self. 'Here,' she said, 'what is this address? Why do you want me to repeat it like a bloomin' parrot, eh? Why should I?'

There was a pause. I leaned against the wall of the corridor and smiled. Had he finished? Had he finally established what was obvious from the start – that my grandmother was not senile? But no, he started again, though I noticed he modulated his voice accordingly. 'May,' he said, 'can you remember your parents?'

'Course I can!' said May, quite angrily.

'What were their names?'

'George and Violet, hard workers they were, honest as the day, Gawd rest their souls . . .'

'Good, good. Right. Now, when you were a child, May, did anyone else live with you and your parents?'

'Course they did – three brothers, two sisters, all passed away now, all a lot older than me. I was the runt of the litter, gave my mum a shock, me appearing, she thought she was on the change. Then one day—'

'OK, May, fine, fine, good. Anyone else live with you?'

'My nan.'

'What was her name?'

'Mrs Pearson, my mum's mum. My mum looked after her, folk did in them days. My nan had a bed in the room me and my sisters slept in, them at one end of our bed and me at the other, lying between their feet, and my nan, she—'

'That's the end of my questions, May. Thank you.'

'Did I pass?'

'Pass? Oh, it wasn't a test, May.'

'What was it, then?'

'Just a check-up.'

I realised as soon as he came out of the ward that the 'doctor' was probably a student. He wasn't big and heavy, and he didn't have black eyebrows. How he came to have such a loud voice when he was so thin and weedy, I don't know – there seemed nowhere for it to come from. But his questions had made May agitated. When I went back in, I saw that her face was flushed. I couldn't tell her I'd been sneakily listening, so had to let her go over what had happened. Jess came in towards the end. 'Oh, him,' she said, taking up her perch on May's bed again, 'you don't want to

71

pay him no attention, he's just a houseman. The one you want is Smith, he's the registrar, nearest to Cooper, he's the consultant, but you won't get near him unless you're worth him fetching his team so he can show them up 'cos they ain't guessed what's wrong with you.'

Should I stay? Jess saw me frowning and restless, and said, 'No good fussing, what's your name? Eh? Funny name. Could be hours till that Smithy comes to look at your gran. You're lucky to have a gran. Mine's dead. Not ordinary dead either – murdered. Honest. Not surprising, the men she went with, my mum says.' On and on Jess went, and May calmed down. It was, I thought, like a kind of music-hall act to her, without the music. She was the perfect audience. Jess paused long enough in her recital of tragedies to tell me to go, she'd look after my gran, why didn't I just keep ringing up them dozy nurses and come back when Smith had been and they'd decided what was what.

So that's what I did.

I wasn't thinking of May when I left the hospital. I was thinking about *her* granny, her nan, Mrs Pearson. I hadn't heard the name before, and I'd never seen a photograph of her, but then May's family was poor and probably didn't have a camera when her grandmother was still alive. Studio portraits would have been beyond their means. Mrs Pearson must have been born in Queen Victoria's reign, say around the 1870s. I thought of her in May's bedroom, her bed squeezed in somehow, and the three girls simply accepting her presence. I wondered if they did things for her, helped her up to use the chamberpot, what a horrible image. May talks a lot about 'pos', as she calls them. Makes her laugh to see people using a po as a plant pot, as though these items were pretty and something to show off to their best advantage.

Does May see herself eventually going to live with my mother? I don't think so. But if not with my parents, when the time comes (as it maybe already has), with whom? Me? That's ridiculous. It wouldn't work. But does May have fantasies that it might? Where else can she turn but to the granddaughter who owes her? The granddaughter whose brain work means she's at home a lot, who could fit her studies round caring for her.

It's no wonder that in my panic at this scenario I almost got run over crossing the road outside the hospital.

May is not going to be in hospital for long. That's the good news. Is it? I quite like thinking of her tucked up in bed there, scandalised by but enjoying Jess's company, and being looked after. She can apparently go home in a couple of days, Mum says, provided there is adequate cover. What exactly does 'cover' mean? It means there must be someone to look after her, of course. She can't be on her own at first. Well of course she can't – she's an old lady who's been very ill. She'll need help, with everything. So it's simple, really: either Mum or I will need to go and stay with her, or else she will have to stay with one of us.

Mum is honest about this. Sometimes I wish she wouldn't be so honest. She doesn't try to pretend that her work would prevent her being able to look after May. She knows she could employ people to help, it could be managed. No, she doesn't plead her career as an excuse for not inviting her mother to live with her. She just says she couldn't stand it, they don't get on and never have done. Knowing this is the truth upsets me – I want Mum and May to love each other and get on famously. How did this sad state of affairs come about? Mum says from her birth. But surely, a longed-for girl after three boys must have meant starting off with a huge advantage. Mum concedes this ought to be so, but all she remembers is May shouting at her and complaining she had her head in the clouds or was daydreaming. Things got worse as she grew up. She says watching May with me was a revelation

– she herself had never known such affection, such devotion. She'd see me sitting on May's knee, being cuddled, and sung to, and laughed with, and it brought back memories quite the opposite.

Mum is fair. She points out that May likes this strange relationship as little as she does, but it's just one of those things, a genetic mismatch that happens all the time. She and May have tried to surmount their basic differences, of temperament, personality, taste, and to a certain extent they've succeeded. Mostly, they can 'get on'. But they can't be easy with each other, as May and I can be, even though there are huge differences between us too.

Mum says it was her father she felt easy with, and probably May somehow resented that. I wish I'd known my maternal grandfather, just to see if it was her father whom my mother resembled, because she certainly does not resemble May. In fact, the physical contrast between them is the striking thing – May small, my mum tall; May fat, Mum slim; May blonde (once), Mum dark. No feature similar. Mum is so contained and reserved, and May noisy and outspoken. It really is extraordinary that my mother is May's daughter. But she is. No need to fantasise that she was adopted, or mixed up at birth in the hospital. May had her at home, the longed-for daughter after three boys. No mistake about that.

It's hard to work out how May and my mother connect except by their DNA. I don't know if my grandmother loves my mother or if my mother loves her. I'm assuming that if the word 'love' is not analysed too closely for its meaning, if it is defined in its loosest sense, then maybe they do love each other, in spite of appearances to the contrary. May is always glaring at her daughter, her expression invariably accusing her (though it is never easy to tell of what), and Mum seems always evasive, never quite looking May in the eye. It's sad, really. I've tried to discuss this with my mother but I never get anywhere. Mum says it is just one of those things.

She and May are incompatible. Considering this, she thinks they manage pretty well. Or they have done, up to now.

Mum is pleased, and relieved, that I am so comfortable with May. I always have been. We are both affectionate towards each other, and we say what we like without fear of offence. May isn't my confidante any more, but I can still talk to her about most things. I am what is called 'close' to my grandmother, even if not nearly as close as I used to be as a child, so when Mum said May was coming out of hospital in a day or so but would need to be looked after, I offered straight away to go and stay with her. There's no reason why I shouldn't do it, every reason why I should. I can carry on working while at May's house, Mum couldn't. And May won't drive me mad the way she would irritate Mum. I'll be her carer until a proper system can be fixed up.

Ian says I'm being a martyr, and glorying in it. He reminds me that I've often told him that May has her wireless, or the television, or both, on at top volume, so I won't be able to concentrate. This is true, but I said my work is hardly brain surgery, so a little distraction won't be fatal. Oh, please, he said, not the self-deprecating bit. You'll just get frustrated and bad-tempered and ruin your beautiful relationship with your granny. I didn't like the way he said that. Did he mean my relationship wasn't beautiful, or is he jealous because he doesn't have a granny to love him the way he knows May loves me? I asked him. He said neither. He said, gently, that he was simply trying to point out what would inevitably happen if I carried out my plan. But I'm going to carry it out. It's settled. I'm taking a load of books with me about Queen Victoria, the obvious ones, the ones not precious enough only to be accessed in the British Library. I'll read out interesting bits as I come across them. May will enjoy it. There she will be, sitting in her battered old armchair, a mug of tea in her hand, and there I will be, with my books and notepad. Very companionable.

IV

MAY HAS mastered the word haematemisis. She takes it syllable by syllable, and pronounces it correctly. She was pleased when I had to ask her what it means. It means, she said, quite self-importantly, 'vomiting blood'. In her case, a large amount of blood, from a gastric ulcer that had broken into a blood vessel. She said she could have been a goner. 'Mind you,' she added, 'at my age, you've got to expect the worst. Seventy-eight is more than three-score years and ten.' There was a significant silence after she said this. She was watching me closely, waiting for my reaction. I knew she wanted me to disagree, to tell her that she was not going to be a goner yet, that seventy-eight was young these days and she had plenty of years left. So I did. I said the Bible was out of date. I said I was certain she would in due course get a telegram from Her Majesty when she reached a hundred. It was the right thing to say, it was what she wanted to hear.

On the first day of my temporary residence at her abode (she loves that word for some reason – 'welcome to my abode' she often says, and laughs), I arrived an hour before Mum was due to collect her from the hospital, so that I could put the fires on in her kitchen and living room and make her bed ready. Mum had already been in and stripped all the blood-stained bedding and dealt with it, so all I had to do was put clean sheets on and open the window. All the sheets in May's airing cupboard were flannelette. She doesn't hold with 'cold' cotton or 'sticky' Terylene – flannelette it has to be, whatever the weather. Same with the lethal fires – they always have to have at least one bar on, however hot the day. I knew I would roast, and had come prepared in the lightest clothes I had.

I was choked up helping her into her abode. Mum held her on one side, I on the other, but even so she staggered. 'I must be drunk,' she muttered, and hoped no one was watching. Once in her armchair, she revived, and thanked the Lord loudly for being in her own home with a decent cup of tea. Mum's leave-taking was, as ever, a bit tense. Mum said that I'd be staying for a few days, and May snorted and said she didn't need anyone, she could manage. Mum said the hospital wouldn't have let her out without being sure she had someone with her. May said they were not the boss of the whole world, and she would do what she liked. The moment Mum had gone, May said: 'It should be her, by rights, not you.' I said didn't she like me, then? She told me not to talk ridiculous.

We listened together, that first afternoon, to several programmes on her wireless and then we had tea, what May calls a cooked tea. Mum had brought some Marks & Spencer stuff, which I heated up. May ate a little of it. She had a diet sheet the hospital had given her and had me read it out to her so that she would be sure to obey its instructions, saying repeatedly that she would have to be careful to avoid another 'do'. But she was too exhausted to eat much and was ready to go to bed by seven o'clock. I had to push her, literally, up her stairs. She helped by clutching the banisters and hauling herself up. We'd considered putting a bed in her living room, but she was adamant that she wanted her own bed in her own bedroom, and anyway there was no lavatory on the ground floor and she didn't want to go back to using a po. God, what a business it was, getting her upstairs, getting her into bed, the pathos of it making me shaky myself. I wanted to cry but knew that would be inexcusable, so I kept up the bright-and-chatty front required of me, making endless crap jokes of the kind she liked, all linked together with her favourite sayings. When she was finally in her bed, sighing contentedly and saying she wouldn't call the King her cousin (one of her more complicated aphorisms), I put her walking stick beside her and told her to thump on the floor with it when she needed me.

She didn't thump at all. I was up several times in the night, peering anxiously into her bedroom, but she never stirred until I was up and dressed myself. I took breakfast up to her, managing the wretched grill this time well enough not to burn the toast, and suggested she stay in bed for the morning. She said this suited her, and so I went downstairs and tried to start on the books I'd brought. Once I actually got into a volume, really into it so that May's claustrophobic, dingy living room receded, I was OK, but it took some effort, and of course I was on the alert all the time for May knocking. I heard her get up to go to the bathroom and held my breath – but she made the trip without falling, which she couldn't have done the day before. So maybe I wouldn't be in her abode long.

Lunch, and then she got up and I helped her to dress and somehow got her safely downstairs. Once she was in her armchair, I sat down with my books spread out, determined to involve her. 'Listen to this,' I said. 'This is Queen Victoria writing: "I hate marriages, especially those of my daughters." What do you make of that?'

'Jealous, likely.'

'Who of?'

'The men, of course, the husbands, taking her girls away.'

'You didn't mind Dad taking your daughter away, you were glad, you said, showed she was normal after all, you told me.'

'Well, I wasn't the Queen. Who else could she trust except her daughters, eh? Being a queen. It ain't easy.'

'I think she was just selfish, thought it was their duty to

78

put her first, especially where the youngest daughter was concerned, Beatrice.'

May gave one of her little grunts, but I thought she sounded pleased. 'You and your books,' she said. 'You and your history. Go on then, tell us some more if you want.'

'Queen Victoria,' I said, 'didn't like having so many grandchildren. She wrote: "I do *not* rejoice in such constant additions." That was after she'd had fourteen, and the fifteenth was on the way.'

'What was wrong with her?' May asked, sounding very cross. 'I wish I'd had more grandchildren.'

'How many have you got?'

'What do you mean? You know how many, asking daft questions like that doctor did. I've got four, counting you, and do I see them? No, I do not. A Christmas card if I'm lucky and that's it. Useless. I might as well just have had the one, you, for all the good the others have done me.'

'Is that what grandchildren are for, then, to do you good?'

'Don't get smart with me, miss.'

The story of May's sons, my uncles, is a strange one, or strange to me. One died when he was just ten. He was the eldest and according to May the spitting image of Albert (the highest compliment she could pay). She won't talk about his death, even now, partly because she blames herself for not recognising the symptoms of meningitis. The other two boys both emigrated to Australia, together, when they were eighteen and twenty. Like their father, they were plumbers, and had a good trade to offer. May never forgave them for going. Plenty of work here for them, she says, there was no call to go skedaddling to the other side of the world. She claims it broke Albert's heart. Whatever. My mum says she's sure her brothers went partly to get away from May, who liked to try to control them. They both lived at home, and Mum remembers terrible arguments between them and their mother. They settled in Perth, and married, and had children, but May has had virtually no contact with them. A Christmas card arrives every year, very early, and a few photographs from time to time, but a letter is a rare event (and usually written by one of the wives). There has never been any mention of either them or their children coming back to the UK, or any suggestion of being willing to pay May's fare for her to visit them. May supposes, bitterly, that they won't come to her funeral just as they didn't come for their father's.

So, what went wrong? Or did nothing 'go wrong'; it's just that the sons wanted their freedom and took it and then not even a bad conscience could bring them home again. My mother remembers being glad of the peace and quiet when her brothers left and glad of the extra space too. She doesn't seem to think they should share responsibility for May in her old age, she doesn't blame them for, as it were, deserting. I asked her if she'd told them about May being ill and she said not yet, there didn't seem any point. I did a May-type glare at her then and said I thought they should be told and encouraged at least to express some concern. Mum just smiled. She said I'd be saying next it was her brothers' duty to respond. Well, I do think it is. Foolishly, I'd said this to Ian and he'd groaned and said there you go again, assuming blood ties automatically bring responsibilities that have to be honoured. I said it was about feelings, emotional ties, which can't be denied. Ian said it was possible they were not there at all. Why, he asked, couldn't I be like my mother, who expected nothing from her brothers, and she was the one who had the right to. I said I wasn't like Mum. I'm like May. 'Unfortunately in that respect,' he said. And we left it like that.

May sulked for a while after I'd irritated her by bringing up the matter of her absent grandchildren and what they could all be doing for her. She said she might have a nap, in her chair. I said I'd read to her, if she liked, it would send her to sleep. I was joking, but May took it seriously and grunted her permission. So I began to read out stuff about

Queen Victoria and her children. I read a description of Beatrice, Victoria's youngest child, making her escape and marrying and having four children, who the Queen admitted brought her great happiness, though she found them a little boisterous. I paused, and said to May that I was trying to find out what kind of influence the Queen had over her grandchildren, especially the girls. 'I know she was very strict about their manners,' I said, 'just like Grandmama Isa was with me.' (A flicker of response from May's closed eyelids – she didn't like Isa being mentioned.) I read on, about a visit made by Wilhelm, Vicki's son, when he was five, to his grandmother. She was going to take him for a ride in her carriage but he refused to sit in the back seat. She thought this showed a disturbing sign of arrogance, which should be dealt with severely before it became ingrained. May nodded.

I carried on reading bits out, choosing the anecdotes most likely to entertain May. I thought she would like that reference to the Queen warning her granddaughter, the Princess of Hesse, against having close friendships with other girls, which she believed led to 'great mischief'. I read the actual quote out to May, and watched her expression closely. 'Why shouldn't the poor motherless Princess be chums with other girls?' I wondered aloud. 'She needed them, all girls do, at some time, don't you think?' 'You can't be too careful,' May said, but wouldn't enlarge on what either she or the Queen might mean. Her eyes were properly open again. She pulled one of the books towards her. 'Any pictures?' I showed them to her. She loved the photograph of the Queen in the garden at Osborne surrounded by her family, taken in 1889, and the portrait of her in her wedding dress by Winterhalter. 'That's how a bride should look,' she said. 'They did it proper in them days, not like today, in and out of register offices wearing any old thing. That's what you'll do, likely. Is that what you'll do, eh?'

My turn to ignore her. 'It worried the Queen,' I read out, 'that the Princess asked too many questions, especially about

81

religion and the meaning of life. She said it was a mistake to try to find an explanation for everything and—'

'Quite right!' May interrupted me.

'Right about what?'

'Too many questions. That's you to a T. Always nagging away, wanting to know things, asking questions there ain't no answers to.'

'Like what?'

'There you are! Like nothing.'

'That doesn't make sense. What I asked was—'

'Don't you tell me what makes sense, the idea!'

'OK, OK. Anyway, what the Queen meant was that she thought there was a spiritual world as well as a material one and that it couldn't be explained, you just had to accept that it was there, and beyond understanding. What do you think?'

'What do I think of what? You talk in riddles, you, talk for talk's sake.'

'What do you think about Queen Victoria's opinion that there's a spiritual life that can't be explained?'

'Don't know what you're on about,' May said, 'and my tea is cold.'

I made fresh tea, sugaring it well. I wanted to persist. May and I never seemed to talk about anything that *mattered*, we just exchanged pleasantries and platitudes, and I wanted to take the chance of really trying to find out her opinions. There she is, seventy-eight, a lifetime's experiences behind her, and I know nothing about how it's made her view life, death, the lot. Once she was vigorously blowing on her tea, I tackled her.

'Granny, do you believe in God?'

'That's my business.'

'But I just want to know if you believe there *is* a God.'

'Where?'

'I don't mean "where" – I just want to know if you believe in him.'

'Tell me where he lives and I'll tell you if I believe in the

82

fella.' She was very pleased with this silly answer and smirked as she sipped her tea. I decided to take her seriously.

'God is believed to be a spiritual power,' I said, 'not actually a person.'

'Well, that's a relief.'

'He is supposed to be an almighty spirit who created the universe and sent his son Jesus Christ to save us all.'

'Very kind of him.'

'But the point is, as I said, he is a *spiritual* presence, or idea . . .'

'Make your mind up.'

'. . . whose existence we can't properly grasp because our mind can't fully comprehend—'

'Oh, for Gawd's sake, stop it! You're making me poorly. Haven't I gone through enough?'

'All I'm trying to say is that some very clever people believe in God . . .'

'Good luck to them.'

'So you don't, then?'

'Don't what?'

'Believe in God.'

'Did I say that?'

'No, but . . .'

'Well then, don't you twist my words.'

I paused, let her finish her tea, let her think she'd won. Then I took another approach. 'Mum told me Grandad Albert had a big funeral,' I said.

'Course he did, a proper send-off.'

'There was a church service, wasn't there?'

'Course there was.'

'Mum says there were a lot of flowers, she remembers that, big wreaths.'

'Course there were.'

'So you must be religious, you must believe in God, or you did then.'

'How do you make that out?'

'The funeral was in a church, and—'

'Where else would it be?'

'Yes, but I'm told there were prayers and hymns and all that. There was a religious service. He could've been cremated, there—'

'Cremated! Your grandad! Burn a good oak coffin?'

'Well, it rots in the ground anyway, there's no difference.'

'Stop it, you're upsetting me. The doctor said I shouldn't be upset, not when I've been ill, not at my age.'

I don't know why we can't ever have a reasonable discussion about such subjects. What's so difficult about saying one does or does not believe in God, that one is or is not religious? Or simply that one doesn't know. But May won't allow it. She pays lip service to religion when it suits her, for the big occasions, and then forgets about it. She never goes to church and I've never seen a Bible or a prayer book receive any attention from her, though I know she has both somewhere in her house and would be indignant if anyone suggested she hadn't. The trouble is, she's superstitious. I'm sure she doesn't believe in God, and has no religious faith, but she's scared to say so in case she's wrong and heavenly wrath descends on her. I'd wanted to talk to her about dying but there was no way I could – that *would* be upsetting her for real, and I hated upsetting her. Hadn't I lied to her, assuring her she was going to live to a hundred when I thought, in fact, she'd die long before?

I let it go. Better to try to get her to talk about love and marriage, though it was just as likely that she'd find that subject impossible to discuss, for different reasons. 'Listen,' I said, reading aloud, paraphrasing, 'Queen Victoria told her granddaughter that marriage was the very reverse of independence because two wills had to act together so all the time two people were having to compromise if they disagreed, or one had to give way. She warned all her granddaughters against marriage for that reason. Don't you think it was odd, when she had such a happy marriage?'

'I had a happy marriage, never a cross word.'

'Then you weren't like Queen Victoria.'

'Eh?'

'She and her Albert had lots of cross words. They had some dreadful rows. There are dozens of descriptions of the Queen in a rage and Albert trying to calm her down.'

'I never had no rows with *my* Albert, we was as happy as the day was long, two lovebirds we was.'

'I don't believe you.'

'You can believe what you like, it don't make any difference.'

'So you both always agreed on everything?'

'I never said that. But we never had rows.'

'And you were never in a rage?'

'He knew how to handle me, if the occasion arose.'

'So you did have rows?'

'What you trying to prove, eh? What you trying to spoil?'

'Nothing. I'm just interested in marriage and how people survive it.'

'Survive? What you talking about? It ain't a disaster, it ain't an earthquake.'

'Sometimes it is.'

'Don't talk daft.'

'What about love, then?'

'What about love?'

'Did you love your Albert?'

'I *married* him, didn't I?'

'But my uncle was on the way, Tom . . .'

I'd gone too far, and was immediately ashamed. Even now, I wasn't supposed to know that May had been pregnant with her beloved Tom (the one who died, aged ten) when she got married. She was more shocked than angry, and that made my guilt worse – awful to see her face collapse and her head

85

lowered, as though she was trying to hide. 'None of your business,' she muttered.

'I wish I'd known you when you were young,' I said, trying to make amends. 'I bet you were stunning.'

'Flattery will get you nowhere.'

'Do you wish you were young again? Do you wish you could go through all your life again?'

'No.'

'Why not?'

'I've done it. Any more silly questions? I'm nearly asleep with them.'

She pretended to snooze, but then I saw that she really had fallen asleep. I put a pillow behind her head and covered her knees with a shawl, and soon she was snoring away. The clock ticked away loudly. An hour until my mother would come to relieve me. I applied myself to my books, rapidly skimming the letters quoted in them, looking for relevant bits about Victoria and her granddaughters that I could follow up. May had never written me a letter in her life, but then I'd mostly lived near her and there had been no need to until I went abroad. She'd never kept a diary either, or any kind of journal. All her memories were in her head and inaccessible to me, except for the well-worn ones she trotted out and had polished until they had become suspect. As for advice, it had amounted to short, sharp commands – do this, don't do that – and had been entirely superficial. There had never been any interesting reflections that I knew of, nothing gleaned from her own experience that had been worth passing on to me. Realising this, I felt depressed.

May snored, I read, the clock ticked . . . I was half asleep myself in the overheated room. Then I came across an odd statement, made after Queen Victoria's death, by her grandson Wilhelm, the one who'd made her so angry with his arrogance and bad manners. He commented, of his grandmother, 'I have never been with her without feeling that she was in every sense my grandmama and made me love her as such.' What did he mean, 'in every sense my grandmama'? How many senses are there, then? I looked at the sleeping May, slumped in her armchair, and wondered if I could agree with Wilhelm that there is more than a genetic connection between my grandmothers and me (which is presumably what he meant). I think he must have been thinking of her authority over him, and of her importance, which in turn made him more important than he already was (he was the Kaiser by then). But what about love and affection? Was that another sense in which he felt she was truly his grandmama? Did he *feel* her love?

I do feel May's. But it comes now at a price, with expectations.

Mum came in quietly, as she does everything. May didn't stir. Mum took off her jacket, put down her bag, and gestured to me that I should go. It was a smooth handover. I piled my books up neatly, to please Mum, and put my notes in a file to take with me. Mum had already settled down, looking through a folder that seemed full of diagrams, but I didn't stop to ask what on earth they were. I left as quietly as she had entered.

What bliss to be out in the fresh air – and it wasn't just the freshness after the hot room, but the lifting of the sense of oppression. I wasn't sure what had oppressed me, but there'd been some weight bearing down heavily while I sat with my grandmother. My head had felt tight, even my clothes had felt tight. May was just a little old woman, but she had some sort of power over me. I was afraid for her. Not of her, but for her. For what lay ahead, inevitably. No good saying that it – dying, death – lies ahead for all of us. That's not the same. May feels, to me, near it, even if she's recovered from this particular illness, and I do not. I feel a kind of panic when I think of what she's so near to, and it's a selfish panic – I know I'm not going to get from her what I want. I've wasted the opportunities to extract from her what I think is there, and soon it will all be gone.

I feel I've got more time with Isa. She's older, but she's healthy. But is there as much there as there is with May? Is *she* 'in every sense' my grandmama? Am I as close to her? And if not, why not?

'Florence Nightingale returns,' said Ian, laughing, 'but for how long? Is this the end of a shift? Will duty recall her within the hour? And how is the patient? Thriving under your tender ministrations?' It was best to ignore him – he can go on entertaining himself for hours in this sort of vein.

It was good to be back in my flat, even for just a night. Mum leaves for work at eight thirty in the morning, so I didn't need to be back at May's till then. And maybe, if things carried on going so well, I'd only need to spend one more night and another day, and then the 'care plan' would swing into operation. I wandered round the rooms in my flat, marvelling at how empty they felt compared to May's, how light and spacious, though measurement for measurement that's probably not true. What these rooms are empty of is memories. That, maybe, is the crucial difference, more important than wooden floors versus thick carpets, blinds versus crimson velvet curtains, and so on. May's house is choked with memories. I'm constantly aware of the life lived within its walls for the last – what? – fifty-odd years. I see her as she was when I was a small child, a little bustling figure, forever rushing around busily putting things to rights, vigorously polishing her best bits of furniture or dusting her many ornaments. And now her belongings hardly know her – they seem to own her instead of May owning them. She can't polish or clean effectively any more, or do a host of small things that would stamp her authority on the place. I've tried to do it for her, but she doesn't want me to. 'Leave it,' she said, when I began picking up her Toby jugs on the mantelpiece to clean them. She couldn't bear to see me taking over. I have to know my place. I don't think May herself knows what that place is exactly. She knows my mother's, her daughter's – that's simple, it should be to look after her – but mine? Am I an insurance against my mother's possible defaulting? Or am I something else?

Yesterday, the first free day I'd had for a week, I had a summons from Isa. She rang and in that high, artificial-sounding voice she has on the telephone commanded my presence. I exaggerate, but only a little – it did sound like a royal command. It was the last day of the Canadian cousins' visit. They were back from bonnie Scotland and leaving for home from Heathrow the following morning. I was to come at five p.m.

They were all in the drawing room (Isa always calls it that, having no truck with sitting rooms, or living rooms, and certainly not lounges), where they had been having after noon tea. The best Spode china was in evidence, and so was the crystal cake stand, bearing a Dundee cake out of which only two portions had been taken. I was annoyed that I hadn't been invited for tea too – Isa knows I love the cakes Elspeth makes for her. I boldly eyed the cake and said it looked delicious, and was eventually, reluctantly ('it is a little late to be eating cake, Isamay, surely') invited to have a slice. Isa asked how Mrs Wright was, and so did Mary-Lou and Beth. I gave them a run-down on what had happened, and on May's condition, and Isa said, 'I have never needed to be in hospital my whole life,' and looked around for applause, or, at least, amazement and admiration.

It wasn't forthcoming. 'Then you've been lucky,' Mary-Lou said. 'It's all a matter of luck, most of it genetic.'

'Well,' said Isa, clearly rather offended, 'I am not at all sure about that. The stock one comes from is, of course, important, but then so is how one lives one's life. I have led a healthy life.

I have never smoked, I drink only in moderation, I exercise daily—'

'Oh, Grandmama,' I butted in, 'you don't exercise!'

'I most certainly do,' said Isa, indignantly. 'I take the air every day in my garden, unless the weather is very inclement.'

'That's not exercising,' I insisted. 'That doesn't get your heart rate up.'

'That's the target, getting the heart rate up.' Beth nodded.

'The Macdonells have strong hearts,' Isa said, proudly.

'Yes, they do,' said Mary-Lou, 'but not such healthy brains.'

'I beg your pardon?' said Isa, eyebrows shooting up.

'Tumours,' Mary-Lou said, laconically. 'Quite a few of the death certificates have brain tumours as cause of death.'

'How very unpleasant,' said Isa, displeased with Mary-Lou.

'What else do the Macdonells commonly die of?' I asked, enjoying the turn the conversation was taking.

Mary-Lou hesitated. 'There were some nasty causes of death on various certificates,' she said. 'Tumours of different sorts, with peculiar names, and in odd sites.'

'Odd sites?' I queried.

'Really,' Isa protested, 'we have just had tea. I really do not think we want to hear about these unfortunate deaths.'

'No,' Mary-Lou agreed, 'they seem to have faded out anyway, if there was any genetic basis to them. But deaths from strokes, especially among the women, have continued. Macdonell women have tended to have high blood pressure.'

'My blood pressure has never troubled me,' Isa said, quickly.

'What is it?' Mary-Lou asked.

'What is it?' Isa repeated, puzzled. 'What do you mean?'

'The reading, what is it?'

'I haven't the faintest idea what you're talking about. Reading?'

It turned out she hadn't had her blood pressure taken for ages, and had never known what it was, leaving 'all that' to her doctor. But he had told her she had the blood pressure of a twenty-year-old when last he had taken it, though she couldn't remember when that was. Isa announced that she kept away from doctors. She thought people who fussed about their health were hypochondriacs. This did not go down at all well with the cousins, who, I felt, saw rather a lot of their medical men and might at any minute start enumerating their ailments. Isa clearly worried about this too, because she suddenly said had they heard that I was writing a dissertation about grandmothers and their importance to granddaughters, and wasn't this interesting. I said that wasn't quite right, and tried to explain what exactly it was that I was working on, but my efforts fell on deaf ears – the cousins, much relieved to have a topic they could be enthusiastic about, launched into their own hopes regarding becoming grandmothers themselves. Mary-Lou was optimistic about her chances, with one daughter married and 'broody', and another about to marry and wanting children straight away. Beth was less hopeful. She had two sons, and neither of them had any intention, they said, of settling down and having children. 'I can't bear the thought,' Beth wailed, 'of never becoming a grandmother.'

Now, this struck me as peculiar, and I picked up on it eagerly. I could understand women not being able to bear the thought that they might never become mothers, but grandmothers? Why did Beth and Mary-Lou crave this role? What was so important to them about becoming a *grand*mother? They both tried hard to explain. There was a lot about second chances, which didn't make much sense to me – I mean, they weren't going to be mothers again, they wouldn't have the grandchildren with them all the time, and they wouldn't be the same children, so what was all this 'second chance' stuff about? Then they went on about 'continuing the line', which was more understandable in a way. They wanted to think of part of themselves going on and on, which I suppose made the thought of their own deaths less frightening. But what fascinated me was the realisation that they both felt that if no grandchildren duly appeared, then this amounted to some sort of failure on *their* part. Grandchildren would, in some mysterious way, vindicate their existence, make them feel that their own lives had been worthwhile. Crazy as I thought this was, Mary-Lou did come out with a comment that seemed worth considering. 'We need to know,' she said, very solemnly, 'not just where we come from but where we are going.' So grandchildren would tell her where she was going? Apparently. How weird.

It was alarming. Long after I'd said goodbye to the cousins, I was thinking about this belief of Mary-Lou's. I decided that it was nonsense. How can grandchildren tell you where you are going when they don't know where they are going themselves? It just sounds good, that's all. I think women want grandchildren, especially granddaughters, simply as a status thing – that and for the fun of playing with babies again, only this time, as everyone points out, without the responsibility. The urge is no more profound than that, and that's my opinion. I tried it out on Mum this evening. I told her what Mary-Lou had said and asked her if she agreed. Well, of course, she didn't – she's a scientist, she isn't sentimental – but she does agree that there is significance in having grandchildren. 'It must be like recharging a battery,' she said. I liked that.

But as a theory, it didn't fit Queen Victoria. Her batteries were always fully charged. No, in her case grandchildren were an extension of her authority. She was a true matriarch, who wanted to see herself reproduced over and over. I was right: she is a standard against which the role of grandmother can be measured only in a restricted, even false, sense. It seems to me that most grandmothers lack the very thing that made the Queen important to her grandchildren: power. No granddaughter could possibly emulate her, or even want to. She wasn't an example to follow but someone far above them, someone intimidating, surely, someone essentially remote. What I'm looking for now is a grandmother who was more of a confidante – friendly, non-judgemental, ready with encouragement, rather than the Queen Victoria brand of advice. That would put the grandmothering role in a different perspective.

I met Dad for one of our lunches, at a place in Covent Garden near where the Theatre Museum used to be. He's always been a theatregoer, which some people find surprising. Isa claims the credit for making him interested in the theatre, though he says that on the contrary she almost put him off by taking him to the wrong things at too young an age. Anyway, he is a committed theatregoer, and for a while he drew me into his interest. Over lunch, Dad said he was worried about Mum. She's depressed, he said. About May, and what is to be done. She's begun to think that, after all, it's her duty to have her come to live with us, he said. We've got more than enough room, and the house could be adapted to her needs. We can afford help, so we don't have to worry about that. But she dreads it, he said. Well, obviously she does. May and my mother . . . they may be mother and daughter, but not *that* kind of mother and daughter. They are not just not close, they are practically alien. As I've already said, they irritate each other all the time. I said all this to Dad, though he knew it anyway. He shrugged. He said that personally he wouldn't mind his mother-in-law living with them. The only drawback would be the effect this would have on Jean. To console him, I suggested that May might well refuse the offer if it was made. She loves her own house, loves her independence. But Dad said events might force her hand – it would become a choice between some kind of home, or living with them, and she'd never choose a home. Who would?

We were sinking into gloom, so to change the subject I yattered on about Queen Victoria, and told him how I needed a different kind of grandmother, one who was more of a friend to her granddaughter. Straight away, Dad thought of

Sarah Bernhardt. He had several books about her, and though he couldn't remember the details, he knew that one of them was written by a granddaughter who had lived with her and been her secretary at one time. I went home with him, though I hadn't intended to, to borrow the books.

Dad was right. Sarah Bernhardt had a granddaughter, Lysiane, to whom she was very close. Lysiane was the second of her two granddaughters, born when Sarah was fifty-four and still at the height of her fame as an actress. Lysiane (daughter of Sarah's only child, Maurice) was aware from the very beginning that her grandmother was famous. She remembered being pushed in a pram by her nurse in the Bois de Boulogne and the excitement all around her when her grandmother's carriage stopped so that Sarah could get out and kiss her. She recalled, too, how she and her older sister used to be taken by their father to lunch with their grandmother (though she was never called that – she liked to be known simply as Sarah). Her studio in Boulevard Pereire was an extraordinary place to the children, packed as it was with curios of every description, collections of ivories, piles of old weapons, and festooned with colourful costumes and drapes. It smelled of citronella and cigars, and was overcrowded not just with furniture but with dogs, who were allowed to run around as they pleased, with inevitable results.

At these lunches they were not the only guests. Even when the girls were very young, with Lysiane still in a highchair, there were distinguished people there whose conversation was far over the children's heads, but Sarah thought it educational for them to learn to listen. She saw her role as grandmother as one of being an inspiration, and exposing them to this kind of company – publishers, actors and writers – was part of it. During the lunches, Sarah sat, dressed all in white, on a throne-like chair, encouraging the little girls to taste all kinds of sophisticated delicacies and giving them watered-down white wine.

Later, when the other guests had left, she played with them, imaginative games in which she would take part herself. Any sign of talent was seized upon and developed. Lysiane liked to write poems, so Sarah commissioned her to write one about her dogs, paying her one louis for the result. The only time she was ever cross was if she caught her granddaughters idle. To do nothing was a sin. 'Do something with your ten fingers,' she would instruct them.

It was no wonder that they adored her, but what, I wondered, happened when they grew older, and so did she? Did they become embarrassed by her? Did she cease to be an inspiration and become a burden? Maybe she even had a depressive effect, when they realised they could never be like her – her fame may have cast a long shadow over their later lives.

I needed to find all this out.

A letter from Mary-Lou, posted as soon as she got back to Canada and containing the birth certificate she'd promised. I love these certificates, the when and where, the registrar's name (even though meaningless to me) – there's something moving about the bare details. Mary-Lou was right. Isa had had a brother, born in 1930, two years after her. I already had a copy of Isa's own birth certificate, and I got it out and compared it. Same registrar, same address at time of birth, same informant of the birth. Could Isa really have had a brother about whom she knew nothing? Whose existence she claimed to be unaware of? She was not quite two years old when this baby was born. Could I remember anything clearly at that age? I tested myself: first memory is of May, of sitting on her knee and being given a barley sugar. I was about two and a half then – it was one of the times I stayed with my granny, because Mum was either having a miscarriage or in hospital trying to hang on to her pregnancy. Since May's method of comforting me was always to sit me on her knee and give me a sweet, maybe I can't remember being two and a half at all, maybe all the occasions have run into each other. I can only be definite about being four, when as well as having a sweet stuck in my mouth, I was told I wasn't after all going to have a baby brother or sister. I was furious and made a great fuss. But if Isa was not yet two, maybe she wasn't told anything about a baby on the way, and then when he died she wasn't told that either, because she wouldn't understand or would be frightened and upset.

But did the baby die? There was a note attached to the birth certificate in which Mary-Lou repeated what she'd already told us: there was no death certificate. She had searched thoroughly, but there was no trace of a male Macdonell who had been born in June 1930 and had died shortly after. So where had he gone? Why hadn't his birth been greeted with rapture – at last, an heir? He could, of course, still be alive, but in that case where had he grown up? Why didn't Isa know about him? My fertile imagination – 'over-fertile', as Ian would label it – ranged over the possibilities. Maybe he'd been mentally backward, as it used to be termed, and had been hidden away, like one of the royal family's relatives, many years ago. Or maybe he wasn't James Macdonell's son at all – maybe Isa's mother had had an affair and her husband had forgiven her but refused to keep the boy. I loved that one. But there could be another reason: maybe the boy is still alive and well, aged seventy-eight. Now there's a thought, there's something to startle Isa, if I suggest it. Which I will do, if I can get my courage up. Isa can be formidable when outraged, and such suggestions would certainly outrage her – I don't know which would make her angrier, the idea that her sainted mama had had a lover and borne his child, or that she could have a brother alive and not know him. It might be cruel to suggest either. I'll have to think about it. What, after all, would be the point? It isn't enough to argue that uncovering this secret is in the interests of family history. That's just pompous. I'd have to find a better justification. If I confront Isa, I might seriously upset her. Would discovering the truth be worth such distress? All I really want to know is whether Isa has been aware all along that she had a brother. Is she concealing his fate because it involves some sort of disgrace or shame? She's capable of it. She's always had her parents on pedestals. She's talked freely of the death of her sister, so she hasn't tried to make out there was no tragedy in her family.

I am getting carried away, as I often do.

It struck me today, as I was walking across Hyde Park, that I don't really fully live in my own times. I often don't see what is actually there. I see the trees, I see the grass, I see the Serpentine – I don't mean that I'm not seeing my surroundings. But I don't seem to see the real people. I wipe away all their reality. Instead, I fill the park with women in long dresses and men in frock coats, and other nonsense. I see children with hoops. Only the horses and dogs stay the same, because they never change. I love the past and live in it too much.

Ian once told me that I was the most unmodern young woman he had ever met. He said I was an anachronism (he said it quite admiringly, I think – it wasn't a complaint). I denied this. I said I drove a car, was that not modern? I use a computer, I send e-mails, I have an iPod; was all this not modern? I wear contact lenses, I have a contemporary hairstyle, I am nearly always in jeans – all modern. What, I asked him, is unmodern about me? He said my language, my thought processes, my mindset – I didn't let him continue, and anyway he was laughing too much to go on. We ended up in bed, in a very modern way.

But, of course, he is right. My mind at the moment is all the time in another century, though I hadn't realised that this showed in my speech and mannerisms. I am *comfortable* in past times. The people are so familiar to me. I like to be with

Queen Victoria or Sarah Bernhardt and all the others much more than I enjoy the company of my contemporaries. What a strange admission. Is it some kind of retreat, some sort of escapism? But from what? I don't think it can be, since there's nothing I want to escape from. I am content with my life. I love my family, I love Ian, I like my friends. It's more a matter of identification, and of being sure of things. The past is so secure, all over and done with, all ready to be explored. The future was always exciting, but it also worries me now. I am no longer in a hurry to get to it. When my grandmothers talk about the past, it all makes sense to me, doesn't bore me in the least. I encourage them, I always want more detail, and I go with them all the way.

I suppose this isn't healthy. I ought to be living more in the present (though what does that mean? It's impossible not to be living in it) and thinking about the future. Planning. Fulfilling my parents' and grandmothers' expectations, settling down and having children.

And I haven't even thought of it.

I can't get on for the moment with delving into Sarah Bernhardt's grandmothering, though another session with Claudia is near enough to mean that I should – I have to take May for a check-up, back to the hospital. 'More of your heroic volunteering, eh?' Ian teases me. He is not so wrong. I did volunteer, knowing how busy Mum is, and knowing, too, that May would prefer me to take her. Mum would be abstracted. She'd be silent, incapable of chat, and this would make May tense. So I am going to take her. I quite understand May's hatred of hospitals, her fear that once inside she'll never get out, and that unmentionable things, over which she has no control, might be done to her. She always – I've taken her before – starts muttering to herself as we get near the building, and the getting her out of the car is an ordeal. But I have strategies to deal with this, oh yes. I'll manage fine.

And I did, on the whole. She was clinging so hard to my arm, complaining she had indigestion something chronic, as we walked into the hospital that she almost unbalanced me and I had to stop and distract her by pointing out the pictures lining the walls of the corridors. She wasn't interested in the art, but the prices gripped her, and she repeated each one as we passed – 'A hundred and twenty pounds for that! A hundred and fifty for that! A cat could have done it.' This way I got her to the lift without having my arm dislocated. Once in the lift, crowded of course, the presence of a man whose face was entirely swathed in bandages, except for holes for his eyes and nostrils, had May beginning to swear under her breath – 'Oh Gawd, damn it to hell, oh bloody hell,' over and over. He couldn't hear her – there were two nurses talking loudly to each other between us and him – but I nudged her and said, 'Sssh,' as though she were a child, and she stopped.

Her agitation increased, though, as we tried to find the right clinic, which was so badly signposted we had to ask a passing nurse to help us. When we found it, there was a woman in a wheelchair almost blocking the entrance and we had to work our way round her, with May acting terrified of falling, which is what she does when she's nervous – there's nothing wrong with her walking beyond a bit of stiffness when she attempts stairs. The small waiting room was crowded, with only one chair free, so obviously May had to have it, and I stood rather awkwardly beside her. I had to let go of her hand, which was slippery with sweat. She'd shut her eyes and was frowning hard.

We waited forty-five minutes. Nobody complained. It seemed to be an exercise in stoicism, and May proved good at it. She barely moved a muscle, remaining with her eyes closed (though they flickered every time a name was called, and she peeped under her eyelids to see who was leaving). The calling-out of a name had such an electrifying effect – people who had been slumped in their chairs jumped up, making a mess of gathering their stuff together, their bags and papers and coats, as though they hadn't been expecting to be called. No one was ever ready and prepared, however long the wait, then suddenly they were on their feet and rushing, as though they were catching a train and not merely walking into another room to see a doctor who wasn't going anywhere.

'May Wright!' The call, when it came, had exactly the same effect on us as it had had on everyone else. May choked on her barley sugar, gasped, coughed, turned red, clasped her chest with one hand and clutched me with the other. 'Take it easy, Granny,' I said, at the same time as catching the sleeve of my jacket in the arm of the chair as I struggled to help her up. 'May Wright!' The call was repeated. 'We're coming!' I called back, and promptly tripped over May's feet as she sat back down again. At last we staggered towards the open door, May still spluttering and me half dragging her into the room. There was a man, quite a young man, sitting sideways at a desk crowded with a computer, folders and papers and an empty mug. 'Sit down, Mrs Wright,' he said, with a pleasant enough smile, and to me, 'Do you want to pull up a chair too?' I pulled one up and plonked myself down. 'How are you feeling today, Mrs Wright?' he said, still with a benign smile, but by then I'd realised it was fixed, he wore it like a tie. At once, May started to lie. All the way there she'd been telling me how dreadful she felt, too dreadful to be able to go to the hospital at all, too ill to be able to do anything but stay in bed . . . Now she said she was very well and could she go home, thank you?

The doctor – Dr Horrocks (his name was on a badge he was wearing, which also said he was a registrar) – said he was delighted to hear Mrs Wright was so well, that was great. His smile took on a different quality. He was amused, he knew May was lying and why she was lying – or, in a more fashionable phrase, why she was 'in denial'. He knew she

100

was so afraid of being whisked off to a ward that she wasn't going to mention that she still had no appetite and had some stomach pains and felt sick. He kept saying good, good, and shuffling papers on his desk and peering into a folder. Then he said she seemed to be making a good recovery after her unpleasant experience but that she should take things easy and be careful what she ate from now on and did she have a diet sheet? May said yes, and it was like being back in the war, no this, no that, but she was sticking to it (another lie). He asked her what she'd had for breakfast and she said a banana, adding that bananas are very good for you, she'd been told. Dr Horrocks gave his real smile again (maybe he has a grandmother?) and said yes, they are, but don't eat too many. It seemed that the potassium level in her last blood test had been a little high, and bananas are full of potassium. He wanted her to eat more protein, some fish maybe if she couldn't manage meat. By this time, May was on her feet, sure that the dreaded appointment was over, and she'd won and could go home. But Dr Horrocks said he'd like to examine her now and would she lie on the examination table. 'Would you like to help her?' he said to me, and turned to wash his hands.

May was back in a state of dread. The doctor had drawn a curtain round the examination bed before he went to the sink, and May and I went behind it. It was quite high, and as she perched on the edge, I had to lift each of her legs and swing it on to the table before she could lie down. I didn't know if she needed to undress, but I took her shoes off, and she lay back, a look of exquisite embarrassment on her face. Dr Horrocks appeared round the curtain and I made to leave. 'You can stay if you want,' he said, so I had to. He stared in some bewilderment, I thought, at May's clothes. She had on her favourite tweed skirt, which came up rather high, the waistband nowhere near where a waist might have hoped to be. I stepped forward and, with a struggle, unzipped it and pushed it down. But underneath lay May's petticoat, a slippery old satin garment, once eau de Nil in colour and now more of a grey. That had to be yanked up out of the grip of the skirt – really he should have given her a gown and told her to strip off. He was beginning to realise this, but went ahead anyway now that May's bloated flesh had emerged amid all the satin and tweed. It was such a sad sight, so humiliating, but May couldn't see herself, and the doctor was used to it, I imagine, so it was I who somehow felt humiliated. I had to keep swallowing hard to avoid weeping – to be old and ill and come to this, all of it inevitable (not, of course, inevitable – but it seemed so) . . .

The prodding stopped. May was pronounced fine. I helped her up, tucked in the slip, pulled up the skirt. She got down herself, saying what a to-do, but looking cheerful. Dr Horrocks said he would see her again in three months' time, but if she had any pain or bleeding she should call her GP immediately. 'Don't leave it too long,' he said. 'Don't ignore what you thought was just indigestion, like last time, will you?' May said she wouldn't. She was all charm now, giving a happy little laugh as I helped her on with her coat, and thanking him umpteen times. She walked quite smartly to the lift, saying she didn't need my arm, there was nothing wrong with her, and hummed contentedly all the way down to the ground floor. I suggested that instead of going straight to the car we should go and have a cup of tea, to celebrate the ordeal being over. She thought that a good idea and we set off to a little Italian café I knew just up the road.

It's a suitably May-ish place. I knew she'd like it and she did – the gingham tablecloths, the waitress service, the proper wooden chairs with padded seats, and the plain chunky white cups and saucers all met with her approval. She drained the whole pot of tea while I sipped an espresso, which I was told would rot my insides. There was no one else in the café, so May's loud belching offended no one. My mobile rang.

It was Mum, wanting to know how things had gone. I said fine, and passed it to May, who held it well away from her because she'd read you could get brain tumours by holding mobile phones too close to the ear. I don't, of course, know what Mum said, but whatever it was, May was not pleased. Her good humour of the last half an hour visibly evaporated. She said 'for the time being' and 'I have to watch it' and a lot of grunts before 'bye', when she gave me the mobile back. Mum had already hung up.

'Typical,' May muttered. 'Her. Ringing up, 'stead of being here.'

'She's very busy at work, she's—'

'Oh, I know that, don't you tell me that, I know she's busy, she's always busy; she's always in that lab place staring down her thingummyjig.'

'It's important,' I said. 'She's doing research into—'

'Don't tell me, I've heard it a thousand times. It should have been her taking her own poorly mother to hospital, but oh no, where is she when wanted, always the same story.'

What a rage she was in, ugly to behold, resentment in every word. There was nothing I could do to placate her except take her home and settle her in her chair and make more tea and put her wireless on. She won't have it that work can be more important than the demands of family (and she won't admit that she'd rather have had me with her anyway than her daughter). It was Jean's job to take her, to put her first, and no excuses are acceptable. Do as you would be done by is her motto, and she fails entirely to see that her daughter *is* doing as she would like to be done by. May feels some kind of code has broken down, and doesn't recognise that my mother is trying to change it. And yet she, my mum, is constrained by May's old standards and expectations. She's struggling against them, and it isn't certain – well, to me it isn't – who will win.

V

Mum found me lying prone on her sofa at three in the afternoon, my hands over my face in best melodramatic fashion. I heard her come into the house, put her car keys on the hall shelf, and drop her briefcase. When I reckoned she was about to come into the sitting room where I lolled, I shouted, 'I had to get out of my flat. I'm going mad.' She made a clucking sound, not unlike one of May's grunts, hard to interpret. 'Was that exasperation or sympathy?' I asked. 'Just a minute,' she said and went off, coming back soon with coffee for both of us.

The thing about my mother, as I've said, is that she is so infuriatingly calm and reasonable. I long to see her panic, lose her temper, launch into wild exaggerations, talk hysterically – anything but this maddening self-control. If that is what it is. She's just never *messy*, as I am. She is always composed, as she was today, coming in to the sight of me lying moaning and groaning about nothing very much on her sofa. She didn't ask what the matter was. She knew she didn't have to – out it would all pour. As it did.

My mother listens carefully, properly, even when, as today, what she is listening to is incoherent. She listens, waits till I've at last stopped talking nonsense, and then she sorts out my incoherence. Well, she tries to. She does a précis first of what I've blurted out, to check she's got the drift of it right, and then she reflects for a long time. Finally, she offers some sort of solution, often so obvious I cannot believe I never thought of it myself. Not this time, though. Anything to do with my MA puzzles her. I know she has never seen the point of my dissertation, though she is too kind to have said so. What puzzles her is that she doesn't see how it could possibly contribute usefully to any existing body of knowledge, and this is what her own work is about, moving the frontiers of science forward and all that. Essentially, her attitude to my kind of research is the same as May's, though she would deny it. I don't think she considers what I'm doing is a total waste of time (as May does), but she would like to be able to see the relevance of it. Dad, on the other hand, doesn't much care *what* I study. He sees my doing an MA as a kind of settling down, and doesn't worry about where it will lead. He sees this sort of academic career as safe, a relief to him after my long time travelling and TEFLing in Japan, then Italy, Spain, and briefly in Thailand. A year of this would've been fine but almost four had been stretching it. But Mum, I think, is a little disappointed in me. She wants me to have what she calls 'a sense of direction', and doing an MA doesn't qualify. What, she occasionally asks, am I going to do afterwards? She doesn't ask this in a hectoring manner – she asks it almost apologetically, as though she thinks she shouldn't be asking. And I can't give her an answer. *I'd* like to have this sense of direction she wants for me, who wouldn't? Beattie and I were always wishing we knew what we wanted to be, to do, and we envied those of our age who wanted to be doctors or lawyers, or chefs, or even 'worthless' things (according to our teachers) like models. But what was our aim? We just wanted our lives not to be dull, all tidy and laid out, the stations along the route ticked off one by one – just not that. Variation, excitement, the unexpected, that's what we wanted. Beattie never got it, but I did. It's just that in the end it became exactly what I didn't want. I was cured.

But not in my mother's opinion, though she never voices it strongly. She still sees me as restless, thrashing about, choosing as an MA subject something amorphous. I've tried to explain that to me there *is* some shape to my quest – well, 'quest' is rather a grand term, but that's what it feels like – if only I could convey this. However lightweight it sounds to her, studying the links between grandmothers and grandchildren may yield some significant knowledge. I repeat, grandmothers are not nothing. They have a place in feminist history. They can't just be ignored. They have had an impact, they have contributed something and that something has had little recognition. It is not as simple as merely giving birth to daughters who have in turn given birth – that isn't what I'm interested in, the straight line of inheritance. No, what I'm looking for are links, consequences, direct connections that have had, and still have, significant results. Grandmothers set in train . . . what? That's what I'm trying to find out, and my mother can't see why I'm bothering, or what difference it would make if I did establish that there was, and is, a pattern. But all she said this time was that what seemed to be worrying me, so far as she could make out, was the title of my dissertation. She suggested it was pointing me in the wrong direction and making me feel I was acting under false pretences because I no longer agree with it. So, she said, why not change it? Why not simply change the title? Think of one that better sums up what you think you're doing. Everything might then fall into place.

I said, at first, it was a stupid idea. Claudia would have a fit. Probably I'd have to reapply to do the MA. I said there was nothing wrong with the title, why ever had she thought changing it would help? But as I hauled myself out of my slump on the sofa, I began to toy with new wording. The title was so imprecise. I could sharpen it up, perhaps. Then Dad came home and I stopped going over and over it in my head, and we all had supper. We talked, inevitably, about

May. I went over the hospital visit, said she seemed fine now. 'It won't last,' Mum said.

'You can't know that,' Dad said. 'She's strong, she's survived this, she'll survive other things.'

'She won't "survive" old age,' Mum said. 'Nobody does. She's seventy-eight, she'll soon start to deteriorate, inevitably.'

'So?' I said.

'So it would be sensible to be prepared.'

'How?'

'Make enquiries, find the best place, get her name down.'

'Mum!'

'What?'

'That sounds so, so . . .'

'Mm. It does. But it's sensible, to be prepared. She need never know till it's necessary.'

'And it might never be,' Dad said, cheerfully.

'Good,' Mum said, nodding.

She's right, of course. Mum is back to rejecting any notion of having May to live with her. Best to make enquiries, be prepared, best to go the alternative route. I wasn't going to accuse my mother of being heartless, because I know she isn't. She's sensible. She knows her own limitations. She knows May. We were all rather quiet, each, I bet, thinking pretty much the same thoughts. Suddenly, Mum said: 'May took Violet, her mother, into our home but she had to be pushed into it.'

'Who pushed?'

'Violet. Just arrived one day, with all her belongings. Her brother brought her. She told May she'd had enough, she couldn't manage any more, she needed help to get up, help to dress, and here she was. I was only four, but I can remember the panic.'

'What did May say?'

'I don't remember hearing her say anything. She was stunned. Violet had always bullied her. When my dad came home he couldn't believe it. Violet was just installed and he hadn't been consulted. Everything changed, to fit in with his mother-in-law, and there seemed nothing he could do about it.'

'Where did she sleep?'

'In the parlour, the downstairs front room. That became her empire. We all hated her. May became her mother's slave, shouted for all day long and half the night to do this, that and the other. Violet wasn't in the least appreciative. All she did was criticise, nothing was ever done how she wanted it done. It was a relief when she died.'

'How, when, did she die?'

'Two years after she moved in. She had emphysema.' Mum gave an odd smile, and a twitch of her mouth, as though she was suppressing with difficulty something she wanted to add.

'What?' I urged her. 'What were you going to say?'

'Nothing.'

'You were, you were going to say something else, Mum. Don't torment me.'

'I've no right to say it. Violet had emphysema, that's a fact. The doctor had been several times, it was officially diagnosed. And she was vastly overweight, with a kidney problem, plus she had diabetes, I think. May was exhausted. She'd been up all the night before, with Violet bawling for her, she'd been up and down the stairs all night long. I remember in the morning how white she was, and the way she said to Albert, "I've had enough."'

'Jean,' Dad said, warningly.

'Yes, I know,' Mum said, 'but I sensed it. It was the way she went into Violet's room that night. I'd got up to go to the bathroom and I saw her standing outside Violet's room. Violet had shouted for ages for her to come, which was why I'd woken up. May stood there, her hand on the doorknob, and she didn't move for a while, then she took a deep breath and closed her eyes. I could see her clearly in the hall light. Then she went into Violet's room. I went back to bed. The next morning, Violet was dead.'

'Mum, are you insinuating that—'

'No, she isn't,' Dad said, crossly.

'Yes, I am,' Mum said, calmly. 'I do think May hastened her mother's death, marginally. She burned the pillows afterwards, two big, soft, expensive pillows . . .'

'Understandably,' Dad said. 'They'd be full of germs.'

'She took them into that little garden even before the undertaker had been, and burned them. I followed her out. The boys had already gone out, but I was off school with what turned out to be mumps. I watched her. All I remember, and it's one of my earliest absolutely clear, reliable memories, is sensing that my mother was frightened and it had something to do with the pillows.'

'Jean,' Dad said, exasperated, 'death *is* frightening. May was just naturally shocked by her mother's death, and burning those pillows upset her.'

'No,' said Mum.

I waited a minute, then I asked Mum if she'd ever talked to May about this. Mum laughed, and wondered how I could ask that knowing May as I do. 'Of course I haven't asked her,' she said. 'What could I ask? "Mum, did you hold a pillow over my grandma's face and press it down hard?"'

'I just thought . . .'

'It's all speculation anyway, all nonsense,' Dad said. 'Imagination run wild.'

But my mother doesn't do imagination. It never runs wild. She is a scientist, she is not fanciful. It was quite out of character for her to say what she had said, and she'd only done so because of worrying about May and what might happen. Did she also worry that she might be tempted to do to May what she believed May to have done to her own mother? Surely not. Mum would organise things

109

so that the circumstances that had driven May to this action would not arise. I wanted to say this, but instead I said: 'Imagine, if May did do something like that, imagine her keeping it secret all these years.'

'If I'm right,' Mum said, 'she won't have seen herself as keeping a secret. She'll have rewritten what happened in such a way that whatever she did was harmless.'

'I'm sure it was,' Dad said.

'I don't know,' I said. 'I mean, I don't know if she would do that, rewrite history. But where would be the harm, if she did?'

'Depends,' Mum said.

'On what?'

'On what effect it had on her.'

'You mean, how she dealt with the guilt?'

'No. If she successfully persuaded herself she hadn't smothered her mother and . . .'

'Jean!'

'. . . and that she'd died quite coincidentally while she was, say, adjusting the pillows, then she wouldn't have felt guilt. No, what I meant was that it may have made her suspicious of what other people could do to her. Especially me.'

It was an explanation, of sorts, of why Mum and May are never easy together. It's possible that May did hasten, maybe just by minutes, her mother's death, so she may well be suspicious of her own daughter.

Supervision tomorrow. Claudia will want to see some progress and there is none. So, all day on Sarah Bernhardt, desperately seeking grist to my mill. I knew I had to get the chronology right first – Claudia's very hot on this. Dates tidy the mind, she alleges. I needed mine tidy, so I applied myself. In 1910, Lysiane Bernhardt's mother, wife of Sarah's son, died. In 1912, Lysiane, after a year spent in England with her older sister, went to live permanently with her grandmother. She was thirteen, her grandmother sixty-eight, and not in good physical condition (though still acting). Sarah's leg, which she'd injured in an accident a few years before (when? Claudia will ask), was very painful and she had been advised that amputation might soon be necessary. In 1915, she gathered her family round her, Lysiane included, and told them she had a choice: suicide or amputation. She'd made her choice: amputation. Her leg was cut off above the knee.

From this point on, her granddaughter Lysiane's help became crucial to how she lived her life. She still went on acting, choosing parts where no movement on stage was necessary, and it was Lysiane who organised all the assistance needed. Still only nineteen, Lysiane accompanied Sarah on yet another American tour (she'd been on three already). To her, it seemed a wonderful adventure but it involved a great deal of planning and patience. There were always complications along the way, such as the time Sarah took a fancy to a lion cub, which Lysiane had to care for. She never saw her grandmother as a burden, though (lesson there for some of us), but as an inspiration, which is what Sarah wanted and intended to be. The message was at all times clearly spelt out by the grandmother to the granddaughter: age could be defied, courage could triumph over adversity. The motto was 'never stop, otherwise you die'. And Sarah had no intention of dying. At seventy-six, she was still said to be attractive (by whom? Claudia will ask), still dyeing her hair, still wearing beautiful clothes, still appearing glamorous. There was to be no such thing as growing old gracefully or any other way.

Now, what does a granddaughter make of this? What do I make of it? Is it how grandmothers should be? That's ridiculous, they can't all be Sarah Bernhardts, with her looks and talent and vitality. But the point is, should Sarah Bernhardt herself be admired or pitied? Is that kind of defiance towards ageing a bad example to set a granddaughter or a worthy

111

one? If young women need role models, is Sarah Bernhardt a suitable one? Or dangerous?

I'm hoping that if I throw all that at her, Claudia will be happy.

She wasn't, of course. God knows what is going on in Claudia's life at the moment – as I've said, we have absolutely no personal chat – but I could tell from the moment I walked into her room that we were going to have a difficult session. She wasn't sitting still, always a bad sign. She was as outwardly composed as ever, but her left foot was swinging slightly. I saw her trying to stop it, and then within a couple of minutes this minor agitation began again. I lurched into Bernhardt, significance of, etc., and she sighed, and then came out with a complicated metaphor along the lines of my dissertation having a scaffolding but that no building ever appears. 'Where are the bricks? Where is the mortar?' she asked. Next, she switched to parallels with detective stories: where was my clear line of enquiry? Where was my connection between subjects? What exactly did I hope to prove? Wearily – she was weary; I was made weary by her weariness – she took me through George Sand, Queen Victoria, Sarah Bernhardt (she ignored Edith Holman Hunt, and I didn't remind her), trying to make me 'elucidate' my argument, as she called it. I couldn't. I just repeated, lamely, that I knew something was there and that I was working my way towards it. 'In the dark?' she asked. I said I supposed so.

Another big sigh, more jiggling of the foot, and then she said she felt the time had come to shed a little light on the murky business my subject matter was proving to be. She said that my approach from the beginning had been far too random, and much too vague. I appeared not really to know what I was looking for and had become too caught up in personal details that had nothing whatsoever to do with what my research was supposed to be about. This had to stop.

I must consider whether I wished to continue, or whether if, in good faith, I had led myself up a blind alley and could not get out. Well, I managed to appear contrite and humble, though it was a huge effort. I knew, after all, that she was right and that her reprimand was earned. I promised to shape up by our next session. Then I left, depressed.

A visit to Isa was overdue, but what put me off going to see her was that I knew it would have to be a long one if I wanted to make any headway with the birth certificate Mary-Lou had sent. It was delicate ground, to be stepped on carefully, or else I'd be warned off for good. So after my supervision with Claudia I rang up and asked if I could come for tea, and as ever Isa said she'd just consult her diary, and then that the following Thursday seemed to be free. I said I'd bring a cake, but was told on no account to do so because her girl always baked a cake on Thursday mornings and would be offended if one was shop-bought.

She'd never for one moment thought I'd actually bake a cake, of course. Quite right. Ian bakes, though. He likes baking cakes, and bread. I thought he was joking when he first revealed this unlikely accomplishment, but soon found out he wasn't. His date and walnut is my favourite. Apparently, his grandmother taught him. It's only the second thing he has ever told me about her, that she made sublime cakes. He claims he can't remember how old he was when this baking lark went on – when he was around eight or nine, he thinks. He had a hand-written recipe book she made for him but he lost it years ago. Didn't lose the skill, though. Isa could have enjoyed one of his efforts if she'd agreed to my suggestion that I should bring a cake. Ian would have been only too willing to oblige. He's always offering to teach me, but I'm happy to let baking remain his department.

Elspeth, Isa's 'girl', is a woman of about fifty. She was leaving as I arrived. 'Mrs Symondson is looking a bit peaky,' she said, as she put her coat on. 'Tired after her party, I expect.' The party had been ages ago, but I agreed that must be the reason.

Isa was sitting in state in her drawing room, the tea tray laid out on the small table at her side. 'Darling!' she said, and held out her arms, and I stooped awkwardly and kissed her forehead. 'My girl has left a cake in the kitchen,' she said, 'and the kettle will have boiled. Can you manage to fill the teapot – she will have left it ready – and bring it through with the cake?' I managed, and was congratulated effusively, as though I'd performed a task of Herculean proportions. Isa did, as Elspeth had said, look peaky, if peaky meant fragile and pale. Her back wasn't quite so ramrod straight, and her hair, though beautifully brushed, had lost its fullness. But I didn't ask her if she felt all right – she doesn't like it. May likes to be asked how she is feeling, and has a long answer ready, but Isa does not. I think it frightens her to wonder if she is not feeling well.

We had the usual bright, vacuous chat, and then I brought up a mention of the Canadian cousins. I said I'd had a nice letter from Mary-Lou, and Isa said she had had one too. I asked her to remind me how Mary-Lou was related to her, and this kept her happy for a full five minutes, going through the familial connection. I wasn't really listening properly, and didn't take it all in, but at what I thought an appropriate moment I said I'd like to have a copy made of Mary-Lou's genealogical chart and could I borrow the one she'd been given. Isa looked confused. Yes, Mary-Lou had indeed kindly given her a copy but she couldn't think where she had put it. She would have to ask her 'woman' (this was how Mrs Roberts, her cleaning lady, was referred to, to distinguish her from Elspeth, 'the girl') to look for it. I asked couldn't I look, but no, I could not (said very firmly).

Half an hour passed, tea had been drunk, cake (Madeira sponge) eaten. Any minute she was going to say she was feeling tired and I would be dismissed. I set my teacup down carefully on the tray and said, 'Grandmama, Mary-Lou sent me something very interesting in her letter. She sent a copy of that birth certificate she told us about.'

'Birth certificate?'

'Of your brother.'

'I had no brother. I had a sister who died. It was all a muddle. I told Mary-Lou. She had muddled up my sister.'

'No, she hadn't. She knew about the sister, she found birth and death certificates for her. But this is another one, for a boy, born two years after you. Look . . .' and I gently placed the certificate on Isa's knee, and handed her her reading spectacles. She studied it intently for a moment or two, frowning, and then rather impatiently thrust it back at me.

'Nonsense,' she said.

'Birth certificates can't be nonsense,' I said, taking great care to keep my tone of voice light. 'I mean, people are legally required to register births and it's done in front of a registrar.'

'Mistakes can be made,' Isa said.

'Very unlikely, Grandmama,' I said, gently, and then, 'It's perfectly possible his birth was something you were not told about. You were not even two. And then later it would have been too upsetting, perhaps, to tell you about it, too painful?'

Isa sat very still, visibly containing herself. She didn't look at me, and her head was bent so that I could see the neat centre parting in her hair. It was as though she were listening, as though she were waiting for some signal. Then she looked up and said brightly, 'I expect you are right.' Relieved, I said, 'But isn't it interesting, to think what might have happened to the baby, why there is no death certificate, or none Mary-Lou has been able to trace? Maybe I should have a go, I could—'

'Leave it alone,' Isa said, suddenly her true self again, staring straight at me, strong and determined, a figure of authority.

115

'But I'm—'

'Isamay, it is none of your business. Whatever happened, happened. That is that.'

'All the same, it's intriguing, it's a puzzle, and I can't bear not to know what *exactly* happened.'

'You will have to "bear it", as you put it. Forget about this certificate, child. I wish Mary-Lou had never found it. It is of no consequence now. Enough.'

It was extraordinary the way a little frisson of fear ran through me, a little electric-feeling charge played up and down my spine. It was gone very quickly, but what shocked me was that it had been there at all – how could an eighty-year-old woman who was my own grandmother alarm me to such an extent? She had no power over me, there was nothing she could do, or would want to do, to harm me, and yet there it had been, the twinge of what I'd recognised as fear. I think Isa saw it in my face. She wanted to make amends, and so she smiled, a genuine smile, and gave a little apologetic cough, and said she was rather tired, she had fatigued herself in the garden the day before, and I must excuse her if she seemed fretful. Then she asked me how I was progressing with Sarah Bernhardt and we had a perfectly amiable chat for another ten minutes or so. Then I left.

I felt uncomfortable the rest of the day, unable to settle to any kind of real work. My brain worried away not so much at the problem of the mysterious brother but at how Isa had reacted. What I couldn't decide was what her anger revealed. She prides herself on being in control at all times, and any exhibition of anger, however mild, shows a lack of control, in her opinion. She had lectured me many times on this – her attitude to my childhood rages was quite different to May's. The more I'd screamed with rage in her presence (and I very rarely did so), the more remote she became, the more she rose above my tantrum, determined absolutely to ignore it. I'd end up in a heap at her feet, utterly exhausted with the effort to claim her attention. And then she would very calmly and sorrowfully point out how my display of anger had weakened me: I was the loser.

But now she had been visibly angry. There had been no shouting or yelling, but her fury was in every one of her few words. So what had angered her? After all, she had never been distressed reminiscing about the death of her sister, never been angry when, in a short-lived morbid phase, I'd questioned her about it. I'd heard loads of times about Clarissa's death, about the big blue eyes closing for ever, about how beautiful she'd looked in her coffin with her golden hair around her head like a halo . . . all that stuff. Isa had been allowed to kiss her – her nanny had lifted her up and she had kissed the dead child on the forehead. Yet now, the very mention of a baby brother who had died and whom she had no recollection of having existed made her angry. She didn't want to discuss it or speculate as to what had happened, and she had forbidden any further investigation.

The point is, am I going to obey her? Has she the right as my grandmother to expect me to obey her?

I told Dad about it. I described the scene (it was like a scene, so theatrical) with Isa, and how angry she had been with me.

'She's suspicious of mysteries,' Dad said, 'unless she's created them herself.'

'And does she?'

'What? Create mysteries? Oh yes, sometimes.'

'I never knew that about her.'

'No reason why you would.'

'Dad, you're being mysterious yourself now. Do you know something about this birth certificate business?'

'No.'

'What do you think happened, then? What does Isa suspect that makes her angry?'

Dad stopped eating his spaghetti vongole for a minute and took a gulp of wine. 'No idea,' he said, and then, very abruptly, 'Do you want ice cream?'

'No,' I said, and then, 'I'm going to find out.'

'Find out what?'

'The truth, about the baby boy. I won't tell Isa, of course, I don't want to upset her, but I have to know. It's like an itch, I have to scratch it, it's driving me mad.'

'Scratching itches makes them bleed,' Dad said. 'It might end up painful.'

'Who for? Not for me. And I won't tell Isa, so not for her. I'll just keep to myself what I find out.'

Dad looked down at his by then empty plate, his arms crossed over his chest, and stared at it as though there was something there visible only to him. A waiter came and asked if we wanted coffee, and Dad shook his head. I didn't want any either, so we were ready for the bill. It was duly produced and slipped under a side plate. Dad didn't touch it for what seemed like ages, and then when I said should we go, he looked at it intently. 'Some mistake?' I asked, smiling. Dad is famous for minutely scrutinising bills. It embarrassed me as a child, but now I see it as an endearing eccentricity. I began to get up, and as my chair scraped on the tiled floor he put his hand out, as though to stop me. 'I think I will have some coffee after all,' he said. 'Keep me company, will you, or have some water or something?'

The coffee came. He was looking at me in that slightly puzzled, abstracted way he sometimes has, as though wanting to check I am who he thinks I am. It amazes me that I still hadn't the faintest suspicion of what he was about to tell me. I was feeling a little impatient with him for fussing over the coffee, making such a production of stirring it round and round, and so carefully measuring out a level teaspoonful of sugar. The sugar alone should have alerted me to something unusual about to happen. He gave it up months ago, saying he was putting on weight.

'Dad?' I said.

'The trouble is,' he said slowly, 'I don't know why I think I should tell you now, why I think it might make you see – no, that's not it – why it's possibly relevant . . .' and his voice faded away.

'Dad, for God's sake, is this about the birth certificate? You know about it, don't you? It isn't a mystery. *Tell* me, go on . . .'

'No, I don't know about it. It is a mystery.'

'Then what are you on about?'

At that moment, a man suddenly stopped at our table and said, 'James! How are you? Haven't seen you for ages.' Dad looked up at him in a dazed sort of way, appearing not to recognise this interloper, or else he was so distracted by the thought of what he had been about to tell me that he was unable to remember his name. But this man was oblivious to Dad's blank look, and continued to stand there, chattering away. I began tapping the table impatiently with a knife lying by my plate, feeling increasingly that I wanted to pick it up and stab the man, just to shut him up and make him go away. Eventually, Dad cleared his throat and collected himself. He half stood up to shake his friend's hand and call him, at last, by his name. There was some exchange of news, while I seethed, and then the man went on his way, with a promise to give Dad a call soon.

'Thank God,' I said. 'Now, come on, Dad.'

'What?'

'You *know* what – the birth certificate, Isa, all that.'

He looked stricken. 'I haven't discussed it with Jean.'

'Why do you have to? Can't you make up your own mind? Why does Mum have to give you permission?'

'She might think it's only going to encourage you . . .'

'To do what?'

'Poke your nose into the certificate thing.'

'I'm going to do that anyway, whatever Isa says. I don't know why you're so bothered when I've promised never to tell her.'

'I'm bothered because it makes me think of other secrets Isa has, other certificates she wouldn't want dug up, I mean looked at. That whole area is so dangerous. She's got enough to hide and I don't see the point in upsetting her. I don't know if this brother's birth and fate is truly a mystery to her, but I know why investigating the past, or sections of it, frightens her. And I want you to leave it alone. I want to persuade you by telling you something about Isa so you'll, well, understand her better.'

Why did he choose an Italian café for this? Was it deliberate? So that the noise and bustle and the very ordinariness of the situation would make what he had to say less dramatic? No, I don't think he thought like that. I believe him. He just suddenly decided, there and then, when I was boasting about what a great sleuth I was going to be, that he would stop me in my tracks. He certainly succeeded. The coffee machine roared, the waiters clattered plates, people around us laughed and talked, but Dad's words came to me across the table perfectly clear – all other sound simply fell away. What he told me astounded me and excited me in equal measure and yet he didn't make a drama out of it (as I expect I would have done). He spoke in short sentences, pausing between each one to check that I'd taken the information in, and I nodded frantically, urging him on. When he'd finished, he spread his hands out on the table and said, 'And there it is.' I stared at him, speechless, my head whirling, the implications of what he'd told me sinking in. 'We'd better go,' he said, and we both got up and wandered out into the busy street, his arm round me. 'Now I'll have to go home and tell your mum I've spilled the beans,' he said, gloomily.

* * *

It's my father's attitude I can't understand, the way he seems not to care, not to be in the least bothered, not to have the slightest desire to discover the truth about half his genetic inheritance. Because that was what his 'confession' was about: Isa is not his biological mother. She is therefore not my true grandmother. I'm shattered by this revelation and its implications, but Dad isn't. To him, it is of no real consequence. Isa is his mother in every sense that matters. He has emphasised that Isa doesn't know that he knows she did not give birth to him and that she must never know that he knows. There must be no hint whatsoever from me. I've promised. I wish I hadn't.

The story Dad told me in the café goes like this: one day, in a science lesson at school, the fact came out that two blue-eyed people cannot produce a brown-eyed child except under very rare circumstances. Brown, he learned, is the 'default' colour for human eyes, which results from the build-up of a substance called melanin. Originally we all had brown eyes, but a mutation affecting a gene in the chromosomes acted as a switch that turned off the ability to produce brown eyes. All blue-eyed people in the world are related to that one individual thousands of years ago in whose crucial gene this switch occurred. Dad took all this in, and then he began to wonder about himself. Both his mother and his father had blue eyes. He thought about his grandparents. One of his grandmothers, he was quite sure, had blue eyes, but he had never noticed the colour of his other grandparents' eyes. He saw both sets of relatives quite often at that time, so on the first chance he had he checked out their eyes. All blue. For a long time he mulled this over, and then one day, on a climb he was having with his father, just the two of them tackling Snowdon, he brought the subject up. He said wasn't it funny that he had brown eyes when everyone else in the family had blue eyes. He didn't mention the science lesson, by then weeks ago. It would have been easy for his father to agree that yes, it was, that he must be a throwback to some forgotten ancestor.

But Patrick, his father, doesn't say that. Instead, he tells James the truth. They crouch on a rock halfway up Snowdon, and while they are resting, he tells his son what happened. He starts with an apology. He says he is ashamed of his own behaviour and he isn't going to try to excuse it. (This in itself is a shock to James, who revered his father and would never have imagined he *could* have any behaviour for which to apologise.) He goes on to say he had an affair with a young woman with whom he worked at the time. Then he changes the word 'affair' – he says James is too young yet (he was thirteen) to understand, but that it was not an affair but an 'attraction' between them. This attraction only happened for 'a short while', but James was the result. He says the young woman (no name mentioned) did not want to have a termination (James didn't know what that was, but guessed) and agreed that the baby would be put up for adoption. Patrick says he is ashamed, for a second time, ashamed that he was relieved. Isa, his wife, need never know. He says he was appalled at the thought of how such a thing would hurt her. She had wanted a baby for the five years of their marriage and nothing had happened. So the whole thing was to be kept quiet. He paid for the girl to go away and be looked after. But then, says Patrick, disaster. The girl died during childbirth (no details given to the adolescent boy).

There was then, Dad said, a long pause. He remembers wondering if he should be asking questions, or saying something, anything, to show he'd heard, but he was mute with embarrassment and didn't actually want to hear any more. But Patrick goes on, half his words now lost in the wind that had begun to whip round them. He says Isa discovered about the baby. How? (James hadn't asked.) Someone phoned her. Who? She would never say. There was a confrontation, Patrick says. It soon became apparent that all Isa was concerned about was the baby – she must have the baby. Patrick was the baby's father; he must cancel the adoption procedure and claim his son. To Isa, it seemed divine providence: here was a baby for her. She was ready to adore him and forgive how his birth had come about. But part of her forgiveness was to be the insistence that no one should ever be told the baby was not truly her own. Patrick sighs at this point, suggests they climb a bit further. James plods along in his father's footsteps, his head in a whirl. He doesn't feel upset so much as astonished and then also fascinated – how had the deception been managed?

They are almost at the top of the mountain when Patrick stops again and finishes the story. James hasn't said a single thing, but his father carries on as though he is being interrogated. He explains that the girl's family lived abroad. They did not want the baby, had no interest in its welfare. In fact, their worry was that they would be expected to look after it. So, that part was easy. The next part was not. Patrick and Isa moved from one part of the country to another. They arrived in London from Somerset with a baby, and since no one knew them there, no one was surprised. But what about family, friends? Patrick asks the question himself. He says it involved a great deal of subterfuge and that yes, he thinks Isa's mother must have known and gone along with the deception, and also someone called Uncle George (though exactly how George helped was not explained). As for his own parents, his mother died at that time and his father was confused anyway.

They complete the climb. They stand on the summit and can see nothing. A mist envelops what should have been a magnificent view. James feels he must, at last, say something. He can feel his father expectant and tense at his side. What he chooses to say is, he later thinks, stupid. He says: 'So she had brown eyes?' His father looks down at him, his face creased with anxiety, and says, 'I don't know. I can't

123

remember. I just don't know.' And James says, 'It doesn't matter anyway. It doesn't matter. I don't care.' And he didn't, he really didn't. His father was his father and his mother was his mother, even if she wasn't. Fine by him. It was never referred to again. On the way down, the mist clears, the views appear, and Patrick says, 'Never let your mother know that you know, will you, James?' 'Of course not,' James says. He remembers feeling happy. They went to a pub and had a drink and crisps, and then they went back to the cottage they were renting, where Isa was waiting. He says he gave her a hug.

Incredible. To me, incredible. The total absence of excitement, of any feverish need to find out about this young woman, this 'girl', who died giving birth to him – his biological mother. I can tell when my dad is pretending or lying. He isn't.

I came home that day and looked in the mirror. For hours. So I have Isa's eyes, do I? Said over and over again, ever since I was a child. Said by myself, quite pleased to agree, since Isa's eyes are her best feature. I've liked being told I have her eyes. But now I know I do not. The only connection between the colour of Isa's eyes and my own is some ancestor common to millions of blue-eyed people who lived thousands of years ago. There is nothing I can see in the mirror that comes from Isa. I am not the image of my paternal grandmother. Genetically, she has nothing to do with me. She is tall, I am tall; she is slim, I am slim; she has blue eyes, I have blue eyes. The combination is that of millions of women.

But what about Isa's characteristics that I am said to have inherited? Is there a case to be made for arguing that, although not genetically inherited, I have 'inherited' them through constant exposure to them? Maybe. Isa is aloof, distant. None of that has passed down to me. But she is also often arrogant and I've certainly been accused of that. She is meticulous, neat, organised, independent, self-contained, unemotional, private – no, I am not like Isa. Neither is my dad. I've always thought him unlike his mother, except in his work, where he too pays great attention to detail. It makes perfect sense that she is not his mother. But as soon as I write that, I see how absurd it is – loads of men are completely unlike their mothers.

I suppose that what I can't get over is that Dad really, genuinely has no curiosity about his real birth mother. He denies he has ever had any. Isa *is* his mother, as far as he is concerned. He'd only told me the few facts about his conception and birth, which he was told to stop me pestering Isa, so that I wouldn't go blundering down paths to the past that I have no business to be on. He told me in order to protect her. I will keep my promise. I won't ever let Isa realise I know she is not genetically related to me. But I can't guarantee that once she is dead I won't try to find out about my real grandmother.

I'd like a name, at least.

I feel so restless. For the last two hours all I've done is what I always do when I can't settle to anything – I wander about, picking up things and putting them down, turning on taps and turning them off, gaping out of the window and counting cars (and sometimes becoming so idiotic as to memorise their number plates). It is literally as though I have ants in my pants. If Ian is here, it drives him mad and so I have to go out and roam the streets, closing people's front gates, breaking off sprigs from shrubs overhanging walls, and carefully not treading on the lines between paving stone – neurotic, obsessive behaviour. But today Ian is out and there is nothing to stop me flitting from living room to bedroom to kitchen to bathroom as if I am demented. Maybe I am. I can't bear not knowing things once I know they are there to be known. I can't stop thinking about Isa, seeing her differently, reappraising her.

I tot up what she has meant to me, what she has done for me, how she has *grandmothered* me. I run my eye over the books she has so generously bought me, big, expensive art books and catalogues. She always indulged me, after she'd taken me to an exhibition, buying the catalogue afterwards if I'd liked the paintings. I have loads of them. I am looking at them now, remembering the outings to the Tate, the Royal Academy, the Hayward, the Courtauld, the National Gallery, and the National Portrait Gallery – every major gallery in London at one time or another. I take down the catalogues of the exhibitions I recall most clearly. I calm down. I turn the pages, I get lost in the paintings, so beautifully reproduced – so beautifully that sometimes the reproductions are more impressive than the actual paintings. Hours pass. I am still, at last.

I stared at a painting by Vanessa Bell. *The Nursery Tea*, painted in 1912. The woman who'd painted it must have been interested in children, I reckoned, and though I wasn't absolutely sure, I thought Vanessa Bell had probably used her own children and their nanny in the portrait. So if she had children, she may have had grandchildren – and I was off doing exactly what Claudia had cautioned me against doing. I felt defiant.

Vanessa Bell was sixty-four when her first grandchild, her daughter's daughter, was born in 1943. Altogether she had seven grandchildren, six girls and one boy, but the one to whom she was closest was Amaryllis, the firstborn. 'What a blessing that they exist,' she wrote of her grandchildren, 'what an incredible difference such small creatures make to life'. She adored having them around, didn't mind the noise and mess a bit, and felt that she could 'fully enter' into their world with no effort at all. In fact, she freely admitted that she preferred the company of children to the company of most adults. She felt more natural, more at ease, more comfortable. There was no need to feel shy (which she was) in the presence of children – they took her as she was and she never had to worry about what to say.

She liked painting them but she also liked doing things with them. At Charleston, when it got to four o'clock and she came out of her studio, she would go down into the kitchen with any grandchildren who were staying and teach them how to make scones. They would watch her take off her rings, and wash her hands, before she weighed out the flour and cut the butter into pieces and rubbed it in, and then they were allowed to do the same. At other times she would gather scraps of material together, colourful fragments left over from the dresses she'd made, and show them how to make doll's clothes. Once dressed, the dolls came to life as she imagined voices and names for them and gave them a tea party.

All this made her a very good grandmother but in a conventional, traditional manner. What was different about her was that she encouraged rebellion in her grand-daughters – rebellion against their parents. The eldest, Amaryllis, her favourite, had lovely long hair, a great lustrous mane, but hated it – it was such a bother to wash and dry and braid and pin up – and wanted to have it all cut off. Her father wouldn't hear of it. He loved her hair, which was definitely, in the case of Amaryllis, a crowning glory. But Vanessa thought her granddaughter's wish should prevail. She took Amaryllis to have her hair bobbed. Now that, for my purposes, is interesting: is it a grandmother's role to side with a young granddaughter against a parent? Is she the superior authority? Did this teach Amaryllis that her grand-mother had power over her father? And what did he say when this rebellious act was discovered?

Then I remembered something about Vanessa Bell that might have made her a more than merely fun grandmother to have. Hadn't she had Angelica, her daughter, by a lover, Duncan Grant? And didn't she have another lover, Roger

Fry? And didn't they all, at one time, overlap? I wonder what the grandchildren made of that? Grandmothers and sex isn't something I've gone into, and maybe I should. Would it have made Vanessa's grandchildren proud of her, to be aware of her history of lovers, or embarrassed? But just a minute: she was sixty-four when her first grandchild was born, so she'd be over seventy before they'd start noticing, if she was still sexually active, if Duncan was sharing her bed as well as Clive Bell (but was Clive still there?). No, it is unlikely the granddaughters would be aware of much, I think – but worth trying to find out. If Vanessa encouraged a granddaughter to have her hair bobbed, what else did she encourage her to do?

I think Claudia might be quite pleased with me if I follow this up.

There was absolutely no point in going to Tate Britain to look at the Vanessa Bells on display – they can tell me nothing whatsoever about her grandmothering – but I went there today all the same, convincing myself it would make me feel more in touch with the woman. What nonsense. I'd have been better off tracking down *Visits to Charleston*, the unpublished memoir of one of her granddaughters. But I enjoyed myself. I like her paintings. I like the colours and the subject matter, everything soft and simple, nothing tricky or violent. There's a peace, a tranquillity, about them.

Afterwards, I sauntered along the Embankment, having one of those out-of-time experiences when I'm not quite sure who or where I am. I got caught up, near the statue of Sylvia Pankhurst, in a party of Japanese tourists. They surrounded me but they didn't seem to notice me, though I was very obvious since I was a head taller than any of them. They were all so excited, talking non-stop, a group of about twenty of them sweeping along towards the Houses of Parliament.

I half wanted to stay with them and put off returning to being myself, but I had to catch a bus to visit May.

Changing buses in Camden Town, I stood with a group of old women. They'd all been to Sainsbury's and were laden with bulging carrier bags, which were deposited at their feet on the dirty, litter-strewn pavement, ready to be picked up again when their bus came. Two of them had those tartan trolleys on wheels, ideal for blocking bus aisles and injuring passengers' ankles. They were probably all grandmothers, still doing their own shopping and not expecting to be looked after. Or maybe I couldn't see it but they were burning inside with resentment at what was expected of them at their time of life, just like May.

She looked better, more alert, more her old self. And she sounded it. 'Here you are,' she greeted me. 'Better late than never.' I thought about saying I couldn't be late because I hadn't said what time I'd be coming, but I didn't. Instead, I told her she was looking well. Mistake. Looks were apparently deceiving. But she made the tea herself, all the while berating the carer, who had put everything in the wrong place. This carer comes in each morning to help her dress and make her breakfast (the word 'carer' was said each time with full sarcastic emphasis). May doesn't want this help but claims it was forced upon her and she has no choice. She has, however, adamantly refused to have meals-on-wheels – 'I'd rather eat grass,' she said. Oh, she was on form again.

We sat in the kitchen, as ever, the heat overpowering. I took my jacket off, and then my sweater, and still I was hot. May said I was looking washed out, what had I been up to? I tried to tell her about Vanessa Bell, of whom she had never, of course, heard – why should she have? – and in whom she had no interest whatsoever. Any talk about art annoys her. She'd told me scores of times that a picture was a picture, some nice, some not, and that was that, why go on about them. My outings in the past to art exhibitions with Isa had made her laugh scornfully. She didn't use the word 'affected' but she didn't need to. I fell silent, thinking of the effect it would have if I changed from twittering on about Vanessa Bell to telling her Isa was not really my grandmother.

'What's up with you?' she said. 'You look as if you've swallowed a golf ball.'

'A *golf* ball?'

'Never mind what sort of ball, you know what I mean.'

'No I don't.'

'Yes you do, madam. What's up?'

'Nothing.'

'Something.'

'Nothing. My work's not going well . . .'

'Your *work*! I meant your 'ealth, what's up with that? You're looking like a little ghost.'

'I'm tired.'

'Tired? Tired? Dear me, at your age – tired! What with, eh?'

'I told you. My work isn't going well, and I've spent hours and hours reading stuff and trying to sort it out and write it up and thinking about it, and it's tiring, that's all. I haven't had time to eat properly or go to the gym, or—'

'Go to the gym! Oh dear, dear me – the gym! In the name of God!'

'Fine. You asked. Mock away, why don't you?'

'You're not telling me something.'

'There's nothing else to tell.'

'Maybe. But you look peaky. You look like your mum looked when she was expecting you.'

I laughed, glad to be able to. I said I was not expecting, she could dream on.

'Your mum and dad would like a grandchild,' she said.

'They couldn't care less,' I said.

'Yes they do. It's natural. You want your kids to have kids.'

'Why?'

130

'It's natural.'

We could have gone on like that for hours – the 'natural' argument was one May employed all the time. If she could say something was natural she felt she had won – it was no good pointing out that a lot of things that are natural are bad. I'd cite endless examples of something that was natural nevertheless not being good, but she would never listen. Anyway, she is wrong about my parents pining for a grandchild. May knows perfectly well – in fact, she holds it against her – that my mum is not the maternal, earth-mother type. She loves me, and wanted more children, that's true, but her work is far more important to her than being a grandmother. If I eventually want to have a baby, then fine, she'll be delighted, but if I don't, she won't make me feel guilty. Unlike May, who definitely will, though she has no right to.

I let her win that one – it's always a case of winning or losing with May. She smirked and pulled her shawl more securely round her shoulders. She's suddenly taken to wearing this shawl though it's far too warm in her house ever to need such an extra layer. It's her new badge of status: look at me, I am old, respect me, or that's how I choose to interpret it. She crocheted this shawl herself, for her own mother – she always tells me this as though implying that I, too, ought to be crocheting a shawl for my mother, or Mum should have done the same for her. We don't crochet, or knit, or sew. She despairs of us.

'You look like the granny in "Little Red Riding Hood" in that shawl.'

'Where's the basket of food you've brought me then?' she shot back, smart as anything.

'I forgot it. Why, is there something you want?'

'You could go and get some eggs,' she said. 'I fancy a boiled egg. I need my protein, see. What you laughing at? Think I don't know about protein? Think I'm ignorant 'cos I'm old?'

'No,' I said, 'the old are wise, especially old women. Do you really want eggs?'

She said she did, and made a performance of finding the correct money for them (with another little contest over whether I knew the price of six eggs, which I did not). I didn't want her money, but it was produced from the Jubilee tea caddy and pressed into my palm. She had a funny look in her eye, one I knew well. She didn't really want the eggs – it was all some kind of challenge for me. There would be a hidden purpose to this apparently simple task. Maybe she'd wanted me to say I hadn't time so that she could use my reluctance to show how little I cared for her. If this sounds unnaturally devious, May *is* devious. Well, I thwarted it by setting off for the eggs.

She hadn't said which shop I should go to, which ought to have been a clue. It was ages since I'd walked along May's street, or any in her area, because these days I mostly drive, but I hadn't even noticed on my way to her house from the stop on Holloway Road that her corner shop had gone. It sold everything, and the family that ran it had been there as long as May. I used to love going on 'messages' there when I was little, May's leather shopping bag in one hand, trailing on the ground, the handles too long for me, and her purse in the other. I was always so thrilled to be trusted with both bag and money – it gave an excitement to shopping that wasn't there when I went round a supermarket with my mother. I stood in front of what is now a video rental shop and thought how sad. May must miss it. Until recently, she could still get to it herself, her daily outing, I expect. Why hadn't she mentioned it had gone?

I walked on, vaguely recalling a larger shop, a sort of mini-market place that I'd noticed earlier. They had no eggs, didn't sell any kind of dairy produce, only some tired-looking fruit and veg, and some tinned stuff. By then I was nearly back at the Holloway Road, where there were plenty of shops.

I bought the required six eggs, but then made a mistake, thinking I knew the area well enough to take a short cut back to May's. I didn't. I came to the overground railway line and couldn't find a way across it and had to go all the way back to the main road and retrace my steps.

'Been watching the hens laying them?' May said. 'The time you've been, blimey!'

'I couldn't find a corner shop.'

'Corner shop? They've all gone from round here. It's a disgrace. Poor old folk like me, we don't have no cars, what are we supposed to do?'

'I never noticed,' I said, trying to be humble.

'Course you didn't, with your nose stuck in books all day. Put them eggs in the pantry and I'll have one later.'

I left a few minutes later, with May now cheerful, having seen me flustered. She told me not to slam the front door as I left or it would come off its hinges. I closed it with exaggerated care. The neighbour next door, Mrs Patel, the one who had phoned for the police, was just going into her house and stopped to ask how Mrs Wright was feeling now. I said she was much better, only just managing not to add better enough to be her old difficult self. 'She has good family,' Mrs Patel said, 'good, good family. You good granddaughter – granddaughter, yes? – good help.' I smiled. May would be observing this interchange from behind her net curtain, longing to know what was being said. I would tell her, when next I visited, that I had been called a treasure and told that my grandmother was very lucky to have me.

May and her shawl – the image persisted for the rest of the day, the way she'd clutched it round her shoulders, the way she used it to flag up her frailty. It isn't a shawl like the one Little Red Riding Hood's grandmother always wears in illustrations to the tale. It's a flamboyant shawl, the colours of the wool clashing violently, shades all the way from magenta

133

to a lurid lime green, because it was crocheted from scraps. May is not like Little Red Riding Hood's granny either, not yet. She's not in bed all day, not dependent on her grand-daughter bringing her food.

It is odd, that. Little Red Riding Hood's granny being on her own, I mean, living in that isolated cottage in the middle of a wood. Little Red Riding Hood certainly wouldn't have wanted to be her grandmother. After all, what kind of life was Granny living, and that's without bringing wolves into it. If I remember correctly, in the original story, the wolf eats the grandmother and there is no woodcutter hanging about to come and cut her free. What kind of inspiration is that? And why wasn't Little Red Riding Hood's granny living with her family, eh? The poor old thing. The more I think about it, the worse the image of grandmothers in children's stories gets. Grandmothers are always peripheral, unlike stepmothers, who are crucial to so many plots and always wonderfully cruel or wicked.

I still have all my childhood books, stacks of them. It amuses Ian. He claims, correctly, that I never look at them, whereas I look at my art books often. So why let them take up so much of our limited shelf space? But I love to have them, to know they are there. I just like to see them – they seem part of me. And they are pretty volumes, artistic, worth displaying for their own sake and never mind the contents. Many are tattered, especially the Beatrix Potters (no noteworthy grand-mothers there). Some – the Arthur Ransomes – are first editions. My dad got them for me and they have illustrations I used to pore over, identifying myself with Titty and her parrot. Ian says those are probably worth something, unlike the rest.

Hans Andersen surely had something to say about grand-mothers, but I couldn't think of one of his stories that featured any of them in major roles. I sat with the two-volume edition I have, the one illustrated by Heath Robinson, and flicked through it, stopping at the drawing 'she was on the whole a sensible sort of lady' in the story of the Little Mermaid – a grandmother, at last. She was the person who told the six infant mermaids about life above the waves. The youngest, who was fascinated by humans, asked if they lived for ever, and her granny said no, they all die, none of them live as long as us, we can live three hundred years then turn into foam. The princess said she'd still rather be a human because they have souls that live on after they die, and that's better than living three hundred years then turning to foam. Her granny is cross with her. She tells her not to be silly, but the princess asks if there is any way a mer-person could get a soul. Granny agrees there is. *If* she can get a human man to love and marry her, then she will have a share of his soul. This, though, is not going to happen because human men find mer-tails repulsive – they want bodies to finish in two ugly pillars called legs . . .

I sat there on the floor and read the whole volume, soon forgetting I was supposedly reading with a purpose. And then, putting the book back, I saw Roald Dahl's *Charlie and the Chocolate Factory,* and remembered the grandmothers in it. Grandma Josephine and Grandma Georgina, who slept together in the same bed with Grandpa Joe and Grandpa George. The grandmas were so old and so tired they never got out of bed (how did they pee? I used to ask Dad, and he whispered that they had bedpans in the bed and I shrieked with disgust). They were as shrivelled as prunes and bony as skeletons. Their faces were hideously wrinkled and their necks scraggy. Not desirable role models, then. It was a field worth exploring, though. But would Claudia approve? Importance, significance of the grandmother in children's literature, etc.? It would give me a very nice time, reading all my childhood books again. I could hear May saying, 'Call that work!'

Claudia might say the same; she might complain I am once

more going off on a pointless tangent. I can imagine her glaring at me and inviting me to clarify my objectives in dredging through children's stories for evidence that grandmothers exert an influence of value on their granddaughters and explain how this supports my main contention, which my dissertation is based on, that . . . that what? Here it is again, this struggle to identify what it is I am about – I *know* something is there, flitting around as ever at the corners of my mind, lurking there, waiting for a strong light to illuminate it. But a strong light might, on the contrary, banish it altogether. Claudia is the strong light. She stares, she raises her eyebrows, she asks one pertinent question and what I think I have almost within my grasp vanishes. Nothing there. Emptiness.

I wish I were a carpenter with planks of wood in my hands, and a hammer, and nails and, hey presto, shelves put up. Instead, I have words and ideas and feelings – it's the 'feelings' that do the damage. Dangerous, insubstantial things. So what is it that I *feel*, in this instance? I'll try yet again: I feel there is a link between grandmothers and granddaughters that is not just the obvious genetic one. I feel this link is to do with experience. I feel a kind of osmosis must take place and that it is important, this unconscious assimilation of what has been endured, that it somehow passes from woman to woman. I feel it is a strengthening force – yes, that's it, a strengthening force. That's what I'm after, what I'm trying to prove. So, how to do it? How to tie everything together?

Ian would say it is time to make a list. He is a great maker of lists. I'm always finding them, stuck in mirrors, in the corner of picture frames, lurking under books. They are usually quite short and abrupt, but always numbered. Ian says the moment he has made a list, his mind clears. The list gives him clear objectives, and even if he doesn't go ahead and obey them, he feels better. Problems appear not so serious, the demands of time not so impossible to manage. So today I am going to write down a list, Ian-fashion, to see if it will help. The fact is, Mum is right, the title of my dissertation doesn't work. I need to re-title it. The existing one is just confusing me. Claudia will be annoyed, but that can't be helped. She is the one, after all, who tells me that my purpose is not clear and I'm floundering. My list will be of other possible titles. But first I plan to make a sort of question-and-answer list – I'll ask the questions bothering me, then try to answer them. I need to be specific to get anywhere. The first question is: can grandmothers have a direct and important influence on grandchildren? I ask it because I read an article recently in which Bertrand Russell was quoted as having claimed that his grandmother 'moulded' his life. I can't remember the exact quotation, though I copied it down and I've got it somewhere, but it was about his grandmother's contempt for convention passing on to him. Her motto had been: 'Thou shalt not follow a multitude to do evil,' and he made it his.

So the answer to that one will be, 'Yes, sometimes.' It's a start.

Ian's worried that I spend too much time in the past. He's wrong. What he sees as pessimism or a negative attitude is my nature. I've done the kind of work that looks to the future, when I was teaching, before I ever met him. I had almost eight years of it, before I came back to studying, and I was never as happy as I am now. My job then was all about the future of the students. I mixed with them all the time, on the surface having 'a great life'. I travelled round the world and I found myself aching for peace and quiet and books and seriousness and a purpose. I had the curiosity to try to find out something, something that interested me, however trivial it might seem to others.

We don't argue about it, Ian and I. I don't try to defend myself. There's no need. He should be more concerned with his own attitude to life. I love the past, Ian seems to hate it to such an extent that he won't allow it to have existed.

VI

CLAUDIA WAS in a mellow mood today, by which I mean she wasn't sitting with her spine so straight it might have had a steel rod inserted in it, and her hands were not clasped tightly on her neatly aligned knees. For her, she looked quite relaxed. Her facial expression was different too. It wasn't that inscrutable stare that I always felt could only have been attained after hours of practice in front of a mirror. She actually smiled as she greeted me, only fleetingly, but I was grateful. I risked a 'Lovely day, isn't it?' but that was a step too far and I only got a nod in return, and then there was the usual enquiring raising of her eyebrows as she waited.

I took a deep breath and said I wanted to change the title of my dissertation. I said it no longer described what I was hoping to investigate and that I felt it was misleading. She frowned. Her back visibly straightened. I held out to her a piece of paper on which I'd written my proposed new title. She took it as though it were something distasteful, holding it by the very tip of the corner of the paper. Then there was a lengthy pause, during which she looked at the words on the A4 sheet and then at me and then back again. Dear God, there were only twenty-three words there, why the scrutiny? There was a sigh, a long pause, and then she said that it seemed a lot of fuss about very little – the new ('new' said with emphasis) title appeared very like the original one, but if I preferred this wording, 'so be it'.

That over, I ran through the work I'd done since I last saw her, including thoughts about grandmothers in children's literature. She seemed quite pleased about these, but less approving when I rambled on about wanting to consider whether grandmothers were more important for their link to the past or to the future. She asked what I meant about this 'link' to the future, how could grandmothers possibly provide such a thing? I said they'd travelled the road themselves and so they could provide a map. 'The road?' Claudia echoed. 'Which road is this?' I got flustered and couldn't explain what I meant (not surprising, as I didn't know). She accused me of being glib. I switched hurriedly to the idea of grandmothers providing cohesion in a changing society. 'Cohesion?' she said, in the same tone of voice. I cleared my throat, and tried to sound confident. I said the whole idea of the family was changing and with it the place of the grandmother within it. One-parent families are common, and families with gay parents, and so the grandmother is crucial to keeping these new sorts of families together. 'How?' Claudia asked.

I didn't bloody well know how, but it sounded good. For the next half-hour I struggled on, trying to back up this claim, throwing in stuff about the new non-nuclear family needing a point of reference and so on. Claudia listened, sighing a lot in that infuriating way she has, the sigh coming out of her nose and not her mouth, the nostrils flaring and unflaring, and the mouth pursed below it. It made her look ugly. My mind wandered, and I thought that if I put a mirror in front of her she would stop doing that. As I floundered on, talk for talk's sake, very full of sound and signifying nothing, she began to pick imaginary bits of fluff off her immaculate skirt. I thought that at any minute she was going to say I was talking nonsense and if I couldn't become more lucid there was serious doubt over whether I should be permitted to continue with this disserta-tion. But she didn't. Instead, she asked if she might be allowed – 'might be allowed', a good one that – to suggest that I should look at the grandmother being not so much a cohesive force but on the contrary an inhibitor of social change in modern society. I admitted this had never occurred to me. How could a grandmother inhibit change? Think, Claudia said, of immigrant communities. Grandmothers arrive with their families not just unable to speak the new language needed but unlikely ever to learn it. It is in their own interest to resist the infiltration of the new language into the family, and this applies to codes of dress and manners and customs, and of course religion. The grandmother fights a losing battle but she fights hard, and what does that do to the family? How does her resistance erode her status within the family?

The Bertrand Russell quote about his grandmother 'moulding' him sprang into my head and I produced it with a flourish at this point. I asked Claudia if this was what she meant, that if grandmothers tried to mould grandchildren, and they were doing this against the grain in immigrant families, then perhaps they became dangerous? Claudia said not necessarily – they could equally become powerless and therefore not at all dangerous. But by then she was looking at her watch all the time. The session was over. As I stood up to leave, she said, 'You quoted Bertrand Russell. Worth looking at his wife Dora, perhaps.'

Claudia is constantly exposing my ignorance, but then I suppose it's part of her job. To my shame, I didn't know anything Dora Russell. She was Bertrand Russell's second wife and an interesting, impressive person in her own right, with a first from Cambridge and a reputation as an influential feminist in the 1920s and 1930s. I liked the sound of her already.

I discovered she had two children by Bertrand Russell and two more by an American she had an affair with while still married to Russell. She was fifty-three when her first grandchild was born, a girl, Sarah, her son John's daughter. He went on to give her another granddaughter, Lucy (and he had adopted his wife's daughter Ann, by a previous relationship). John and his wife lived in the USA, so Dora didn't see much of her granddaughters in their early years, but later on her son moved to London and she got to know the girls as teenagers. She was by then living in Cornwall and was proud of keeping open house for her family. She wanted the younger members to know that this was a place they and their friends could come and be accepted as they were without fear of being judged. But when they did come, especially Lucy and Sarah, she was shocked by their appearance and attitude. They were, she wrote, 'like mendicant friars', clad in an assortment of rags, arriving hungry and expecting to be fed, depending on free hospitality and giving nothing back in return. Sarah, who had once pleased her by getting a scholarship to Oxford, had dropped out of her course, and Lucy gave up her place at the Sorbonne. Their grandmother argued fiercely with them, trying to persuade them that education was the starting point for everything and should not be spurned, but she couldn't persuade them. Their rejection of education was to her the most awful waste and an insult to everything she held dear. How could such clever young women just drift about, apparently with no purpose? It was a mystery to her and she tried to think of an explanation. What she came up with was the theory that they had been affected by the Hiroshima bomb. It had made them conclude that nothing mattered, nothing was worthwhile. Dora disagreed strongly with this nihilistic attitude. It was everyone's duty, she said, to protest against iniquities like nuclear bombs – they ought to be doing what she herself was doing, i.e. leading anti-nuclear demonstrations.

But try though she might, her words had no effect on these girls. Their grandmother, far from moulding them in her own image, appeared merely to convince them that she was misguided and there was no hope. Far from growing out of her tramp-like existence, Lucy, who had become a Buddhist, seemed to grow more and more unhinged. She said she was

141

going to become a Buddhist nun. To her grandmother's (and everyone else's) horror, she then burned herself to death, emulating the example of some Buddhist nuns and monks in Vietnam. Strangely, though Dora mourned the loss of such a 'lovely young woman, brave, gifted in mind and spirit', she thought that her granddaughter after her death belonged 'to those we honour without medals'. Even though Dora could not agree with her, she reckoned that Lucy had acted out her convictions, and by drawing attention to the bombing of Cambodia by the Americans at the time, had made a protest she considered important and worthwhile.

At first I couldn't get past the manner of poor Lucy's death to think about Dora, and how she'd reacted to it, but then I began to see the challenge she as a grandmother had faced. There was very little detail in Dora's account of how, where and exactly when Lucy had committed her dreadful act, and it worried me. Dora found all this too painful to write about, but the information must be available. Somehow, without it, the whole death seemed unbelievable. The ordeal for Dora didn't end with Lucy's death. For a woman who prided herself on her understanding of young people, and who had been so tolerant of their waywardness, it was a blow to her pride as well as being a tragedy. She obviously felt she had failed the girl. Like so many grandmothers, she hadn't always approved of how her grandchildren were being brought up, and now she felt she ought to have tried harder to exert more influence. She wasn't the sort of woman to keep her opinions to herself but perhaps she hadn't, in the case of Lucy, voiced them loudly enough. Whatever – she never stopped grieving for Lucy for the rest of her life.

Then, pondering all this until late in the night, it struck me that the Dora/Lucy relationship might indicate that there is a gulf between grandmothers and granddaughters that can't be bridged because the grandmothers can't grasp the nature of the problems the granddaughters are grappling with – they remain in their own world and can't comprehend the modern one. Dora Russell thought, I'm sure, that she had moved with the times, but had she? Maybe Lucy didn't think so. But my argument, such as it was, is weakened now I know the story of Dora and Lucy Russell. The grandmother as an influence, the grandmother as a cohesive force, the grandmother as mentor . . . I don't think so. What, then?

Surprisingly, Ian was interested in the Dora/Lucy history. He knows a bit about Buddhism. He says there's nothing in it that calls for the sort of death Lucy gave herself. Ian says Buddhism is about destroying greed and hatred, and through doing so attaining enlightenment. Lucy wasn't going to attain any enlightenment by burning herself to death. 'It was a form of protest,' I said, 'against what the Americans were doing in Cambodia.'

'A pointless form of protest,' Ian said.

'Well, it called attention to what was happening, and—'

'And did no good whatsoever.'

'At least she had principles, she was brave, she—'

'Rubbish. Like her grandmother said, people with principles who want to defeat evil fight against it. They don't kill themselves. That's defeatist, it's the easy way out.'

'Easy? Burning yourself to death? Please! Think of the pain, the agony, the fear . . .'

'She was probably on LSD, doped to the eyeballs.'

'You don't know that.'

'It's a reasonable guess, it would fit.'

Neither of us knows much about Lucy Russell, but it's strange the way Ian and I interpret what happened differently. He is on the whole contemptuous of her. He sees her as mad, or at the very least mentally unstable due to taking drugs (though he has no evidence that she did). Her death doesn't upset him. It doesn't even really puzzle him – she was mad, mad people do mad things, end of story. But I feel for her.

My skin crawls just with reading the little her grandmother writes about her death. I imagine the smell of the petrol she poured over herself, I imagine the whoosh of it taking fire, I imagine the heat, and then the beginning of the pain . . . I torture myself by trying to imagine it all. Then I think of Dora. How did she hear about it? She doesn't say. Her mind would be flooded with memories of Lucy, happy ones, disturbing ones, she'd hear her voice, see her young face, and nothing would make sense. She would surely feel she had passed on nothing to her granddaughter. Lucy had ignored her, she'd gone off at a wild tangent, rejecting Dora's brand of idealism.

There must be this hopelessness built into the role of grand-mother when such tragedies overtake their family. Their own living must seem a sham. They can't stop anything, they just have to witness events, some so terrible they have never envis-aged them. I said this to Ian. He shrugged his shoulders, but didn't say anything in reply. 'What does a grandmother do if she sees something going wrong with a grandchild and the parent isn't doing anything about it?' I was just pondering aloud, not expecting him to make any comment.

'She can't do anything if the child doesn't ask her.'

'She could remonstrate with the child's parents.'

'Some parents can't be remonstrated with. Some parents are shit.'

He said this so angrily that I knew at once this was personal, but in view of how Ian had always resented any enquiry whatsoever about his family, I didn't dare pick up on it. I tried to do it sideways, though. 'They aren't shit for no reason,' I said, 'and the grandmother would know the reason.'

'Oh, don't give me that rubbish. Reasons aren't excuses.'

'You mean grandmothers know the reasons but they make excuses?'

'No, I don't mean that.'

'What do you mean then?'

'How did this start? Never mind, it doesn't matter. All I

meant was that grandmothers can't always do anything about bad situations to do with their grandchildren. They might want to, but they can't.'

'So they suffer silently and watch the grandchild suffering . . .'

'I'm bored with this now. You're getting all hypothetical. We were talking about Dora Russell, that's all. I know your game, Issy, and I'm not going to play it, so don't think you're being clever and leading me on to confession time. There's nothing to confess, OK?'

No, it wasn't OK, but I stopped. I stopped, but I filed away in my mind Ian's reaction. It was easy to deduce he had something to hide on the subject of both parents and grandmothers. I will bide my time.

Isa has left a message. I haven't seen her since Dad told me his story, and I realise I've been putting a visit off because I'm nervous, knowing how much I must conceal. Suppose I give something away? Suppose something shows in my eyes, a flicker of the doubt I now feel, or even a suggestion of accusation. She is no longer the grandmother I thought she was, in every sense. I won't be able to be my usual self. Will she spot the change in my attitude, however hard I try to hide it? Well, I can't go on not visiting her. I listened to her message again. She would like me to come and visit her, and would I please ring her to arrange a convenient time. 'That is the end of my message. Have you understood it?' Her voice sounded unusually shaky, but maybe just because of her age. May's voice still sounds young – not *young* young, but sort of fifty-ish – whereas recently Isa's voice betrays her years more than anything else about her. Maybe it's an accent thing too – Isa is so refined, she enunciates every word so carefully, whereas May never pauses and there's still an energy about her delivery. May, of course, hates people who 'talk posh'. She says there's no need for it. If I point out that they can't help it, it's how they were brought up, it's the schools they went to, she won't excuse them. The young princes, William and Harry, please her very much by not talking too posh – she's heard them being interviewed and they spoke 'very nice, proper but not posh'.

Ringing Isa back, I got the faithful and deeply irritating Elspeth. 'Mrs Symondson is not so well,' Elspeth said, in a definitely accusatory tone of voice. 'She hasn't been so well since your last visit.' Why Isa thinks Elspeth so marvellous I can't imagine. She's odious, a creepy sort of woman, appearing deferential when that is the last thing she is. Her role in Isa's household is quite odd. She doesn't clean – Mrs Roberts comes twice a week to do that – but she does some dusting; she doesn't cook dinners, but she prepares light lunches and bakes cakes – baking is her speciality and she's very good at it. In many ways she's like a sort of latter-day lady's maid, fussing over Isa and ever ready to be called for to do something minor. Elspeth has a low opinion of me. She clearly thinks I am not nearly attentive enough to my grandmother. I bet she's careful never directly to criticise me to Isa – it'll just be a word here and there, letting the odd suggestion drop that I don't visit often these days, etc. Will Isa pick up on her sneaky words? No, I don't think so, but they'll register if repeated often enough.

Isa, when I arrived, still looked a little paler than usual, but she was as dignified and regal as ever in the way she greeted me, or rather allowed me to greet her. She likes an air kiss on her right cheek, and that's it. I sat down, and automatically looked for the sherry. No sherry bottle on the table, no glasses, though it was sherry time. Was this an indication that I was in disgrace? I made no comment, and neither did Isa. I willed myself to be humble, and careful about anything I said. I must not rise to provocation, I must let Isa get away with any fantasies she wished to project. She is old, she has rights. I am not sure what sort of rights, only that they exist.

We exchanged pleasantries, as we usually do, about the

weather, about the traffic on my way there, about our health. Isa was as polite and attentive as ever, listening gravely to the banalities I came out with. She enquired how May was – 'How is Mrs Wright?' (not how is May, or how is your granny, or how is your mother's mother) – and I told her she was making good progress. Once this was over, she then surprised me. 'Isamay,' she said, 'you are a very dear girl to me.' I said she was very dear to me too. 'Very dear,' she repeated, 'but capable of getting into a muddle.' 'Too true,' I said, cheerfully, 'all the time.' But honesty was not what she apparently was after. She was clasping and unclasping her hands, I noticed, the fingers first locked together and then separated. What was she working up to? She didn't, though, seem nervous, even if this gesture suggested she might be, but on the contrary quite composed. Her voice was now confident, measured, no hesitation in her tone. She was, as she liked to be, in control. She was going to tell me something, I was sure, and my heart began to beat a little faster.

Suddenly I wanted to stop her telling me anything at all. She'd regret it, whatever it was, I instinctively knew she would. People do. People like Isa always regret revealing secrets. First, there's the relief, of not holding in whatever it is, no longer having to worry about the secret being revealed, but then there's the price to pay. You can't tell how it will be received, how you'll be forever altered in someone's eyes. And there's the wider damage, which can't always be limited, the effect of confession on others involved in the secret, who you've perhaps betrayed. I make myself sound experienced but I'm not. It's more that I've been told secrets, not that I've had any to divulge. Take the most recent example, my dad telling me his secret about Isa not being his real mother. It changed him for me – I still haven't readjusted to his history. I feel a peculiar kind of pity for him that was never there before. He doesn't want, or need, my pity, but it's there. And since knowing this secret, I can hardly look Isa in the eye.

She's always been a model of propriety. I would never even *imagine* her being capable of telling a lie, or acting out such a deception, yet since my dad told me his secret I know she's been so adept at both that no one has ever suspected anything. Her cunning, her ability to sustain deception, astounds me.

I started talking, to stop her, blurting out about her being right, I did get into muddles, and launched into a convoluted account of muddles I've been in – but she held up a hand in protest. 'Isamay,' she said, 'quiet.' So I was quiet. (God, for once I'd have welcomed the horrible sherry.) 'Human beings,' Isa said, 'are storytellers. We all need stories, do we not?' I nodded, wondering if she was possibly going to quote Mrs Gaskell, and others. If I'd been my usual self, I would have asked her what she meant by 'stories', and enjoyed splitting hairs with her over the definition, but I wasn't and didn't. 'We need stories to explain who we are and where we come from, do we not?' I wanted to say no, not really, but I nodded again. Where on earth had she got this Christmas-cracker wisdom from? 'But stories are not facts,' Isa went on, 'they are inventions woven round facts.' It was as though she were reciting something she'd memorised – she had that look on her face that people have when they are concentrating on something learned, a look of strain as they try to get each line right. 'Especially when stories are about family history,' she continued, 'because such stories are complicated. Many of them are myths. They have been told so often, and in the telling, details have changed. The facts the stories are based on become less vital and what surrounds them takes over.' Then she stopped. This wasn't Isa, all this stuff. I couldn't think where she had picked it up – from some programme on the radio? Some magazine? In any case, she'd now forgotten what her point was. I wondered if I should help her out, but suddenly she got a second wind and was off again, giving examples of how family history stories change. Somehow, she'd jumped to my own birth, describing the event

148

as I'd heard it described every Christmas Eve. 'That is a factual account,' Isa said. 'I was there, your other grandmother was there, your parents were there. We all have a clear recollection. Facts. Indisputable. But there are other stories where the facts are not known.'

She was actually trembling slightly, her whole body quivering in the most disturbing way. I asked her if she was cold, and looked around for something to wrap round her shoulders, but she said she was not cold, she was perfectly all right and I should not fuss. The quivering stopped, and she took a deep breath. I started to say something – I was going to ask what on earth she'd been hinting at – but she held up her hand, in the well-known manner, to tell me not to speak. I couldn't read her expression. Her eyes, her still so bright blue eyes, appeared vacant – it was quite frightening to observe. I began to get goose pimples and my mouth went dry. 'Grandmama,' I said, 'what's wrong? You look so odd.' She didn't reply, but some recognition seemed to creep back into her expression. She put a hand to her head and kept it there a moment. 'I am the keeper of another story,' she said, 'and I have kept it long enough. You have got in a muddle, Isamay. You have brought this about.' Totally confused, I asked *what* I'd brought about, was she referring to the brother she hadn't known about? 'You have got in a muddle, and forced my hand,' she said.

I studied her carefully, half afraid to move or speak, wishing for once that Elspeth would come creeping in, but she'd gone, or that a phone would ring – anything to shatter the weirdness of the moment. But there was silence except for Isa's breathing, rapid and surprisingly loud, and my fidgeting as I rubbed at the arms of my chair to try to conceal my anxiety. I was counting as I did it, one-two rubbing forward, three-four rubbing back, a pointless motion that soothed me. 'Upsetting things,' Isa suddenly burst out, making a fist with her right hand and banging her knee. She'd gone from

149

appearing hardly to be there to being very present and now angry. Colour crept into her pale face and she frowned in a way she never allows herself to – frowning creates lines – and there was a renewed strength in her voice. 'It is time for the lying to stop!' she announced, melodramatically. 'Who's been lying?' I asked before I could stop myself. 'Sssh!' she said. 'This is quite difficult enough.'

And then, just when I didn't want the interruption, which only minutes before I'd been desperate to happen, the telephone on the table beside Isa's chair rang. It has an old-fashioned ring, hard and loud, no personal tune for Isa. It's an old-fashioned dial telephone, rather large and cumbersome, taking up too much room on the table, but she won't switch to a neater, push-button sort. She would never not answer it, either. So when it began its insistent double-beat ringing, Isa gave a start, and then reached out her hand for the black receiver. Her face changed the moment she heard the voice. 'Darling!' she said, and smiled. She listened, nodded, said 'Of course, of course,' and then 'Yes, she's here,' and rather reluctantly handed the phone to me. It was Dad. He said he hadn't known I was visiting, he was just checking on Isa because Elspeth had said she wasn't too well, and how did I find her? With Isa watching and listening, all I could say was fine, and I'd ring him later.

That was it. When the receiver was replaced, Isa said, 'Where were we?' in an absolutely normal tone of voice. I said she'd been talking about lying, and then, predictably, we got into a complicated conversation about who had been lying and why, and in the end Isa agreed she couldn't remember what she had been going to say. It had all been so tiring, first Isa's strangeness, then her apparent resentment about something or other, and lastly the sense that she was going to make some unpleasant announcement, or divulge some shocking news (though that bit may have been my imagination). Nothing could have been more different from my normal sessions with her – they had always followed a reliable pattern, boring maybe but entirely dependable. I knew more or less what she would say, I knew how to respond, what she wanted of me. Now I was bewildered. She'd definitely summoned me to tell me something but I hadn't the faintest idea what it was, and thanks to Dad calling, she had herself forgotten.

There was nothing to do but leave. 'Oh!' Isa said, when I rose to give her the regulation farewell kiss on the cheek. 'You haven't had your sherry!' I said it didn't matter, but she said she'd been 'remiss' and had forgotten her manners, and how could she have done? She saw me to the door and her walking, though stately as ever, was very slow, as though she feared she might fall. Her hand reached out to hold on to the hall table as she passed it and the little lace handkerchief she'd been clutching fell to the floor. I bent down and picked it up. It was damp, and I remembered she'd been twisting it earlier, over and over – it was damp with perspiration from her hands. This touched me. It was all wrong that an old lady should be in such a state and that somehow I had caused her distress. I hesitated when we reached the front door, wishing Elspeth was still in the house. Was Isa safe on her own? I wasn't at all sure. But when the door had been opened, the rush of fresh air from outside seemed to revive her. 'Oh!' she said. 'What a lovely evening,' and she stood on the doorstep with her eyes closed, breathing in and out in the theatrical manner she sometimes adopted. I felt reassured. She was still standing at the door by the time I got to my car, parked outside her front gate. She looked so elegant in her blue dress, one hand still raised in a courtly wave. To my relief, she closed the door before I started the car. Elspeth would have left her supper for her. She would slip into her beloved routine and, with luck, remember nothing of the previous half-hour.

When I got home, Ian was already there. He said I looked shaken, had something happened? I told him I wasn't sure

151

what indeed had happened, and tried to explain about Isa. He's only met her once, but I've talked enough about her for him to be familiar with what she's like, and of course I've gone on about the brother thing and Mary-Lou's research, so he knows about all that.

'I just feel that whatever is wrong with Isa it's somehow all my fault,' I said.

'Yup,' he said, which annoyed me.

'What do you mean, "yup"?' I said.

'Well, like you said, you and the Canadian cousin have started something off, even if you don't know what. Just memories, maybe. Ones she's suppressed and doesn't want to surface again.'

'Memories of what?'

'*I* don't know. Maybe she doesn't either, maybe there's all sorts of stuff just swirling around and she's confused. She's eighty, she's entitled to a bit of confusion. I don't know why you're all so scared of her.'

'What do you mean, scared? We are *not* scared.'

'Yes you are. In awe of her, then. The way you talk about it, always nervous of offending her, worrying about what she'll say or think.'

'Ian, you're making this up. You've only met her once, you've only seen me with her once . . .'

'That was enough.'

'. . . and you've never seen the rest of my family with her.'

'I don't need to. I've listened to you, that's enough. It's obvious Isa makes your mum nervous and your dad isn't comfortable with her.'

'Oh, you'd be the expert of course on mother/son relationships.'

'I'm an expert on you, anyway. The way *you* behave with her it's as though she's made of china and you are afraid of smashing her. She's probably the only person you seem not to be cheeky to, from your own accounts, or sarcastic. From the sound of it, you do the good-little-girl act, and she treats you like some kind of favoured acolyte she's anointed—'

'That's not fair. I'm her granddaughter, she treats me like a granddaughter.'

'Except you're not. You're not her granddaughter.'

'The birth thing doesn't make any difference. I *am* her granddaughter.'

Ian shrugged. I wanted to challenge everything he had said, but I felt stopped in my tracks. I am not Isa's granddaughter. Knowing this makes me doubt all kinds of things I was once sure of. The doubt is creeping into my work.

Ian came home this evening and silently passed me a newspaper cutting he'd taken from his jacket pocket. It was all scrunched up and I had to smooth it out to see what it was. He has this sneaky habit of tearing items that interest him out of newspapers he reads in the cafés where he has his lunch.

I ought to have screwed up the pilfered cutting as a matter of principle but I didn't. I'd caught sight of the photograph. It was obviously of a grandmother and granddaughter, the likeness clear in spite of the age difference and contrasting styles of dress. The caption under this photograph read: 'Found at last, after 28 years'. So it was irresistible to me, as Ian had known it would be – I had to sit down and read the whole thing. I read it rapidly, then twice more, slowly. It was about a group of grandmothers known as the Abuelas de Plaza de Mayo, who got together to search for the missing children of their own children who had 'disappeared' during the military dictatorship in Argentina during 1976–83. These grandmothers had persuaded the post-dictatorship government to set up the National Bank of Genetic Data to facilitate the tracking down of missing people. The children of the grandmothers were usually dead – tortured, then killed – but *their* children were very often alive and being brought up by people who they did not know were not their real parents. The article said that so far eighty-two grandchildren had been traced. Often, it seemed the grandchildren had been shocked and resented the exposure of their real parentage; they had been happy with their adoptive parents (usually members of the previous dicta-torship's regime) and had been brought up in luxury. To find that they now belonged to much poorer families presented all kinds of problems, and the love of the grandmothers was not enough to overcome them.

I stared at the photograph a long time. The grandmother was said to be eighty but looked much older, very frail and bent, and the granddaughter, much taller than her, was twenty-eight, almost my age, but looked younger. She'd been six months old when her parents (her mother a student, her father a lecturer) had disappeared. They had both been arrested at their home and taken with the baby to an undisclosed destin-ation. From the first, the grandmother, a seamstress, had been certain they had been murdered for their part in demonstra-tions against the regime, but she could not believe the baby had shared their fate. Her joy at discovering that this young woman was indeed her granddaughter – all it took was a blood test (though it wasn't explained how the young woman came to be traced in the first instance) – was overshadowed by the realisation that it was not shared. The granddaughter hadn't been keen to meet her. She said she had a grandmother already and would always regard her as her true grandmother. The reunion was not the happy occasion it was expected (by the blood grandmother) to be. No wonder that in the photo-graph they both looked stern-faced and sad – and yet the resemblance was truly striking. Both of them had the same high forehead, the same long, slim nose, and most noticeable of all, a distinctive upper lip with a pronounced bow in the centre. The granddaughter was wearing lipstick, so the upper lip really stood out, and the grandmother was not, and her mouth was sunken – false teeth, or missing teeth? – but nevertheless the strong similarity was clear.

There were so many unanswered questions in this article, and the last paragraph was missing, due to the carelessness with which Ian had torn it out, but it didn't matter. There was enough there to demonstrate how important grand-mothers are – *they have the knowledge*, and not even a military dictatorship can make them forget it. It doesn't 'disappear', as their children did. This made such a deep impression on me, the thought of how the genetic claim could not be denied, that I almost forgot that the granddaughter hadn't wanted to be found and claimed.

Whenever I visit May, she likes me to prattle on non-stop, yet when I do that she complains that I never pause for breath and give her a headache. Today, she was actually out in her little garden when I arrived, which was a good sign, watering the tubs. The watering can is just a cheap plastic thing she can handle quite easily. I always thought it ugly and once bought her a pretty metal one, on sale at the Sainsbury Wing shop in the National Gallery, after a Monet exhibition. It was pale grey with water lilies painted on it. May never used it, said it was too heavy and the lilies didn't look anything like water lilies, but what had really turned her against it was the price, which I hadn't noticed – the sticker was still on the bottom, £12.50, and it enraged her.

I'd remembered to bring my key this time and let myself in, shouting a greeting. When I realised she was out at the back, because the door at the end of the passage was wide open, I went and stood there, waiting for her to catch sight of me, so as not to alarm her. She looked so sweet, concentrating on her watering, both hands gripping the old can as though it were much heavier than it possibly could be when it held so little water. She held it as a child might do, as I myself had held it under her direction. I noticed how much weight she'd lost since being in hospital – it didn't suit her, this new thin look. I wanted her to be round and plump again. And her hair was thinner too, not as bouncy as it usually was. It hung lank and a bit wild. She hadn't had one of her perms for ages.

Finally, she noticed me. 'Oh, it's you,' she said. 'Have you put the kettle on? I'm worn out.' I went and put it on. I asked her if we should sit outside, since it was so sunny and warm, and offered to bring a couple of chairs out. She said I must be mad to think of such a thing at this time of year, but didn't enlarge on this pronouncement. We sat, as ever, in her crowded kitchen. There were the usual traps everywhere, things she could fall over, but she negotiated them expertly, clinging on to the backs of chairs, clutching the corner of her cooker, avoiding the trailing wires of her electric fire – it is lethal having that fire there at all, but she will not part with it. She claims it warms her kitchen 'in two ticks', and wants no truck with any other form of heating.

She produced a new packet of digestive biscuits. 'The Body got them,' May said. 'Gets paid for doing it an' all. Fancy, paid to buy biscuits for poor old folk.'

'I expect she does a bit more than buy biscuits.'

'Oh, she'll have degrees for it,' May said, giving a little snort of contempt. 'In my day, we helped each other out, but now you need a degree to buy digestives.'

There was absolutely no point in challenging this ridiculous statement. Instead, I said, 'Is she nice?'

'Who?'

'This Body with a degree who buys biscuits.'

'I give her the money, mind, it isn't her money.'

'I'm sure you do. But is she nice, do you like her?'

'She talks funny. She's from somewhere foreign. I can hardly make her out.'

'She probably thinks you talk funny.'

'Well, that's her funeral, she'll have to learn. I got a shock when I saw her. Nobody told me she'd be black.'

'Why should they?'

'So as I wouldn't get a shock,' said May, at her most indignant. Was this another thing, not to challenge?

'You know plenty of black people,' I said, 'and you like them. Look at your neighbours . . .'

'They ain't black, they're brown.'

'It's the same thing – brown, black . . .'

'Yellow.'

'What?'

'And yellow, Chinks, Japs . . .'

'Granny!'

'What?'

'You don't say Chinks.'

'I do if I want. Prince Philip does, he said they had slitty eyes, it's no more than the truth.'

'It's insulting, offensive.'

'Oh, get on with you. I'll say what I like in my own kitchen. Nobody's listening except you, and you know it don't mean nothing. I can say what I like.' And a fourth digestive was crammed into her mouth and satisfactorily crunched.

I gave up the battle. I hadn't come to argue about her carer's qualifications or skin colour. Maybe I was being far too self-righteously virtuous, correcting her choice of words. She was right – I did know she didn't intend to be insulting. I decided to change the subject, and told her about the Argentinian grandmothers and what had happened in the Argentine during the military dictatorship there. May seemed reasonably interested, which is to say she didn't interrupt during my little résumé of events, and she didn't yawn ostentatiously. I was encouraged. I described how people who demonstrated against the regime were arrested, imprisoned and tortured, and then often killed. May asked if it had been on telly, all this. I said I didn't know, I was only a baby when it was happening. Then I told her about how the babies of the protesters were given to people on the side of the dictator and brought up not knowing these were not their natural parents. 'But the grandmothers never forgot,' I ended my spiel dramatically. May nodded, sagely. 'They never gave up hope of finding their lost grandchildren.'

'I should think not,' May said.

'Would you have tried to find me?'

'No need.'

'I know, but if there'd been a military dictatorship here . . .'

'Don't talk silly!'

'. . . and Mum and Dad had been arrested . . .'

'What for?'

'Anything, going on a demonstration, say, or—'

'They wouldn't be so daft.'

'They went on the peace march against invading Iraq.'

'I told them then they shouldn't.'

'But they did, and they might have done the same if the situation here had been like it was in Argentina.'

'Well it wasn't.'

'I *know*, but just supposing they had been arrested and—'

'I don't like this kind of talk.'

'All I'm asking is whether you'd have acted like these Argentinian grandmothers if—'

'I ain't Argentinian, thank God.'

May does this all the time. She pretends not to understand the point of something or other when she's grasped it perfectly well. She's not stupid, but she's quite prepared to give the impression that she is if it will cut short a conversation she doesn't like. It's easier than arguing back. Her method is to turn questions round so that they become meaningless, or else to reply to those not being asked. I often think she has a brain that works in such a perverse way she could have been brilliant – say, as a barrister – if she'd had the necessary education. As it is, she jumps about mentally in non sequiturs, which are maddening and successfully avoid giving away what she really thinks.

She was smirking now, convinced she'd put me off, but I was determined to force her to answer properly. I tried again.

'If I'd been taken away and given to someone else after my parents were killed—'

'Oh, stop it, it's bad luck, that talk.'

'How much would finding me have mattered to you? Come on, Granny, that's a straightforward enough question – how much?'

'Flesh of my flesh,' she said.

'What's that supposed to mean?'

'What it says. You're flesh of my flesh. It's in the Bible.'

'So?'

'There's a bit that comes after that but I can't remember it. I never read the Bible. Have you read the Bible, being clever? You should think about it, do you good.'

'So, just because I'm flesh of your flesh you'd have wanted to find me?'

'Don't know how.'

'There's a genetic bank . . .'

'A what? A bank?'

'Not the sort of bank where you have money, another sort, where they store your DNA.'

'I've seen them going on about that on the telly. It's all twisted veins, looks horrible.'

'No, it isn't to do with veins, it's what's in them, what's in the blood. Your blood and my blood match, the genetic profile contained in it, I mean.'

'Double Dutch.'

'Anyway, you could trace me through a blood sample, or a hair from your head, or—'

'I can't spare one. It's thinning, my hair, something chronic. I used to have lovely hair, thick and curly, don't know where the curl has gone either. You've got it only you won't let it show. Why is it so short? Doesn't suit you, you should be proud of your hair, it's a woman's crowning glory . . .'

She was off, a long rant about hair and how it should be treated and worn and brushed. I gave up. All the way home,

I was imagining what it would have been like to be claimed by May as her lost granddaughter at the age I am now – a nightmare. How could we have made even the most tenuous connection? I would never have believed in, or accepted, the relationship. Flesh of my flesh? No, surely not. I looked up the quotation as soon as I got in. It's from Genesis: '. . . bone of my bones, flesh of my flesh . . .' I am of May's bone, I am of her flesh, via my mother. But what about the rest of this genetic inheritance? How far does it go? Bone of my bones, flesh of my flesh . . . what does it mean, apart from the obvious?

Ian says I should be trying to understand the science behind DNA, or at least how the tests that determine it work, how it could be proved that I am bone of May's bones, etc. (but not of Isa's). He is right, I should. All I know is that somehow a sample of my blood, or hair, or (I think) fingernails could be subjected to some sort of examination that would prove, or not, my genetic connection to my grandmother. What I don't know is how exactly the testing is done, what process these samples go through, and how definite the results are.

So, I've looked up everything available to a non-scientific person such as myself. Acres of information on the internet, from which I've absorbed the following: the certainty that a grandchild belongs to a particular grandmother would be 99.95 per cent if their DNA matches. Pretty definite, though I suppose a neurotic (me?) might fret over that .05 per cent of doubt. The tests are haematological, and there are four of them. They determine genetic markers from blood groups; HLA, or histo-compatibility; seric proteins; and blood cell enzymes. I still have only the faintest idea what all this means. Blood groups, yes, that's straightforward enough. I know there are four main ones, A, B, AB and O (though I don't know which either May or I belongs to). But there are apparently lots of other rarer groups, of which the only one I've heard is rhesus negative. How important is the blood group match as part of the four tests package? I must find out.

As for the other tests, my understanding of them is still vague. I know what a protein is, but what is a seric protein? And enzymes are chemicals, aren't they? Or are they proteins too, and produce a biochemical reaction? I'll have to ask my mother. But I've already learned enough to realise that these tests must be pretty thorough and complicated and can only be carried out by people who know precisely what they are doing. I think I'd trust them. I doubt, though, whether May, if she had found herself in the situation the Argentinian grandmothers did, would have managed to discover how she might be able to trace me. I'm not sure what it involved, but it must surely have meant having blood taken by a medical person in some sort of medical establishment, and May, with her fear of needles and hospitals, would have been reluctant to do this. Also, she would have been suspicious – she wouldn't have understood about DNA and wouldn't have believed in it.

But Isa would have done. There's the irony. Isa could have coped. She'd have read about, or heard about, the genetic bank and the possibilities it offered. Having a blood test would have held no fears for her. And she would have been persistent, endlessly checking that everything that could be done was being done. On the other hand – and now my imagination runs away with me – she could just as easily have been one of the women to whom a child of murdered parents was given. I can see her as the wife of some regime-supporting official. And then she would have done everything in her power to thwart any tests. She would have brought up the child as she has brought up my father, and as she has, to a certain limited extent, brought me up, to believe they were hers. DNA would have had no chance against Isa. She would have outflanked it.

VII

THERE'S THIS constant little voice whispering away in my head, saying why wait until Isa is gone to find out about your dead grandmother and her family? Where's the harm? Isa will never know, Dad need never know. I wouldn't be breaking my promise. The promise was only that I wouldn't ever let Isa know I knew the truth about my father's origins. But the time to begin any investigation is not right. How will I know when it is right? I'll feel it, I know I will. The conviction will come over me that it's OK to begin. It might come over me quite suddenly, or just creep up and I'll be surprised to recognise that it's been there for some time. Meanwhile, the existing grandmother, the one who took the dead one's place, needs attention. Elspeth, the self-righteous Elspeth, tells me so. She rings up and says that Mrs Symondson 'seems lost' at the moment and needs company. She, Elspeth, tries to stay a little longer each day she's there, but she has other responsibilities and it is becoming a little difficult. She wonders if, since I live fairly near and have a car and I'm 'not tied to set hours', I could perhaps pop in more often to cheer my old grandmother up. All this is said in a breathless kind of way over the phone, the tone striving to be apologetic but failing. Elspeth just loves pointing out to people how good she is and how far from good they are.

So I have started 'popping in' on Isa, though I know, and

Elspeth ought to, that Isa does not like being taken unawares. I don't spend long with her, twenty minutes maximum, and I make a point of leaving some small evidence that I've been so that Elspeth will know – a bunch of flowers, some fruit, that kind of thing. It isn't that I want to earn Brownie points from Elspeth, more that I think she is right. I've discussed Isa's changing mood with Mum and Dad. Dad doesn't see any real difference, but Mum does detect a slight slackening in Isa's general controlling behaviour lately (and is glad of it).

I think it *is* worrying and we do need to keep more of an eye on her. During one of my visits Isa was reading a review in her *Times* of a biography of Lloyd George, and she went on from telling me about it to talk about other prime ministers whose biographies she'd read – and one of them was Herbert Asquith.

So, it is Isa's fault that I may have wasted time on Cynthia Asquith. I thought she'd been Herbert Asquith's wife, but of course she was his daughter. By the time I'd found that out, I'd got interested in her and was desperately trying to think how I could use her. Part of the attraction was that she was so nicely modern, in historical terms, and I need more variety in my range of grandmothers if I'm to make a general point. (Times change, grandmothers change, etc.) Another instance of not being able to confess to Claudia how I came to select her, but I put that to the back of my mind – I'd think of something. She sounded a bit odd, Cynthia Asquith (1887–1960). The role of grandmother certainly didn't appeal to her. She had no Queen Victoria type ambition to be a fount of wisdom, George Sand's desire to stuff her grandchildren with happiness, or Sarah Bernhardt's resolve to be an inspiration. Was this a more usual kind of grandmother then? Definitely not.

She had six grandchildren, the first (Annabel) born when she was fifty-two. In spite of not welcoming her new role, she had written books and articles that might have indicated that she would revel in it. One series was for *The Times* – 'Children

and the Doctor' and 'Seaside for Children' – full of advice
for parents and showing what looked like a great love of children. But Cynthia's attitude was very Edwardian: children
belonged in the nursery, with contact designated to a particular, and brief, part of the day, especially when it came to
grandchildren. They called her the Choccy Lady, because
when she visited she distributed sweets. After that she was
at a bit of a loss, though she tried to amuse them with jokes.
These 'jokes' were very strange. One of them consisted of
inking a face on to her bare knee and then swaddling her
skirt round it, pretending it was a baby. Not surprisingly, the
grandchildren weren't sure whether to laugh or be appalled.
But what was referred to as Granny's 'puckishness' was part
of her, and accepted as such. It pointed up, I thought, the
element of embarrassment in relationships with grandmothers. There was lots of scope for this with Cynthia Asquith
as your grandmother. Her clothes, for a start. She wore
flowing garments and liked to sport striking headgear. Once,
she appeared with a band round her head that had the blunt
end of an arrow emerging from one side and the sharp end
from the other, making it look as if her head had been pierced
(a friend who'd bought this at a funfair had sent it to her).
Not someone a grandchild would want to be picked up by
from school, then. But luckily Cynthia never did such a
mundane thing, nor did she join her grandchildren for meals.
She was an eccentric who had very little idea of how to relate
to her grandchildren, and yet, at the same time, she was
fond of them. I'm attracted to Cynthia, but is she worth
including? She doesn't appear to have had any influence
with her grandchildren, or to have wanted any. What would
she be an example of? What would her style of grandmothering illustrate?

I recite their names over and over again – Elizabeth Fry,
George Sand, Sarah Bernhardt, Vanessa Bell, Queen Victoria,
Edith Holman Hunt, Dora Russell, Cynthia Asquith – no, *not*

Edith, not Cynthia, they are now rejects. These women crowd in on me, all with their piece to contribute, and though I can hear them clearly when they speak individually, it is the collective voice that doesn't harmonise. I tell myself there is no reason why it should, but if it doesn't, there is no point to my dissertation. Is a 'point' necessary? Of course! Claudia, though, wouldn't use that word. She would say there has to be a 'focus', I have to add something meaningful to what is already known. I look at 'my' grandmothers, the ones I'm interested in, and what these women are known for is not for being grandmothers. They have been selected for a whole variety of reasons other than their status as grandmothers. However famous they have been, their links to the next-but-one generation have been mostly ignored, this influence hardly discerned. As for power, the idea that these grandmothers had any is doubtful. Prove it, critics would say. I'm trying to. And I have this conviction that my own relationship with my grandmothers comes into it – I ought to be learning something from how I regard, and have regarded, Isa and May. My life has been influenced by them. Their example – no, not example, the direction their lives have taken has in some subtle way directed my own life. Now, is that true? So, what direction has Isa's life taken? A predictable one for most of the way. Born to a pretty well-off family, educated at a private school not known for academic success, then stayed at home afterwards helping her mother and going to dances and other social occasions until, at the age of not quite twenty she marries the soldier hero Patrick. After that? Nothing. Being a wife, trying to have a baby. And then that glitch, that stunning overturning of how she had been brought up (to be honest and truthful), the great deception. Once it has been carried off, with the move to London, the easy life with Patrick, the dinner parties, some travelling with him, and then widowed when she was fifty. A great blow, but one from which she recovered, cushioned by having no financial worries and by having a devoted son and his wife living near her. And a granddaughter.

I honestly can't see anything I've taken from this uneventful (excepting always that one irregularity) trajectory of Isa's life, and yet I still feel there must be some discernible influence. Until I was eighteen, I was with her a great deal and must surely have picked up some sort of wisdom. Manners, I suppose, the importance of having good manners, but that's hardly 'direction'. I absorbed more from May. Her example shows me how tough life can be and how hard one has to fight to stay afloat. I haven't had to fight, of course, but being aware of how May's life has, in the past, been hard has stopped me becoming complacent or smug, I hope. On the other hand, I could argue that May's waste of her own abilities has directed me to be ambitious. I don't look at May's life with that touch of scorn I reserve for Isa's, but with a sort of regret, I suppose. Born into a working-class East End family, worked in a factory, married when she was pregnant, looked after her family, worked for some years as a cleaner, widowed at forty-eight, deserted by her sons but with a dutiful daughter at hand, and enough money to 'manage'. What kind of direction does that give me? In what way has my life really been directed by my grandmothers? I have yet to find out.

Walking down the street today, I heard a girl say in a bad-tempered way, 'Oh, for Chrissake, get a life, Ella,' then she quickened her pace and left 'Ella' behind. I badly wanted to get a look at Ella, so I quickened my pace too and when I was abreast of her sneaked a look. She was an unremarkable-looking girl, about fifteen I'd say, wearing the uniform of a local school. Short bobbed hair, neatly brushed. Quite well developed under the hideous jumper. She appeared unmoved by the insult hurled at her by her departing friend. Maybe Ella thought she had a life already.

I've had it said to me, often – 'Get a life, Issy.' Beattie used to say it, usually when I said I had too much work to do and couldn't go somewhere or do something. It's often the truth – I do have too much work to do – but sometimes it is just an excuse to avoid telling the truth, i.e. that I've travelled and lived abroad enough, and now I'd much rather stay at home and get on with whatever I'm doing instead of going to the cinema/for a drink/to a club, whatever. That's when friends have said 'Get a life' in a tone of exasperation, or even contempt. I can see what they mean. Doesn't look good at my age, nose stuck in books and all that. Has never stopped me having boyfriends, though. I have lifted my eyes from books occasionally, with interesting consequences. Boys/men have ended up saying it too: 'Get a life.' But not Ian.

Ian likes feeding me more books, more printed matter. It amuses him that I never fail to snap up whatever is offered. He says he finds me particularly attractive when I am engrossed in some book or pamphlet or article, and that's when he pounces. 'I'm reading,' I say, and he laughs, and says yes, yes, he knows I am and I do it beautifully and he can't resist me, go on reading, he urges me, and when I do, he lunges and I have to stop reading. Just because I'm a serious reader – and how solemn that sounds – doesn't mean I'm like a nun.

Well, I can't read. Today, the print jumps, it swims.

Glasses. Maybe it's just that I need specs for reading. What, at my young age? Surely reading specs are for the middle-aged, and I'm not quite thirty. Nobody in our family had specs at thirty. Mum still doesn't need them for anything, and Dad only wears them for watching telly or at the cinema. Isa – but it isn't relevant now to think about Isa. May, then. Yes, she has an ancient pair of specs for reading, but she's in her late seventies, and anyway she never uses them because she hardly ever reads anything, not even a newspaper. If she wants to read a label on a packet or tin she holds it a long way away and squints and manages to make it out, all the while cursing out loud that she can't find her specs, somebody's pinched them.

It isn't my eyes. I know that really, but I'm clinging on to that as an explanation. I know the print is swimming because I feel dizzy, light-headed, and I'm not focusing properly. If I lie down, the swirling around stops. I reach for my book, a biography of Frances Hodgson Burnett, and hold it up in front of me. Good. While I'm lying down and not moving, the print behaves itself. Relief.

Frances had her first grandchild when she was sixty-six, a girl, Verity, daughter of her surviving son. Verity, her grandmother claimed, seemed to have been born 'by magic, so quietly and beautifully'. I wonder how her daughter-in-law managed it. She was also, writes Frances, 'so wonderfully well and radiant'. Frances resolved to invent a new category of grandmother, the Fairy Grandmother, 'before whom the Fairy Godmother will pale in comparison'. She was another who made doll's clothes, for Verity and her sister Dorinda, and romped with them, and play-acted, and wrote little notes to them . . .

I sit up to make a note myself at this point and this time the whole room lurches. And now the phone rings and I really can't get to it. I wait for it to switch to the answer phone, and when it does, I let Frances Hodgson Burnett fall to the ground as I lie back and close my eyes. The obvious has occurred to me, of course. I'm not so wrapped up in books that I don't notice such things. It is possible. Not probable, but possible, and so I must act quickly, as I have done before. Not yet, though, not until I can stand up safely. I lie and think about Fairy Grandmothers. It makes me feel even more queasy. I have this vision of May in a pink net dress, and with gossamer wings attached to her back, prancing around her kitchen waving a wand and scattering fairy dust . . . grotesque. Maybe Frances fitted the image, but not May. Not Queen Victoria. Sarah Bernhardt? Yes, she'd throw herself into the role. I go through all my grandmothers, checking out who could have been a Fairy Grandmother . . .

Cautiously, I get up. Good. Quite steady. I listen to the phone message. It's Mum. Can I go to Isa's? She's 'in a state' and Elspeth can't cope, and Mum, as ever, can't leave what she's doing or not for another hour, and where Dad is she doesn't know, his mobile appears to be switched off, and can I ring her back the minute I get her message.

I drove over to Isa's, hesitating only a minute, wondering if it was safe to drive when I had felt so odd, but my eyesight seemed normal again, so off I went. The roads were fairly empty and I knew all the short cuts, so I was there within twenty minutes. As I parked, an ambulance was leaving the next-door house and I could hear from within a child, a young child by the sound of it, screaming. It made me shiver. Elspeth answered the door clutching dramatically at the collar of her blouse, as though she herself were having a heart attack, and began at once on a breathless description of how she'd found Mrs Symondson with her eyes 'popping out', her complexion 'white as a sheet' and, apparently, 'in a trance' (this was amended from 'in a coma' when I queried that rather sharply). The shock of her discovery, said Elspeth, had given her palpitations. In fact, she still had them.

Isa was sitting beside an open window, looking out of it. She turned to face me. I wouldn't have said her eyes were popping out exactly, but they were certainly bulging a little, and were wide open and staring ahead. She didn't reply to my cautious greeting either. I wondered if she might have had a stroke, but my knowledge of such catastrophes is pretty limited. Isa just looked as though something had startled her into a catatonic state. I experimented by snapping my fingers in front of her. She blinked. I did it again, and she frowned and jerked her head away. Not a stroke then, surely. I took hold of her hands. They were cold. I told Elspeth, who all this time had been hovering over us, to go and make some tea, and she scurried off. Gently I squeezed Isa's hands. Equally gently she squeezed mine. Hers looked so white against mine, her manicured nails a reproach to my bitten ones. I kept looking into her eyes, trying to identify some response, but as yet there was none.

Elspeth returned with the tea. She poured some for Isa, who ignored the cup. 'Do you think we should call for the doctor now?' Elspeth whispered. Suddenly Isa seemed to snap to attention. 'Doctor?' she said. 'What are you talking about – I do not want a doctor. Why ever would I want a doctor?' I smiled and told Elspeth to leave us for a minute. I waited for her to go, though she seemed reluctant to do so and had to plump up a couple of cushions quite unnecessarily before she did, and then I tried to talk to Isa.

'You seem to have had some sort of . . .' and I stopped. Some sort of what? Elspeth's term 'a bit of a turn' didn't seem right, but neither did 'odd episode', so I started again. 'Elspeth was worried, she said you didn't know she was there, you were staring into space and your eyes were blank.'

'Nonsense,' Isa said, and, releasing her hands from mine, placed her right hand across her forehead. 'I had a shock,' she said, 'that is all. I am perfectly all right, thank you.'

'What kind of shock, Grandmama?' 'The usual kind,' she said (quite sarcastically, I thought). I handed her her cup of tea, but she shook her head and said she had had her tea. 'What I meant,' I said, 'was what was the cause of this shock?'

There was a long pause, during which she seemed literally to return to herself – the back straightened, the chin went up, the sharp intelligence returned to the eyes. She coughed a little, and shook her head to and fro, as though shaking water off.

'Dear me,' she said, the voice definite and strong, 'most

unfortunate.' Then she gave me one of her usual stares, her eyebrows raised very high. 'Isamay!' she said, as though just recognising me. 'What brings you here at this time of day?'

'Elspeth rang Mum, and Mum rang me.'

'Whatever did Elspeth do that for?'

'She was worried about you. She thought you'd had an attack of some sort. Mum couldn't leave work for another hour and Dad couldn't be contacted.' Isa made a sound that could've been either of irritation or exasperation. 'So I came. I was glad to come.'

'And all for nothing,' Isa said. 'How provoking for you.'

'I'm not sure it was for nothing,' I said. 'Elspeth isn't stupid. She thought something was wrong, and so did I when I got here. You did seem very strange, Grandmama, not yourself at all.'

'Well of course I was not myself, as you put it. I had had a shock. I simply looked shocked, I imagine. Is that so strange?'

'But so far as Elspeth knows, and she was with you, nothing had happened to shock you.'

'How can she possibly know that?'

'Because she was here, in this room. You went suddenly stiff, your eyes were popping out of your head . . .'

'Oh, do not be so vulgar, Isamay!'

'It's what Elspeth said.'

'Well, do not repeat it. Repetition doubles the insult.'

'Sorry. But Elspeth *was* worried, and something must have happened to make her worried.'

'She worries about everything. She is a worrier. Nothing will cure her, I am afraid.'

'What was the shock?' I said, abruptly, determined to try one more time.

'It is private.'

I smiled. 'A private shock,' I repeated. 'How interesting. It took place in your mind, then?'

171

'Almost,' she said.

'Were you frightened?'

'Yes. Temporarily.'

'So it was an hallucination.'

'It was not. Did I say that? No, I did not.'

'But you saw something?'

'No. I heard something.'

'What?'

'That is private. It would mean nothing to you. Now, Isamay, I am grateful that you came, supposedly to my rescue, but I have things to do and I'm sure you have your work to return to. I am perfectly all right, and you should go.'

There was no escaping Elspeth. She was waiting in the hall, not exactly barring my way but giving the impression she was an obstacle that would have to be negotiated. I said that my grandmother seemed fine, in full possession of her faculties. Elspeth was not pleased with this verdict – she seemed to think it cast aspersions on her judgement. I thanked her and then I left.

I didn't go straight back to my flat. I thought some fresh air and exercise would do me good. It was a beautiful morning, so I didn't want to get back into the car. I left it in Isa's road and walked from there on to Hampstead Heath. It was still only midday and there was no one around as I skirted Whitestone Pond and crossed the road. I followed the path above the Vale of Health and made towards Kenwood House. I was thinking about Isa's 'shock', of course, and the 'something' she had heard that had set it off. I'd asked Elspeth if she'd heard anything – a car backfiring, perhaps, or had she dropped something in the kitchen? That was a mistake – Elspeth never dropped things, she was very careful. We both agreed, though, that the sound Isa had heard could very well have been a far-off police siren, or the ambulance I'd seen leaving, sounds familiar enough at any time of the day

172

anywhere in London. But then they were familiar to Isa too, and therefore unlikely to have given her a shock . . .

I smiled to myself, remembering that she had said that the shock, and the mysterious sound that had precipitated it, were 'private'. A favourite word of hers. She was always using it, and not always appropriately. If there was any question she didn't want to reply to, then the information she was not prepared to divulge was 'private'. Sometimes it was quite funny. 'Grandmama, where did you get this scent from?' 'It is private.' I think she just meant secret. If she'd laughed, and said it was a little secret, it would have made some sense. 'Private' didn't.

Is that being pedantic? I don't think so. Isa meant something quite clear to herself, if not to others, when she described her shock as 'private'. It set me thinking, as I walked through the trees, of how little privacy there is for old people. Isa has always employed people to do things for her – cleaning ladies, housekeepers, gardeners – but she's always been in charge until recently. She still thinks she is, I'm sure. And no doubt Elspeth, if discovered and challenged, would always be able to come up with a plausible excuse for her snooping. All that is truly private for Isa now is her past, her memories. Neither Elspeth nor anyone else can take those away from her. So I reckoned, as I walked, that Isa's 'shock' was to do with a sudden overwhelming memory of something long forgotten. What did she hear to trigger it? What kind of noise connected with a memory so unpleasant or frightening that it had shocked her into a temporarily catatonic state?

When I got home, I rang Mum and reported that Isa was fine. Then I surprised myself by ringing Beattie, my old school friend. I don't see much of her, but that's my fault – I'm lazy about keeping in contact. If Beattie doesn't make the running I don't bother, I just depend on her to do it, and eventually she always does. Her life is different from mine and sometimes it makes the gap seem too big to cross – she

173

married young, has two kids, lives in Pinner – though when we do get together again, and she's managed to meet me on her own, we can quickly slip back into our old easiness. The reason I broke a lifetime's habit and was the one to ring Beattie was because of her grandmother. She's an extraordinary woman, quite unlike either Isa or May. She was a spy in the Second World War, parachuted into France, and then afterwards set up her own travel company, just at the beginning of package holidays, and made a fortune. Beattie adores her (though I think she might be a bit of a disappointment to her grandmother). I thought I could talk to Beattie about Isa, and invite her and Jack, her husband, to supper. So I rang her and she was lovely, as she always is, and I invited her over. Then I told her about Isa's 'shock'. Beattie knows both Isa and May, though she hasn't seen either of them for years, so she could imagine what I was describing, how Isa would have looked. She decided that Isa had had 'a senior moment', one of those sudden mental lapses when the brain seems to freeze momentarily, and then recovers and returns to normal operation but having lost the frozen time. Plausible, but I didn't think it fitted. We chatted some more. I asked how her grandmother, now ninety-two, was – off on a trip to Scandinavia with one of her sons – and then fixed a date for her and Jack to come to supper, if she could get a babysitter. I'd much rather have arranged to see her on her own, but that's too difficult to organise somehow – she always ends up bringing both babies and we have to talk over them.

I told Ian when he came in. 'Good,' he said. He likes Beattie and Jack, but he doesn't like going to their place. It isn't because of their children, and all the crying and fussing that goes on; it's their house, the set-up there. He says he feels he's looking at a fate – the semi, the neat garden, the attached garage – that he hopes will never be his.

He said he'd cook roast lamb, we hadn't had any real meat

for ages, and at the mere suggestion I felt nauseous. I closed my eyes, and shook my head. Ian asked what the matter was; I looked pale, he said, and asked was I sick. I said not sick, exactly. Silence. I waited for him to pick up on the 'exactly'. After a good while, I opened my eyes and found him studying me, in that infuriatingly calm, appraising way he has. 'Well,' he said, carefully. 'Not well at all,' I said. 'Awkward, then,' he said, 'but not . . .' he paused, wanting to find words that wouldn't offend me, 'not something you don't know how to deal with. You told me you'd—'

'I know what I told you.'

'So, you know what to do, how to get it done.'

'Do I?'

It was only then that he seemed to realise there might be something going on he hadn't bargained for. His expression changed, from one of a vague sympathy to wariness. He didn't want to make a mistake, and waited for me to explain. I'd so have liked him to come and put his arms round me and comfort me, but he didn't. He just stood there, waiting. 'I'm not sure,' I said, at last, and repeated this, my voice sounding weak and plaintive. I was experimenting, trying to get near to saying out loud what I was beginning to dare to think: I could have this baby, I think I *want* this baby. Terrifying words I hadn't yet the courage or the conviction to come out with. I cleared my throat and tried again. 'I want to think about it this time, Ian. I never needed to think about it the other times. But this time . . .' My voice trailed off.

'Come and sit down,' he said. It was such a relief to be on the sofa beside him, his arm across my shoulders. 'This time isn't any different, Issy,' he said. 'You don't really want a baby. Think about it. You're doing an MA, you're hoping to go on to some academic work, it would be disastrous. And then there's me. I don't want children. I told you from the beginning I didn't want a family, and you said you agreed, you'd never wanted children, and—'

'I believed it,' I said, 'but things change. *I've* changed.'

'I haven't.'

'No, I know. But I want time to think, I don't just want automatically to have a termination. Something, this time, is making me hesitate. It's to do with studying all those women who—'

'Oh come on, you're romanticising now.'

'Maybe. But – don't laugh – I see that I could be a link in a chain, carry on a line—'

He did laugh, though it sounded strained and false. 'And whose line would that be?' he asked.

'Well, I think of May and—'

'So you're considering having a child to let May's genes, or some of them, trickle down the ages?'

'I feel some sort of need, I suppose; the so-called biological urge.'

'Which you have never had. You've boasted about not having it.'

'I have not.'

'Mm, you have. You've scorned it, you've called it "the biological urge". You have.'

'OK, I have, but that was because I hadn't felt it. I didn't know what I was talking about.'

'And you truly feel it now?'

'Not exactly.'

'There you are then.'

'Where?'

'Back where you started, not really wanting to have a baby but tempted by the idea for purely romantic reasons and all because you've fallen in love with grandmothers and their alleged impact on grandchildren, which so far you haven't been able to prove, and that sort of stuff. You'll be telling me next that you think it is your duty to have this baby, that it was *meant*.'

He'd gone from being calm and reasonable to being scornful

176

and impatient with me. I'm not sure what might have been said if Dad hadn't rung at that moment. Abruptly, Ian left the room, and then the flat, as soon as I'd answered the phone. Dad said I sounded odd, did I have a cold? I said no, no, and launched into telling him about my latest visit to Isa, and her shock, etc., so that I didn't have to tell him why I sounded so shaky. He didn't seem in the least bothered about Isa's 'turn'. 'She's eighty,' he said. 'These things are bound to happen, it's all part of becoming old.' I said we weren't talking about mere forgetfulness, we were talking about a shock temporarily freezing Isa. He still wasn't worried. In fact, my anxiety made him irritable – he said I sounded like Elspeth. Then he asked if Ian and I could come for Sunday lunch. May was going to be there and it was going to be as like 'the old days' as Mum could make it, with roast beef and all the trimmings. I said Ian wouldn't be able to make it, he had a football match, but that I'd be there.

The rest of the evening I just lolled on the sofa watching rubbish on telly – high-class rubbish, but rubbish all the same. It was some kind of spy thing and I hadn't the faintest idea what was going on. Half an hour later, Ian came back, and sat down beside me and made some comment about what I was watching. After that, neither of us said a word. Companionable? In a strange sort of way, considering the tension, yes. We *are* good companions as well as everything else. But hanging in the air was the implicit question: why change things? Why let a baby interrupt this companionship? For the moment, it seemed something too dangerous to discuss again.

Sunday lunch with May . . . it used to be so commonplace, so ordinary, so much part of our family routine, and now it has become an event. May herself is very aware of this. She resents the fact that an invitation to Sunday lunch has to be given when once it was simply assumed that she would be picked up at her house around midday and returned to it about half past four. She liked her neighbours, even the ones she didn't know, to see her being ushered into a car. The short drive was all part of the treat, almost as important as the meal itself. The food, of course, had to be the kind May liked, and it was probably the need to provide big roasts that Mum couldn't stand. I'm not quite sure exactly how or when she broke the tradition, but broken it was and never resumed in the same way – the feast became movable. May was upset. 'Not wanted in my own daughter's home on a Sunday,' she said to me, but quickly had to add, 'Not that I care, I can look after myself.' This announcement was followed by a lot of sniffs. Sniffs always punctuate May's words when she's indignant, like loud full stops.

Dad was just pulling up in front of the house when I arrived. I leapt out of my car to open the door of Dad's so that May could get out. 'Lovely to see you, Granny,' I said. 'You could see me any time,' May said. 'You've got my address, you lazy lump.' But it was said affectionately. I gave her a kiss and she told me not to mess up her hair. We could smell the beef roasting the minute we stepped into the hall, which made me instantly feel nauseous. 'Smell that!' Dad said. 'I will,' May said. 'I haven't smelled a smell like this for a long time.' We trooped into the sitting room and not down into the kitchen/dining room. This was a state occasion. May liked the formality of being given a drink first in the upstairs room, where she could sink into an easy chair and look out on to the garden. Mum didn't appear. She shouted hello and said she'd be up in a minute, she was making the Yorkshire pudding. 'Hope she don't mess it up like she can,' May said. 'You could go and show her how,' I said, and got a disdainful look in return. 'I've shown her hundreds of times,' May said, 'and she can't seem to get the hang of it, she's so clever.'

It was like an old-fashioned stage set, May in her armchair, centre left, Dad near the window, standing beside the drinks table, and me on the sofa, near the door. I found myself consciously trying to think of something to say, and was shocked. For years as a child I'd chattered away to May, and now there was this silence, which I had to strain to fill. Being in my parents' house and not in May's cluttered kitchen made the strain worse.

Luckily, at that moment Mum called out that lunch was ready. Dad helped May to her feet, and for once she didn't refuse, but clung to his arm and didn't let it go. I offered to take her other arm but she said she wasn't incapable yet, so I picked up her drink and followed the two of them down the stairs. May only managed them by turning sideways and going down crabwise, with Dad now preceding her so that if she fell she'd only fall on him. I stopped being cross with her. Suddenly I felt overwhelmed at the thought of becoming old. 'What's that long face for, miss?' 'Nothing,' I said, and went to help Mum carry all the stuff across. May smiled, a smile of pure delight that she couldn't suppress. 'Now that,' she said, surveying the beef on its oval platter, surrounded by roast potatoes, and the dishes of carrots and peas, 'is a grand sight.'

We were all pleased that she was pleased. Everyone relaxed and began eating. May was in full reminiscing mood and went on and on about the glories of the Sunday lunches she herself had provided in her time. I knew without needing to ask Mum that they hadn't been as May described. May had cooked a roast all right, but then used to rage because Albert was late coming back from his drink at the pub (his particular Sunday treat) and the boys were either fighting or else just arriving back themselves from playing football. Only Mum was sitting there, captive, and May was in a fury with the rest of her family, whom she judged lacking in appreciation. It was even worse when May's mother was still alive, because she would apparently criticise her daughter's

179

cooking, finding fault with almost everything. But May has forgotten all the tension. 'This takes me back to the good old days,' she was saying for the tenth time, 'when Sunday lunches *were* Sunday lunches. Slaved over them, I did.'

'Bet you were glad when you stopped, then,' I said. I couldn't have said anything more stupid.

'Glad? *Glad?* Course I weren't glad!'

'I just meant glad you didn't have to slave any more.'

'Who's talking about slaving? It was hard work, that's all, and I was glad to do it, looking after my family properly. Women did then. We had our family round the table of a Sunday, feeding them proper, and glad to be doing it.'

There was another silence, while we all ate busily. But May was not eating as heartily as usual, in spite of her relish. Normally, she would have scoffed everything on her plate in double-quick time and would have been ready for seconds before anyone else had finished. Instead, she was picking at the meat, had eaten only half of a potato and hadn't touched the other vegetables. It was proof, I thought, that she was taking heed of what the doctor had advised. Yet she was asking already what was for pudding. 'Oh, the puddings I made,' she said. 'The apple crumbles, the spotted dick – grand. Remember them, Jean? Proper puddings. What we having for pudding, then?' 'Fruit salad,' Mum said. 'Fruit salad?' May echoed. Mum told her it was all fresh fruit: strawberries and raspberries and melon and . . . May cut her short. She sighed, and said she supposed fresh fruit was healthy, and then asked if there would be cream to go with it. Mum said yes, if you want. Nobody spoiled her pleasure by saying she shouldn't be having cream. Mum brought the fruit salad and the dishes to the table, together with a jug of cream. Though May had nothing like finished her main course, she pushed her plate away and helped herself to a little fruit and a great swamp of cream, and ate the lot in something of her old style.

We had managed, throughout all this, to have a stilted sort of chat, each of us politely waiting for the other to finish talking, totally unlike our usual way of conversing, which involved constant cutting across each other and virtually never waiting for anyone completely to finish what they were saying. May had concentrated on her fruit salad, contributing nothing, but after she'd slurped up the last of the cream she looked at me and said, 'You could do with some cream, by the look of you.'

'I hate cream. It clogs your arteries anyway.'

'It ain't clogged mine. You need some fat on you, all skin and bone you are.'

'I've always been slim . . .'

'Skinny, you are, like one of them girls what starve themselves.'

'I don't starve myself.'

'Well, you look as if you do. Nice little fat baby you were, and now look at you. You must take after your dad's family, 'cos you don't take after ours, not now, not in the looks department.'

I took some fruit salad, ostentatiously pushing the jug of cream away. May glared at me. I glared back. Then she suddenly leaned forward across the table and said, 'Is this the thinning before the fattening, then?'

'What does that mean?'

'Are you up the duff?'

Could I have lied? Of course I could have. I could have out-stared May easily. I could have laughed convincingly and said she must be joking, and that would have been that. But for a second, a mere second, I hesitated, and to a beady-eyed observer like May, hesitation is proof. I saw the triumph in her eyes – she'd scored a bull's eye, she was sure. She sat back in her chair and said, 'Well I'll be damned!' and then 'I'll be a great-grandmother' and 'I never thought I'd see the day.' Soon she was chuckling away, and shaking her head, and altogether giving an exaggerated display of delight. Mum and Dad still hadn't said a thing. 'Isamay,' Dad eventually said, 'is this true? I mean, it's wonderful news, but is your granny right?' 'Course I am,' May interrupted. 'Oh, I knew all right, minute I set eyes on her today.' Mum put her hand over mine and squeezed it, and waited for me to confirm or deny what May had said. It seemed impossible to tell them that even though I thought I was pregnant, yes, I hadn't decided whether to have a termination or not. They'd be shocked. It was too cruel. So I said it was early days. I said I was about five minutes pregnant and anything could happen, and I'd rather not have told them. May boasted again that she'd guessed, that I couldn't fool her. 'I knew you'd fall in the end!' she cackled, and then, 'It'll be a boy, I can tell. What you going to call him? Albert, after your grandad, eh? Albert James, after his great-grandad and his grandad.' There was nothing I could do to stop her babbling on, her previous grumpy mood forgotten. She said she thought she might still be able to knit, if she took her time, if she picked a good day when her arthritis wasn't too bad. She said she wanted to buy the pram. She hadn't much money but she had a bit saved, just for this occasion. 'How much do prams cost these days?' she asked. None of us knew.

It was hard to get away. I would have liked some time alone with Mum, to tell her how I was really feeling, but May was clearly determined to get her fill and stay all day, so I left about three o'clock with instructions to look after myself, and put my feet up, while she followed me out of the door. Dad saw me into my car. 'Lovely news, sweetheart,' he said, 'I'm going to enjoy being a grandfather.' I must have looked miserable, because then he asked anxiously if I was happy about it. 'It wasn't a mistake, was it?' he asked, leaning down to look at my face through the car window. 'Or was it?' I said that of course it had been but that it didn't mean I was necessarily going to get rid of it. At the words 'rid of it' he flinched. 'Well,' he said, 'whatever you decide. Take care.' I drove off, furious at how I'd mishandled things – I *should* have lied, at least until I'd really left it too late for there to be a choice. Now I will upset my parents and most of all my grandmother if I have a termination – the distress it would cause is so unnecessary. Suddenly I realised there was still a solution that would avoid this distress. It involved lying, but I'd just agreed with myself that lying would have been preferable and still is: I could quite easily have an early miscarriage. Happens all the time. I could be brisk and sensible about it – God, the last thing I want is for my lies to reap misplaced sympathy.

This way out of the mess I've got myself into appeals to me. I'll think about it.

I've got a postcard of a photo of Vanessa Bell stuck up in front of me, just above my computer, and one each of Sarah Bernhardt, Queen Victoria, George Sand and Elizabeth Fry. I haven't been able to find one of Dora Russell and I've taken down Cynthia Asquith. It helps to look at them, though it hasn't so far helped enough. I've studied photographs in all the relevant books and watched my subjects age as they became grandmothers, but what I'd really like is a sequence of snaps or portraits of each of them, one for each decade, so that I could flick through them like through a pack of cards and watch the changes in them accelerate.

I think photographers today try to catch the personality of the sitter. The formal pose still exists, but even that attempts to create atmosphere. Vanessa Bell does this in her paintings, but I wondered if there were a woman photographer who did the same. I wondered aloud, as I often do. Ian heard this particular wondering as he was on his way out and said, 'Julia Margaret Cameron . . . Bye . . . won't be home until late, remember.'

I wrote the name down, but then spent the best, shocking

part of an hour thinking about Ian and the embryo still within me. Actually, I think it is a foetus by now, not an embryo. With distinguishable arms, legs, etc. I am nearly at the end of the first trimester. I've been promised, in the books I've consulted (reading them in Waterstones, a little furtively), that in a couple of weeks I won't feel sick any more or have these worrying dizzy turns, but will I feel any less slow? Slow? I mean *stupid*. My mind wanders, my concentration is wrecked. The books – there are loads of them – say this is normal. I hope this changes, if I'm to stay pregnant, that is. I want my brain back in full working order, I want this fog to lift. I keep having these strange images of waterfalls, but instead of water, it is DNA cells that are thundering down – it's mad. I see this great torrent cascading down the years, unstoppable, with more and more tributaries being fed into it, and I am part of it, my DNA is joining the flow. Why am I letting it happen? *Why?* I listen hard, carefully, for the answer. I want to be truthful. I didn't intend to become pregnant. So? Why haven't I dealt with it? I hate to admit that I am keeping this child – though am I going to? – because I can't resist the chance to see what I can create. Curiosity – what an answer. I don't yearn for the cuddling bit. What I feel is an intellectual curiosity, and a desire to be part of a mysterious process. That's appalling.

What I can't understand is why Ian doesn't share this curiosity. Maybe he does, and is just refusing to allow himself to admit it. And of course it isn't growing inside him, which makes a difference, though theoretically it shouldn't. He notices me being sick, naturally, and is solicitous, bringing me cups of tea in bed and that kind of thing, but he doesn't say anything. If I do, if I groan and say I can't go on with this, he doesn't tell me to do something about it. The whole business is turning into some sort of silent battle in which Ian's strategy is to give me enough rope to hang myself – and now I'm being melodramatic as well as choosing unfortunate metaphors. Work is the only refuge from all this endless fretting about what to do.

I stared blankly at the name written down in front of me. Julia Margaret Cameron. Yes, I knew who she was, I'd seen some of her photographs in various biographies. But how would she fit in? Was she even a grandmother? It was a relief to have something easy and definite to do, something my sluggish brain could cope with. Julia Margaret Cameron, born 1815, married 1838, had six children – promising already. Only one daughter, Julia, who gave her a granddaughter in 1859. So, a young grandmother. But she – Julia Margaret – didn't have a camera of her own when Charlotte, her granddaughter was born. She didn't get one until Charlotte was four and she didn't take her first successful photograph until 1864. She was smart. Right from the beginning she began to copyright her work. Lots to look into, then. I felt that little spark of excitement, though 'excitement' is too strong a word, at the thought of being on the trail of something interesting.

Then another wave of tiredness came over me: I fell forward on to my desk, and drifted off to sleep.

I went to the GP. Finally. This afternoon. Note that I went to see 'the' GP, not 'my' GP. I registered with a practice when I moved to this flat, just to satisfy Mum, who fusses about such things. I've seen two of the five doctors there, briefly, but never Dr Fraser, who is apparently my designated doctor.

Sitting in the waiting room, I knew my mind had to be made up. It was no good breezing into Dr Fraser's room and saying I was just about twelve weeks pregnant and hadn't decided whether to have a termination or not. Time was short – it would have to be full speed ahead in the case of aborting this foetus (horrible words, 'abort' and 'foetus': I don't like the sound of them at all). But I felt my mind had been made up for me by my very inactivity. I'd done nothing, now possibly there was nothing that could be done. I stared round the room looking for signs. There were only five other people waiting, all elderly. They were no help. Then the outside door opened and in came a young woman pushing a buggy with a child in it. The child was asleep, well wrapped up, though it's warm today, sunny and mild. Quite a pretty picture, the attractive mother – blonde, slim, nicely dressed – sitting looking anxiously at the sleeping child. Boy? Girl? I couldn't tell. Couldn't tell the age either. What do I know about children . . . ?

I haven't, thank God, had much experience of doctors, but Dr Fraser was enough to put one off them for life. Distant, distracted, massively bored. I told him I'd done a pregnancy test three times (I'd thought I'd better have evidence) and they had all confirmed I was pregnant. He asked if I wanted him to examine me. I mean, *he* is the doctor, he should decide. I said not if there wasn't any need. Right, he said, you need to make an appointment with our midwife. Which hospital do you want to have it at, she'll book you in. And that was that. I don't know what I'd expected – some concern as to how I was feeling, perhaps? – but his briskness shook me. The receptionist was equally offhand. Told me which day was antenatal day and made the appointment for me. I felt unimportant. Well, that's a clue, shows how *self*-important I'd begun to feel – look at me, I'm pregnant, I'm going to have a baby, everyone! Cut down to size, that was me, the size of a shrimp. For a moment I thought dammit, I'm going to have a termination after all, so there, Dr Fraser, you've lost me. How petty.

I rang Mum, who for once was at home. She was very soothing, said Dr Fraser was probably having a bad day, over-worked, etc., and he'd probably thought I was matter-of-fact and had mirrored my approach. 'You can seem a cool customer, Issy,' she said. 'You can sound brisk and uninterested yourself.' Then Mum reminded me that I hadn't yet told Isa my news and that I should, she'd be so pleased and might be hurt not to have been told. I promised to go and see her, but I haven't rung her yet. I need to get everything clear with Ian first, now that I've seen Dr Fraser, and I have the other appointment and am in the system. Never mind Isa, I haven't actually told Ian that I am definitely going to have this baby. I have to spell it out, just in case he is clinging on to the hope that I will 'see sense', i.e. still have a termination. He's made his opinion, and his position, plain, but I haven't told him I am going ahead in spite of his opposition.

His disapproval over the last couple of weeks has expressed itself in various ways but most of all in his silences. They are not sulky silences, or hostile ones – it's simply as though he cannot bring himself to talk about what I want him to talk about. He always seems to be on the verge of saying something, and then he looks at me and decides not to. I interpret this look as meaning it isn't worth his effort because I'm not up to any kind of proper discussion. Too true, but he could try. I feel disappointed in him, though I've no right to be. I wanted him to share my new feelings about having our child, especially the curiosity I have. Is that so wrong, to feel curious? To let curiosity influence me? Best not to provoke an argument about it. Ian would win easily.

187

VIII

JULIA MARGARET Cameron wrote that 'the eyes of the first grandchild should be more beautiful than any flower'. *Should?* Apart from the gushing tone, this sounds so silly. But she was far from a silly woman. On the contrary, she was clever and ambitious, and not above using her grandchildren for her own purposes in the career she built for herself as a photographer. Perhaps because she knew she might well do that, she was careful not to get too close to them. When her first grandchild, Charlotte, was born (Julia was then forty-four), Julia wrote that though she intended to cherish the child, she was 'building bulwarks round my heart to prevent myself getting too fond of her'. The bulwarks seem to have stayed in place. None of her grandchildren are on record as adoring her. Instead, they were wary of her. To them she was rather scary-looking, short and squat, dressed in dark clothes stained with chemicals from her photography, and smelling of them, too. In manner, she was bossy and controlling and sometimes made them model for her when they didn't always want to. Modelling was a tedious business for them, which involved staying still for inordinate lengths of time, but they didn't dare disobey their grandmother.

Bossy and controlling grandmothers are surely fairly common, but I hadn't come across one quite like Julia Margaret Cameron. Queen Victoria was bossy and controlling but then she was a monarch and had the power to be, and she used that power, so far as I had discovered, for the benefit of her grandchildren. I suspect that Julia Margaret Cameron may have used her relationship with hers to serve her own ends. Or is that too harsh? I need to read some of her letters, which are in the Bodleian Library and at the Royal Photographic Society. I imagine they'll be fun to read – someone commented that 'she lives upon superlatives as upon her daily bread'. And I must look at all the photographs available in which her grandchildren appear. The only one I've seen is 'My Grandchild', taken in 1865, a picture of a baby of about a year old (I think), lying asleep. Nothing bossy or controlling about it.

I have to think about Julia Margaret Cameron and her significance as a grandmother. Something about her is disturbing. I read that in order to get the right expression of grief, or similar, she was capable of shutting a child she wanted to use as a model into a cupboard for a while. A woman dedicated to her art, then, but at what cost to the children?

At last I rang and arranged to visit Isa. It was an unseasonably hot day when I went, and Isa was in her garden pruning roses while her 'man', Mr Pinkerton, was doing a last clipping of the hedge at the bottom of the lawn. Isa looked like an illustration in a book called *The Lady Gardener*, elegantly dressed in a long pale green skirt and a white blouse, her head covered with a straw hat, which had a ribbon round the crown matching exactly the green of her skirt. She was wearing immaculate pale cream gardening gloves, and over one arm she had one of those shallow baskets, which I could see contained two last, perfect yellow roses. She was concentrating hard on her pruning and I didn't want to alarm her by shouting a greeting so I sat on the stone steps and just watched her for a while. I liked watching her. She looked so graceful, if frail, nothing crabbed or disturbing about her. She looked like everyone's ideal old woman, serenely tending her flowers, her faithful

189

retainers – her 'man', her 'girl' – discreetly keeping her under observation. What could be more reassuring? If this was old age, I thought, how charming it could be.

I got up from the steps as Isa finished her task and turned to go to another rose bush nearer the house. I waved. She stood still, facing me, and I went towards her, calling out 'Hello, Grandmama!' For one worrying moment I thought she didn't recognise me, but then she smiled and said my name. We went up the steps together – no, she did not need a helping arm, she said – to the sheltered corner of the terrace and she called for Elspeth to bring out some tea. It was brought promptly, and there was the usual fuss setting out the china and the tea strainer and covering the milk jug with one of those net things that have little beads round the edge to give them weight and keep the flies off the milk. 'Isn't this pleasant?' said Isa. Mr Pinkerton's genteel clippers sounded faintly in the distance. Would a bee soon hum contentedly overhead? Yes, it did and then buzzed off. A butterfly (only a cabbage white, but still) fluttered past. Isa gazed about her, pleased with nature. She sat in her basket chair, her back ramrod straight as usual, her skirt draped over her knees, almost covering her ankles. Her ankles are her weak point. They grieve her. Tall and slender though she is, her ankles are thick. She could hide them by wearing trousers, but in Isa's opinion, no lady wears trousers, not even in the twenty-first century. She may be the last woman in England to stick to dresses and skirts, but so be it.

Isa was charmed with herself and the setting. All was well in her world, mysterious shocks forgotten and a grand-daughter's tedious probing about an alleged brother forgiven.

'Grandmama,' I said, 'I have some news for you.'

'Good news, darling?'

'I think so.' I knew I mustn't use that word I don't even like myself: 'pregnant' – Isa thinks it common, quite unacceptable – and instead I should say 'I am expecting a baby' if I couldn't bring myself to use the archaic expression 'anticipating a happy event', which she would prefer.

'I'm going to have a baby,' I said, 'next March.'

Now truthfully, what kind of reaction did I expect? Delight at the very least. I thought her face would be flooded with a huge smile and that she would let out a little cry of pleasure perhaps. I even thought there might be a tear in her eye. Instead, she seemed startled. Her mouth opened slightly in evident surprise, and she put a hand to her cheek. 'Oh dear,' she said, 'oh dear, dear!' I was puzzled. I thought perhaps she hadn't heard me properly, or that she'd somehow misunderstood me. So I repeated that I was going to have a baby, next March. Still no response, just a slight shaking of her head. It was baffling. 'Well,' I said, 'you don't seem happy about my news.'

'Happy?' she echoed.

'Yes, happy for me.'

Did I sound resentful? Did I say this in a whiny voice? Possibly. Probably. I suppose I felt cheated, disappointed. The longer she was silent, the more restless I became, ending up fidgeting in my chair in a way I knew would bring forth a reprimand. It did. 'Do sit still, Isamay,' she said, but in an absent-minded fashion.

'I'm going, actually,' I said, and stood up.

'So soon?'

'Well, there doesn't seem much point in staying; you don't seem to want to hear about the baby.'

Again, the silence, the air of abstraction, as though I were speaking to her from a long way off, or that my words were somehow muffled. At least, that's what I deduced from Isa's face, from her vague, dreamy look, so unlike her usual poised, carefully arranged expression of either intelligent interest or concealed boredom. Her eyes in particular were devoid of feeling, not blank but deliberately not registering any thoughts she might be having. It was the same expression she'd worn when she had her 'shock' and Elspeth had been

191

so alarmed. It occurred to me to remark on this, so I asked her, straight out, if she had had another shock. She nodded slightly. I sat down again. I tried to be sympathetic and gentle. 'What has shocked you, Grandmama?' I asked. 'Are you shocked that I am going to have a baby?'

'No.'

'What, then?'

'It is private.'

I laughed. 'Private again? But I was here, nothing happened. You couldn't have heard a noise, there was no noise.' She cleared her throat, and blinked several times. A sharpness returned. She frowned and fussed with a button on the cuff of her dress.

'Very well,' she said, 'you are going to have a baby.'

'Yes. In March.'

'I see. And who, may I ask, is the father?' She sounded as if she genuinely did not know. There was no hostility in her tone, nothing like that, but I was wary.

'Ian, of course. My boyfriend. You've met him, remember?'

'Your boyfriend.' There was no question at the end of the words – it was just a flat statement, a repetition, as though she were checking she'd heard correctly.

'Yes. We've known each other four years; we've lived together most of that time.'

'But you are not married.' Again, a mere statement.

'You know we're not.'

'Will you marry now that a child is to be born?'

'No. I don't want to get married, neither does Ian.'

'Whose name will this child take?'

'I don't know. I haven't thought about it.'

'Then had you not better think?'

What was wrong with her? She was spoiling everything. Why couldn't she be like May, thrilled to bits and not bothered about husbands or names? I wanted to flounce out, but what kept me there was trying to work out what Isa was really saying. What was going on in her head? There was a subtext I couldn't quite read. So I tried again.

'What is it that worries you about my having a baby?' I asked her.

'What are you going to do with the child?'

I was shocked. '*Do?*'

'Yes. Are you going to give it away?'

I simply stared at her, speechless. I couldn't even attempt to reply. I felt insulted and angry, though perhaps I had no right to be, and had to struggle to control myself. After a long pause, during which we held each other's stare, I managed to say, 'Why, *why* do you imagine I would have a baby then give it away?'

'Women do.'

'Women *used* to, because they had to, because they hadn't intended to become pregnant . . .'

'Did you?'

'What?'

'Intend to conceive?'

'No. That's not the point, I—'

'It is very much the point.'

'No, it is *not*! If I had not wanted this baby I could have terminated the pregnancy, I could—'

'You could have murdered it, you mean?'

'No! Grandmama, stop this. I became accidentally pregnant but I do want this baby and I will not be giving it away.'

'Perhaps you should.'

'*What?*'

'Perhaps you should think about whether this child might not be better off with another woman who has a husband and can care for it in a proper manner.'

There. It was out. Of course. Now I felt sorry for her. This was all about the past, her past, the past none of us was supposed to know about. It was so tempting to blurt out that I knew why she resented my having a baby when I wasn't married and hadn't wanted one – it wasn't fair, she couldn't stop envying women like me. She was old, long beyond the years when she hadn't been able to conceive, but she was still unable to get over it. It was silly to allow myself to become upset over the tortuous workings of Isa's memory. It was up to me to behave sensibly, until the confusion was overcome, as it surely would be, so I didn't say anything else, just got up, kissed her and said goodbye. I left her sitting motionless in her chair. I felt let down. But it was more than that. Somewhere in my subconscious I'd envisaged an emotional scene in which I listened to Isa confessing the truth about my father's birth. I'd seen myself comforting her – for what, precisely? – and admiring her. There would have been a new intimacy between us, a bond of a kind there had never been before. Instead, there was now a rift.

All this time, I had been putting off telling Ian what I hoped he had by now surely realised: I had decided to have the baby. I couldn't justify my decision, and dreaded arguments, and attempts to dissuade me. But I knew I had to tell him, to leave him in no doubt. I dreaded his response. Anger was one thing, but distress was another. What if he became upset and pleaded with me? He is so good at consoling and comforting me, but I've never been challenged to do either for him.

I told him, choosing my time carefully. He held my gaze, and I was the one who had to look away. Then he said I was making a big mistake. It made him weary, thinking of the mess I was getting into. A little spark of rebellion flared in me, and I started to list all the women in history who had had children they hadn't planned to have, and hadn't thought of them or their lives as a mess. Ian said their experiences were irrelevant. He took hold of my hand and begged me, 'Don't do this to yourself.' I let him hold my hand a minute longer, and then I took it away. 'Sorry,' I said. Afterwards, I was ashamed I'd said sorry.

*　　*　　*

194

When the twelve-week scan was due, I told Ian about the appointment. I didn't seriously expect him to offer to come with me, but I suppose I hoped he might. He didn't, but he asked what was the point of the scan. I said it would give an estimate of the date of birth, and reveal any abnormalities. He asked what I'd do if there were any abnormalities, and I said I'd have a termination. He approved of that. 'It still isn't too late to have one anyway,' he said. 'I'd go with you. You don't have to go through a termination alone, Issy. I'd be with you.' I shook my head. 'No,' I said.

We were both sitting very still, across the table from each other. I felt we should get into an arm lock, put our forearms against each other, clasp our hands, and then each try to force the other's arm down. But he'd win, obviously. He has strong arms. They look like tennis player's arms, as though they could swing a racquet to devastating effect. I struggled to lighten the atmosphere.

'I wonder if our child will have your arms,' I said.

'Don't try that.'

'What?'

'You know what very well.'

'Couldn't be that you're afraid to see the baby on the scan, could it? Couldn't be that you're afraid you might become emotional when you see—'

'Emotional? You've got the wrong man, Issy. Me, emotional? I'm not emotional over problems. I'm logical, I think them through. I thought you did, too.' He seemed so sad, and that made me resentful.

'I did. I always have done. But being pregnant doesn't come under the same heading as other problems. I've tried to explain, it's different this time. I'm, well, I'm following an instinct, that this is—'

'An instinct? Oh, come on! A whim would be more accurate.'

'I wouldn't have a baby just on a whim. If you think that's what I'm doing, you can just leave.'

'Leave? You want me to leave? Seriously?' He was incredulous, but then he said, 'I suppose it might be as well. I couldn't cope with a baby.'

I started to laugh, hysterically. *He* couldn't cope with a baby living with us? Neither could I, or not without him. What had I said? I wanted to take it back, but I couldn't find the words. And yet, at the same time, the belief that I would, should, could go ahead and have this child grew curiously stronger in me. Was it because of Ian's opposition? If he'd reacted differently, said OK, if it's what you want, it'll be interesting . . . If he'd said something on those lines, would I have had a termination?

Confused was not an adequate word for how I felt.

And then I had the scan, and the confusion left me. I couldn't make out a damned thing on the screen but I was told all was well. 'It's a lively one,' is what the nurse – doctor? technician? – said. 'Want to hear the heartbeat? I nodded, dumbly. The heartbeat . . . how it thumped, how determined and regular and unrelenting it was – Me! Me! Me! it said. I must have had tears in my eyes without realising it, because the woman operating the scanner smiled and patted my hand. I was in a trance leaving the room, barely able to straighten my clothes and pick up my bag. I remembered, with what felt like shame, the other occasions when I'd been pregnant (though never as pregnant as this). Suppose I'd had scans then? What would I have done? Changed my mind? No, not then, not at those times. I was a different and much younger person from the person I am now. But it would have made it harder to go ahead.

I so desperately wanted Ian to have been with me. I know it would have made him feel differently – whatever he thinks,

196

it would have made him *feel*. That is what I am doing, feeling. Feeling is proving stronger than thinking.

It suited my mood to spend this morning looking at Julia Margaret Cameron's photographs of children posed as cupids, cherubs and angels. She eventually had to seek models outside her own family and found some children of a Royal Artillery soldier who lived nearby, and another child, son of a local fisherman, who were willing. Loads of studies of Alice, Elizabeth and Kate Keown, and of Freddy Gould, to me the most appealing. I thought how May would enjoy them. She is back in hospital. No drama this time. Her GP recognised the signs of another imminent disaster and had her admitted. We're back to taking turns visiting. The last thing I want to do is go again to a hospital, but it has to be done.

I visited her this afternoon. She's in a four-bed ward, like last time, but this one is part of a much bigger unit. When I arrived, she looked asleep. I studied her. Closed eyes, obviously, make a huge difference to how anyone's face looks, but in May's case the result was dramatic. Everything about her seemed shrivelled – her skin was collapsed in on itself, with all kinds of dips and hollows appearing. I suppose it's just that if you're looking into someone's eyes you don't notice the detail of what surrounds them. Her face was suddenly like a paper bag that's been screwed up and cast aside. Her hair had been brushed, though not by her. May brushes her hair off her face, with a parting on the left. Someone had brushed it flat to each side, with a parting in the middle. Stray strands had been pushed behind her ears. It isn't all white, May's hair. There's still quite a bit of brown mixed with grey. The white is only noticeable when it's windy and she's outside and it blows about showing the patches underneath.

* * *

I wondered how much May knew about what was wrong with her. All the stomach trouble, which was supposed to be due to a treatable ulcer, had now turned out to be something possibly more sinister, a growth/tumour – they seemed to alternate the words – that might, or might not, be malignant. May hadn't asked. She hadn't asked anything except when could she go home, though suspicions had clearly occurred to her – she did say to me that she might not live to see her great-grandchild. 'I might never know if it's a boy or a girl,' she said. I asked if that would matter and she got cross with me, saying that of course it would matter, she thought it would be a boy but wanted a girl. I told her that quite soon, in a few weeks or so, I'd be having another scan, which would show the sex of the baby. 'Bloomin' marvellous,' she said. I promised that I'd come straight to her and she'd be the first to know. She repeated that she hoped it was a girl, for *my* sake. 'You have a son till he takes a wife,' she recited, 'you have a daughter, you have her for life.' This, she informed me with pride, was 'a wise old saying'. She's always coming out with what she claims are wise old sayings, most of which I'm convinced she's just made up, but this one sounded more authentic.

The funny thing is that what May said makes me want this child to be a boy. I don't want to keep any child for life. But then maybe I'm defining 'keep' and 'life' wrongly. I don't know anything yet about the nature of the relationship between a mother and a child, from the mother's point of view. Obviously, it's complicated, but to May, it's simple, summed up satisfactorily in one neat little rhyme.

It's been ages since I had lunch with Dad; my fault, not his. He's invited me to meet him often enough but I just haven't felt like eating, or watching him, and others, eat. But I met him today, and we had a snack at the Tate Modern, not what he calls a real lunch but it suited me fine. Great views over the Thames from where we sat.

Dad, of course, wanted to talk about the baby, or more particularly about Ian and the baby. There didn't seem much point in concealing the truth.

'He's moving out when the baby's born,' I said.

'Oh, sweetheart,' Dad said, squeezing my hand. 'Why don't you come back home? No need to struggle on your own.'

'Who said I'm going to struggle?'

'Well, you'd cope, of course you would, but it'll be hard, and—'

'I don't actually want to talk about it, Dad. There's no need to worry about me. Millions of women look after babies on their own. And anyway, I won't really be on my own. Ian isn't abandoning me, he's just . . .' And I stopped.

'Moving out,' Dad said.

'To get some peace.'

'Noble of him.'

'No good being sarcastic, Dad,' I said. 'He's entitled to. He doesn't want this child. I made the decision to keep it.'

I tried to think how I could explain my confused feelings. I tried to tell him that it is all wrapped up in my work. I don't know how, but I know it is. I started quoting lines of hymns May used to sing, stuff about time's ever-rolling something or other, and more incoherent nonsense about feeling powerless, in the grip of fate, etc. Dad looked more and more anxious, so I decided to change the subject fast. I asked him how Isa was. He sighed and said not so good. Elspeth is talking about giving in her notice because 'madam' is acting increasingly 'funny', and Elspeth's nerves can't take it. Dad doesn't think Isa is showing symptoms of senile dementia or anything like that but he admits she isn't her usual self. She's been what Elspeth calls 'funny' with him too. The other day, when he visited her, she started talking about his father in a way she had never done before. Up to now, Dad said, Patrick has always been spoken of in reverential terms – war hero and all that – but now Isa told him

199

that his father had not been all he had seemed. This was said in an almost threatening manner – Isa, he said, appeared to wait for a response from him, leaving her words hanging in the air. Dad was uncomfortable and made some remark about none of us perhaps being as we seemed. He rather dreads his next visit.

We walked together back along the South Bank, all the way to Westminster Bridge. Dad put his arm round me and I put mine round him, and we sauntered along slowly, stopping every now and again to lean on the balustrades and watch the boats go by. I thought how I never seemed to do this kind of thing with Mum – it's always with Dad. Mum's forever working, she doesn't have time to have lunches and walks. Will I have time? That's what I was wondering. I'll have to, because there won't be a dad in my baby's life to do this kind of thing. My work will not be able to come first, not for years and years. I almost panicked at the realisation – for my child's sake I'll have to snap out of my obsession with the past, my endless ruminations, and as a normal person of my age would say: 'get real'. But I don't want to get real if it means the sort of life I think it will mean. Tough. Maybe I should have become a nun, or a secular version of one, shut myself up in an ivory tower, withdrawn from 'real' life.

Not that I came out with any of this to Dad; it would only have worried him more. We parted outside the House of Commons, quite reluctantly. I do like being with my dad. Watching him stride off – he has this odd, erratic walk, alternately shortening and lengthening his pace – I felt suddenly tearful and had to struggle not to cry. Pure self-pity, or rather pity for my unborn child, with no daddy to put his arm round it and take it out to lunch and . . . Oh, stop it! I stopped. Hormones, that's what it was all about. Hormonal activity was making me drown in sentiment, and I had to get it under control. I have a supervision tomorrow, for which I'm nothing like prepared. I'd meant to look into the life of the anthropologist Margaret Mead and come up with some wonderfully original idea, but all I've done so far is outline the chronology of her work. This will hardly satisfy Claudia.

IX

MY SUPERVISION with Claudia was on Thursday at two p.m.
I'd been reading about Margaret Mead half the night and felt
terrible when I woke at nine o'clock. At ten, Elspeth rang
Dad and reported that his mother had received a letter that
appeared to have upset her very much. No, Elspeth hadn't
read the letter herself, but Mrs Symondson was still in a
terrible state and she thought one of the family ought to come
round. It was the usual story, Mum and Dad both with very
important work that morning, so I was the 'one of the family'
who went over.

When I got there, Isa did look stricken, it was true. She'd
been weeping, not something I've ever seen her do, and her
face powder had run. It made me feel peculiar to see the
streaks down her cheeks – I was embarrassed and shocked.
The offending letter was lying in her lap. I thought she might
object if I just picked it up and read it without asking her
permission, so first of all I sat down next to her and took
hold of her hand (which felt quite daring enough). I could
see the headed notepaper, and that the address was in Hatton
Garden. After a few minutes, during which there was no reaction from Isa, who was sitting quite still, staring into space,
I asked if I might read the letter. She didn't reply, so very
gently I manoeuvred the sheet of paper round until I could
read it without needing to pick it up. My first thought was

that it was a con. I felt instantly relieved – not bad news at all. Isa was distressed for no reason, and I felt angry with these con merchants for upsetting an old lady.

According to the letter, a relative of Isa's had died intestate, leaving some money, and she, Isabel Clara Symondson, née Macdonell, could claim it, as his next of kin. I told her there was nothing to worry about and that I'd ring these people and give them a piece of my mind. 'No,' she said, 'do not ring them. I do not want to know. I shall tear this letter up.' She then seemed to make a huge effort, said how foolish she'd been, apologised, and did indeed begin to tear the letter up into very small pieces. 'I shall burn it,' she said. 'Where are the matches?' I couldn't stop her – with a sudden impressive rush of energy, she was on her feet and over to the fireplace, looking unsteady but determined. She groped around for a matchbox on the mantelpiece. The fire was laid, as it always was, and she set fire to it by hurling first one match on to it, which went out, and then another and another. When the paper under the twigs and logs at last began to burn, she scattered the torn-up letter like confetti, and only when every little piece had been incinerated did she relax. 'There,' she said, smiling oddly, 'all done.'

I was stunned. What was this about? First her distress, then her agitation, and now this false good humour. She couldn't wait to get rid of me. 'Off you go! Alarm over,' she kept saying, in this hearty, cheerful tone. 'I do apologise, darling, for causing such a fuss, off you go.' So I went. I went straight home and phoned the number I'd memorised. Once I'd said who I was, and had given my grandmother's name, and complained about their letter, I was passed over to someone who said he was a case manager. He was very polite, answering all my barely civil questions patiently and calming me down. The firm, he assured me, was a highly respected business. It finds hidden beneficiaries of wills and unites them with the cash which they are entitled to claim before the government does so. Ten million pounds or so, he told me, slips into government coffers every year simply because nobody claims it. The government apparently publishes lists of unclaimed estates, and firms in the heir-hunting business choose which people to try to find. Macdonell, he said, was a name unusual enough to give them a good chance of tracing a descendant. They'd found Isa quite easily. Their letter hadn't given details of who had died intestate, or of how much there was to be claimed, because they first of all negotiate a fee for doing the finding. I asked how much, thinking this was the catch, and was surprised at how reasonable it seemed. 'The thing is,' I said, 'my grandmother doesn't want to know about it. She's burned your letter.' 'Then perhaps her children do,' he said, 'or you yourself?' I said I'd call him back.

She hasn't any children. Her son is not *her* son. She hasn't any grandchildren. Her granddaughter is not *her* granddaughter. Dad and I are frauds. If Isa doesn't want the money, we can't claim it. But whose is it anyway? Why doesn't she even want to know that? Well, it's obvious. It must be her brother, the one she'd denied had ever existed. She'd always known he had. But where? And why conceal his existence? He hadn't tried to contact his sister, not so far as we knew (though Isa, I could now see, was perfectly capable of hiding anything she wanted). But maybe he hadn't known he had a sister. These heir-hunters could hardly know what a complicated history they were uncovering – or maybe they did know it, maybe such deceptions in the world of blood ties are commonplace to them.

I want to uncover the truth, but without Isa's co-operation I don't see how I can. It's not that I want the money (though if it's going begging, why not?); I want to know what happened to my grandmother's brother, why he was banished from the family and why his sister lives in such fear of this other secret of hers being exposed. But do I have any right to make her tell me – why should she?

It isn't my family. That's what it comes down to. Blood ties. The deciding factor. Yet I've made no attempt to find out about my 'real' grandmother. It's strange. It's Isa's fault, somehow.

I could hardly bear the thought of my supervision and almost cancelled it but in the end knew it was too late to let Claudia down without good reason. So I went, my mind full not of Margaret Mead, the grandmother I now want to consider, but of Isa's mysterious brother, his legacy.

Someone was coming out of Claudia's room when I arrived, five minutes early, a much younger woman than me. She was flushed, and might, just might, have been on the edge of tears. Anyway, she was in a state, dropping the papers she was holding in her hand as she tried to stuff them into her bag while hurrying along. I bent down to help her. I could see there were red marks, in Claudia's startlingly neat italic handwriting, all over the pages – lots of question marks, too. 'Oh God, oh God,' the girl kept saying. 'I feel sick, I'm going to vomit in a minute.' I asked if she'd like me to go down to the cloakroom and get her a glass of water, but she said no, she'd be fine once she got out into the fresh air, and off she scurried.

I can't imagine anyone actually being scared, or upset enough to feel sick after a session with Claudia, but then maybe that shows how little I know about how she treats other students and how they react to her. I was, as usual, dreading my own session with her, but not enough to make me sick. Somehow, seeing the agitation of that other young woman made me feel *less* apprehensive about what Claudia was going to think of how I was progressing. I wouldn't give her the satisfaction of reducing me to a wreck. So I went into her room with my head up and a bright smile on my face and said, 'Good afternoon,' rather loudly. She inclined her head graciously, looked at her wristwatch and said, 'Well?'

I took a deep breath and launched into Margaret Mead. I told Claudia that the best thing about Margaret Mead, for the purposes of my dissertation, was that she had addressed herself as an anthropologist, as well as a woman, so directly to the importance of grandmothers. According to her, no woman could think of herself as 'a full human being' without access to grandchildren – a pretty bold claim, and on the surface absurd. Her very description of the role of grandmother seemed to me inaccurate. She saw the grandmother as 'standing in the middle of the past and future'. But surely it is the *mother* who does that? What did she mean? 'Past and future merge in the relationship' (between grandmother and grandchild), she declared, 'and any society that ceases to recognise this is greatly endangered.' This theory had partly come from spending her working life tracing patterns among what she termed 'primitive peoples'. In cases where there were no written records, these people had only themselves and their families to embody what they were. Grandparents were therefore of tremendous significance and value.

But she'd also come to this conclusion, about grandmothers being so important, because of her personal family experience. She wanted to emulate her grandmother, who had been a teacher, and it was from her that she gained her sense of self-worth as a woman, and the self-confidence to do what she wanted to do. One of her aims was to become an anthropologist but another was at the same time to become a mother – a combination unusual, still, in the first half of the twentieth century. She planned to have six children. But in 1926, during her first marriage (she was married three times), when she was twenty-five, she was told that because of her retroverted womb she wouldn't be able to have children – if she did conceive, she would miscarry. And miscarry she did, once during that first marriage, and then repeatedly during her third. Most of her miscarriages happened early in the pregnancies, but in 1939 she had a late, bad, miscarriage and

206

thought her chances of ever carrying a baby to full term were finished. But in that same year, 1939, on 8 December, she gave birth to a daughter. She was thirty-eight.

Naturally, as an anthropologist, she was even more fascinated than a normal mother by the emergence in her daughter of traits and dispositions that could be attributed to one member of the child's family or another. She knew how dangerous and misleading this game could be, but she couldn't stop playing it. When, at the age of sixty-nine, she became a grandmother to her daughter's daughter, she played it even more intensely during the brief spells when they saw each other. In fact, because her daughter lived in Europe, Margaret's grandmothering was hardly put to the test, and in any case the child was only six when Margaret died. I hadn't yet been able to find out much about how she developed as a grandmother, but that didn't seem to me to be as important as knowing what she thought and why. I said to Claudia that Margaret Mead's conviction that grandmothers were vital in society was something my whole theory, my whole dissertation, was based on.

There was the most unnerving silence after I'd stopped talking. I swear I could hear my own breath going in and out of my nose, so laboured and heavy, as I waited. Then Claudia finally spoke. 'Theory?' she said, as though it were a dirty word. 'Theory? What is this? It is beginning to sound more like a romantic novel than a dissertation.' She closed her eyes and seemed to shudder slightly, repeating 'theory' with disgust. Then she sighed and said that after all this time I still needed to narrow down my broad subject matter – 'the importance of grandmothers in women's history' had to have behind it a proper rationale. What exactly was my research question? She still was not clear. And what was the relationship between the question, whatever it was, and the nature of my sources? I had to decide if these sources – was I talking just diaries, letters, autobiographical fragments?

– presupposed certain horizons, certain limits, to my investigation. She didn't doubt my genuine interest in how the role of grandmother had developed and how it has influenced the growth of feminism, if it has, but what she very much doubted, as she had by now constantly repeated, was the direction in which my interest was leading me. I *must* sort out the relationship between my material, my methodology and my intention. In short, I lacked self-reflexivity. I was becoming tiresome.

It's an offensive word, 'tiresome'. It suggests a reprimand to a whining, snivelling three-year-old. To use it to describe the behaviour of an adult is contemptuous. I'd rather be called stupid, but maybe that is because I know I'm not stupid, whereas I hate to think I might indeed be tiresome. I hung my head, bright smile gone. There was another prolonged silence. Claudia, of course, uses that kind of silence as a weapon. Usually, I break it, trying to snatch the initiative, to show I'm not cowed, but today I didn't. I was thinking bugger it, I'll just drop this whole charade and become a full-time mother. Claudia was talking again. She was saying that she would like to see a draft of my dissertation. She presumed, she said, that a first draft had long since been completed. She presumed wrongly. I hadn't written a word of the thirty thousand she was expecting.

I said I would deliver something next week.

There are 10,000 trillion ants in the world. There are about 6.6 billion humans. Ants live and die for the good of the colony. Isn't that noble?

It's the kind of information that sidetracks me. I think about the ants and their altruism, and then I think about humans and, on the whole, their lack of it, and I struggle to make something of it. I'm not a myrmecologist, so why does it interest me? Because of the genes thing. Humans pass on their own individual genes. Ants apparently pass on group genes – their altruism starts with family members. It is more important to them that the group, the family, survives than that the individual does.

I am convincing myself that I am behaving like an ant.

Well, that came to me in the middle of the night, when I couldn't sleep. Ian was sound asleep beside me, so I couldn't ask him questions, not that he is a myrmecologist either, but it is his fault I was thinking about ants and their altruism. He came home yesterday with one of his pilfered cuttings, about some scientist who has this theory about the replication of genes. He thought it might help me with my dissertation. The idea was so bizarre it made me laugh, a little hysterically, but still – it was good to laugh when all I wanted to do was weep.

I was tired. I'd been to see both Isa and May, and it was too much, but I felt I'd neglected both of them and I felt bad about it. I resolved to spend at least an hour with each of them before getting my head down and starting the draft of my dissertation, because once I do start – and that will be a miracle, I've put it off so long – I'm not going to do anything else. I'm going to hole up and *think* and straighten out my thoughts and then astound Claudia with a clear, concise, intriguing outline. I am.

It was a risk, visiting Isa without phoning her first and without knowing what kind of state she was in, after the letter episode, but if she was going to give Elspeth the pleasure of relaying the news that she wouldn't, or couldn't, receive me (Isa always 'receives' people, even family), I would at least be able to say to myself that I'd tried. But I was given a true welcome, which startled me – it was as though Isa had forgotten about her disapproval of my pregnancy, or even that she'd forgotten about my being pregnant at all. This was the Isa pre-'turns' – gracious, kindly, eager to converse. The relief . . .

What she wanted to converse about was her father's car. She'd found a photograph of his first motor car, a 6hp Oldsmobile, registered in January 1904. It had cost £150. But what Isa remembered hearing about the car wasn't the price but the fact that it had travelled extensively in the service of the suffragette cause. It was Isa's aunt Mabel, her father's sister, who thought women should have the vote. Her interest in the suffrage movement started in 1906, when she met some ladies at tea in Bath. In July of that year she joined the Women's Social and Political Union (WSPU), formed by Mrs Pankhurst in 1903. She was only eighteen at the time. Surprisingly, said Isa, her parents were sympathetic and her brother positively enthusiastic – 'very odd'. It was James, Isa's father and Mabel's brother, who drove her to meetings during the next six years. Mabel never took part in any violence – Isa shuddered at the thought – and was never imprisoned. Her main activity was distributing leaflets. But she met Christabel Pankhurst and Annie Kenney and Mrs Patrick Lawrence, and other prominent suffragettes.

Isa carried on talking about Mabel, and though I was interested, my mind wandered, as it seems to all the time at the moment, and I felt sad. It was nothing to do with hearing about Mabel's fate (she died aged twenty-six of TB) but with thinking that this interesting-sounding woman had no connection with me. Before I knew that Isa was not really my grandmother, I would have been thrilled to have such a relative, someone who had actually had the nerve to become a suffragette. But now the thrill is not there. I don't carry Mabel's genes. My admiration for her isn't personal. I can't boast about her.

'He loved Mabel,' Isa was saying, 'loved her dearly. I do believe he never got over her death.'

'Shame,' I said, vaguely.

'My mama looked like Mabel. That was the initial attraction for my father, I'm sure.'

'How incestuous,' I said, still vague, still not concentrating.

Luckily, Isa didn't seem to have heard my remark, which surely would have offended her, and I had time to pick up the photograph of the car and admire it, and then, though I was hardly listening, I think Isa chatted away about all the cars her father and her husband had had, and I was able to smile brightly and nod, and the hour flew. I wondered if I ought to mention being pregnant again, just in case she really had forgotten, or not taken it in, but I decided not to. And there was the legacy business to discuss, but she was in such a good mood and I didn't want to spoil it. Then, just as I was about to start preparing to go, she came out with the strangest remark. 'Men never can know,' she said, 'that they are truly the father. Women have the advantage there.'

'What?' I said. 'What did you say?' I realised I really hadn't been listening to her properly. Somehow we'd finished with cars and the suffragette cause and moved on to establishing paternity.

'Men,' Isa said, serenely, 'terribly difficult for them, don't you think? They can never be certain. They have to believe the woman.'

'Well,' I said, not sure quite how to take this up but desperately keen to, 'well, I suppose men do know who they've slept with, and what the chances are, and—'

'Ah yes, the chances,' and she smiled.

I stared at Isa. She looked back at me, quite steadily. I thought she seemed expectant, geared up for some sort of challenge, perhaps. 'I suppose,' I said, carefully, 'it's about trust. If a man trusts a woman. If he believes he's been the only one.'

'Oh yes, in my day,' Isa said, then added, 'but not always, even then. A man could not be absolutely sure unless he'd kept the woman locked up, and she was a virgin to start with.'

211

'Grandmama,' I said, 'I think I'm lost; I think I can't have heard something you were saying . . .'

'Mabel,' Isa said.

'Yes, I remember that of course: your father's car and Mabel and the suffragettes and your mother looking like Mabel, but—'

'You said it sounded incestuous.'

'Yes, I did.'

'My mother told me that she wondered if my father loved her because she looked like his sister. That would have been a sort of incest, would it not?'

'Well, I don't think so, not really.'

I was still lost. Somehow Isa had gone from speculating about why her father was attracted to her mother to reflecting that men could never be sure that they were the true father of their child. Any connection was so glaringly missing that there was no point in pretending I understood. She seemed quite pleased that she had baffled me. 'I was remembering,' she said, slowly, enjoying her sense of advantage, 'my father loving my mother because she looked like Mabel. And then you made your remark about incest and I recalled hearing a tale of an adopted boy who had unknowingly fallen in love with his natural sister and they produced a child before they discovered their relationship. Now, in those days it was very shocking, but when my mother told me this story she did not seem shocked. The child, it turned out, was perfectly normal. But then my mother said that though this woman *said* the father was the man she later found to be her brother, he may not have been. Men can never be sure. I didn't know these people she was talking about; I didn't know their names or who they were or where they lived. My mother may have identified them – she made it clear that she had known them, that this was not gossip – but if so, I have forgotten. But I have not forgotten how strangely she smiled when she pointed out that men can never be sure. That has stayed with me. It worried me then and it worries me now.'

Was she trying to tell me something in the only way she knew how, the convoluted way, the roundabout way? Definitely she was waiting, watching me intently, gauging my reaction. I was frowning. I could feel the frown. Usually she would have told me not to frown, not to disfigure myself – the skin of the face should at all times be relaxed, neither frown nor smile allowed to settle in too deeply. I felt that anything I said would be dangerous, and yet I so badly wanted to be blunt and ask questions – I was bursting with questions. But Isa didn't wait for me to speak. She said, very quietly, almost absent-mindedly, 'Your grandfather had a secretary once. Quite a young girl, pretty in a rather old-fashioned way. She had a baby. Nobody knew who the father was. Names were bandied about, but it seemed she had had several boyfriends in spite of her youth. She named the father but she couldn't prove it and many did not believe her, many thought she was naming the one man who could provide for her if he could be convinced he was the father. Shocking, really. I'm sure it happens all the time. Fathers can't be sure.'

I knew what to say this time. 'They can now, Grandmama, with a DNA test. You've heard about that, haven't you? It's quite simple. At least, having the test is simple. You only need a blood sample, or a hair from a baby's head, or—'

'Ah, but if the man is dead, it is too late.'

'No, no, it isn't. A blood relative will do. Look at Prince Philip and how he was used to prove that an American woman was not Anastasia. Exciting, isn't it?'

'Prince Philip?'

'His family was related to the Russians, to the Tsar's family, so they shared a genetic inheritance. Whatever sample Prince Philip gave didn't match the sample this impostor gave. Their DNA was different, so she couldn't be Anastasia.'

I could now see, of course, exactly where this was going,

but what I couldn't see was how to bring it into the open and get rid of all this beating about the bush. Did Isa truly want to know if my father was really the son of her late husband? But why? For what possible reason? If her husband had believed my father was his son, wasn't that enough? Why cast doubt on this, after all these years? What had got into her? But she was calm and composed, there was calculated thought behind what had at first seemed a case of mere reminiscing. She had always intended, I was suddenly sure, to end up getting as near as she could to telling me she had doubted the truth of my father's parentage, and now she was waiting to see if I saw through her pathetic ploy.

Except it wasn't really pathetic. I realised that. I sensed she wanted to expose doubts about my father's paternity as some sort of twisted revenge. I'd upset her all those weeks ago, going on about a brother she either hadn't known existed or whose existence she still wanted to conceal, and her resentment had festered. Into her mind had crept a way of getting her own back. She knew how I felt about family and she was taking half of it away from me. My father was to be made anonymous, with his mother dead and her family wanting nothing to do with him right from his birth, and now he was to be robbed of the man supposed to be his father. Was there no option for me except to be brutally frank?

Before I could, Isa again took me by surprise. 'Your young man,' she said, 'the father of your child, is he sure it is his?'

'Of course he is! Really, Grandmama . . .'

'He has no doubts?'

'No! How can you ask such a thing?'

'Then why does he not marry you? Why does he not do the proper thing by his child?'

'There *isn't* a proper thing . . .'

'Or is he married already? Have you thought of that?'

I was so exasperated I could hardly stop myself from shouting at her. There she sat, a complacent smile on her face, imagining that she had somehow cornered me, and it was all so ridiculous and twisted. I caught myself just in time, and saw that instead of being furious I should be amused. My laugh didn't come out very convincingly, but it helped. 'Grandmama,' I said, at my most formal and polite, 'I must be going. We seem to be at cross-purposes today.'

'Indeed,' Isa said, 'but you should pay attention.'

'To what?'

'To me. To what I am warning you of.'

'Warning?'

'The dangers. For the child you are carrying. The confusion there will be.'

'*What* confusion? For God's sake . . .'

'About the father.'

'There *is* no confusion. Ian is the father. He knows he is. The child will know who its father is.'

'His name will be on the birth certificate? He will pay for the child's upkeep? He will help rear it? He will love it? He—'

'Grandmama, stop!'

She stopped. I stared at her in amazement – her voice had risen hysterically. I could hear Elspeth opening the door, and it was a relief instead of an irritation to hear her ask if everything was all right. I managed to say I wasn't sure if it was or not. Elspeth hurried to Isa's side and said she looked flushed. She did. 'There, there, Mrs Symondson,' Elspeth said, 'I'll get you a glass of nice cold water.' She scurried off, and I got to my feet, feeling shaky. Should I kiss Isa or not? Even the regulation peck seemed too much, so I just patted her hand and said I would see her soon. I didn't say anything to Elspeth, who was coming back into the room with the water as I left. I escaped before she could interrogate me to find out what had upset madam.

I wouldn't have been able to tell her anyway. Back and back I went in my mind, trying to trace the course of our

215

conversation and being unable to. Writing down what I remember of it now, it is obvious that some link is missing. While my mind had wandered, there had been a change of direction, and of mood, and I'd become a victim of Isa's long-buried anger with her dead husband. But am I right to think that? She hasn't actually said to me that she always doubted that Patrick was James's father. She hasn't ever confessed what I know, and my father knows, to be the only truth: that she is not his mother. Everything has been obscured by hints and insinuations. She has depended on all of us letting her maintain the façade she constructed so long ago. We have conspired with her to let things stay as she wants them to stay.

Or is that wrong? Trying to get into Isa's mind, and under-stand her thinking, is impossible.

I didn't go straight on to May's – how could I, in such a state? – though I'd intended to. I came home first, for an hour or so, just to give myself time to get over feeling so disturbed. Unusually for that part of the day, Ian was there. I wasn't sure that I wanted him to be, but in the end I was glad. He was all concern, said I looked pale, insisted I put my feet up and had something to eat. It was comforting – comforting enough to make me tearful.

I hardly told him anything of what Isa had said, and he didn't press me. Probably he guessed it would be stuff about the baby, and he wouldn't want to go over the same old ground again, especially when he could see I was in a funny mood. So we chatted a while, about nothing, and I sipped the tea he'd made, and composed myself. I didn't even ask him why he was at home, just grateful that he was. I know Ian will not desert me. He won't fade out of my life just because of the baby. Of course he won't. If he moves out when it's born – there, I'm pretending it might not be true that he will – he will still come and go. And he'll put his name on the birth certificate, I'm sure. There's no need to ask him.

May came back home last week. She's on some drug that stabilises her condition. She still doesn't seem to want to know what that condition is. Serious, anyway. When I arrived she was knitting. She'd found some wool at the back of one of her drawers and thought it would do because I wouldn't fuss about colour. The wool she'd found was a lurid lilac shade. 'Lucky,' she said, 'it'll do for either a boy or a girl.' I reserved judgement. The needles she was using looked too small and delicate for her knobbly hands, but she was feeling her way carefully, knitting by touch rather than sight. Since she'd come out of hospital again she looked frailer but stronger in spirit, I thought – all due, Mum said, to the news about the baby. She is completely obsessed with thinking about my baby and won't talk about anything else. She wants it to have a name already, before I've even had the scan to tell the sex. When I say I haven't the faintest idea about what to call it she is scandalised – she always had her names ready. 'Your other grandma will be wanting it to be called after her, if it's a girl, I suppose?' I said Isa hadn't mentioned names. 'She'll be biding her time,' May said, 'you'll see. She's got something to leave, that one, something in the bank to pass on. She'll be wanting a family name, like James or Patrick, you'll see, and Isabel for a girl.' I said I didn't think Isa was interested in names. May couldn't believe this. It was only natural.

She switched to my diet. I wasn't still a veggie, was I? Because meat was good for the baby, full of iron. I should be eating liver once a week, and drinking a pint of milk every day. I said liver, and all offal, was not recommended for pregnant women now. May was shocked. She'd forced herself to eat half a pound of lamb's liver every Thursday, Thursday being the evening Albert worked late and she ate on her own.

She hated liver, Albert hated liver, but liver it was for her when she was expecting . . . I closed my eyes. Why were we talking about liver? With all the things I wanted to know about May, why had it come down to talking about liver?

'You're tired, I can see,' she said, accusingly. 'What have you been doing, in your condition, eh?'

'Working,' I said.

'Oh, not that bloomin' reading and scribbling again, sitting in them libraries all cramped up – I've told you again and again, it ain't good for you, squashing your organs, putting pressure on your bladder . . .'

'Whereas of course you were doing the perfect thing for a pregnant woman with your first baby, standing at that factory bench, wasn't it? On your feet for hours and hours every day, giving yourself varicose veins.'

'None of your lip.'

'It isn't lip. It's a fact. You've told me yourself how physically hard it was, and how women today have it soft.'

'You have to think of the baby.'

'The baby will be fine. Nothing I'm doing is harming the foetus.'

'The what?'

'Foetus. A baby is an embryo first and then a foetus.'

'It's a baby, that's all. Little miracles they are. You're a very lucky girl.'

'Why? Because I'm having a baby?'

'Yes. Some women can't.'

'And some women don't want them.'

'Then they're silly. What else is there in life to match having a baby?'

I was about to make some mocking remark, along the lines of what a philosopher she was, how profound I don't think, but I stopped myself just in time. She was being sincere, and I thought maybe she was presenting me with a way into a proper discussion, of the sort I'd always wanted to have, about her thoughts on her own life. I let her laboriously knit another row of whatever this alarming lilac wool was to become, and then, very quietly, I said, 'Do you really think that, Granny? That there's nothing in life to match having a baby?'

'Yes.'

'Do you mean the actual having of it, the experience of it growing inside you and then giving birth, or . . . ?'

'I mean the baby. When you see it, and you think: look what I've made.'

'So it's pride?'

'What?'

'There's nothing to match it because you're so proud of what you've achieved?'

'I don't know what you're talking about, muddling things up, wrapping everything up in words.'

'I didn't mean to.'

'You don't mean a lot of things. Wait till you've had your baby. You'll change your mind, madam.'

'About what?'

'You'll know what.'

There it was again, the same going round in circles, the same irritation coming off May in waves. Babies were miracles. Babies were the best experience in life. And she didn't want to discuss it.

I didn't stay long after that. When I got up to leave, she didn't make her usual comment about me always rushing off, hardly stopping to warm a seat, etc., but instead encouraged me to go home and put my feet up. She asked if 'that Ian' was looking after me. I said he was. That pleased her. I'm sure Albert never looked after her, but my dad had looked after my mother and she had been amazed to witness it. Modern fathers met with her approval in this respect. She asked me when I was going for the next scan and I told her the date again, and repeated that I'd come straight from the hospital to tell her first whether it is a boy or a girl.

219

The scan is next week. Before then I must, I *must*, complete a draft of my dissertation for Claudia. I feel as if I am Bob the Builder. A refrain runs in my head, going, 'I cannot do it, I cannot do it' and I answer myself, 'Yes you can, yes you can.' It is *essential* that I do it. I will not have this baby turning my mind into mush – and there I am, using pregnancy as an excuse when it is no excuse. All I need to do is read through my research material and then think. Think clearly. Think constructively.

Everything will then fall into place.

Think clearly. Simple words, simple instruction, but a very difficult task. Thinking, in my case, always seems to lead to dreaming. I start off well enough, but then the thinking can't be held on a tight rein – it becomes wayward, undisciplined. Lists help at first, but then I stray from those too.

Think clearly. But nothing is clear, that's the point. I can think deeply, I can think intensely, but aiming for clarity defeats me. Nothing *is* clear, but does that mean the idea behind my dissertation is invalid? I truly don't think so. I will try again.

I've printed it out. A first draft of my dissertation. It looks professional. Neat, tidy. And it reads well. I am quite flushed with success. I did, with a huge effort, manage to think clearly, and it shows. It wasn't beyond my capabilities after all. But of course that is the easy bit, the first draft. I still have to write the whole finished dissertation. The ideas have to be fully developed.

Like a baby, really. The baby has to grow, to develop, or it's nothing. Everything is there from the beginning, ready to grow, but it might not. It takes time. The woman's body has to work hard to feed it and then produce it . . .

But there is no comparison between the writing of a dissertation and the growth and birth of a baby. I am romanticising an ordinary activity, trying to make it something more important than it is. May is right: there is nothing in life to equate with producing a baby, nothing quite so strange and mysterious. And I haven't even done that yet, nor completed a dissertation.

I got lost in the hospital, God knows how. I thought I was being clever, going in at a side entrance, sure there would be plenty of signs telling me how to get to the maternity unit, but there weren't any. I seemed to wander along empty corridors for miles without meeting a soul, and what dismal, dreary corridors they were, nothing on the walls but dirty paint, and the floors lacking any hint of polish. In the end, I had to go all the way to the main exit and then start again, this time seeing and following the signs.

Even then, I went first by mistake to the postnatal ward, which scared the hell out of me. I shouldn't have been allowed in there in the first place – there was a locked door, but when the man in front of me was let in I just followed on, not realising it was the wrong place. I swear the impression was that I'd come into a battery-hen farming shed – well, not exactly a shed; it was a long, narrow room with beds either side, tightly packed in, with red and white patterned curtains drawn round all but one of them. I walked the full length, not a nurse in sight, until I came to the end and saw a woman breastfeeding a baby, so I about-turned smartly and walked straight back out, hearing whispered voices behind the curtains and the odd birdlike screech from a baby. This is where I would be in another twenty weeks, packed in like this, no privacy. I'd go mad.

'You're very pale,' the nurse said, when I finally found the right clinic. 'Have you been eating properly?' I said I had. I said it was just that I'd got lost and was afraid I'd be late. This seemed to amuse her. She indicated a row of women sitting in the corridor. 'Plenty of time,' she said. I sat down on the only available seat, clutching a pager I'd been given. After nearly an hour of other women's pagers pinging, but never mine, I started wondering how much it would cost to go private, though Dad would be disgusted with me. He doesn't do any private work, never been tempted, even though he knows the NHS is overburdened and he never has enough time in his own clinics. It isn't just the waiting itself that I'd like to avoid, so much as the herd-like, helpless feeling it fills me with. I feel pushed into a group where I don't count as an individual. But I couldn't even begin to afford private health care, quite apart from the principle thing, so my next thought was whether I could have this baby at home. Why not? I was born at home, accident though it was, and May had all four of hers at home. (I suddenly remembered asking Isa where she gave birth to my dad, and her careful answer that he was 'born in hospital'.)

If I had the baby in my flat, I'd need help. Could I ask my mother? No, it wouldn't be fair. And supposing something went wrong . . . My pager went off at last and saved me from any more mental meanderings of this sort. I was directed to Room 6, where a woman dressed in a green smock and trousers was sitting in front of a scanner, a computer screen, I supposed. The room was in half darkness, and though I wasn't in the least worried – I'd had the earlier scan and knew how easy it all was – I began to feel faintly excited. The woman told me her name, which I didn't take in, and said she would talk me through what she saw on the screen and if I'd any questions she'd answer them if she could. Then I lay down, as before, and the gunge was plastered over my belly. She tilted the screen slightly so that I could watch, and at once the shape of the baby filled it. 'There you are,' she said, 'there's the head, there's the neck, now I'm going to follow the spine and through the buttocks . . . Do you want to know the sex?'

Did I? There was May to consider. She might not live until

the baby is born, and she so wants to know. But did *I* want to know? The operator was asking again. 'Do you want to know the sex? If in doubt, you should say no.' I asked her how certain it was that she could tell me accurately. She said it was never a hundred per cent certain but that in my case she could see it clearly, or else she wouldn't have asked if I wanted to know. I lay there, thinking. Did I care about what she claimed was the tiny margin for error? I decided I did. If she'd said the prediction *was* one hundred per cent certain, I would have said yes, tell me. But that minute possibility for error somehow made me say no. 'No thank you, I don't want to know the sex.'

May will just have to live, and wait.

X

ELSPETH HAS gone. This is catastrophic. She didn't even give notice, but then as she's never had any contract she wasn't obliged to. Seems she rang Dad this morning at work on his mobile and said she was very sorry but her nerves were 'frayed to bits' and her doctor had forbidden her to leave her flat. She said she would not be returning to Mrs Symondson's house – not ever. She had been treated with ingratitude and contempt and it was more than the frayed nerves could stand – in fact, Mrs Symondson's treatment of her over several months now, though she had never complained about it, was what had caused the fraying of the nerves. Dad said she was weeping. Nothing he could say would console her.

He's already sent her flowers, plus a cheque and a letter. And now he is going round to Isa's and would like me to join him, if I'm free. Of course I'm free. He hardly ever asks me to do anything for him and I wouldn't dream of refusing, but I do wonder why he wants me there. He knows things have been a bit delicate between Isa and me for a while now, so he might imagine my presence would aggravate her if she's in a touchy mood as a result of Elspeth's sudden departure. Does he, I wonder, feel suddenly nervous at tackling Isa about Elspeth's accusations? Does he perhaps want a witness in case she says things to him he wants someone else to hear?

* * *

The front door was locked, from the inside, with the key still in the lock. Dad tried to push the key out with his own key but of course this didn't work. We rang the bell repeatedly and could hear it ringing inside, and then we banged with the brass knocker and yelled through the letter box. I used my mobile to ring Isa while all this was going on, but there was no reply. Dad said he'd have to break in. We stood and surveyed the house, wondering which window it would be easiest to break and gain entry through, and also easiest to get a new pane fitted in afterwards. Isa's house is detached, with a good number of ground-floor windows, but a lot of them have bars on them (the pantry, the downstairs cloakroom, the utility room). Round and round we went, several times, then just as Dad was settling on the glass panel of the side door, even though it had bars inside (reckoning he could stick his arm through and open it, because the key was always left in the lock), I saw Isa looking down at us from her bedroom window.

We stood back on the lawn and waved and smiled. Isa stared back at us but gave no corresponding wave. We groaned as she turned her back and disappeared from view, but then we could see her going down the stairs – there's a window halfway down on the landing – and next she appeared at the patio doors. She didn't open them, but stood right up close to them and peered out, shading her eyes from the sun, which was shining into them. Dad went closer, shouting, 'It's me, Mama, it's James come to see you. It's James, Ma, can you open the door and let me in? Can you? See, Ma, it's me, James. OK?' He was almost pressing his nose against hers by then. Still she made no move to unlock and open the doors, but at least we could see that she wasn't lying somewhere with a broken leg or something. I wondered if my being there, at Dad's side, was making her uncertain, so I backed off, leaving him standing there on his own. He stepped back too, just a little bit, and didn't call out again. He stayed still, his hands clasped in front of him in an oddly pleading way, quite unthreatening. After what seemed an age, but was probably only a couple of minutes, Isa slowly reached up and loosened the bolt at the top of the glass doors and then equally slowly, and with obvious difficulty – this bolt, we knew, was stiff – undid the bottom one. All she had to do now was turn the key, but she hesitated. She was saying something. Her breath steamed up the glass. Dad went closer, and whatever she had said was a question, because he nodded. The key was turned and the door opened.

I still kept well back, on the lawn, waiting. Dad didn't enter the house at once. He let Isa study him, almost in the way it's wise to let a dog sniff you, and then I heard him say, 'Ma,' and I could see her smiling and holding out her hand in that regal way she has. They went inside, away from the doors, but not before Dad had given me a little wave and indicated with a nod of his head that I should go round the side to the front door (or that was how I interpreted the gesture). When I got there I didn't know whether to ring the doorbell or just wait, but as I was deciding the door opened and Dad was there. 'She seems fine,' he whispered as we walked together into the drawing room, where Isa sat in state. 'Isamay!' she said, with every appearance of delight, and offered her cheek for a peck. I pecked (one side only, as the rules dictated). 'Now, this is a pleasant surprise. Both of you together, how unusual.'

'Well, Ma,' Dad said, 'we were worried.'

'Why would that be?'

'You haven't been answering the phone, and—'

'I expect I was busy when you called. You cannot expect me to sit around ready to answer the telephone, James.'

'But the front door was locked, and my key—'

'One cannot be too careful these days. You have told me so yourself.'

'Yes, but locking it and leaving your key stuck in the lock means no one can get in with their key . . .'

'Precisely.'

'But you might have been ill, or had a fall, or—'

'Really, James, you are full of gloom and worries.'

'Sorry, but—'

'Now, shall we have some tea? Isamay, go and find Elspeth and ask her if she will be kind enough to bring us some tea.'

'I don't think Elspeth is here,' I said.

'Not here? Of course she will be here.' Isa looked at the clock ticking away on her mantelpiece. 'Three o'clock. Elspeth does not leave until four, sometimes five. She is reliable.'

'She was,' Dad said.

'Is she dead, then?' Isa said, very cool, no panic at all in her voice.

'No. But she's given in her notice, or rather she's said she won't be coming again.'

'How thoughtless.' Isa sighed. 'I will have to find someone else. There are agencies, are there not?'

Dad was silent. So was I. What were we dealing with? Amnesia? Or something more sinister? Isa seemed quite unconcerned about Elspeth's defection, except for the thoughtlessness of it. She clearly had no intention of being distraught, and nor was she going to admit what a huge problem there would now be. Devotion such as Elspeth's is rare, but Isa didn't show any signs of appreciating this. 'I was wondering,' Dad said nervously, 'if maybe you could persuade Elspeth to return?' Isa looked shocked. 'Why ever would I wish to do that? Dear me, how mortifying that would be.'

'What happened?' I risked asking, 'Why has Elspeth left so suddenly?'

Dad looked alarmed, but it was absurd, I thought, not at least to try to find out if Isa even remembered what had happened. She didn't seem offended by my question either. Just puzzled. 'Happened?' she echoed, disdainfully. 'I am afraid I do not know of anything "happening" with regard to Elspeth. She was here yesterday, I am sure. She performed her usual duties.' If the situation hadn't been so serious

227

I would have laughed at the hauteur with which Isa said this, as though she were talking about a butler.

'She told Dad—'

'Isamay! I do wish you would not use that term. If you will not refer to him as your papa, please call James your father.'

'She told *Father* that you had treated her with ingratitude and contempt – that's right, isn't it, Dad, I mean Father?'

'Ingratitude?' said Isa, absolutely astonished. 'Why would I owe a servant gratitude?'

'For good, loyal service?' I suggested.

'But it is a servant's job to serve . . .'

'Oh, come on, Grandmama, Elspeth wasn't a servant in any real sense, and even if she had been you could still be grateful that she did well what she'd agreed to do.'

All this time, Dad hadn't said a word. He was tapping his foot impatiently; it was obvious he wasn't pleased with me. He cleared his throat and stood up and said maybe I would go and make some tea, we all needed it. So I shrugged and obeyed. The drawing room is quite a distance, of course, from the kitchen, so I didn't hear anything that was said between them while I was boiling the kettle and setting a tray with cups and stuff. I must say, the kitchen was immaculate, though I think that's due to Mrs Robert's tender care rather than Elspeth's – she surely didn't do anything as lowly as clean kitchens. It's a purely functional kitchen, nowhere to sit and eat, though there's one stool in front of the worktops. I perched on it while waiting for the kettle to boil, staring out of the window at a bird table, where there were two chaffinches squabbling over what looked like bacon rinds. Then I filled the teapot and lifted the tray. God, it felt heavy, what with the pot, three cups and saucers, milk jug, sugar bowl, and the tray itself wasn't light. I bore it back to the drawing-room, grateful that such times have, for most women, gone. It's mugs in the kitchen, and milk straight from the fridge, and none of this palaver.

Isa asked where the tea strainer was. I said we didn't need one. I'd found some tea bags. 'Tea *bags*? In my kitchen?' she said. I nodded. She looked pained. 'Elspeth's, or Mrs R's,' she said. 'They must bring them to use themselves.' I poured the tea, expecting her to say it was undrinkable, but she drank it without complaint. 'So, Mama,' Dad said, 'you say you found Elspeth opening a drawer in your desk and—'

'James, I found Elspeth opening a drawer she had no business or need to open. That is a statement of fact. You cast doubt upon it by the way you phrase it.'

'OK, Mama, you found Elspeth opening a drawer.'

'I did. I caught her in the act.'

'Of doing what?' I said.

'Of opening the drawer, child.'

'What was in this drawer?'

'It does not matter what was in it. The point is, Elspeth had no right to open it, and I told her so.'

'What did you say to her exactly?' Dad asked.

'I forget.'

'Did you raise your voice?'

'I may have done. One would have been entitled to.'

'And what did she say?'

'She said she was looking for an envelope in which to put . . . something, some form, something.'

'What kind of form?' Dad asked.

'I have no idea.'

'Had this form, or whatever, come in the post? Had you looked at it?'

'I may have done.'

'And handed it to Elspeth? Maybe it was important, maybe—'

'James, stop. You are complicating what is simple. Elspeth opened a drawer she should not have opened on the pretext of searching for an envelope. I reprimanded her. She took offence. This is a fuss about nothing.'

Dad and I both studied Isa. She was not quite as confident as her words implied. It was tempting to press her to recall what this 'form' was, but on the other hand it didn't really matter. I believed absolutely, and I'm sure Dad did too, that Elspeth really had been looking for an envelope, for whatever reason, and that she had inadvertently opened a drawer Isa wanted kept shut. But why? What had she been afraid that Elspeth, with her sharp eyes, might see? The very thing Isa had said did not matter mattered most. But we would never get it out of her. Dad obviously recognised this. He sighed and ran his hand through his hair, and said that the important thing was that Elspeth had left and was refusing to come back unless Isa apologised, and maybe not even then.

Isa stared at Dad. 'I cannot believe,' she said, 'that a son of mine would suggest I needed to apologise.'

'Well, if you shouted, and—' Dad muttered.

'I do not shout,' said Isa, almost hissing with anger. 'Now, can you please stop harassing me? Let us talk about something else. Isamay, how is your thesis progressing?'

I wanted to tell her not to change the subject, but humoured her instead. 'It's hard to talk about. I'm studying a woman photographer, Julia Margaret Cameron, who used her grandchildren to pose for photographs, and Margaret Mead, the anthropologist . . .'

'I think I'd better go,' Dad said, 'I've got—'

'James, sit down.' And Dad sat. He is fifty-five years old. He is an orthopaedic surgeon. But when his mother told him to sit down, he sat, even though he needed to be somewhere else.

The fact that he sat when bidden pleased Isa. She was mollified. Her expression brightened, and she switched back on the 'charming' smile she habitually used, an empty smile, with no true warmth in it, but nevertheless it was a relief to see it after such an uncomfortable interchange. She looked steadily at Dad, and then at me, and her smile grew more genuine.

'A strong likeness,' Isa said. 'Mrs Wright may say you resemble her side of the family, but it is quite untrue. You look like James, and like me. You are your father's child, undoubtedly.'

'I know that,' I said, flatly.

Isa carried on as though she hadn't heard me. 'You have your father's ears, pretty ears for a man, so shapely, and his hair, the same colour, the same texture. There is nothing of your mother or your maternal grandmother in your appearance. You are like your father, except for your eyes, of course, which are mine.'

'Odd, isn't it?' I said, daringly.

'I really do have to go, Mama,' Dad said. 'I've got a clinic and I should be there now . . .'

'Go, my son,' said Isa, giving a dismissive wave of her hand.

Dad pecked her hurriedly on the cheek, and as he passed me he squeezed my shoulder. Quite an unnecessarily hard squeeze. A warning?

'Odd, isn't it?' I repeated, when he had gone.

Isa looked vague, but she was alert. She wasn't going to ask me what was 'odd' and give me the chance to tell her. She sensed danger, I was sure, and was going to avoid it. I knew she was going to change the subject – of family resemblances – even though she had brought it up herself, and she duly did. 'Your father works very hard,' she said.

'So does my mother,' I said.

'Oh, your mother,' she said, as though my mother working hard was somehow a different thing altogether. I was delighted to have the opportunity to take offence.

'Don't you admire Mum for working hard, then?'

Isa looked startled at the idea. 'Admire her? Well, of course, Jean is admirable. She is my daughter-in-law.'

'*That* doesn't make her admirable in itself, does it?'

'I would never criticise my daughter-in-law.'

'But you want to, don't you? For working hard, for having a demanding career . . .'

'Isamay! That is quite untrue.'

'Sorry.'

'You seem determined today to be contrary, you are unlike yourself.'

'You don't know my *self*.'

'Don't be absurd. Of course I know you, you are my grand-daughter. I was there when you were born, I have—'

'Yes, yes, but you don't really know me *now*.'

'What is there to know that is different?'

That would have been my chance. I could have broken my promise and said it then. I could have told her that I knew she was *not* my blood grandmother and that knowing this made me feel very different indeed. But I didn't. She looked so innocent, suddenly so open, so vulnerable, and yet she is far from any of those things. She's guilty of a massive decep-tion, possibly two deceptions. She is emotionally closed up tight, and she has a carapace of aloofness that protects her from too much contact with others. I simply could not chal-lenge her. I was afraid to, afraid of the possible consequences. So I made some facetious reply, and she accepted it, and put on a good show of being amused, and soon afterwards I left.

I need to think more clearly about Isa. About Isa herself and about her significance for my work. That's where I need to think most clearly of all.

Claudia is pleased with me, or rather she's pleased with the first draft of my dissertation, which I delivered to her last week. She sent me an e-mail – very short, just saying she had read the draft and thought I had sorted myself out and she could now see where I was going. Good.

But her approval makes me lazy. Right, I think, I don't need to worry about work for a bit now, though of course I do. There are only five months left before the whole dissertation needs to be presented. It will be a race between delivering the baby and delivering the dissertation, and if I don't manage to do the latter before the former I'll be in real trouble. I ought to be galvanised into action by Claudia's blessing but I'm not. All I've managed to do today is put all my research notes into chronological order – by order of grandmother, that is. I go by the date they first became a grandmother, so Elizabeth Fry comes at the beginning and Margaret Mead at the end. Having done that simple task, I then spent an idle few minutes deciding who I like the sound of best as a grandmother. Maybe Vanessa Bell, though Sarah Bernhardt sounds fun . . .

I'll start tomorrow, doing the real work. Or the day after. I have to do something about the legacy business too.

The red light on the phone was winking when I got home from college, but I didn't rush to attend to it. Let any message wait until I'd made myself a sandwich. I felt like Isa, refusing to let the phone come first. Like Isa, I thought, and it was true, I *am* like her, even if she isn't a blood relative. All kinds of my attitudes and habits can be traced directly to her. It is no good rejecting her or denying her influence, just because she isn't 'really' my grandmother.

I fed myself, and then went to listen to the messages. There were two. One from Beattie, giving me her new mobile number and asking me to text her, and the other wasn't for me. It was for Ian. A short message, abrupt and sharp. A distinctive Scottish accent, a woman's voice but rather hoarse and deep. 'Ian,' the woman said, 'Ian, ring me.' No 'please'. It was an order. I played it again and again. It was not the voice of a young woman but definitely an older one. She didn't leave a number. Whoever this was assumed Ian had her number. So, was it his mother? His grandmother? My curiosity made me restless. I paced up and down, peering out of the front window to look for Ian coming home, which was mad because it was only four o'clock. I convinced myself something dramatic had happened – never, in all our four years together, had Ian been rung up by anyone except friends, male friends, of his own age, and work colleagues. So far as I knew, there had been no calls from his family.

The caller, who left no name or number, who was Scottish, who expected to be automatically recognised, must be family. I had to struggle not to ring or text Ian at work. He wouldn't like being disturbed when he was in the middle of something just to be told a woman with a Scottish accent had rung him and wanted her call returned. It could wait a few hours. But I had convinced myself it was his mother. Someone had died or was seriously ill. She needed him. I got more and more anxious imagining this woman sitting there waiting for her son to call her – she'd be pacing up and down, frantic, maybe smoking cigarette after cigarette (her voice sounded like a smoker's), hours to go and that poor woman waiting . . .

I tried to settle down to looking at my George Sand notes again. So awful, that rift with her daughter, and the things she said about her. I wanted to bring out how becoming a grandmother gave her a second chance and how this was a characteristic of grandmotherhood that emerged strongly through the generations. I successfully concentrated to such an extent that when the phone rang I really did jump, pulled sharply back into my own life. I lifted the receiver and said hello in such an absent-minded way that the caller must hardly have heard me. There was silence, which made me attend more closely. I said hello again, and then gave my number and asked who was calling. The receiver at the other end was put down without a word being spoken. I instantly rang 1471 and found that the number was withheld. I hate people who withhold their number.

Three hours had somehow gone by. I was back at the front window again, watching, all thoughts of doing any more work given up. Though I was still sure the mystery caller had been Ian's mother, I'd changed my mind about her. I didn't feel she could, after all, be so distraught. If she was, surely she would have spoken to me, surely she would have blurted out whatever was wrong and why she needed to speak to her son. I wished I had used her name, said Mrs Scott, this is Isamay, can I help? (Though that was presuming the caller *was* Ian's mother.) I'd lost the chance, maybe, to talk to her, something I'd wanted to do for a long time, but Ian wouldn't allow it, he wouldn't even acknowledge he had a mother alive.

He came cycling round the corner just after six. He is always so neat and careful in everything he does. He didn't leap off his bike in a hurry. He stopped at the kerb, took his helmet off, detached his bag and carried the bike slowly up the steps. Suddenly he looked vulnerable to me. I worried for him, not knowing what awaited him. He would not like hearing that a woman I'd thought must be his mother had called, and needed him. Ian did not want to be wanted by her. His absolute insistence on being free of all family ties had always shocked me, but I'd learned at least to pretend to accept it. I waited anxiously, hearing the main door into the house close. The bike has to stay in the main hall because there is nowhere else to put it. He is scrupulous about putting it right up against the wall, in the corner, and has an old blanket on the floor there so the wheels don't dirty the tiles. He loves that bike, an affection that goes way beyond liking it because it gets him to and from work and keeps him fit.

I hardly waited for him to get through the door. 'A woman left a message. I think it was your mother,' I said, trying, and failing, to suppress my excitement. 'She's left a message telling you to ring her.' Predictably, Ian ignored my tone of voice, only nodding slightly and raising his eyebrows and then making his unhurried way to the bathroom, where I could then hear the shower running. Patience. I had to have patience. The keener I was to get him to respond to his mother's message (if it was from his mother), the longer he would take. So I settled myself on the sofa and made a feeble play of reading a book. Even when he finally appeared, showered and dressed, he had to open a bottle of wine and pour himself a glass before he sat down to listen to the message. His expression gave nothing away. He only listened once, and then he sat and thought. 'Are you *pondering*? Was it your mother?' He nodded. 'Then what are you waiting for? It must be urgent. Someone must be ill or—'

'Always expecting drama, Issy,' Ian sighed.

'Well, considering your mother has never, ever rung you in the years you've been living here, it *must* be something dramatic.'

He didn't reply, only smiled slightly. I couldn't understand him. 'Ian,' I pleaded, 'come on, you have to call her back.'

'No, I don't.'

'But she sounded so agitated, so—'

'She's always been agitated.'

'But she obviously needs you, and—'

'Oh, you're right on that one, but it's no good, I refuse to be needed.'

'You can't, you're her son, it isn't your choice . . .'

'Yes it is. It is my choice, and I made it a long time ago.'

'Then tell me, explain to me.'

'No.'

'Why not? Are you ashamed? Or is it too awful, too—'

'More fantasies, Issy? Abuse, maybe? Is that what you're imagining? Scenes of horror? Maybe a—'

'Well, if I am, it's your fault, it's only natural I should start to think something terrible must have happened to you as a child to cause this attitude to your mother. Did it?'

'No.'

'Well then, what did happen?'

'Nothing.'

'Ian! This is so stupid.'

'Yes, it is, and if you're going to go on like this just because I refuse to call my mother back, for my own good reasons, then I'll go out.'

He didn't shout. He didn't sound particularly angry.

He just sounded tired. I went into the kitchen and started cooking. Maybe if we ate, Ian might change his mind and realise that he must reply to his poor mother's message. His 'poor' mother – that was how I was thinking of her. Ian had grown in her body as my baby was now growing in mine, and she'd gone through the agony of giving birth, and the intimacy of feeding him, and *now he wouldn't even return a phone call*. I hadn't believed that his detachment could be as extreme as this. He'd told me virtually nothing about his childhood, but I did once ask him if he'd never loved his mother and he sighed and said no, not that he could recall. He'd added that I just had to get it into my head that some people feel nothing for their mother, and that I was wasting my time trying to make him feel guilty about this.

This makes Ian sound such a cold, hard man, but he is not. I asked him once if he would have liked to feel about his parents the way I feel about mine, and he admitted it had certain attractions. I suggested that in that case maybe he could try harder to foster family relationships, but he got annoyed then and said he'd spent years trying, and he'd failed. Distance, and time, hadn't made him feel any differently. So I'd learned not to go on about his lack of any contact. But now I felt outraged on his mother's behalf. I begged him as we ate to call her back. Finally, wearily, he said he would, but later. We chatted amiably for a while longer. The tension I felt was making me stutter. He asked about Isa, and whether anything had been done about the legacy business. I said I hadn't had time to do anything about it yet. When we'd finished supper, I pleaded with him again to ring his mother. He said he would, but that he knew she'd call again anyway, he'd just give it another half-hour. When the phone rang, about nine o'clock, he gave me a little smile, knowing perfectly well what I was thinking. He let it ring until it almost switched to the BT answering service – that's twelve rings – and then he went over and picked up the receiver. He didn't say anything, not even hello, or his number. He just waited. After a moment or two, he gave a small grunt, which must have been an agreement to some question.

I wondered if I should leave the room and let him have this conversation in private, though what I wanted to do was lift the extension in our bedroom and listen in. But since Ian didn't seem to be saying anything at all – this was a monologue on his mother's part – there was no need for me to go. I sat at the table instead, still nibbling the fruit we'd ended our meal with, skinning grapes ever so carefully with my teeth, watching his face. I decided it wasn't quite expressionless, though that was what he was aiming for. When you know a person really well, when you've been their intimate companion for a long time, no facial expression can really be blank. Ian wasn't smiling, he wasn't frowning, he wasn't contorting his features into any show of boredom or impatience or irritation. His face was quite still. But his eyes gave everything away. He had narrowed them, dropped his eyelids, so that anyone who didn't know him as I knew him might have thought he was falling asleep. It wasn't that at all. When Ian lets that happen he is angry and he is trying to hide his anger.

I saw him pick up a biro and scribble something on the notepad beside the phone. 'Yes,' he said, and 'Tomorrow, if possible.' There was a pause. 'Because I don't know if it will be possible,' he said. Another fairly prolonged silence, with the earpiece held a little way from his ear so that even across the room I could hear the loud Scottish voice. It stopped. Ian still held the receiver until there was a click at the other end. Carefully, he replaced it. 'Well?' I said. He shrugged and walked off into the kitchen, carrying our empty plates. I followed him with the rest of the used dishes and said, 'Well?' again, and at that moment the phone rang again. This time I went to answer it – Ian was shaking his head and I knew he wouldn't – and I was suddenly desperate to talk to his mother myself.

238

But of course it wasn't his mother. I don't know why I'd been so convinced that it would be. It was May. She'd been thinking about me and was everything all right? I said fine, everything's fine, and how come she was making phone calls so late, why wasn't she in bed listening to her wireless, all snug with her hot-water bottle? She said because she was worried and knew she wouldn't sleep and it was better to wander about until the worry settled. I asked her what had suddenly made her so anxious about me and she said it wasn't sudden, she'd worried about me all my life and always would because that's the way she was made, that's what being a mother and then a grandmother did to a woman . . . I listened as patiently as possible, repeating all the time that I was very well, and so was the baby (though how could I know that?), and eventually she was satisfied and said she was off to her bed. The last thing she said, after one 'Good night, love' and before the next, was that I should remind her to show me something the next time I came round.

'That was May,' I said, out loud, when this was over. 'Just fussing about how I'm feeling.' There was no response from the kitchen, and when I went back to it there was no Ian there. He was in the bedroom, packing. Well, not exactly packing. He was standing in front of the chest of drawers, the drawers all open, staring into them.

'It'll be cold,' he muttered, 'it always is,' and he picked out his thickest sweater, a black and grey thing with a polo neck. This went into the bag he'd already got out of the cupboard. 'So you're going to your mother's?' I asked. No reply. 'What's wrong, then? Has there been an accident?'

'No.'

'What then? Is she ill?'

'No.'

'So?'

'It's too boring, too complicated.'

'If it's complicated it can't be boring, Ian.'

'Yes it can. Complications can be immensely boring.'

'I won't be bored. Tell me.'

He hadn't put much into the bag but he zipped it up and put his jacket on quickly. Then he checked his pockets, counted the cash in them, and slung the bag on his shoulder. 'I haven't time,' he said. 'I'm getting the train. I'll be lucky to catch it.'

'Where to?'

'Where do you think? Glasgow.'

'So it *is* an emergency?'

'Not in my opinion.'

'But in your mother's?'

'Yup.'

'I thought I heard you tell her you'd have to see if you could get time off work.'

'That was so I get the advantage.'

'How?'

'Arriving before she expects me.'

'Ian, you are odd, really you are. I don't understand this.'

'You don't have to.'

'Oh, come on, surely you're not going to leave without filling me in just a bit . . .'

'I will when I get back, when everything's sorted. Bye.'

I followed him down the stairs, right to the front door, begging him to give me a clue, but he wouldn't. As he opened the door to leave, I was so cross with him that I said something deliberately to annoy him. 'Don't forget,' I said, before the door closed on him, 'to tell your mum she's going to have a grandchild' – the last thing in the world he would tell her. It was spiteful to make that my parting shot, but then I have a tendency to be spiteful when I'm thwarted, unlike Ian. I was sorry the minute I'd said it, and opened the door to shout after him, telling him so, but he'd gone. I rang him immediately on his mobile but he had it turned off, so I texted him, apologising.

Usually when I'm on my own in my flat, there is a sense of relief at having it to myself again. It's not that I don't want Ian there – we wouldn't be living together if I didn't – but that I like gaps, the sort of short gaps that happen naturally. I never have to say to him look, can you give me a day or two on my own, a couple of nights maybe, because he realises I have this need and he absents himself quite unconsciously at just the right moments, saying he's off on some cycling trip, or going to an away football match and will stay overnight. So it's not unusual for me to be on my own, and I like it. But that night I didn't. I was shocked to find I felt lonely, deserted. I wanted Ian there, sharing with me whatever his mother had told him. The way he'd behaved seemed suddenly to underline how far he was moving away from me just when I didn't want him to. And it was my own fault. I was going to have his baby, the child he did not want. I was going to be with it on my own. I was sure he was going to move out. I knew all this, I'd accepted the consequences of going against Ian's wishes, but what I hadn't taken into account was how I would change because I was pregnant, and by changing need him in a way I had never anticipated. Pregnancy was making me feel dependent on him.

Now, this had nothing to do with Ian not disclosing his mother's news – seeing it as private, and none of my business – but it started something off that I didn't like. He wasn't going to let me, or his child, anywhere near his mother or anyone else in his peculiar family. He was probably terrified that I would somehow contact his mother and tell her I was carrying her son's child. It wasn't fair, on me or my child-to-be, to know nothing about her. My child was going to be as deprived of knowledge of its true genetic inheritance just as surely as my father had been deprived of his.

We have two desks in the flat. Ian's is just a basic IKEA job, but it fits neatly under the window on the landing, leaving mine to occupy the tiny box room. Ian doesn't ever really work at his desk – he just needs it for storage, and to use his laptop there occasionally. It has three drawers, none of them very deep, but he keeps most of his stuff on the surface, spread out. I wasn't expecting to find anything interesting or personal in the drawers – I knew there wouldn't be diaries or letters, Ian being the sort of man he is (or who I think he is). But I did find something underneath his passport. It was a tiny photograph, about 5x3cm, in a cardboard folder. It was very old, the black and white turned grey type, and it didn't show much. Just two faces, neither distinct, one of a woman with white hair and one of a boy. I couldn't be absolutely certain the boy was Ian. The photograph wasn't large enough and the image not clear enough to see any distinguishing features, but it was easy to persuade myself that the boy's rather square face was Ian's, and so were the heavy eyebrows. I took it over to the window to get a better look. Both boy and woman were smiling, happy to be photographed (not at all like Ian now). I turned the snap over. No names, but a pencilled date, 1984.

If it was Ian, he would've been eight. But who was the woman? Somehow, I didn't think it could be his mother. I know nothing about his mother; I don't know her age or any other detail, but this woman looked too old, at least sixty, maybe older. Could it be his grandmother? But he had never given the remotest hint of loving, or being close to, a grandmother. He had told me that one little anecdote about her teaching him to bake, and had told May about the tea ritual, but beyond that no suggestion that he was devoted enough to her to keep a photo of the two of them – and keep it secreted away, never showing it to me. I was hurt. Why hide it? He knew I would love it. I replaced it. My heart was thudding slightly, not so much with excitement at unearthing the secretive Ian's secret photo but with a strange sort of nervousness.

I kept thinking, how well do we know people who are not

part of our family? Well, I agree, how much do we know about those who *are* family, but it is somehow different. You've grown up with family; you haven't grown up with people you meet outside it. I met Ian four years ago, when he was twenty-eight. There are twenty-eight years of his life I don't know about. He doesn't reminisce, he isn't into that kind of sharing, and he has moved geographically a long way from where he was born and brought up so nothing can be known by me from observing him in his natural habitat, as it were. And now he has gone off to a mother he barely refers to for a reason he won't divulge.

I suddenly wanted the comfort of my own family. If I'd had a sister, I'd have rung her, but I don't, so the choice was only between my parents and, I suppose, Beattie. I hesitated a long time before ringing Mum, ashamed that all I wanted was some kind of reassurance it wasn't really possible for her to give – she knows Ian even less well than I do, how can she explain his attitude? But I had to talk to someone *safe*, and none of my friends, not even Beattie, came into that category. By 'safe' I mean someone I could trust not to get carried away and enjoy the drama of the situation too much – I didn't want their speculations. And I didn't want to lose face. My pride wouldn't let me confide in them. Ian is the one I confide in. Nobody else has filled the same need for the last few years. So, eventually, after another hour of pacing up and down, and making tea I didn't drink, I rang Mum and unloaded all my anxiety and bewilderment on her.

She was sensible. I know I mock how invariably sensible she is but it is very soothing. When I was younger, it enraged me, but now it is what I want. Ian, she said, would be dealing with his own emotions and was probably unable to be coherent about whatever had happened to make his mother call. As he'd told me, it might all genuinely be so compli-cated he wouldn't have known where to start. And he was hurrying to catch a train. He'd had no time to sit down and start explaining. I was, she thought, being unfair to him, which was understandable, but still. She said that one of my faults was constantly to imagine that other people fitted into their families the way I fitted into mine. Ian had made it plain from the beginning of our relationship that he was not a family man. He had removed himself from the family set-up. Pulled back into it now, for whatever reason, he would be fighting his reluctance to give way to the pressure being exerted.

I listened, and was calmer. I had her sensible voice in my ear and that was all I needed – it wasn't as though she was actually saying anything I hadn't thought of anyway. I lay on the bed, duvet up to my neck, warm and, at last, relaxed, the phone on the pillow beside me. 'But what about the photograph, Mum?' I said. 'Why go to the lengths of keeping it hidden like that?' She said probably because it was so precious, or maybe it was wrapped up with something too sad or distressing to talk about. I said I was hurt that he'd never shown it to me if it was so precious, what did that signify? 'You ask too many questions, Issy,' Mum said, 'that's what it signifies. Ian couldn't face the inquisition, I expect.' She sounded tired, as well she might be. She works so hard, and there I was moaning away when she should be asleep. So I mumbled my thanks and said I was sure she was right, and hung up.

But I didn't sleep straight away. I do ask too many questions. I do start asking more when someone is trying to answer them. It makes Ian's head ache. The thing to do was *not* to badger him with questions but instead to wait, to be receptive to his mood, and see if this would encourage him to volunteer what he would not let be dragged out of him by excitable questioning.

See, I can be as sensible as my mother.

XI

Woke up feeling much better in every way. Showered, dressed, had a decent breakfast and left for the British Library resolved to put in a full day's work and not think about Ian and his mother at all. I waited patiently in the queue to hand my coat in when I got to the library, and then had to wait again to get a chair in the Reading Room, which was crowded and not nearly as quiet as I like it to be, but once my books arrived, after twenty minutes, that other life became mine. I was content, immersed in *Coming of Age in Samoa* and another Margaret Mead publication I thought might be relevant, *Letters from the Field*. I forgot I was pregnant. My baby couldn't dominate me in that place. I was happily living in my head.

And then, after about an hour, I felt it. A beat, a pulse. Low down in my stomach, a quivering. I held myself absolutely still. I waited. Nothing happened. Slowly, I relaxed, cautiously turning a page. But then it began again, the beat, the pulse, the quivering. Three times in succession I felt it, stronger each time. Of course – the quickening. It was what I'd been told would happen. The child stirring, the child telling me what a fool I was to think I could forget it. The flutterings ceased, but I couldn't get back to concentrating. For half an hour I simply sat there, head bent, furtively watching the bulge under my green sweater to see if it moved, but it didn't. I packed up my stuff, handed the books in, and left the Reading Room.

I felt upset out of all proportion. What was going to happen to me if this child could already distract me before it was even born? I struggled on to the hellishly noisy Euston Road, suddenly appalled at my irresponsibility. Ian was right. There I was, fancying myself scholarly, supposedly loving research, and choosing to go ahead and have a baby I had not planned. A pattern familiar in the history of women, which I enjoyed studying so much. I didn't need to go in search of examples of my behaviour. They tumble down the ages in hordes, women bearing children they had had no intention of giving birth to, and yet for over half a century there's been contraception available, and access to terminations has been allowed now for decades. The cars and lorries and buses hurtled past me as I stood at a bus stop doing sums in my head. Was it really too late to get rid of this baby? Yes, it was, absolutely, definitely, completely impossible for me. I was twenty-two weeks pregnant. I stood there and wept.

A bus came. I had no idea which bus it was, or where it might be going. It was just a bus, getting on it was something to do. I clambered on to the top deck and sat right at the front, and carried on quite openly crying in a self-indulgent, slow, unembarrassed way. It was as though I was just leaking grief. Can a grown woman really be so childish? Apparently. And the awful thing was, I almost wanted someone to notice me. Anyone, a complete stranger, just someone who registered my distress and bothered to stop and console me. But it was London, the Euston Road. I'd have had to collapse, literally fall flat on to the filthy pavement before anyone noticed, and even then I'd have been approached warily. The most a passer-by might have done was ring an ambulance. And there I was full of self-pitying resentment that nobody cared about my tears, sitting on the top of a bus going God knew where. How could I have a child when I couldn't control myself?

The bus turned out to be a 390. When I'd finally stopped

snivelling, I began to recognise the route. It could take me near to my grandmother's house. May would say it was meant. I'd been guided on to that particular bus for a purpose and that purpose was her. I got off at the stop nearest to the street where she lives and felt immediately happier. I had the prospect of comfort ahead, as well as the inevitable tea and biscuits. I walked along, remembering being dropped off at May's by my mother, who'd picked me up from school because they'd called her telling her I wasn't well, and she had only enough time to collect me and take me to my granny's. May had a set routine for such occasions. She'd take me into her kitchen and put two chairs together, and cushions on them, and then lie me down and cover me up and give me a hot-water bottle to hold against my tummy, regardless of what was wrong with me (or of the weather). I loved it. If I was really not well, it always made me feel better, and if I wasn't – if I'd been pretending for some reason – it helped my state of mind.

She wouldn't be able to put me on two chairs now (the big, squat leather one and the battered straw one, both squashed into corners in that small, overheated room). It would have to be the settee, in the front room, and that room wouldn't be heated, so May wouldn't want to put me there. Maybe she'd make me go and lie down in her bedroom, underneath her slippery pink eiderdown, and I didn't want to do that. No, I'd have to settle for the leatherette armchair, and let her put my feet on her stool. That would do. She could still cover me with a rug, though. I'd allow that, but not the scratchy tartan one, I'd never liked that one even as a child. She had another one, a chenille one, I'd prefer that . . .

I can't have been in my right mind. Half an hour later, there I stood, on May's doorstep, tear stains still damp on my cheeks, mouth trembling a bit, I expect, ready to unload my misery, and suddenly I caught hold of myself – what was I *thinking* of, about to treat my sick, old grandmother like this? I stepped back, found a tissue in my pocket and tried to wipe away the evidence of all that silly weeping. I'd have to pretend I had a bad cold. I found another scrunched-up tissue and dabbed at my nose. I rapped the knocker. Shuffle, shuffle, then there she was, peeping at me through the lace curtain in her front room. I lifted the flap of the letter box and called out, 'Granny, it's me, Isamay. I've forgotten my key.'

There was no flinging open of the door and cries of delight, but then I hadn't expected them. But I'd hoped for some sign of pleasure, visible in a little grunt and a half-smile and an instruction to get myself in and she'd put the kettle on. Nothing, at first. A stare, a frown. 'It's me, Granny,' I said, 'Isamay.' And then she did half smile, and she did tell me to come in and she'd put the kettle on, and I followed her down the passage. 'I thought you were someone else,' she said, 'a girl I used to know. You looked just like her.' 'What was her name?' I asked, not because I really wanted to know, just to keep her chatting. 'Cora,' she said. 'What happened to her?' 'She died.'

That finished that topic off. The kettle boiled, the tea business was managed, and we each sat down. 'Let's have a look at you,' May said, then, 'You look under the weather.'

'I'm fine.'

'You don't look it. You look like you used to look when you dodged off school.'

'I didn't dodge off school.'

'And the Pope's not a Catholic. Proper little actress you were, the time of them bullies. Couldn't stand up for yourself. Tell your gran, I used to say, and out it would come. Shall I go and bash them? I'd say, and I'd get a saucepan and say I was going to go and bash them, and you'd cheer up.'

'I don't remember being bullied.'

'Well, I do, miss. So who's been at you?'

'*At* me?'

'You know what I mean. Is it that whatever-she's-called teacher? With a man's name?'

'Claudia, you mean? It isn't a man's name. And Claudia never bullies me. We're two grown women, for heaven's sake.'

'Your fella, then, that Ian, is he being rough?'

'Rough? Ian? Granny, please!'

'It was a manner of speaking. Is he being good to you? You know what I mean.'

'He's always good to me.'

'Then what's the matter? It's not good for the baby, you being peaky. Are you eating proper, eh? You need your strength, you need to eat for two . . .'

That's when I started crying again, crying and laughing at the same time (or hysterics, as it is commonly known). 'Oh, my good Gawd,' May said. 'This isn't good for the baby. Settle down now, settle down.'

It's hard to cuddle or hug someone if they are sitting slumped in an armchair, but May did her best. She perched her bottom on the luckily broad arm of the chair and leant down towards me, bracing herself with her hands clutching at the back of the chair. It was a very awkward position, which she couldn't hold for long, fortunately – the tea fumes were wafting strongly over me and making me feel sick – and soon gave up. 'Oh my Gawd,' she gasped, 'my back. Get yourself out of that damned chair or I'll fall on top of you. All this carrying on ain't good for the baby, so stop it, stop it.' She sounded angry but I knew she wasn't – she was beginning to panic, afraid she wouldn't be able to console me. 'I shall have to ring your mum,' she said, 'that's what I'll have to do if you don't stop. Here, here's a hanky, dry them eyes, come on, it can't be that bad, whatever it is, I've known worse, I'll bet.'

The tears only stopped because I was exhausted by then. My head ached and I felt my eyeballs themselves were raw.

But I didn't move from the saggy old chair. May patted my hand and peered at me, and I croaked that I'd like a glass of water if she wouldn't mind. The tap ran for ages until she was satisfied that the water was cold and fresh enough and then she produced the glass, a slice of lemon floating on the top, as she knew I liked it. That was a concession – May thinks it a waste of a lemon, and a lemon itself a luxury. She watched approvingly as I sipped the water. 'That's better, down the hatch with it,' she said. 'It's good to drink water, you carry on drinking it.' I drained the glass. 'More?' I shook my head. 'Sorry,' I said. 'We'll forget it,' she said.

'It was just . . .' My voice trailed off.

'Doesn't matter,' said May, hurriedly. 'Best forgotten if it upsets you.'

'But I can't forget it.'

'What is it, then?'

'I'm having a baby. It moved today.'

'Well, so it should. How far on are you? Halfway, isn't it? It should be kicking, that's nothing to cry about.'

'But I've made a mistake.'

'What about? What the devil are you on about, Isamay?'

'I don't want this baby. I've made a mistake.'

'This is daft talk.'

'No, it isn't. I've made a terrible mistake.'

'Then you have to live with it, that's all.'

May's tone was harsh and definite. She stopped patting my hand and hovering over me and went across to her dresser, where she started banging plates about, her back to me. I snivelled, and closed my eyes. God knows what I'd thought I was doing, coming to my grandmother. What had I expected? Tea and sympathy? But I knew perfectly well that to May, babies were sacrosanct. Not to want one, especially when it already was halfway to being born, was heresy of the vilest kind. I'd heard May's views on abortion many a time: murder, no other word for it. Suddenly she turned back to face me, her hands clutching a plate before her like a shield. 'You, madam,' she said, sternly, 'don't know how lucky you are. That's your trouble, you and your mistake, calling the baby that, well, I know a lot of mistakes and they are glad to be alive and their mothers are glad to have them and wouldn't ever let them know they was mistakes, so just get on with it and stop bleating on or don't never come here again. Now, you should eat, after all that bawling. What will it be? Toast and cheese? A ham sandwich? You ain't leaving this house without a bite to eat.'

I chose the toasted cheese. She cut the two slices into triangles for me and I ate them daintily. She said my nose was red and my eyes had disappeared and I couldn't leave her house looking like that or the neighbours would think it was her fault. Then she put her wireless on, very low, some sort of music station, and said she wouldn't be a minute, she had to go upstairs and get something she wanted to show me, to cheer me up, she said; it was what she'd told me, on the phone, to remind her about. I heard her plod up the stairs, talking to herself, and then the dragging of something across her bedroom floor and a bang as something fell. Then there was a silence, and I began to worry that the bang had been May falling, but I knew it hadn't been loud enough. I called out, 'Granny?' rather feebly, but didn't move. Eventually I heard the bedroom door being closed and the sound of May descending.

I expected photographs, or a photograph. She'd probably unearthed some blurred snap, like the one Ian had hidden, and I'd be obliged to peer at it while she identified the could-be-anyone people in it. But she wasn't holding anything that looked like a photograph or an album. She was carrying a cylindrical cardboard container, holding it like a cosh, as though she were about to bash me over the head with it. Her expression, too, was quite threatening, but that wasn't unusual. 'Now,' she said, coming to stand in front of me

(I was still flopping in the armchair), 'now, madam, what do you think this is, eh?' I said I'd no idea. 'What does it look like?' I said it looked like a container for a poster, something like that. 'You're getting near,' she said. 'Go on, then.' She held it up for me to see better, then tapped it on the arm of the chair. It wasn't as long as it had seemed when she'd come into the room brandishing it. It was only about thirty centimetres long, so if it held a poster it was a small one. I really couldn't be bothered to guess any more, but May was insistent. 'A certificate?' I said, 'Something like that?' 'Now we're getting somewhere,' she said, and handed me the cardboard tube. 'Go on,' she urged, 'look inside it,' and she stood over me, waiting, with this strange, triumphant look appearing on her face.

The tube was closed with one of those hard plastic discs. It was stuck in firmly and obviously hadn't been opened for a very long time. I picked at it, lazily, until May was becoming impatient and annoyed with me, and I tried harder and got a fingernail underneath the rim and prised the disc off. 'There you are,' May said. 'Now fish it out and see what it is.' I fished. The paper was tightly scrolled, and though I slid my finger in easily enough, it didn't move under the pressure I was able to exert. 'I don't want to tear it,' I said. 'I should think not,' May said. 'Give it a tap.' Obediently, I tipped the tube up, and knocked on the bottom, but the scroll of paper didn't budge. 'Oh, for Gawd's sake,' May said, exasperated. I tried harder, this time wedging two fingers inside the rolled-up paper, quite far down, and slowly I could feel the scroll beginning to slide out. Another tap on the bottom end and an inch or two was free. I extracted the complete thing and saw it was tied in the middle with what looked like thread, black thread, wound round and round. There was no apparent knot. 'Do I break the thread?' I asked May. 'Well, you'll have to, won't you?' said May, and 'I've plenty of black thread.'

I put a finger under the thread but it didn't snap, and in

trying to make it break I'd dented the paper. 'I need scissors,' I said. 'Of course you do,' May said, crossly. 'I've plenty of scissors, haven't I?' and she went over to her dresser and pulled the middle drawer out and came back with two pairs. 'Scissors!' she said. 'Take your pick!' I snipped the thread. It came apart, but the strands stayed together as though glued, sealed, I imagined, with age. 'This had better be good,' I said before I unrolled the scroll. I was feeling more cheerful, taking part in this little charade, though I'd been so reluctant to take an interest, and realised that May was concocting a sort of game, just to distract me, and that what was finally being revealed would turn out to be nothing much, something of no significance at all, and I'd have to act as though it was extraordinary, to please May. I peeled open the scroll, but it had been rolled up so tightly for so long that it immediately sprang back. 'Careful,' May said. 'I *am* being careful.' I unrolled it again and placed the flat of my hand over it. My eyes were blurry, as they often are when I've been crying (or 'carrying on', as May would say). And I was still slumped in the squashy depths of the armchair, the leather sides of it casting gloom on the scroll's writing, which in any case was hard to decipher. It was the old style ornate sort, full of loops and twirls, and written with a thick nib. 'What is it?' I asked May. 'You can read, can't you?' she said. 'It's plain enough.' I blinked, but the writing still swam before me, and I blinked again, and tried to open my eyes wider. 'Goodness gracious,' May said, irritably, 'are you having a fit, or what? Stop it. Sit up. If you can't see there, move to the table. You should get your eyes tested. All that reading's done for them. Here, I'll put the light on. What a waste, needing the electric when it's broad daylight.' I got up, clutching the scroll, and went to the table. It was only a step away from the armchair, but my legs felt wobbly and it was a relief to sit on one of the hard, upright, solid chairs round it. 'There you are,' May said, once I'd sat down. I concentrated.

253

I read what was written on the scroll twice. It was a Pitman's shorthand certificate, with an oval photograph of a bust of Sir Isaac Pitman himself at the top. It said that Muriel Wright had been examined on 19 October 1916 by the undersigned examiners and had proved her ability to write Pitman's shorthand at the rate of 100 words a minute. I stared at this document and asked the only safe question: who was Muriel? My grandfather Albert's sister, apparently. 'Well,' I said, weakly, 'very nice.' 'Nice?' said May, scandalised. 'Nice? She was *clever*, that's the point. Learning shorthand like that, in them days. It's where you and your mum get it from.' I said, stupidly, that neither Mum nor I could do shorthand, and May got cross. 'It's the brains I'm talking about,' she said. 'There was brains there already. See?' I said I saw. 'No you don't,' May said. 'Muriel, she was a mistake. Turned out the cleverest of Albert's lot, but she'd been a mistake. Like me. Her ma caught out by the change. We was never intended. And you talking about getting rid of your mistake, the idea!'

May was shouting, and the shouting was making her breathless, and it scared me. I went close to her, to put my arms round her, half fearing she would hit me. But she let me encircle her, and gradually the heaving stopped, and she started pushing me away, but gently, muttering to herself that she didn't know what was going on any more. Then she freed herself and tottered back to the armchair and picked up the cylindrical container the scroll had come in and handed it to me. 'Put it in again, nice and tight,' she ordered me, and I rolled the certificate up again and did so. 'I've got another certificate of Muriel's,' May said. 'Don't know where it is. She passed something with her violin, too. She sang lovely, played the piano and the violin. A neighbour took an interest and taught her the beginnings and then she passed her on to this music teacher she knew and Muriel paid for the lessons by doing shopping for people and working Saturdays at the paper shop . . .' May was happy again, rambling on about my great-aunt Muriel, relishing all the detail. I did listen, and I was interested, but I felt that none of Muriel's story had much to do with me, and yet I was the one so obsessed with genetic inheritances. Anyway, I thanked May for putting up with me, and went home soon afterwards.

Still no Ian, and no news of him. His mobile is turned off and I'm tired of leaving messages for him. It's embarrassing constantly to text him, so I've stopped.

I tell myself this is good practice for learning how to live on my own again. I'm fine until about six in the evening, and then the silence around me seems to change its nature. It becomes denser, my ears sing with it. I find myself clearing my throat noisily when I've no need to. It isn't that I am nervous, afraid of someone breaking in or anything like that, but the silence becomes so acute it needs to be dealt with. Each time I turn over a page it is like a statement – here I am, yes, me, on my own, sitting reading. My ears go on singing and I feel I can hear myself breathing. The silence is suddenly a weight, and though I am not crushed by it, I am aware of being cowed. I try to imagine what it would be like if the extreme quiet was to be broken by a baby crying. Would it shatter the silence in such a way that it would never be complete again? Would that be a good thing? Have I outgrown the solitary life?

I fell asleep, and when I woke, after half an hour I suppose, my neck was stiff and I felt cold and the flat hummed with small noises I hadn't heard before. I registered them with relief: the odd creaking of floorboards as Maisie, the upstairs tenant, walked about, the ticking of the central heating as the water went through the radiators, the faint constant whirr of the freezer, the drip from the tap in the bathroom, which needs a new washer. All the tiny sounds never noticed either when Ian is here with me, or when I've withdrawn into a kind of suspended life and shut everything out. Now I was OK. So, the flat was quiet but not alarmingly so. It was how I like it. The peace to think in, not disturbing at all. I could cope. I could more than cope. I could relish it.

I was very glad, when Ian returned, that I had had that experience. It did me good to know that I can, and will, manage on my own and that his presence is not as important to me – though it *is* important – as I'd started to believe it might be. There was no need to panic about the baby. I could be a family of one. Well, not just of one. The child will have grandparents and great-grandmothers.

I was working steadily when Ian returned, at about four o'clock. I carried on writing notes when I heard the door of the flat being opened. No rushing to greet him, no shout asking him where on earth had he been and why hadn't he rung each day? None of that. 'Hi,' he called. 'Hi,' I replied, as casually as I could. I heard him go into the bedroom and heard the thump of his bag as it was dropped on the floor, and then the squeaky cupboard door being opened. Seconds later, the sound of the shower in the bathroom. It ran for a long time, longer than it needed to if he was just getting clean. He'd be standing underneath it, with the water very hot, to ease his fatigue, I imagined. I thought about getting up at that point and going to make him some tea, but I didn't. He made it himself. I heard him go into the kitchen and boil the kettle, and then the clatter of mugs and teaspoons and other tea-making sounds. 'Tea?' he called. 'Yes please,' I called back.

So far so good. I was being polite, receptive, but above all else detached. I smiled as I walked into the kitchen, to show I wasn't sulking. The smile was wasted. He was sitting with his back to me, looking out of the window, the mugs of tea steaming in front of him. It was a shock as I moved forward and saw his face: he looked haggard, wrecked. He hadn't shaved and the stubble was black and heavy, and with his wet hair brushed flat his head looked odd, as though it was moulded in clay. 'Oh, Ian,' I said, and put my hands on his shoulders. No response. 'Do you want something to eat?' I said, picking up my own tea. He shook his head. Carefully I sat down at the table and sipped the tea. It seemed crass to ask what was wrong when so much obviously was, so we sat in silence until the tea was drunk. We both were looking anywhere but at each other. The pattern on the mugs, the grain in the wood of the table, the tiles on the wall behind the sink – they'd all become apparently fascinating to us. We sat there, rigid with tension. I felt I had to wait for him to say something, and eventually he did.

'There wasn't a chance to phone you.'

'Don't worry, didn't matter.'

'It did. I'm sorry. I just . . . I get . . . I just can't handle it. I never could.'

He knew he was talking in riddles, but I sensed that talking at all was hard for him, so I didn't ask questions.

'I won't be going back to Glasgow, ever,' he said. 'If she ever rings and asks for me, just say I've moved and you don't know where I've gone.'

'And if she turns up?'

'Turns up?' He laughed. 'Oh, she won't turn up, no worries there.'

Cautiously, I risked a harmless direct question. 'You mean your mother, I take it? You're talking about her? What did she want?'

'I don't want to talk about her.'

'But I do, Ian,' I said, very gently. 'I'm completely in the dark.'

'Good place to be.'

'No, it isn't. It's a horrible place to be. I don't understand anything, and I want to. I hate to see you so upset and not to know why, not to be able to help.'

He grimaced, and got up and refilled his mug with tea, then he went and stared out of the window. I didn't know whether to get up too and go and put my arms round him, to comfort him – he was so clearly miserable. But I dreaded him shaking me off, and so I stayed where I was and felt ridiculously rewarded when he came and sat down again and said, 'Sorry, it's my fault.'

'What's your fault?'

'Not being able . . . not talking to you about it. I just don't want to, that's all. It's embarrassing, stupid. I want to ignore it.'

'What? What's this "it".'

'My mother and everything to do with her, and me. She's no business intruding into my life. I'm thirty-two, I'm not a child.'

'But you went to her.'

He hesitated, seemed about to say something, but changed his mind, I thought. 'A mistake. I'm always making the same mistake, but it's years since I made the last one and I won't make another.'

If he'd been angry – and I can recognise when Ian is full of fury as opposed to distress – then I would probably have given up at that point, or at least bided my time, waited for a better opportunity to press on. But he was not angry. He was disturbed and uneasy and resentful, not the same at all. So what I said next was that I'd done something I was ashamed of while he was away. I said I'd been so mad when he went off in the way he did that I'd been determined to find out where he'd gone, his mother's address or something, and so I'd searched all over, his clothes, his desk, his belongings. I'd found an old photograph. I said I wanted to know who the woman was, and why he'd kept the snap and why he'd hidden it. Couldn't he at least talk about that even if he couldn't talk about his mother? I said I couldn't stand even more mystery.

258

'You snooper,' he said, but quite amiably, 'going to those lengths. Where else did you look? In my socks? Find anything tucked inside? You're blushing, and so you should.'

'I'm ashamed. I'm sorry.'

'It's of my grandma. My mother's mother. She took me in.'

'But why hide it?'

'I don't like anyone looking at it.'

'Not even me?'

'Especially not you.'

'Oh, Ian!'

'It might give you ideas. I'd never hear the end of it. I'd be cross-questioned about her – I know you.'

'I'm hurt.'

'I knew you would be. Well, it's your own fault. You shouldn't have been so sneaky.'

He'd moved away, of course, from what I'd meant should be the main topic of conversation. I'd expected anger, and I'd hoped, once fuelled by it, he'd let me lead him on to telling me why his mother had called and what had taken place in the last few days. Instead, my confession had given him the opportunity to concentrate on something else. He wasn't angry, because he was relieved and pleased. He didn't mind in the least telling me about his grandma. So all I could do was pick up on 'she took me in'.

'When did your grandma take you in?'

'When I was about fourteen.'

'That old.'

'Yup, that old.'

'And why?'

'I needed somewhere to live.'

'So you wanted to leave home?'

'I *had* to leave what was called home.'

'That bad?'

'That bad.'

We were still sitting at the kitchen table. It was as if we

259

were playing a game of chess, each of us making deliberate, controlled moves. The word not to mention was 'mother'. I mustn't ask him about his mother. What I must do, I told myself, was get behind that forbidden word and then move closer to it, catching him unawares, like in another game. The Yes or No game. I needed to ask innocuous questions that he wouldn't mind answering and that might add up to some revelation he hadn't intended to make.

'Where did your grandma live?'

'Near Glasgow.'

'But Glasgow is where you were born, where you lived, right?'

'Right.'

'So you hadn't run away very far.'

'I didn't say I ran away.'

'You said—'

'I said I needed somewhere to live.'

Steady, I told myself, remember not to use the 'm' word. 'What did your grandma say when you asked if you could live with her?'

'I didn't. She offered.'

'How old was she?'

'Sixty-something.'

'In that snap she looks older.'

'They all did, those women of her sort, with her life. Old before their time.'

'Quite hard for her, taking in a bolshie teenager.'

'I wasn't bolshie. I was quiet, studious. No bother to anyone.'

'But you had to leave home.'

'I had to leave home.'

'Curiouser and curiouser.'

He smiled. Not exactly a happy smile, more of a rueful one. 'How have you been?' he asked.

'Fine.' He nodded at this, as though it were the answer he

260

expected. 'Actually,' I said, 'I haven't been fine. I got in a state, about you. I worried about you, and I saw what it was going to be like living on my own again, without you. But I got over it, my panic, I mean. And I'll be fine.'

'Course you will. And you've got your family, you're not on your own.' There was a pause. 'What about food?' he said. 'Shall we go and shop? Or I could go, let you rest.'

We went to Sainsbury's. I got the fruit and vegetables, he queued for the fish; we chose a chicken together. Then we came home and cooked. It was pleasant, companionable. Everything was back to normal. And I still didn't know a damned thing about why his mother had called, why he had gone to her, what had happened. I lay awake for ages, Ian breathing steadily, rhythmically beside me, his hand lightly covering my own until I turned over on my side. The baby inside me jumped. I put my hand on the place where I'd felt the movement and then I turned back again, to lie flat, and put Ian's warm, inert hand there too.

But the baby refused to move again.

I have written the first five thousand words of my dissertation, the final version. I've printed it out, and there it is, a neat twenty pages. But I'm not going to read it again, not just at the moment. I read it so many times on the screen, making loads of small improvements, and I can't bear to have to recognise that I should have made even more. I feel good about what I've written, it is going to work, and I don't want that feeling to be spoiled because I am off for what will be my last supervision with dear Claudia.

This was the kind of 'last time' I like – last time I'd have to wait outside Claudia's room fretting over how to cover up how little I'd achieved since the last session; last time I'd be seething over her lack of warmth; last time I'd be humiliated by her exposure of my inadequacies. A good 'last time'. But

261

when it came to it, there was some regret too. I did, after all, respect her utter concentration. No one else has ever listened to me quite so attentively, even if critically. And I admired her detachment as much as I resented it – whatever else, Claudia could never be accused of letting personality influence judgement. She didn't, I'd decided, like or dislike *me*. It was my ideas and thoughts she liked or objected to.

It was a satisfactory session. She said she thought I had at last straightened out my confused thinking. An argument was now emerging and I was well on the way to proving its underlying point. I'd collected a lot of worthwhile evidence, presented it well, and the only danger now was that I might force a conclusion that was still open to doubt. It was good, she said, to take a strong line but not good to push aside anything that contradicted it. However, she was confident that my completed dissertation would earn me my MA. She reminded me of the date by which it should be handed in, and how many copies of it would be needed.

'Well, Miss Symondson,' she ended, 'I'll say goodbye,' and she stood up and formally extended her beautifully manicured hand. I shook it, aware, as ever, of my own bitten nails. Was she really not going to refer to my pregnancy? But at the last minute, after I'd mumbled my thanks to her, she said that she hoped I was feeling quite well and that I would finish my dissertation before giving birth. I said there was no doubt about that, the baby wasn't due for another three months, a little more than that in fact. 'Just as well,' she said. 'I found childbirth very distracting.' I'd hardly had time to take in those astounding words before she was smiling her polite smile, walking me to her door, opening it, and saying goodbye.

I had to sit down for a minute. Claudia had had a baby? Had I got that right? So all this stuff I'd been pulling out on grandmothers and their importance, their role, might have had some personal resonance for her. Maybe, if she had a child – boy, girl? – she was a grandmother herself. She was old enough, just. I'd estimated she was in her late forties, maybe even early fifties, so if she'd given birth in her early twenties, as my mother did, she could easily have a daughter who had made her a grandmother. Realising this had a strange effect upon me. I felt exhilarated, as though I'd been given hope. I could be a Claudia. It wasn't as though I hadn't known of plenty of women academics who had families but none of them were like Claudia.

I thought back over how hard she'd been on my ideas, especially at the beginning. She'd seemed to rubbish everything I'd suggested and never once had she indicated that she had personal experience. Well of course she hadn't, it would have been unprofessional, but nevertheless no little hints or involvement had escaped her. Claudia as a mother was startling enough, but as a (possible) grandmother? I desperately wanted to go back in and ask her so many questions, but the next student had arrived and, anyway, I wouldn't have dared.

Then, as I went home, I became annoyed with myself for being so affected by Claudia's admission. I was falling into the stereotype trap, imagining I knew how a mother, and a grandmother, should look and behave. Claudia was nothing like May, only remotely like Isa. It proved nothing.

The next time I visited Isa, still thinking about Claudia as a grandmother, a stranger opened her door. She looked Spanish, or Italian, around forty maybe, wearing a black dress and over it a white waist apron, for all the world like a maid in a Noël Coward comedy. I expect my astonishment showed on my face. 'You are granddaughter?' the vision asked. I nodded. 'I am Cosima,' she said. 'This way, please.' I was led into the drawing room, where Isa sat in state, in a very good mood, smiling and extending her arms, but, as usual, dropping them as I approached. Cosima didn't just go, she definitely 'withdrew'.

'Where on earth did she come from?' I whispered.

'An agency, darling.'

'Not Central Casting?'

'I beg your pardon?'

'Joke, Grandmama. She looks unreal – that frock, that apron!'

'Her choice, and I rather like it. Her English is far from perfect, but we manage. Her references are excellent.'

'Is she living in?'

'Good gracious, no. She comes in the afternoons and helps.'

'With?'

'With what I need, of course.'

'Does Dad know?'

Isa looked puzzled. 'Your father? Why ever should he know?'

'Well, he was worried when Elspeth—'

'Oh, all that fuss! I am tired of hearing about Elspeth. Cosima has been engaged on quite a different footing.'

At that moment, Cosima appeared, bringing tea. I was about to ask for some water, but saw there was already a carafe of iced water on the tray. 'Thank you, Cosima,' Isa said, with one of her most gracious smiles. The smile deepened as Cosima gave a little bob before leaving.

'Does she come every afternoon?' I asked.

'Heavens, no, only three afternoons.'

'The same as Elspeth, then.'

'Isamay, please, I have heard quite enough about Elspeth, who was not in any case a maid. Cosima is trained. She will be a great comfort to me.'

'Do you need comfort, Grandmama?'

She stared at me, teacup halfway to her lips, and then put it down. 'Is there a hidden meaning in that question, Isamay?'

'No.'

'Good, because a girl of your intelligence knows perfectly well that everyone needs comfort at some time. Cosima provides the sort of comfort I need at the moment.'

'Well, that's nice. What nationality is she?'

'Italian. I have always liked Italians, and their country, especially the city of Florence. Have you been to Florence?'

'No. Rome, I've been to Rome, and—'

'Quite different, Florence is much more beautiful. Your grandfather and I had our honeymoon in Florence.' She drank some tea, and then added, 'If your father had been a girl, I should have named her Florence.' It seemed such an open invitation. What more natural than, having been given this lead, to ask her if she had wanted a girl? So I did, making my enquiry elaborately casual.

'I wanted a child,' Isa said.

'You were how old when Dad was born?'

'Twenty-five.'

'Very young still.'

'It was not thought especially young. My mother had her first child at nineteen.'

'And you'd been married how long?' I asked, very, very cautiously, ready for Isa to be outraged at what she might interpret as a suggestive question.

'Five years,' she said, and paused. 'A long time,' she added, 'to wait for a child. Or so it seemed.'

'I can imagine,' I murmured.

'Can you? I don't think so, Isamay. You know nothing about waiting and hoping.'

Now what was that supposed to mean? But I didn't dare press for an explanation – I was so afraid of upsetting her again. And so I changed the subject, making a feeble link between her comment that I knew nothing of waiting and hoping and one of my own about *waiting* until I'd finished my dissertation, *hoping* it would be satisfactory. She asked me to remind her how far I'd got in my research, and I tried to sum up. I said I had almost decided I'd been mistaken in thinking hereditary factors were more important than those of environment and example; that it was what granddaughters remembered grandmothers as doing and saying that was an influence, not the inheriting of character or personality traits. The hereditary thing only influenced appearance, but—

She interrupted me. 'You have my eyes,' she said.

'I have eyes like yours, yes,' I said, choosing my words so as not to challenge her but at the same time to make a clear distinction between what she'd said and what I was saying.

'Exactly the same unusually violet blue,' Isa said, dreamily, 'and with that slightly darker shading round the iris.'

It was almost as though she were tempting me, as she had done before, but I still hesitated, unsure how far I could go.

'My mother had the same kind of eyes. A family trait.'

'Yes, in your family.' I put only the slightest emphasis on 'your', but it was picked up immediately.

'My family, yes,' Isa said, staring straight at me, 'but not my husband's family. The blue eyes in his family are quite different. Ordinary, really, the Symondson blue. You are lucky to have my family's colour of eye.'

'Millions of people share it, I expect.'

'Millions?' She seemed startled.

'Well, all over the world. I mean, if all the blue-eyed people were examined there would be bound to be millions with our shade of blue.'

Isa frowned. I had the impression that this inane conversation wasn't going the way she had intended, even though I had no idea what her intention was. As usual, she was trying to steer me somewhere I was unconsciously refusing to go. But then she seemed to come to a decision. She stopped talking about eyes. She gave her head a little shake, just a quick movement, barely perceptible, but I saw it because I was watching her so intently, and then she took a deep breath and gripped the arms of her chair as though steadying herself. I had no idea what was coming, only a sense that whatever she was about to say was costing her some peculiar effort of will.

'I want to talk to you about that letter,' she said. I didn't ask what letter, no need to. I felt guilty that I still hadn't got round to finding out more. She turned from looking at me to staring out of the window at the other side of the room, so that her fine profile was all I could see – she wasn't going to look directly at me, which I registered as significant. 'I have contacted those people myself. It seems,' she said, tone of voice a touch scornful perhaps, 'that these, these *people*, have uncovered a relative. A man in an institution, who has died.' She raised her chin higher until it looked as if she was straining her neck horribly. 'He was apparently well cared for, there is no need to imagine maltreatment.'

'What kind of institution? Was he insane?'

'No. I gather he was in some way disfigured. Badly.'

'In some way?'

'I have not enquired. There is no need to imagine an unpleasant story, Isamay. He was said to have been quite content.'

She turned from looking out of the window to looking directly at me, but only for a moment. I couldn't quite decipher her expression – was it defiant, or hesitant? – but I knew she could read mine. I could hardly contain my horror. I swallowed hard, sipped some water, and as the very images she had told me not to imagine filled my mind, I said, 'A man, in an institution, who was . . .'

'A relative,' she said, quickly.

'Was he your br—'

'A relative,' she cut in abruptly, 'that is all I know.'

'But . . .'

'I really do not wish to discuss this, Isamay. He was a relative. He was left some money the year before he died, and I have apparently inherited it. I shall not accept it, of course. I will see that the institution he resided in receives it.'

I was silent. I could see that Isa was relieved by my sudden silence but that she distrusted it. She was waiting for the questions I could not bring myself to ask. And why couldn't I bring myself to ask them? Because they were too enormous to frame, because I was afraid that any answers I forced out of her might appal me. The tinkling noise of Isa's china cup going back on to its saucer relieved the tension a little. 'Can I pour you more tea?' I asked, my voice sounding hoarse, as though I'd been shouting. 'No thank you, darling, I can pour my own.' She sounded so gentle, she was being kind to me because she knew I'd let her off an inquisition, though she didn't know why. It was because I'd realised I could find out about this 'relative' myself. We went on to have some idle chat, and then I left. As I said goodbye, and was leaning over her, she murmured, 'Lovely eyes, just like mine.'

I thought she looked defiant.

XII

IT WAS incredible the way everything seemed to slip back to normal between Ian and me. There seemed to be some kind of unspoken agreement that we wouldn't let any of our worries interfere with our day-to-day living. We were, perhaps, excessively careful with each other, a touch over-considerate (not our usual style), but that was the only indication that there might be more going on under the surface than it appeared.

Then, one afternoon when I was back from the library early, this apparent calm was interrupted. I was tired, sleepy, quite a pleasant feeling, not at all that awful, draining exhaustion I'd experienced early in pregnancy. I decided to go and lie down on our bed instead of slouching on the sofa. It isn't a big enough sofa to slouch on anyway – my legs hang over the end. I pulled the blind, one of those wooden slatted ones, because the sun was making the room harshly bright. I took off my shoes but I didn't take anything else off. I just lay on top of the duvet and almost immediately started to drift. My thoughts trawled idly over what I was writing, over my almost completed dissertation, and then they wandered round my family, little images of them all popping into my head. I was just beginning to try to conjure up a vision of my baby, trying out different faces, different colours of hair and eyes, when something brought me out of my reverie. It was nothing like any kind of noise – it wasn't a doorbell ringing or a telephone – but something else. I lay there feeling suddenly alert. I can't say I was frightened. Our flat is in the middle of the house, with a heavy front door to the house itself, and then another, less substantial, but still solid wooden door into our flat. If someone had broken in downstairs they had a long way to go before reaching me.

I settled down again, convinced I'd simply been on the edge of sleep and had jerked myself awake. There'd been no sound of a door being forced or a window broken, just that feeling of some kind of change in the atmosphere. I couldn't drift off again, however hard I tried, so I gave up and decided to make myself something to eat. As I got up and went into the kitchen and stood with the fridge door open, wondering what was in there that might appeal to me, there was a knock on our front door, the door leading on to our landing, that is. I thought it would be Maisie, who lives above us. Maisie is a nurse. She works shifts, coming and going at all kinds of odd hours. We don't really know her, though we're on friendly enough terms. Twice I've rung her doorbell when I've lost or forgotten my house key, and she's obligingly let me in, and several times I've taken mail in for her (she seems to buy things mail order rather a lot). That's not much interaction in four years but it's enough to make us feel we can depend on each other for help. So I thought it would be Maisie, all apologetic, wanting to ask a favour. I went to the door thinking this would be a good opportunity to invite her in for a cup of coffee – after all, now I was going to have a baby I needed all the friends I could get, especially if they were nurses.

I flung open the door with an extra bright smile on my face and already saying, 'Maisie, why don't you . . .' but it was not Maisie. It was a woman I'd never seen in my life before, a complete stranger. She was tall, taller than I am, well built and with very obviously dyed blonde hair, parted in the middle and tied back, dark roots showing. She stared at me without saying a word. I was still somehow connecting her with Maisie. 'Oh,' I said, 'sorry – did you want Maisie? She lives in the flat above, but she might be at work. Do you want to go and see?' The woman shook her head. I waited, confused. 'Well then, can I take a message?' Now why I said that, I don't know. The woman hadn't even said she wanted Maisie. She hadn't said anything. 'Who is it you want?' I asked, stupidly, wondering if this visitor could possibly have got not just the wrong flat but the wrong house. But someone had let her in. That could only be the Baxters on the ground floor, an elderly couple who kept themselves very much to themselves. If one of them had let this woman in, she couldn't be visiting them.

I began to close the door, starting to feel vaguely uneasy. The woman hadn't answered my query, but to my alarm she put her foot out to stop the door closing. 'Excuse me,' I said, 'I don't know who you are, but—' 'I'm Ian's mother,' she said, 'I want Ian. I want to see my son.' There was a moment of shock, a leaping of my heart, and I put my hand on my chest to quieten it. 'Ian's mother?' I repeated. She nodded. I had registered the Scottish accent. 'Well,' I said, 'you'd better come in – yes, come in, please, but Ian is at work.' 'I'll wait,' she said. There was no hint of a smile or any attempt at conversation. She followed me into the kitchen and I put the kettle on. She didn't sit down, just stood there, stiffly, her handbag clutched with both hands in front of her. 'Please,' I said, 'sit down. Would you like some tea, coffee?' She shook her head, but did sit down, lowering herself with great caution on to the chair as though it might explode on impact. I cleared my throat, and said I was going to make myself a sandwich, would she like to join me. Again, that mutinous shake of the violently blonde head.

It doesn't take long to make a sandwich, but I managed to stretch the simple process out for several minutes, trying to put off sitting down with this woman, who seemed determined to be unfriendly. 'I'll text Ian,' I said, 'and tell him you're here.'

'No!' she said. 'I'll wait. I'll wait till he comes.'

'That might not be for ages.' I looked at the kitchen clock. 'He sometimes isn't home until eight.'

'I'll wait,' she repeated, and clutched her handbag tighter.

'Well, maybe you'd like to wait somewhere more comfortable,' I said, and got up to lead the way to the sitting room.

'I'm fine here.'

'On that hard chair?'

'I'm used to hard chairs.'

'Won't you at least take your coat off?'

'I'm all right.'

I hesitated. I'd offered her food, a drink, a comfortable chair, and they'd all been rejected, and rejected quite brusquely. She wasn't a pleasant woman, for sure. But I wasn't going to be trapped in my own tiny kitchen, obliged to sit upright across the table from her. I gestured to my bump, though there should have been no need to. 'I'm going to lie down,' I said. 'I need a rest. Make yourself at home.' She nodded, looking for the first time slightly uneasy. 'You go along,' she said. 'I'm fine.' So I went. I went back into the bedroom but I didn't close the door. The kitchen is across a small hallway opposite the bedroom, with the door to the sitting room completing a square. Lying on my bed, propped up by pillows, I had a clear view of Ian's mother, still sitting at the table, with her back to me. It struck me that I hadn't shown her the bathroom, but it wouldn't need much investigation to find it – my door was open, the sitting room door was open; the only closed door was the bathroom's.

The scene was as still as a painting. The straight, black back of her, surmounted by the gleaming slick of yellow hair, and beyond, the plain white wall, unadorned save for the round wall clock, itself with a black rim, black figures and white face. The light comes from the north in the kitchen, from the window on the left of the seated woman. It cast no shadows. Her outline was sharp and somehow sinister.

I shivered, though the bedroom was not cold, and pulled the coverlet, lying over the bottom of the bed, across myself. I was aware of doing this as quietly as possible, straining not to draw attention to myself. I wished I had closed the door – it was unnerving constantly having that unbending figure in my vision. I thought again about texting Ian, but I was afraid he might not come home at all if he knew his mother was waiting for him. I closed and then opened my eyes constantly, willing her to move, do something, anything. After about twenty minutes she did move. She laid her handbag – an old-fashioned black leather article with one of those vicious metal clasps – on the kitchen table and pressed upon it. The click echoed through the flat, making me jump. Then out of the bag she drew something I couldn't see. There was another sound, a sound I knew perfectly well, but didn't immediately identify until I saw the smoke rising. She'd lit a cigarette.

I was on my feet in an instant. 'I'm sorry,' I called out, 'you can't smoke here.' The smoke went on rising, and I saw her hand, holding the cigarette, resting on the table before being lifted again. I went to confront her, repeating that I was sorry but she couldn't smoke in our flat. 'We don't allow it,' I said, knowing I sounded impossibly prim. 'We never have done, even before I was pregnant. I hate smoking and so does Ian.'

'Does he now?' she said, and deliberately took another puff. 'I'll just finish the one,' she said. 'I don't like waste.'

'I'd rather you didn't. I'd rather you stubbed it out and saved it for later.'

'It's nearly done,' she said.

But it wasn't. She'd only taken three pulls at it and there was still half of a long cigarette left. I couldn't credit that she could be so brazen, behave so outrageously in the home of someone she had never met. But I couldn't think what to do. Suppose she turned violent, suppose she knocked me down if I moved to snatch the cigarette from her – I didn't want to provoke an incident like that. So I did the only thing I could do. I went to the window and opened it wide. It's only a small window but it can be opened wide on a latch, and I opened it to its full extent. A gust of air blew in at once, sending the things pinned on the noticeboard fluttering and turning the pages of the book left on the table. Ian's mother was entirely unmoved. She went on smoking until her cigarette was finished and I went on standing stupidly by the window. 'Have you a saucer?' she asked, calmly, when she'd finished. I passed a saucer to her. She stubbed out the cigarette end very thoroughly. 'There,' she said, 'you can close the window now and get back to your bed, sweetheart.'

The 'sweetheart' was said with such a sarcastic emphasis that I blushed. God knows what I would have done or said if the phone hadn't rung at that moment. It was my mother. The second I said, 'Oh, Mum,' she knew something was wrong. 'What is it?' she said. 'What's happened? Is it the baby? Are you—'

'No, no,' I said, 'I'm fine. Ian's mother is here.'

'Ian's *mother*?'

'Yes.'

'Heavens. Can you talk?'

'Not really. Later, I'll ring you later. I'll ring back.' And then, ridiculously, I said, 'That was my mother.'

'I heard.'

'I'll have to go and call her back.'

'You do that, dearie.'

There was that same unpleasant stress on the 'dearie' as there had been on 'sweetheart'. I looked at her for a minute, trying, but failing, to outstare her. 'I don't know your name,' I said.

'I'm Ian's mother.'

'That's not a name.'

'It's all you need to know about me.'

'How unfriendly.'

274

She gave a little grunting laugh. 'I'm not here to be friendly, darling.'

'Why are you here?'

'I want Ian. I want to see my son.'

'You've just seen him.'

'No, I haven't.'

'But you rang, and he—'

'I rang but he didn't come.'

'He hasn't been in Glasgow with you?'

'He might have been in Glasgow for all I know but he wasn't with me.'

I believed her. Everything she said, she said with such absolute conviction, firmly, no room for doubt in the way she said it. So where had Ian been? I tried to remember exactly what he'd told me when he came back: very little. It was true he hadn't actually said he was with his mother. I felt so stupid – Ian lived with me, he was my lover and friend, the father of my child, but what did I *really* know about him? I tried to tell myself that I knew all the things that mattered. I knew he was kind, thoughtful, intelligent, considerate, honest – honest? Honest about everything except his past, about where he came from, how he had been brought up, who he had loved, how he had fitted into his family. I'd accepted his argument that these 'details' were irrelevant to who he is even though I didn't agree with him. I'd accepted him as he'd wanted me to accept him: as himself, now. But faced with this alarming woman who is his mother I suddenly realised, with a sense of fear, that I'd been wrong to do that. This woman, and her place in Ian's life, could never be described as irrelevant to him.

She was sitting there, confident and complacent. I couldn't bear it. 'Excuse me,' I said, and this time as I left the kitchen I closed the door, and then once in my bedroom closed that door too. I had to speak to Ian, actually *speak* to him. I rang his mobile. It was turned off. I thought about ringing his work number but I didn't have it – I'd never needed it, I'd never thought of asking for it, I always used his mobile. So I rang my mother instead. 'I'm coming round,' she said, after I'd blurted out an account of the interchange with my visitor, and rang off before I could object.

Mum has her own keys, both to the main house door and to our front door. Ian's mother would think it was Ian coming home when she heard Mum coming up the stairs – briskly; she's very fit and does everything briskly – and putting her key in the lock. I wasn't going to warn her. Why should I? *She* hadn't had the courtesy to tell me her name. I'd let Mum have the advantage. She'd take this rude woman on and deal with her. So I lay there, now very wide awake, and waited. It normally took Mum about twenty minutes to drive over, but if the traffic had begun to build up already then maybe half an hour was more realistic. I listened intently for the sound of her car coming down our quiet street. She has a Peugeot, which has a distinctive engine noise I know well. As soon as I heard it, I would get up and be ready (though ready for what? I wondered).

Mum didn't arrive within half an hour. But Ian did.

It is hard to put all the things that happened that evening into chronological order, even though they didn't happen simultaneously and it should be simple. Order vanished, the way it does during any kind of drama, and these events were dramatic. But though I didn't learn of Isa's death until the end of that day, I have to record it first because it wiped out for a while everything else that had taken place.

What happened was this: Mum was just getting ready to close her front door, to drive over to me, when the phone rang. It was a very frightened Cosima asking her to come quickly. She thought that Mrs Symondson had had a heart attack. Mum went straight to Isa's, but by the time she got there, Isa was dead. Cosima had phoned 999 and an ambulance came remarkably quickly, but Isa could not be revived. There is to be a post-mortem because Isa had not seen a doctor for a long time and had seemed in excellent health. To say, as I repeatedly did, that I didn't believe it could be true was feeble – where was the grief I should have been overwhelmed by? – but it was my genuine reaction. I didn't believe it, partly because it seemed impossible for my grandmother, whom I'd spoken with so recently, now to be silent for ever, and partly because there was so much I needed to know from her. The impossibility of now ever being able to know it couldn't be accepted. After the initial distress, I felt dismay, even anger, not grief, which was all wrong, and I was ashamed.

So, that was the reason Mum didn't arrive at my flat in half an hour. She came round eventually to break the news, but by then we'd had the Big Scene. That was what it was like, a theatrical performance with the actors giving it everything they'd got. I was the audience, spellbound, in the front stalls. First: the sound of the downstairs front door opening. Oh good, I thought, childishly, getting up from my bed, Mum's here. Then the sound of rather heavy footsteps on the stairs. Not Mum's, I thought, unless she's wearing wellingtons. Then I heard the sound of a key in our own front door, by which time I was out of the bedroom. I saw Ian. I pointed at the still closed kitchen door and mouthed, 'Your mother!' He looked puzzled, said just one word, 'What?' and that was enough for his mother to emerge.

So there we were, all three of us, standing in a tight triangle. Me in the bedroom doorway, Ian with his back to the closed front door, his mother in the kitchen doorway. 'Here you are,' she said. 'About time.' Ian stared at her. He stayed absolutely still, not a flicker of response. 'Cat got your tongue?' his mother said. Ian ignored her. He seemed to collect himself together, and without acknowledging his mother in any way walked past her into the living room, where he went and stood looking out of the window. 'For God's sake,' his mother said, irritably, and marched through to join him. She stood directly behind him, up close, and she was whispering, but I couldn't hear her words. Whatever they were, Ian was not replying. Then she raised her voice. 'You listen to me, son, I'm not going away until I've had my say.' Still no movement, no speech, from Ian. I didn't know what had rendered him so mute, but I couldn't bear his mother's bullying tone, and I couldn't bear, either, being a mere spectator to such a bewildering scene. 'Look,' I said, joining them, 'why don't we—' 'You shut up,' his mother snapped. 'This is between me and my son.'

And then Ian did turn round and speak. His face had changed. He was frowning, red-faced and angry. He told his mother not to speak to me like that, how dare she. Then he told her to sit down and try to be civilised. She started to laugh at him, but the laugh turned into a cough, and she did sit down. Her coat was still buttoned up, the bag clutched now to her chest as though I might snatch it. She sat on a battered old chair my father had passed on to me when he bought a new one. The upholstery had split on one of the arms and I'd never done anything about it. Once over her cough, she looked at the stuffing leaking out as if it might contaminate her. I stared at her, examining her feature by feature. I could see nothing whatsoever of Ian in her – not a trace, no fleeting resemblance, no vague possibility of a shared genetic relationship. But I knew this was meaningless. She was Ian's mother. She'd said she was, he hadn't denied it. He must look like his father, a man he once said he'd never known. He told me to sit down, and I did, my knees shaking.

'Leave,' Ian said to his mother, 'before I say something you won't like.'

'Huh! You've already done that scores of times.'

'And you've deserved it.'

It will sound so like a ball being bashed back and forth across a net, all regular and even, thump, thump, first one

278

of them, then the other, but it didn't sound like that at all. There were deadly pauses between the things they said to each other, and the tone of each voice varied from the ultra-soft and menacing to the shrill and venomous. I felt sick listening to them, feeling the hatred between them and yet still having no idea what it was based on. I started to speak but only got as far as 'please' before Ian's mother told me to keep out of this, it was none of my business, she was talking to her son.

'He knows what I want,' she shouted.

'You are a fantasist,' Ian said, very slowly.

'You're no fantasy!' his mother raged back.

'You're a fantasist and I refuse to aid and abet you.'

'Oh, a fantasist, am I? Then where do you come from? You can settle this *fantasy* easily.'

'No.'

'Take the test!'

'No. I refuse.'

'I'll make you.'

'You can't.'

'Oh, see if I can't.'

'Leave. This is Isamay's flat.'

'She asked me in.'

'She asked you in because you are my mother. She didn't know you're a complete fantasist.'

'I am not! I can prove it! All you need to do is—'

'Leave. Now.'

I could see his mother was trembling, either all the aggression was suddenly gone or else she was about to change tactics. She took a cigarette out of her bag, and a lighter.

'No smoking,' I said, feebly. She ignored me, flicking the lighter on, lighting the cigarette, and taking a deep drag. 'Ian?' I said.

'Oh, don't appeal to that one,' his mother said. 'He's a coward, he'll no' do a thing. Scared, he is, aren't you, son?'

But Ian stepped forward, snatched the cigarette from her and stubbed it out viciously on a plate left there.

'My,' his mother said, 'what've you been feeding him, eh?' And she calmly took out another cigarette.

'Look,' I said, desperately, 'I don't know what's going on, but please don't smoke here. Why don't you just tell me why you've come, and what you want?'

'I might do that.'

'Go ahead,' Ian said.

She lit the second cigarette, and I thought if it means getting her to talk, and then leave, what does it matter? So I said nothing, and neither did Ian. He just walked back to the windows and opened both of them wider. The wind blew in, rattling the blinds, and Ian's mother shivered ostentatiously. 'My, it's gone cold in here,' she said. She smoked. One, two, three, four pulls on the cigarette, but they were puffs, not drags, puffs of defiance. 'Well now,' she said, 'it's a long story. Settle yourself, sweetheart, eh?'

I didn't move or speak. I was sitting down anyway. I tried hard to look Ian's mother in the eye, to show her I wasn't afraid of her, though I was. I was afraid of what she was going to tell me. Ian was still near the window. I wished he would come and sit with me, hold my hand, so that we could face this hostile woman, and whatever she was going to say, together. It seemed horribly significant that he had made no move to do so. He went on standing by the window, not even looking directly at his mother, who sat opposite me. I wanted to move but there was no other seat in the room, and she had begun her story. It was, as she'd warned, a long one. She took me back to her childhood, describing exactly what kind of place her family lived in. She said she was pretty, and boys paid her attention from the first. She said she liked the attention and she liked getting away from home, especially away from her mother, who was 'a religious nut' and made her life a misery. At seventeen, she met Mick and fell pregnant. He married her and she had two children by him before she had the sense to go on the pill. They lived in Glasgow but there wasn't much work about and Mick took a job on an oil rig. Good money, but he was away for months at a time and she was still young and she liked to go for a drink with her pals on a Saturday night. And then she met Ian's father. 'And that,' she said, at this point, 'was the result,' nodding towards Ian.

Ian said not a word. I kept turning round, waiting for him to interrupt, at least to hurry her on, or tell her to stop, but he was by then quite detached. I was the one practically in thrall to her, and she knew it. 'Well now,' she said, 'Mick came home one day and there I was, in the family way again, and he knew it couldn't be his bairn, and he said he'd divorce me. He went mental. Threw me out of the house, after he'd slapped me about first, wouldn't let me have my two wee girls, sent them to his mother's, and said that if I used his name on my bastard's birth certificate he'd kill me.' She paused, put her head on one side and, though I hadn't spoken, said, 'What? You're wondering what happened to the pill? Oh, that's easy. I'd stopped bothering, with Mick away so long, and then I got taken by surprise, oh, I did.' And she laughed, and leaned towards me. 'Swept off my feet I was by Ian's dad, he was a very passionate fella all right.' There was another stagey pause, before she again leaned forward and whispered, 'I didna know I was pregnant, see, I came on just the same for four months, not as heavy, but still the bleeding—'

'For God's sake!' Ian erupted, and now at last he did move and stood in front of her. 'Finish the fairy tale and go,' he said.

'I'm talking to your lassie woman to woman,' she said, attempting, and almost attaining, an aggrieved, dignified air. 'I want her to understand how you came about, I have to give her the details.'

'No you do *not*. She doesn't want to hear this stuff.'

'Oh, she does, look at her, she does.'

'I just want to know why you're here. What it is you want from Ian,' I managed to say, speaking very quickly so that I wouldn't give away to Ian, as I'd already given away to his mother, that yes, yes, I *did* want every tiny detail, however distasteful, however much they disgusted him.

'We're getting to that,' she said, and sat back in the chair. 'Are you going to block my view, or do I have to move?' she said to Ian. 'The lassie will want to watch my face, she'll want to see I'm telling the truth.'

'Ian,' I said, 'please sit here, beside me.'

He did. I took his hand. 'Aw,' she said, 'sweet, holding his hand. Now, where was I? Oh, yes, telling you about falling pregnant and never catching on until I was nearly four months. Why didn't you have it seen to, you'll say, it wasn't too late, not these days, but it wasn't these days, it was those days, and in Shettleston even in the 1970s it wasn't easy, it wasn't straightforward, or I'd have done it, I'd have seen to my little mistake, don't you worry. But nobody would help me. My doctor was a Catholic bitch, she wouldn't send me to the right people, and I'd no money to go private and my own mother wouldn't help me, *especially* her. So. I had to go through with it. I had a terrible time, terrible, not like the other times.' Ian started to stand up again, furious with her. 'Sit yourself down. I'm not going to go into it, not when she's expecting herself. So. I had him, and then what could I do? I was stuck back at home again, nowhere else to go, and preached to every bloody day and no money, and I couldn't get my wee girls back.'

Ian made a dismissive sound, not unlike one of May's grunts.

'Oh?' she said, 'You think I didna try?'

'I think you didn't care,' Ian said.

'And how would you know that, my wee man?'

'I know.'

'Look,' I said, 'can we . . .'

'Just get on with it,' she finished for me. I nodded. 'So,' she said, 'no money, living at home with my saintly ma, and what way out did I have? Eh? You won't guess? You think you can guess? Well, you'd be right. I met another fella, Sammy. Worked on the railways. He was older, been married before, like me. He had a place in Caldercoats, in Glasgow. I moved in, with Ian. He was a good man, Sammy, wasn't he, Ian?'

'This has nothing to do with anything,' Ian said.

'Well, maybe on that one you're right. Sammy has nothing to do with your father and why I'm here, which is what this lassie wants to know. So, Sammy died. He was fifty-four, and he had a stroke at work and he died five days later in hospital. I wasn't his widow, I didn't get the pension, I hadn't—'

'Stop!' shouted Ian, and this time he stood up again and began pacing about. 'What she's going to drag you through,' he said, 'is how she went from man to man and I was the big handicap until suddenly I was a possible asset if she could convince people I was who she said I was, who she says I am, which she can't because it's a complete fantasy. There isn't a shred of proof.'

'Then take the test,' his mother said, quietly.

I must have looked as I was feeling – completely confused and lost. Ian's mother smiled. Somehow she seemed to think she was winning whatever game she and Ian were playing, with me as piggy in the middle. 'Do you know what test I mean?' she asked. I shook my head. 'A DNA test,' she said. 'It's a way these clever scientist boyos have of—'

'I know what a DNA test is,' I said.

'Right. Well then, that's all he has to do. Take the test. Prove I'm right. Prove that his father was who I've told him it was. Where's the harm?'

'The harm,' Ian said, 'is what it does to me, but you

wouldn't care about that, of course, you wouldn't even recognise how I might be harmed.'

'You're right there, sonny. You should be proud to know you're the son of—'

'For God's sake!' Ian roared, before she could get the name out, and then he said, 'Isamay, please, go into the bedroom and close the door. *Please.*'

Ian's mother laughed. 'Oh, dearie, dearie me,' she gasped, 'what a state he gets in! Afeared of the very name! All right, all right, don't send her away, poor lamb. I won't say it, I won't say the name. I'll get on with it. When you were five, I saw his photograph in the paper, when he had the accident and died, and I thought my God, it's him, and—'

'The pound signs flashed,' Ian said. 'But it didn't work, your ridiculous scam.'

'No,' his mother said, 'nobody believed me and I couldn't prove it. But now I can. I could've proved it the last twenty years, if only I'd known about DNA sooner. Oh, it's dangerous, isn't it, Ian darlin', when the likes of me gets educated in such things? Eh? All I need is you to oblige . . .'

'And I won't. I've told you that again and again. I don't want to know who my father was, and especially not now, when I know exactly why you've started all this crap again. Isamay, *please* let me have five minutes on my own with this woman, please.'

I got up and did as he asked. His mother made no objection, no attempt to stop me. I closed the bedroom door and lay down on the bed, relieved to do so. With the sitting room door shut as well, I couldn't hear a thing. They weren't shouting, anyway, or I'd surely have been able to hear some sound. I looked at my watch: 6.10. At 6.32, I heard the sitting room door open, and then there was a short interchange, maybe a couple of sentences each, between Ian and his mother. I could hear their voices without being able to make out the words. Were they angry? I debated their tones of voice with myself. No, not exactly angry so much as firm, on Ian's part, and threatening on his mother's. There was the squeak of the hinges on the door that opens on to the landing. So Ian's mother was leaving. Would he see her down the stairs and into the street? Yes, I could hear him go. I waited. He came back up the stairs very slowly indeed. I waited again. He seemed to hesitate outside the bedroom door. 'Ian?' I called. He came in and took his shoes and jacket off, lay down beside me and took my hand.

I don't know why I still felt so frightened. She'd gone, but what she'd left behind, the atmosphere in the flat, scared me. 'Ian,' I began, but he put his hand lightly over my mouth. 'Sssh,' he said, 'later. Rest, sleep for a bit.'

Surprisingly, I did, and so did he, I think, because when Mum arrived, to break the news about Isa, we were both still lying on the bed. The shock was awful but it was somehow numbed by what had already taken place that evening. I couldn't tell Mum about what Ian's mother had said, about the scene there'd been, not in front of Ian, and in fact she was too wound up about Isa's death to ask many questions. Ian made us all tea but I didn't drink mine. Mum said I looked shattered and I should try to sleep and we'd talk the next day. I didn't think I'd be able to sleep – my mind was racing, going over and over everything that had happened – but after Ian had seen Mum out, he came and lay beside me again, held me, and I calmed down, and eventually sheer physical exhaustion took over, and I did sleep.

I slept for fourteen hours. Ian had gone when I woke up at almost ten in the morning, but there was a note on his pillow. It merely said what I'd have known anyway, that he'd gone to work, and he'd see me later, lots of love. Nothing else. It depressed me that he couldn't at least have promised to explain everything when he came home – surely he wasn't going to carry on this not-really-talking business. I could hardly get out of bed but I badly needed to, and forced myself up. The sun coming through the frosted glass of the bathroom window dazzled me, and I stumbled and hit my hip on the corner of the bath. I had to sit down to stop my legs shaking – I just felt so feeble and weepy, and resented Ian not being there.

Eventually I pulled myself together enough to shower and get dressed, then I drifted into the kitchen to make the coffee I didn't feel like drinking, just to make things seem normal. But of course things were not normal. The last twenty-four hours had been wildly abnormal. I needed to reclaim some semblance of normality, but how? The only way I knew: by working. By sitting down at my desk and steadily working through my notes. By taking myself away from the memory of Ian's mother, and everything she had said, and concentrating on other women, my grandmothers. But then I was distracted when it struck me that my child was going to have Ian's mother as one of her grandmothers. Of course, that's how it would be, Ian's mother in the role of the Bad Grandmother, a woman whose genes had already been passed on to her. We couldn't get rid of her. Ian hadn't managed it. My child had no chance.

Inevitably, May had to be told about Isa's death (the post-mortem revealed she'd died of an aortic aneurysm). I was afraid she might glory in it, be almost triumphant that she had survived 'Lady Muck', but she was clearly shocked and, without being ghoulish, wanted to know every detail of what had happened. 'You never know,' she said, 'you never know the minute.' She said it in awe of Isa's fate, her face creased with concern. I thought she'd be eager to go to the funeral, but no, she said she'd 'gone off' funerals.

I don't know why Mum had told her about Ian's mother turning up – maybe to take her mind off death – but May rang me up in a great state of indignation.

'What's this? What's this I hear?'

'I don't know what you've heard, Granny.'

'About that woman turning up, about the carry-on.'

'Oh, it was nothing.'

'Nothing? Don't sound like it. Bloomin' cheek, fancy her barging in like that, and you carrying her grandchild, scandalous.'

'Granny, don't let it upset you.'

'Was she right in the head? That's what I want to know. Is she barmy?'

'Not really.'

'Well, what's this bee in her bonnet about? What's this about your fella's father?'

'I don't know. She's confused, she—'

'Confused? Blimey, she's more than confused if she's taken all this time to tell the boy who his dad is.'

'It wasn't quite like that.'

'What was it like, then? What was she doing there? What is she after? Is there money somewhere, eh?'

'Could be.'

'Bound to be. I knew it. Has your fella's dad just died or something?'

'I don't think so. Ian hasn't explained yet.'

'Well, he'd better. It ain't good for you and it ain't good for me, all this. I'll be going the way of your other grandma any minute, I will.'

I slept again all afternoon. I was still lying there when Ian came home.

'I *have* been up,' I murmured, thinking he might imagine I hadn't stirred since he'd left.'

'Good. And have you eaten?'

'Yes.'

'Good.'

'And now I'm ready to hear it all, Ian, every little bit, OK? No more putting off.'

'Am I allowed some food myself first?'

'Only if you're quick.'

He came and sat on the bed with a plate of food and ate steadily while he related his history in a straightforward way. He spoke slowly, in short bursts, pausing while he ate some more, and then starting again. It seemed to help him that he was consuming food, engaged in a simple activity, and not just talking, and I think it helped, too, that because I was lying down, and he was sitting beside me, we were not staring at each other. He'd told me before he started not to ask questions till he got to the end, so I didn't, though from the beginning of his recital they crowded in on me. The story of his childhood was told flatly, but even so it was distressing to hear, and the fact that it was sadly familiar enough didn't make it any less so. His mother always had some man living with her after Sammy had died. Ian's first memory of a stepfather (though since his mother never married again these men were not real stepfathers) was not of Sammy but of Pete. Pete must, Ian reckoned, have stayed about two years but he dominates Ian's earliest recollections. Pete drank, his mother drank, there were fights, though Ian himself was never struck. He learned, as such children do, to keep out of the way, which often meant under the bed, or, as he grew older, and other stepfathers behaved in much the same way, out of the house. His only ally was his maternal grandmother, who sometimes came and took him to her home. She lived in two rooms in a tenement block with a bed set into an alcove in each of the rooms. Ian was happy with her but he was never there long. His mother, instead of being glad to get rid of him, as might have been expected, kept wanting him back. It wasn't, he was sure, through affection or consideration for his welfare. She just seemed to want to own him. But then, when he was about fourteen, a new man, Stuart, came into his mother's life. He was, said Ian, a very nasty piece of work. There was no need, he said, to go into the nastiness, and he personally didn't suffer from it. The point was, eventually he could no longer stand it. It had taken him a long time to work out what was happening, but then he was young, only fourteen when it started. Stuart would bring a 'mate' home. The mate would stay the night and be gone in the morning. These mates didn't like Ian being around, so his mother would tell him to go to his room and stay there, which he was only too glad to do. Sometimes there would be weeks without Stuart bringing anyone home, and then it would start up again, this 'bed and breakfast' as Stuart called it. So far as Ian could tell, his mother didn't seem to object. Every time a strange man stayed, Stuart would buy her new clothes or jewellery. But then one morning, Ian, still in his room, heard his mother shouting at Stuart, and Stuart shouting back. The words were indistinct, but he could tell his mother was objecting and Stuart was threatening. Ian crept to the top of the stairs and peered down, into the kitchen. He saw some banknotes on the table. Stuart was giving his mother some of them and his mother was trying to take more. Suddenly, he understood. As soon as he could, he went to his grandmother's. He asked if he could stay for good. She said of course, but that his mother would come and claim him, and she warned him that she had the right.

So Ian prepared himself. He carefully wrote down an account of Stuart's behaviour and sent it to the police station near where his mother lived. Social workers appeared. Ian was closely questioned. A court order was issued. He was allowed to live with his grandmother. He remained with her for four years, until he went to university. His mother did keep appearing but he managed, as he grew bigger and stronger, to face her down, and of course there was the court order on his side. Once he left his grandmother's home and came to London, he didn't see his mother for ten years, till just before he met me.

So far, so good, meaning I'd understood what Ian was

telling me, even if I had loads of questions to ask. But the next bit was difficult to make sense of. Ian was well aware of this. He'd finished his food, and was sitting with his arms crossed and his eyes closed, as though forcing himself to stay still and concentrate. 'She said she had something to tell me, "in your interest", as she put it.'

'How did she find you?'

'I don't know. Anyway, she did find me. I was living in Vauxhall. She turned up, just like she did yesterday. Luckily, I was on my own, my flatmates were out. I didn't even recognise her straightaway, I really didn't. It had been ten years, more than ten, and she looked very different, her hair, her clothes, and she'd put on weight. She said she wanted to get to know me, let bygones be bygones, she was my mother after all. I said I didn't want to know her. I forget how I put it, but maybe that's because I want to forget, it was all so embarrassing and somehow humiliating. I just wanted rid of her, but she wouldn't go. She said I should try to see things from her point of view, now I was grown up and "a man of the world". I didn't say anything. Then she asked me if I'd ever wondered who my father was. I said I'd never been interested. As far as I was concerned, he didn't deserve to be known. She said she'd tell me if I wanted. I said no thanks. I actually said "no thanks" as though she'd offered me a sweet. She just wouldn't go, sat there smoking and staring at me and rambling on. She said I got my brains from my father, he'd been a clever bastard too, she should have known the type – and I stopped her. She said right, she'd done her best to "make amends", "heal the breach". She said I'd regret not taking the opportunity to learn where I came from, whose blood I had, who I was. I said I knew who I was, and she laughed. "You've no idea, son," she said. And then she gave me a name. I'm not going to repeat it. She said that this man with the famous name had been my father. I knew instantly it was a fantasy.'

He was nearly at the end. For a while, he stopped talking and I didn't know if I was going to have to press him to tell me why his mother had turned up again. I ought to have guessed, of course. Ian's father, the man whose name he refused to repeat, had been killed in a car accident, years ago, but *his* father, Ian's alleged grandfather, had only just died, at the age of ninety-one, and he'd died intestate. If Ian took a DNA test and proved he was this man's grandson, he could claim the estate, or at least part of it. And his mother expected him to share it with her, 'for all I've suffered', as she'd put it.

Another long silence. I was appalled by what Ian had told me about his mother, but eventually, shakily, I said, 'Permission to ask questions now.' He smiled slightly, a tired smile, and said, 'Go on then, but not too many.'

'To begin at the end,' I said, 'what did you say to your mother yesterday, how did you make her leave?'

'I reminded her about my name, all the complications. My name on my birth certificate is Wallace, because she was still married to Mick Wallace when she gave birth to me. I changed it by deed poll later. Mick had thrown her out, but the divorce wasn't yet through. My alleged father's name isn't on the certificate.'

'But her point is still that a DNA test would prove who your father was, so it wouldn't matter.'

'It might. There are other claimants, and it could even weaken my claim. It would be clear that my supposed father had rejected me, denied I was his, didn't want my mother's offspring to have anything to do with his family. And then I reminded her of the cost of a legal battle. She has no money – obviously that's why she's doing this, to get money – and I have none, and even if I had I would never make this claim.'

'Did she still want you to have a DNA test?'

'Of course. Which makes me suspicious. She *says* this man was my father but I think there's a hint she isn't absolutely sure. If she had been so sure even pre-DNA testing, I think she'd have tried harder.'

'What could she have done?'

'I don't know. Turned up at his family home, it's a famous enough place – something like that. She did nothing else until his father died. She's a chancer, that's all.'

'Do you think she really believes you'd get some money? And that you'd share it with her?'

'Yes, in her fantasies, if she can prove I'm his grandson.'

'She *is* a bit, she's a bit . . .'

'Unbalanced is the kindest word.'

'Don't you feel, well, sorry for her, in a way?'

'Which way?'

'I don't know. Just, it sounds such a mess of a life.'

'She made the mess.'

'You're very certain. But how can you be?'

'My grandmother.'

'That's not an answer – your grandmother what?'

'My grandmother wasn't the religious bigot my mother says. She wasn't a bitch. She was a good, kind, decent woman who brought her daughter up well.'

'You know that, do you?'

'Yes.'

'But you weren't there, you weren't alive, you can't know what went on.'

'All I'm saying is that my mother had a good start. Whatever she did, once she grew up, was her own doing.'

'Maybe she was "unbalanced" because it was innate, a genetic—'

'Cut the lecture, Issy.'

'It wasn't going to be a lecture. I was just saying that if there was nothing in your mother's upbringing to make her what she seems to be, then, logically, she was born that way, unpleasant, nasty, a fantasist, according to you, and so perhaps it isn't her fault.'

'I'm getting tired of this blame the genes stuff, Issy.'

I wasn't, though. I can't think of anything else except all the unknown genes floating in my baby's system. There are enough *respectable* unknowns on my own side of the family, but on Ian's there's a weird mother and a truly unknown father. I wish Ian would take the DNA test so that at least the man his mother said was his father could be ruled in or out.

But he won't.

It suddenly struck me when I woke up in the middle of that night that Ian still hadn't told me where he'd been in Glasgow. His mother said that he hadn't come to her, which is why she'd had to come in search of him. So where had he been? Why had he come back so drained and tired? As soon as we woke up, I was on the attack. 'Ian, where did you go in Glasgow? I know you didn't go to your mother's. Where did you go, and why, and why did you deliberately give me the impression you *were* going to your mother's?' I was beginning to sound tearful.

'All right, I'll answer part one of that if you promise not to harangue me about the rest.' He was up and dressed by then, ready to leave the bedroom and have his breakfast and set off on the long ride to work. I thought I'd shock him into telling me what I wanted to know. 'You have a wife in Glasgow, don't you, Ian?'

He spun round, his expression one of absolute bewilderment. 'A *wife*?' he said. 'Are you mad?' I shook my head slowly. 'Oh, come on, Issy, you know that's bonkers. Of course I haven't a wife in Glasgow or anywhere else. What the hell are you playing at?'

'What are *you* playing at, Mr Mysterious Visit to Glasgow? Don't you see, if you don't tell me, I'd be tempted to believe anything. *Of course* I don't think you've got a wife in Glasgow, but . . .'

He was angry, but also, I could see, relieved. He'd certainly thought for a second that I'd believed he had another woman. I thought he might be too annoyed with me now to tell me where he'd been, but he sat down on the bed again and said, 'I went to see my grandmother.'

'Christ, I thought you said she was dead!'

'No, I never said that, but she might as well be. She's in a home, in a bad state. She doesn't know me, really.' I choked back all the questions that rushed into my mind, knowing Ian would clam up if I asked even one. 'I went to see her then because . . .' He stopped. 'I thought maybe . . .' and again he halted. Finally, with a huge effort, he said, 'I thought I ought to ask her about, you know, *him*. I've never asked her, she's never mentioned a name. But I'd trust her. I thought it might be a way of putting an end to my mother's fantasy. Or, yes – before you say it – confirming it. I don't want to know who he was but it just seemed . . . she won't live much longer, it just seemed something I should have heard from *her*.' He got up again. 'Shall I bring you some coffee?' His back was to me, so I couldn't see his face, but his voice sounded upset. 'Yes, thanks,' I said. But he didn't leave the room at once. I hadn't asked a single thing. 'She wasn't able to speak,' he said, 'she just mumbled. I haven't visited often enough for her to know me as she used to. My fault. She's not demented or anything, but nothing I was talking about seemed to make any sense to her. I'll make the coffee.'

I wished I hadn't forced him into telling me about going to see his grandmother, but on the other hand it showed me so much about him that he hadn't wanted me to know. Later, without any encouragement, he told me more about her (though he still wouldn't tell me her name for some reason). It distresses him that she's had to be in a home for the last few years, but there was no one to look after her, and Ian's mother hadn't been near her for nearly twenty years. Ian had sent money to a neighbour, to go in to see his grandmother every day, but it wasn't possible to arrange the twenty-four-hour care she needed. He'd only visited her twice a year (times, I realised, when he went off on cycling trips), feeling guilty but doing nothing, in effect, to lift the guilt. It was all so sad. He said he could hardly bear witnessing the care Isa and May received, especially May, when he thought of his own grandmother and her circumstances. Talking about it would have only hurt more, and have made him feel even more ashamed. His grandmother had done everything for him, and here he was, virtually abandoning her when she needed him.

Eight in the morning is not the time of day to make this kind of confession, but if Ian hadn't blurted all this out then I don't think he ever would have done. There was no chance to talk to him about it before he had to rush off, late, for work, and when he came home he wouldn't discuss it – the shutters were down again, the whole topic forbidden once more. I was left to do what I am always doing, speculating, trying to fit the pieces together.

XIII

THE DAY before I was due to hand in my completed dissertation, I suddenly decided that the conclusion, the final few pages that should have drawn the whole thing together, weren't working. They strained for effect and ended on a flat note. So I ditched them. Then I sat at my computer, staring at the blank screen in a state of near panic. It was uncomfortable sitting there anyway, in such an advanced state of pregnancy, but the physical misery was nothing compared to the mental torture. Ideas and words would not come. I only knew in the vaguest way possible what I needed, and I was waiting, helpless, without any confidence that given time (which I didn't have) the words I wanted would appear.

They formed themselves around midnight, in that beautifully serendipitous way that can sometimes happen. Ian, in the background, in the other room, was watching something on TV about the President elect Barack Obama, whose memoir *Dreams from My Father* he'd been reading that week. I'd picked the book up myself, and read some of it, the early stuff, and I suddenly remembered a passage about Obama's grandmothers, which had, naturally, attracted my attention. That's all it took. I went and got the book and read it again, the bits about his maternal grandmother especially. He stressed how important she had been when he was still so unsure of himself and his ambitions. 'What is a family?' he asked, and then considered what the definition might be. A family could simply be a collection of people linked by a genetic chain; a family could be a social contract; a family could be an economic unit. It could be one or a combination of all three. But what grabbed me was Obama's other, alternative suggestion: a family could be 'a reach across the void'. That void was time. His grandmothers, in very different ways, had done the reaching. He'd lived with his white grandparents as a child, and had watched his grandmother leaving the house very early each morning to catch a bus to the bank where she worked, as a clerk, to support her family. She had expected from her grandson the same hard work and determination she had shown herself and demonstrated to him. She reached across the void to teach by example. His paternal grandmother, whom Obama didn't meet till he was an adult, set another example. Hers was one of endurance in the face of catastrophe. It seemed to him that both grandmothers had expectations of him. He felt there was nothing simple about the genetic chain – his grandmothers had forged the strong links that bound him to them, and he could not, and did not want to, break them. The message in his case, he decided, was one of determination and stoicism – 'They all asked the same thing of me, these grandmothers of mine.'

It was a bit romantic, but I felt I could take from his feelings enough to pull together the strands I hadn't quite succeeded in plaiting strongly enough myself. The whole point of my dissertation had been to try to establish that grandmothers provide a continuity of a spiritual as well as a genetic sort, that there *is* some 'reaching across the void'. I had to work hard to make all that sound connected to everything that had gone before, but finally I did it. I rewrote those last pages four times before I got rid of the slightly portentous tone, but in the end I was pleased. My conclusions were clearer and carried conviction.

Whether I believe them myself is another matter.

* * *

297

Dissertation done, gone, I have nothing to do but loll around, if I want, waiting for the baby to be born. But it is the wrong time of year to be so free – I long for summer, so that I can be in the open air, because it isn't much fun roaming parks in this grey, drizzly weather. I can't seem to apply myself to what I should do next. I'm drifting, making my condition the excuse. I long for invitations, to anything, to go anywhere. I've met Beattie a few times, gone with her and her children to the playground near where she lives. A disaster. I don't know whether her kids are particularly demanding or not, but they never seem to leave their mother alone for a minute, always clutching at her, calling for her, interrupting anything she attempts to say. I didn't know what I was doing there. 'You soon will,' Beattie said, a trifle grimly, I thought, and after one afternoon spent in her house and not the playground, because of the rain, I saw what she meant – being in the open was definitely preferable.

Lunches with Dad were always something to look forward to, but now they've become glittering dates in my empty diary. I had lunch with him yesterday, but it wasn't as enjoyable as usual. I arrived at his café of choice to find him unusually morose, sitting with an untouched glass of wine in front of him, staring at the menu chalked on a blackboard as though he couldn't understand it. He asked me what I would like, and I said he could choose for me, but he shook his head and said no, you choose for me, I can't be bothered. I ordered the meze. Some pitta bread and olives, his favourite sort, arrived while we waited but he left them alone. Gloom seemed about to settle. Luckily the café was busy, quite full, and the general noise and bustle covered our silence. I didn't ask what was wrong. Isa had only been dead three weeks. I felt depressed myself. Dad's low spirits would also, I was sure, have something to do with Isa's brother's legacy, about which, for weeks now, there had been a lot of trouble. I was right.

The problem was that Isa had in fact received the legacy

before she died but she had not had the time to make it over to the home where her brother had lived all those years. It should have been simple for Dad to do this for her, but for some reason it was proving legally complicated. But quite apart from all that, it emerged, as I ate my food greedily and he picked at his, what was bothering him was an uncomfortable feeling that he should go and inspect this institution that was to benefit from the money. He felt that it was his duty to make sure that what was a fairly large sum should only go to a decent establishment. This was what his conscience was telling him. And he was tempted to tell it to shut up.

'Guilt, is it?' I said.

'Suppose so.'

'But it isn't your guilt. None of whatever that poor man had to endure is your fault. It's got nothing to do with you. You didn't even know he existed.'

'I ignored signs.'

'Signs? What signs?'

'I think there were hints, and I ignored them.'

'What kind of hints? From whom, how?'

'Oh, little things, even before that Canadian cousin, what was her name . . .'

'Mary-Lou?'

'Mary-Lou. Even before she came up with that evidence that Isa had had a brother, I'd shut my mind to certain puzzling remarks my mother used to make.'

'Such as?'

'She'd refer to bothersome letters that were annoying her and I never showed any real concern – I just thought she meant letters about finance of some sort, to do with her stocks and shares, which she was often fussing about. But I know now that I'd sensed they were not. She was nervous about these bothersome letters in a way that was different.'

'That's hindsight. I don't believe you sensed anything at the time.'

'Well I should have done. I should have checked she didn't just mean letters about money. I never did.'

He sighed, and said he would have to visit the place. I said he didn't need to go himself, he could easily get it checked out, or he could get someone to go for him if he felt a personal investigation was essential. I said I could go, I wasn't doing anything, but he shook his head at the idea. No, he would have to go himself.

'Where are these letters anyway?' I asked. 'Have you read them?'

'No. I didn't find any. She must have destroyed them.'

'Are you sure it was her brother writing to her? I mean, how did he have her address? He'd never even met her. How did he know he had a living sister?'

'I've no idea.'

'Well, anyway, he wasn't mad, or disabled enough not to be able to write.'

'Apparently not.'

'What was wrong with him, then? Why was he hidden away like that? Why wasn't Isa happy to hear she had a brother? When *did* she hear, when did these letters start?'

Dad groaned, and rubbed his eyes till he must have made them sore. He said he didn't know the answer to most of my questions, questions he'd asked himself ever since he learned of the legacy, and that was what shocked him, his own ignorance. He ought to know, and he didn't.

'Well,' I said, gently, 'you can find out. Now Isa's dead, nothing you discover can hurt her. It should be simple, I would've thought, getting most of the answers. They're pretty obvious questions.'

'But that's the awful thing – I don't *want* to know the details. I ask myself the questions, as you do, but I don't really want the answers. The thought of them appals me. It's a scandalous story.'

'You don't really know that the story *is* scandalous.'

300

'Putting a child into an institution, letting him live there all his wretched life, and all the time ignoring his attempts to communicate with them – how could that not be scandalous?'

'But you don't know the circumstances. Think how your own history could be interpreted. There may be explanations you can't even guess at that would make the fate of Isa's brother far from scandalous. That's why you have to find the answers to all your questions even if you dread them.'

He shook his head, said he'd been through all this with Mum, who said just what I did. We might be right, but it didn't make him feel any differently. I offered again to help. I said I didn't need to visit the home, if he was so opposed to my doing so, but what about my going down to Somerset and seeing some of the relatives who'd come to Isa's party? They would surely know something.

'No,' Dad said, 'I don't want old people upset.'

'You don't know they would be upset.'

'Raking over the past is always upsetting when it's that kind of past.'

'But Isa's dead.'

'Yes, but it was her behaviour while alive that we'd be uncovering, and that remains shameful.'

'There would be no need to tell them about the letters or that Isa ignored them. I'd only talk to them about her parents, see if they knew about the brother and what happened to him.'

'No. I don't want you to. I have to deal with this myself.'

I know he won't. I'm going to carry out my own investigation, though. No need to tell Dad. I know how his mind works, and what would upset him. I know how he will slowly begin to convince himself that there is no need to visit the home. He will not even imagine the unpleasant scenarios that are constantly invading *my* mind. He will tell himself that there is no point in attempting to uncover what is at best a sad story and at worst a shocking one. He does not suffer from my insatiable curiosity. A sense of a story unfinished will not bother him for long. It will go on bothering me. His conscience troubles him at the moment, but soon it won't. I know my father.

The man I am finding I still know even less well than I thought is, in spite of recent revelations, Ian Scott. I don't know a simple, basic thing like his surname. Why did he really change it? What is the significance of his having changed it to Scott? Surely it wasn't just because he *is* a Scot? And added an extra 't' for the look of it? But he keeps his original surname hidden, together with everything else about his background. He won't tell me his mother's name. It is, he says, of no consequence. Well, it is to me. I need to know her name because I want to find out all I can about her, I want to understand what has made her into the horrible woman she seems to have become. Ian laughs at the idea of any information explaining his mother's behaviour. I said maybe he is right, but I have to start somewhere. 'No,' Ian said, 'you have to *stop* somewhere, Issy.'

But I can't, and won't. I have my child to think of.

Ian's mother's name is Moira. Moira Janet Macpherson, born 8 November 1956. It wasn't too difficult to find out, as Ian should have known. She'd told me herself that she'd got married at seventeen to Mick Wallace, so although Wallace is a common surname in Scotland, I had something to go on.

Moira's mother, Ian's grandmother, the one who took him in, is called Janet. Her father, Ian's grandfather, was Hugh Macpherson, an engine driver. It pleases me so much to have even this kind of basic knowledge of Ian's family. Pleases me, but also makes me greedy to find out more. What about those half-sisters? I am so tempted, and yet I hesitate. Ian never knew them, they were never part of his life. And maybe they have turned out as unpleasant as their mother. I think maybe I ought to leave that one alone, for the time being, anyway.

Finding out information about Isa's brother was more difficult. Thanks to Mary-Lou, I had his birth certificate already and it was straightforward obtaining the death certificate. Cause of death was lobar pneumonia and heart failure, which told me nothing about how he came to have lived in an institution, how long he had been there, or why his sister appeared not to have known of his existence until she began receiving his letters when she was around sixty (that's when Dad roughly dates the beginning of Isa making references to bothersome communications). I spent a long time on the phone tracking down the name of the home where James Macdonell had resided (though he'd actually died in hospital) and even longer finding someone to talk to who knew how he came to be there, and what was wrong with him. There seemed to be a strange reluctance to go into details, and nobody seemed to know exactly what had happened, or even when. I said, when finally I was able to speak to the warden, that surely there must be a file on James Macdonell, notes of his condition and so forth, and some history of where he was from and how he'd been treated. I was told these were confidential and I would have to prove I was related and then apply for access, which would involve a fee. So I applied. Six weeks went by before I heard anything at all, and I began to think of resorting to plan B – going to Bath and visiting one of the relatives. But that would have meant directly disregarding Dad's wishes, and I was reluctant to do this.

The medical file when it arrived was thick. What it told me explained a lot but still left a great deal mysterious. I learned that James Gavin Macdonell was born very prematurely, at twenty-eight weeks, and suffered oxygen deprivation at birth. He weighed only 3 lb 6 oz. He was kept in hospital for three months, finally being discharged when he'd reached

7 lb 2 oz, though he still had mild respiratory problems. One month after he arrived home, he was badly scalded. The burns were mainly over his face and left shoulder. There were masses of entries about his injuries and what was done for them, but the language was mostly too medical for me to understand. He was in a burns unit for nearly a year, and then there is a gap in the notes until he was four, when he broke his right leg. The records of numerous illnesses follow, but I was so numbed by this catalogue of tragedy that I hardly took them all in. I concentrated instead on tracking addresses, where given. I quickly realised that poor James had not been in the home near Bath for long. He'd been in a series of other homes across the south-west of England. Some of the earlier ones were schools – School for Disabled Children, School for Physically Afflicted Young Adults, a whole list of Dickensian-sounding institutions. It was a litany of misery.

But I still didn't know how baby James came to be scalded, or what effect the oxygen deprivation at birth had had, or why his well-off family couldn't arrange care at home, or why his sister was never told about him. Medical records don't reveal that kind of thing. Maybe today there would be reports from social workers included, but not then. It seemed to me inevitable that I'd have to consult either Uncle George or Isa's sister-in-law, whose name I couldn't remember. They could fill in the gaps, maybe. Still I hesitated. I contacted the warden of the home again, but she was suspicious of my motives even after I'd said who I was. My father, I was told, was in possession of all the facts. I should ask him.

Everything I was learning about James Gavin Macdonell was unbearable to know, and yet I don't regret knowing it. Is that because I am so far removed from any connection with the tragedy? I try to imagine it, but even that seems shameful. Suppose this baby of mine . . . but that's a route it is too dangerous to go down. Isa, of course, closed her mind to any inkling of what those bothersome letters might mean.

Somewhere, though, she had that 'private' memory tormenting her decades later. Of a baby screaming? Of a nursemaid shrieking? Of a mother howling? Of general chaos, pandemonium in the house? But then I thought of the very existence of letters. James Gavin Macdonell could apparently write, or else was sufficiently intelligent to dictate letters. Oxygen deprivation at birth could not have entirely damaged his mental faculties – he had been capable of composing a letter, and he apparently knew he had a sister.

It is very difficult to forgive, or to understand, Isa's attitude. She hated any kind of disfigurement – even warts on someone's face had her shuddering – but if she didn't know about her brother, how did she know, when he wrote to her, that he was so badly facially scarred? Did he tell her? Possibly, but if he was hoping to meet her, he would hardly have dwelt on his appearance. I think the very sight of his name at the end of any letter must have caused her great alarm. She didn't want a man coming out of the past to claim her – she was perhaps instinctively afraid. That's the best excuse I can make for her. It's still an excuse.

Another excuse is needed for my 'real' great-grandmother, she who, according to the story Patrick told my father, was only too relieved to let the wife of her dead daughter's lover claim him. I know her name – oh, how the names are gathering! She was called Gladys Walker. Her daughter, my 'real' grandmother, was called Elizabeth. Elizabeth when she died soon after giving birth was twenty-seven. I had a bit of luck there (I mean, trying to find out about Elizabeth). At Isa's funeral I met a man who had served in the same regiment as Patrick, my grandfather. Never mind his name, there are enough names already, but the point is that he turned out to have known about Elizabeth Walker. I didn't, of course, bring her name up – at the time, I didn't even know it – but in his ramblings about Isa, he did. 'A fine woman,' he said, 'fine woman, stood by her man in times of trouble, no hesitation.'

I said did he mean the war? He was very deaf, and I had to shout the words again, asking him if he meant during the war. He was impatient, said no, no, good heavens, no, he meant after the war, 'over the little secretary and all that hoo-ha'. I nodded politely, desperately keen for him to spill out more indiscretions and wondering how I could prompt him. But he needed no prompting. Old age seemed to make him feel free to recall anything he liked without worrying about possible consequences. I wasn't the only one who heard him remember my grandfather being 'infatuated, swept off his feet by that girl, the Walker girl, pure madness, but his wife stood by him when it was over, a fine woman'.

The sleuth work was easy on this one. My real grandmother was born in 1926, in Nottingham. Her father was an optician; her mother, Gladys, a nurse. Her father was killed in the war and the widow Gladys moved with her only child, Elizabeth (aged fourteen), to London, to live with an aunt in Putney. Gladys got a job at St Bart's Hospital, but when Elizabeth was twenty-two, her mother emigrated to Australia. I imagine Elizabeth had the chance to join her but she apparently chose not to. The address on Elizabeth's death certificate is in Kilburn. I went to look at it, though I've no idea what I thought looking at a building half a century and more later would reveal. But it did seem to reveal something. It is still a house full of bed-sitters, and from what I've been able to piece together, using the local history archives, that is exactly what it was then.

But back to Gladys. Once in Australia, in Perth, she became a sister in the general hospital there. She married a doctor in 1951 and I imagine, though of course I can't be sure, that the last thing she wanted was to be burdened with her dead daughter's illegitimate son. Maybe she never even told her new husband about Elizabeth's disgrace (which is what, in 1953, it would still have been). Can I blame Gladys? On the one hand yes, on the other no. I don't think she and Elizabeth can have been especially close. The news of her daughter's death in childbirth must have been an appalling shock, though. Maybe she'd known nothing of the affair, nothing of the pregnancy. It's possible. Excuses, again. But I suspect there was an unfeeling streak in Gladys. Not to have attempted any kind of contact with the people who had taken her grandson, not to have shown any concern, sounds unfeeling to me. But then again, maybe this was part of the bargain, Isa's bargain. My father had to be totally hers.

I won't try to discover anything else about my real grandmother. I think her short life may have been quite sad. Even her love affair with Patrick Symondson, for which she paid such a terrible price, sounds sad.

I spend a lot of time with May now. We go for walks, my pace suddenly so slow it matches hers. There's a little park near her – well, it isn't so much a park as an open area, a square, with some grass and a sandpit and a couple of baby swings. It has railings round it and a gate into it and no dogs or people without children are allowed. But with May being an old woman and me heavily pregnant we are no threat to anyone and nobody has ever stopped us sitting on the benches. At the moment, it's mostly too cold or wet to consider sitting, but we make this area the object of our ambling and on the odd mild sunny afternoon we perch a while and watch the children. It makes May supremely content.

'You've got no park near you,' she said, yesterday.

'I've got a car. I can drive to one.'

'Not the same.' Pause. 'You could move to my house, the two of you, when it's born. You could bring it here every day, get the exercise and fresh air and have somewhere safe to sit.' I laughed. 'What's so funny?'

'Just the idea.'

'What idea?'

'Of me pushing a buggy here every day, of that being the highlight of my day.'

307

'What do you think you're going to do, then?'

'Not that.' I didn't add that the mere prospect made me shudder.

'You've got high and mighty ideas, you have, madam. You need to come to your senses, sharpish.'

'OK.' Another pause, and then May said, 'I'll be leaving you my house in my will. It's all done proper, signed and everything. Your mum's got enough, and my boys and their lot don't deserve nothing. So you could move in, knowing you wouldn't have to move out.'

I waited a fraction too long before telling her how overwhelmed I was, and she took offence. 'O' course, you might not like my kitchen, you might not want to live in a house with an old-fashioned kitchen, though it's good enough for me.'

'I love your kitchen.'

'Well, then. Suit yourself. I've made the offer. You can make your own mind up. It'll stay open. I don't mind babies crying, it won't bother me. It'd be three generations together, think of that.'

I thought of it. Three generations . . . it should appeal, instead of alarming me. 'One generation missing, though,' I said, playing for time. 'One generation skipped.'

'Oh, your Mum would never come home.'

'Well, she's got her own very nice home.'

'I know that, clever clogs. You know what I mean. We ain't comfortable, Jean and me. Nobody's fault.'

'I'm flattered.'

May grunted. 'So you should be.' She nudged me, and we both laughed as though some joke had been made. I laughed out of nervousness. I don't know why May laughed.

I said, as we walked back to her house, that I'd think about her suggestion, see how things worked out with Ian. He hadn't moved out yet, and we had four months' rent paid in advance between us. That seemed to satisfy her. I don't think she felt rejected. In fact, maybe she was quite optimistic that I would move in with her, which will make the realisation that I never will all the harder. It makes me feel guilty.

Ian has heard of a flat he could take over for two years while a friend of his is in America. It's only a fifteen-minute walk from my flat here, so it would be 'very convenient for popping in', as he puts it. I told him to take it, if he wanted to, it made no difference to me. But of course it makes a huge difference (and not just because of the rent), it makes his threat of moving out a reality. Though I'm using an ugly word like 'threat' when what he'd said he would do wasn't meant as such at all. He'd merely, at the time, been stating what his decision would be if I went ahead and had our baby. *My* baby. He would have to move out, he'd said, provoked by me, and now with the birth imminent, he was going to. Yet I sensed he was waiting for a reaction from me that might influence his decision. Telling him to do what he liked wasn't what he expected, or even wanted, to hear.

He said he'd settle things with his friend and start moving his stuff in soon. I shrugged, determinedly offhand. I chose that inappropriate moment to ask if he was going to be with me for the birth, knowing perfectly well what the answer would be but still masochistically wanting to hear it.

'No,' he said.

'You're not frightened, are you?'

'Of what?'

'That the "miracle of birth"' – I put on my best mocking voice – 'will make you wonder how on earth you could not have wanted this child to be born.'

'No, I'm not afraid of that,' he said, quietly.

'Heart of stone and proud of it, eh?'

Sensibly, he didn't bother replying to that cheap jibe. He knew that I knew he hadn't a heart of stone. But I hadn't finished trying to provoke him, trying to hide my distress (as he realised) by being sarcastic.

'So, Mr *Scott*,' I said, 'are you going to let your name appear on this child's birth certificate?'

'Yes, of course. Issy, I've never tried to deny I'm the father.'

'But you don't want anything to do with *it*, right?'

'I don't know, I think . . .'

'Ooh, so if the baba is very good and very clever and very beautiful and a credit to you, you might graciously say hello now and again?'

'Issy, Issy . . .' He sighed, and shook his head, knowing quite well that I was lashing out stupidly because I was upset.

'They can make you contribute to *its* upkeep, you know.'

'I'm happy to do that, as you know.'

'So what is it you're not bloody happy to do?' I was shouting, on the edge of tears, wanting him to say that of course he wasn't going to move out, he'd never meant to anyway.

But he didn't, and how could I expect that he would? Instead, he repeated that he was going to take his friend's flat but still see me often, and he'd wait until he'd sorted out his own feelings, about the paternity thrust upon him, to decide what to do. He wasn't going to abandon me, he still loved me, but he just didn't think he could pretend to love a baby as well – he hadn't wanted one, and he was full of resentment that I'd completely ignored his wish that I should have a termination. He said he had to wait, at a distance, to see what happened to that resentment. 'Fine talk,' I sneered, but I understood, I really did, and do. Ian doesn't feel what I feel. He hasn't had the family, the upbringing I have had, so how can he be expected to? But he has a grandmother, who helped make him the man he is. That should count for something.

He is still here. Four weeks to go, and he hasn't moved out, though he's made one or two half-hearted attempts to take some of his stuff to his friend's flat. He's very considerate, looking after me in all kinds of ways. No one would ever know he is a reluctant father-to-be.

* * *

I have a lot of time to think at the moment. I sit for ages at the front window, watching what goes on in the street below. It's a quiet street, but a surprising amount of activity, however ordinary, goes on: vans delivering things, traffic wardens ponderously writing down numbers, people using the street as a short cut between two main roads. It means the street is rarely completely empty and I can always rely on something or someone to watch. Sitting there makes me think of being ill or old, stuck, dependent on whatever passing show might come my way. I would adapt well, I think, to the sitting still bit anyway. I am far too fond of sitting still, daydreaming. I don't obey Sarah Bernhardt's instruction to do something with my ten fingers. They rest idly in my lap. I don't grow restless, like Elizabeth Fry, when I am at home. It would have annoyed Isa to see me slumped here at my window, but it pleases May, so long as I don't have a book in my hand (which I do) – sitting still, in her opinion, is good in my condition, though reading is not. She will never accept that reading, my work, is not physically damaging, she would never agree with George Sand that the love of work can save us from everything – 'I bless my grandmother for having me acquire the habit'.

What do I bless my grandmothers for? Plenty of time to ponder that one. Isa, I think, tried to teach me two things: to be determined, to aim for what I want, at all costs, and to adapt events to my own needs, not quite the same. I suppose her philosophy could be seen as a belief in being ruthless, if necessary, not allowing anything to interfere with the smooth trajectory she wanted her life to take. I would say she failed, but Ian might say she succeeded, that I have gone ahead and let my wishes transcend his. Victory to Isa, then. But when I look at the example she set me, I know I reject it. I might be wrong, but I feel I could never pretend a son was my own if he was not. I could not ignore the 'communications' of a brother, no matter what his state or circumstances.

May's influence, her legacy, is different. She is a stoic. She puts up with things, even if she moans about them. Her words, so often repeated, 'it can't be helped' enrage me, because very often they are an excuse for not taking action. It almost makes her happy that 'it can't be helped'; it means she is not to blame. There is no element of that in me. But May can also be honest, sometimes brutally so, and I have absorbed that trait as well as her obstinacy. I am having a baby whose conception was an accident and whose father does not want it. I think I've been honest with Ian, though maybe he wouldn't agree.

I am beginning to wonder if Ian is right about it being better to ignore the past. He has tried so hard to shake it off, reinvent himself, disown his parents, whereas I have done the opposite, clung on to it, tried to make it responsible for so much, tried to 'reach across the void'. Right now, that reach fails; the void is deeper and wider than ever.

Not long to go now. Sixteen days maximum. They are going to induce the baby if it is not here by then. I like the idea of that, of having a set date when I know something will definitely be done. Waiting does not suit me any longer.

Ian is in his friend's flat. It was part of the deal, that the flat shouldn't be left empty, and that Ian should move in the day after his friend left. He – Ian – was quite reluctant to go, which must mean something. He's left a lot of his stuff here, which I don't mind, I like seeing the evidence that he hasn't vanished. 'Vanished?' he said, when I remarked on this. 'What do you mean? I'm not going to vanish, you know that. I'm just down the road.'

'You might. Mr Mystery Man, the man with no past. I could easily vanish from your CV, just like others did. Isamay Symondson? Never heard of her, what a peculiar name.'

'Amuse yourself, then.'

'I will. Now, let's see, when did your life start, again? Not before you were born, I know that, that's not permitted, and not *when* you were born, though your mother says differently. No childhood acknowledged, I know you're firm about blanking that out, so shall we say eighteen? Nineteen?'

'I'll indulge you. Eighteen.'

'Right. So at eighteen, what?'

'You know – uni.'

'That doesn't tell me much. You've never talked about your uni days. Chums? Interests? Work? All you've said is that you went to Glasgow University and took a degree in physics.'

'All there is to be said. I don't do reminiscing.'

'Of *course* not! I'll be asking if you use Facebook next. Let's move on then, see how far you'll let me push you. After Glasgow, London, yes? Imperial College? Then a bit of travelling, India, Japan, before—'

'Why are you doing this?'

'I'm just taking a personal history, checking I've got it right.'

'But these things don't tell anything, stuff about where people studied, where they lived, their jobs – none of it is important.'

'What is, then?'

'The person. As he, or she, is.'

'Don't make me laugh, Ian. It's like saying a cake is just a cake and doesn't consist of flour and eggs.'

'And fat.'

'What?'

'Fat – butter, margarine. There's usually fat in a cake.'

I don't know why I wanted to go on with such an absurd argument. Maybe I'd always wanted to have it, after the charm of being with a man who tried never to mention anything to do with his past had worn off. I know now about Ian's mother, and the bare facts about his upbringing, and the existence of his grandmother, but I still yearn to know more. There is so little to pass on to my child – but then perhaps it will be like its father, and not want to know.

Perhaps I will get written out of its life too. S/he will tell people s/he is herself/himself, and there is nothing to be known.

But there is. There always is.

I was sent home from the hospital the first time. What a fool I felt. I was so proud of managing to get there on my own (breaking my promise to call my parents), but when I was examined they said I was only one centimetre dilated in spite of what I'd thought were contractions every ten minutes. They said I'd be better off at home until labour had progressed. The second time, Maisie took me. She was on her way to start a night shift when she found me outside the door of our flat, clutching on to the banisters during a strong contraction. She drove me to the hospital and helped me in, and when we reached the maternity unit she asked if I wanted her to call Ian. Groaning with pain, I said yes, and gave her his number. He was the only person I wanted and needed at that moment.

It was two in the morning. He came straight away. By the time he got there, I was in agony, half hysterical with the kind of pain I'd never anticipated. Ian held my hand and talked to me. What about? I've no idea, but the mere sound of his voice did help. When, at last, I was taken into the delivery room, he didn't come with me. I was beyond caring, my body entirely given up to the struggle. But he waited outside until I'd given birth, and he'd been told all was well. He asked a nurse to tell me that he would be back soon.

I am in a room of my own. One hundred pounds (Ian paid) for this blessed privilege, and worth every penny and more. The bed is comfortable. There is a window that actually opens. The walls have recently been painted, the floor is spotlessly clean. 'My,' May said, when Mum and Dad brought her in, 'this is posh.' There is a chair beside my bed and she took it eagerly, so that she could hold my baby in her arms. It was

314

a touching sight, May bending her white head over the baby, peering at her, and of course the identification process started at once: her nose was her grandfather's, her chin her grand-mother's, the shape of her head her great-uncle Tom's. 'She's a beauty,' May said, 'just like her mum.' I laughed, and said I was no beauty. May looked fierce and said, 'If I think you are, you are.' And then, surprisingly for her, she became senti-mental. 'Thank God I lived long enough to see her, my own great-granddaughter. I can die happy.' We all protested that she was not about to die, that she shouldn't talk nonsense, but she repeated her words very firmly and said, 'I know what I know,' which, in all its enigmatic glory, at least sounded more like her true self.

I know what I know too. Now I've given birth, I know how it feels to be pushed into the future; I know, all the same, how the past keeps on pulling. I am already thinking what to tell my daughter about her great-grandmothers and her grandmothers (both of them, even Moira). If she wishes, my daughter will have the means to find out more and make the connections I see so clearly and which her father would like to deny are of any importance.

Ian did come back, as he'd promised. He's seen his daughter. He didn't coo over her, didn't ask if he could hold her. He simply stood by her little crib and stared down at her, for a long time, his expression impossible to decipher. I thought I saw respect there, perhaps even a touch of awe, but I could be mistaken. Then he sat down beside my bed and looked at me. I held his gaze. This time, I knew I was not mistaken about what I saw in his face. I could read his expression perfectly. I smiled, with relief. He held my hand, lightly, and said I'd certainly been through it, he'd hated seeing me in so much pain. I said it had all been worth it. Before he left, he stood and looked at our baby again, and this time he touched her, just stroked her cheek with the tip of his finger.

I lay there, after he'd gone, feeling that some sort of test had been passed. I felt that in some strange way I understood what those grandmothers I'd studied had tried to articulate, and what May and Isa had tried to tell me: there *are* connections between the generations of women that matter. I accept, as Ian does not, or not yet, that though my daughter will be herself, she cannot be that self without those traces of me and my mother and her great-grandmothers counting for something.

The connections are there, and they are still strong.